HIGH PRIORITY

A Tiffany Chanler Novel

Suzanne Eglington

If everyone is thinking alike, then someone isn't thinking.
—GENERAL GEORGE S. PATTON

Prologue

"Don't worry unless you have something to worry about. We are fine."

"You're bad luck."

"That's impossible. Luck has nothing to do with it."

"This company was doing fine before you showed up."

"Look, Jason, I know you tried to transfer. I'm sorry they denied you, but I have a vision here. I love the concept of our service. It has a lot of potential; I want to grow here."

"Grow here? All you young kids are the same. You want to change everything. It's working fine the way it is. You seem to be a magnet for trouble. I like it simple and just want to retire, alive."

He made me grin. "Stop being a baby. I'll start the generators. The base is sending another truck. Thirty minutes tops, so just relax."

I made my way to the back.

"Hey, Chanler, looks like we got company."

I started the generators and stood up watching the van that pulled in front of us. Their brake lights softened, signaling they must have parked. I watched from the back. Our cabin lights were on illuminating the inside, giving visual advantage to anyone outside.

Two men exited the van one from the driver side, the other from the passenger side. We watched as the guy from the right crossed behind the van to walk with the other guy. My heart rate sped. I heard Jason mumble "She is bad luck."

Then there was a knock at my window, with the man asking in a friendly voice, if we needed help. I leaned back, answering, locking the back doors at the same time. "We're all set. Please, return to your vehicle. The police are on their way."

He signaled Jason the thumbs up as he turned and walked back. I scanned the windshield; the generator was too noisy to listen for anything.

"Jason, do you see the other guy? There were two of them?"

"Like I said, you are bad luck Chanler."

He was turning to the right; his door window exploded as a club bashed through.

"JASON!"

CHAPTER ONE

I landed new employment all on my own. This is my ticket out. I took a moment, looking around, fighting a grin. Soon, I would only be a visitor here.

Glancing toward the stairwell door, across the spacious lobby entrance, I contemplated running up all sixteen flights. Vern acknowledged me touching his index finger to the brim of his hat "Miss Chanler," he smiled.

I grinned, turning my gaze toward him. "I've got great news, but I have to get up there. I am already late."

"I look forward to hearing all about it."

Distracted by the empty elevator's doors opening, I waved to him. "I'll be back down later." Darting in, touching my key card against the scanner and pressing my floor's button. I shifted my weight side to side, working out the final details in my head, of how I would announce this.

I wanted to shove it in their faces. They no longer called the shots in what I was doing with my life.

The elevator slowed to a stop on the fifth floor, which housed high-end office suites, ending any luck that I would have this ride all to myself. If they were continuing up, it required a key card because living quarters occupied the sixth floor to the penthouse.

I had kicked out my fair share of passengers "forgetting" their key cards. Rules were rules, especially after that estranged wife incident a few months ago. They allowed no one to be neighborly.

The doors opened and, Mitzy Wellington paused her forward motion, making wide eyes. My inner voice grumbled. I did not have time for her snooty, better than everyone, attitude. My finger was in route reaching for the button. "Well? Am I moving on?" she had one second.

Mitzy, slumped her frown even lower, rolling her eyes as I spoke. Her collagen injected bottom lip stuck out like a ten-year-old that didn't get her way.

Stepping in, she sneered the left side of her upper lip, swiping her bedazzled key card, pressing the number twenty-two. Stepping back, she snipped, "You moving on, Tiffany? We couldn't possibly be that lucky."

She then took her time, scanning me from top to bottom, her face frozen in that same expression. "I see you are still a six-week loser with no job."

I laughed, elated by my change in news. "I have a job. It's not as useless as yours, though."

She swiped and tapped her phone, not replying. We were almost to my floor. I had a few seconds to get in another jab, "What are prostitution rates these days, Mitzy?"

"Ha! You're just jealous Tiffany, that I landed the position as Mr. Emerson's personal time manager." She said that so proudly like it was the job of the century.

"Time Manager? What even is that? Oh, my God, do you have to time yourself with him?" I laughed at my clever spin.

The elevator bumped to a stop; I stepped forward with Mitzy shifting over toward where I was standing. She sounded like that ten-year-old's attitude telling me, "Get a job, loser, and move. You don't belong here. You never did."

I turned, leaning in, making her back up a step, forcing the doors to stay open. "For God sakes, at least use protection. Not even Emerson deserves to share what's been in there." I said, pointing toward her crotch.

"Well, at least I like men. I heard you turned gay after doing it with Blake."

Not worth it, not worth it, not worth it! "You've been misinformed as usual, but you had sex with Blake; it's a miracle I didn't jump ship, right?"

I stepped back from the doors to hear her protest, "Loser!"

Hearing Blakes name shot down every happy feeling inside me. I shivered, slowly letting out a breath, repeating my mantra not today, not any day. You are dead to me.

* * *

Growing up with the branded name, "Tiffany Chanler," created a constant battle for my identity. My parents had substantial expectations for me right from birth in their high-society social status.

Only I was the little girl who jumped in puddles, seeing how big of a splash I could make, even though I was forced to wear uncomfortable puffy dresses that cost more than some kid's braces.

Mother insisted I learn ballet. I argued that I wanted to learn karate, making me gain negotiating skills at an early age. Ballet enhanced my martial arts performance leading into one of those rare occasions where we both ended up content.

My father is the longtime CEO of Henshaw Logistics, a $500 million-dollar enterprise. He has been trying to mold me to work for him since grade school. This was my future in their eyes: only I didn't want it.

I was shipped right from preparatory school off to college. They picked my business degree and the only reason I stuck with it was that my college was far enough away, giving me plenty of excuses not to come home. About the only thing Father and I have in common now is the transportation business.

The day I walked in telling them I had found my dream job was the start to my breaking away from their institutional high-society lifestyle.

I had turned down my father's offer after graduation and now he wanted to know what I would do for a living.

I will never forget our conversation. I can still recall the feelings that were bubbling inside me, standing in the hallway, facing the door to the grandiose living quarters I grew up in, disregarding the conversation with Mitzy, when she called me a loser that day.

It was six weeks since my graduation. I was going nuts being back here.

I could now afford my own place and I knew exactly where that would be. My Fairy Godmother had sweetened the deal in favor of me accepting my father's job offer, but when I turned him down, she gave me the ultimatum that she would only hold the condo for two months. Time was ticking.

I held the doorknob for a moment, pulling back my emotions to stay on target, repeating to myself just to play it cool. I stepped onto the carpeted, marble tiled grand foyer, knowing both my parents would be home and wondering why I was late. I was pushing the mandatory arrival time by twenty minutes.

It was nearly seven o'clock on Wednesday evening. We considered this "family night" in the Chanler suite, consisting only of cocktail hour and then a meal before being allowed to disappear to a separate room.

I don't know why this was a requirement to be here; we did nothing special. We were all just under the same roof, one night a week.

I stopped, distracted by breathing in Mother's savory roast, instantly activating my salivary glands, cueing my mouth to water, making me now realize that I was hungry. Mother is a fantastic cook. She studied in France the summer I went off to college.

I had to concentrate and focus my attention back on my announcement, not on my stomach.

Sounds of their conversation echoed from the living room around the corner to where I was standing. Mother talking about some new Martini recipe she had tried earlier today from her bi-monthly, cut throat, rich bitch, wives' luncheon.

I knew exactly where they were standing, both at the bar area, drinks must have started.

Mother's voice was now moving, emphasizing that Mary vowed it was the blueberries that gave this its special touch.

I have to admit, most women from her earlier lunch group made me cringe. Sometimes just hearing their names stirred bitterness in me.

They were spoiled, rich, meddling, shallow, condescending women who had nothing better to do than gossip, rip each other apart, and sleep with each other's husbands, brothers and other relations.

My mother didn't belong in this group. It forced her to conform when she married my father just like it forced me to grow up with all their rotten children like, Mitzy and Blake.

Two women in her clique had amnesty in my eyes. Mary being one. The other being my godmother taking her role to heart.

Mildred Jones, who I often referred to as my Fairy Godmother, made her fortune on her own in real estate. I knew where I stood with Mildred as did everyone else. I learned what I know today about commitment, self-assurance and motivation from her influence. She was the one standing strong through all my bumps, bruises, and frustrations.

My damp sneakers squeaked against the marble flooring, alerting them I had arrived. They watched me turning the corner, fresh from the gym.

Father's monotone pitch called my name, "Tiffany." Mother added to his sentence asking if it was still drizzling outside and why wasn't I wearing a raincoat.

Then she went into sheer routine asking about my day, turning back to her drink. I think she had given up on any news happening in my life.

I heard them talking a few nights ago about sending me back to college. Their brief silence broke out into laughter at the idea that I could become a professional student.

Yes, that was just hilarious. I would rather pump gas for a living than go back to school at this point.

A six-week post Master Graduate still without securing a job. Well, I was until five hours ago. My college advisors were more concerned about my unemployment than anyone.

It was looking bad on their records that they had produced a business graduate who was still jobless.

Mother's Wednesday luncheon meant that all the other women pulled out the brag cards on how their children, husbands, or relatives were succeeding, exaggerating the details. These women went out of their way to one-up each other. Unfortunately, my mother had nothing since my graduation, and the news I was about to drop, proved another move in my life they could not control.

I tied my thick mousy-blonde hair back in a ponytail. I sported my favorite T-shirt that echoed my college states logo of Live free or Die along with my running shorts and favorite pair of sneakers, fresh from my workout. I was fighting not to smile, my inner conflict battling between pride and self-assurance. I needed to stick it to my father. I didn't need his money. I am doing this on my own.

I decided to role-play, mimicking one of my professors, a very serious and calculating speaker. He was well-known on campus and mocked by many. I used to copy him frequently, driving my friends crazy.

Morphing into character, thinking about one of his classic speeches, I began, "As you know, I have been diligently researching the market and posting my resume, just as my college advisors have suggested as they've been guiding me through the process."

I paused a moment to hear any comments. Neither one of them spoke, but I had their attention. I continued, "Finally, I received the one call I was waiting for. This has been my pick for employment right from the start. They are expanding and hiring four new employees. I went to their interview today."

My parents adjusted, Mother giving me more attention. Father asked, "And how did this one go Tiff?"

Mother raised her left eyebrow, as she studied me. She knew something was up.

I remember his tone, a little too wary for my liking. I smiled regardless because I already knew what they thought about the last four offers I had turned down, not including my fathers at his company. I knew our week-long argument about Henshaw Logistics still disappointed him.

I knocked off the act and answered in my voice. "They offered me the position, Father; this is my dream job. I know I will grow with this company. It is exactly what I have been holding out for. I accepted after negotiating an extra five-thousand dollars above their third-tier starting salary, which I am well-qualified for."

That's all I had to say. Mother lit up. My news had promise for something she could bring to her next luncheon.

"This is wonderful dear. Come, tell us about it. Let's all have a seat. Tiffany, what is the name of this company?" She motioned toward the couches, touching my father's arm, reassuring him that this was good news.

She signaled him to hurry, waiting, before they both took their seats.

Father took another weary sip. He did not smile. I could see the conflict he was projecting. I was certain he was thinking...what job would be greater than working for his company?

I was positive that he also thought I would cave and work. I knew he didn't expect that I could do this without him. Mildred's offer was about to expire, and he knew how much I wanted to be out on my own.

I joined them dropping my gym bag next to the opposite sofa, confidently removed my sneakers and plopped myself comfortably. I was positive Mother would address how I just did that. She hated bad posture and the way I could drop myself on furniture. I could make her eyes burn when I sat on the coffee table. Watching for the tipping point, I folded my legs to my side, answering Mother's question, "Angel Wings."

They both glanced toward one another, repeating the name having a small discussion back and forth between them, bouncing the name for any recognition. Neither one of them had heard of it. Father turned his head quizzically with one eyebrow up and the other slightly narrowed down, aiming right at me.

"What is Angel Wings, Tiff? I never heard of this company. Is it nonprofit?"

He was guessing; I think from the name.

I sank back into the cushion contemplating the category classification of my new employer, drawing out this moment for as long as I could for dramatic effect. I learned this in my speech class and right now seemed like the perfect time to test this method out. I was now tapping my chin with my right index finger.

My fingernail touched my skin. I examined my fingers briefly, noting it was time to trim my nail. I looked up, answering Father, bringing my attention back to them.

"You know, that was something that did not come up. Never asked. I don't think it is. Had the impression it is the private sector. Going to find out. Anyway, it's a transportation service, Father."

He grinned. "Finally coming into the transportation business, are you? Why don't you come work for me? I can teach you everything. In two years, you could run your own department, make good of that degree I paid for."

I lowered my head snickering "Thanks, but I didn't get hired for an office job. I'm a driver."

I was watching, waiting for that to sink in. Boom, their expressions changed.

Mother went from joyous to discontent. She stood up with her hand on her hip, pointing to me with her other hand. "Tiffany! You are a Chanler. We hire people for those positions not fill them ourselves. You have an MBA. All those years of education! Why would you settle for this?"

My grin spread a little wider while watching my father calm her down. "I also have several black belts Mother; Karate, Jujitsu, and I'm training hard in grappling right now. You shouldn't exclude those after announcing I have an MBA. I worked just as hard training and studying to earn them. Honestly, I think they were more of a challenge."

My father said something to Mother; she reacted with a wave of her hand in the air assuring him she would have an open mind as she reached for her drink, taking a big sip and sitting back down.

He turned back to me. "What does 'Angel Wings' transport?"

Now, we were getting down to it. This was where the real fun began.

"Precious cargo."

Mother let out a sigh of relief. Now, my job sounded like it had merit. Dad grew suspicious though; he knew logistics all too well and me even better. "Tiffany, what kind of cargo will you be transporting?"

I paused, wetting my lips; relying on the skills I have practiced with them for years. With a slight raise of my chin and a sudden unexpected playful grin, I at last answered. "Body parts."

CHAPTER TWO

I was ready. If I beat Kyle on this course, I would be a top driver. If they ever paired us up one day. I would be senior to him.

My heart rate quickened, willing that light to be on my side. Every second counted, controlling my breath, impatiently waiting to react. I visually saw it turning green as I counted down, trying to be one with something I had no control over. "Three, two," waiting another second it went green, "one." My foot pressed as much as the acceleration allowed. I had to feel this ambulance's diesel engine. We had to start with a different model year on each challenge.

The trick was a steady acceleration, as the ambulance adjusted to the movement. This one was an older model, very different from the first two in this challenge. I had to win. It would kill me if Kyle beat me. The first corner came up, and I couldn't help it. The weight distribution was heavier than I expected. I was tipping. "Damn it!"

The next corner now to the left. I was behind Kyle's time by several seconds. I needed to stop over thinking and get my head here and now.

The third corner came up, and I over-steered too wide. I was tipping; I could feel the wheels coming off the ground. No way I would lose this.

Pulling the steering wheel to straighten out, I knocked through some barrels. I would rather take another few seconds off the clock than dump this on its side. Knocking more barrels out of the way, to get back on course, I accomplished not dumping this beast. Surely, that had to count in my favor.

I tuned out everything else and just listened to the engine. I had forgotten that this was one of the first things Greg had taught me in the shop.

Recovering through the bends, there was a rhythm going. I felt it. Turning the last right angle was the finish line. I was one with my truck.

We picked up speed, the needle climbing and gaining momentum; we had a chance. I could smell sweet victory.

My panoramic vision spotted a car coming from my right to left. It was now skidding to a stop, blue lights flashing as I slammed on my brakes, turning the wheel to the left to avoid crashing.

It reversed the last second from my path, only I was already off course crossing the finish line ten yards off target. It pissed me off.

As soon as I shifted the ambulance into park, I unbuckled, jumping out, verbally protesting. They didn't do that to Kyle. Why me?!

The instructor was trying to speak, holding his hands out, pumping them in a downward motion for me to calm down. Only I didn't let him get a word in as I continued in my rant.

He finally threw down his clipboard, telling me to shut my damn mouth as he said I had scored higher.

I won. I won? I beat Kyle? I WON!

* * *

I knew Kyle was waiting for me to make the first move. This had been his childish game ever since I beat him on the driving agility course. He cut me off causing me to slam on my brakes within inches of hitting him. A sinister grin stretched across his face as he leaned out his driver's side window seeing how close I had come to backing into him. I swore out loud as he sped away up the ramp.

I've now been employed for three years with this organ transport service. My partner, Michael, looked over telling me to relax.

I glanced over at Michael. He flashed a wide grin. I liked almost everything about him, except for his annoying ability to argue. He is particular about his name. He is not a Mike, Mikey, Mick, or Mitch. He is a Michael and will correct you most irritatingly until you get his name right. I have personally experienced this. It's not pretty.

The rules in my truck are, I drive, and I am the boss. Michael, so far, holds the record of being my partner and I think we will work out just fine.

My ambulance is also very important to me. So much so, that I spend a fair amount of my downtime at the garage, learning the mechanics and maintenance for it. When I first started here, I had a breakdown that put my first partner and me in danger. I vowed that would never happen again.

Now you may wonder what sets me apart from other ambulance drivers. Well, the first noticeable difference is that I carry a gun but not the size I want to wear. They only allow us to carry a 9mm. My preference would be a larger gun. I mean, if you carry one for personal security, why not carry one with real firepower?

Regardless, I am allowed to wear it out in the open on my waist just like a cop, so you can imagine the looks I get when I step out of my ambulance and go into a restaurant or store.

A gun showing on your waist is still a statement that catches people's attention when you are not a police officer.

It wasn't just the gun I carried that drew notice, because the one thing I could not reject from my parents is the body they made for me. I stand five-foot-five, have dull blonde hair that is usually up in a ponytail, and I have my mother's vibrant green eye color. The green complements her auburn hair but sometimes contrasted with my blonde shade, depending what colors I wore. I knew black drew a lot of attention to my features so I tried to stay away from that color.

Where I got the blonde hair from is a mystery. Neither side of the family has blonde hair. If I didn't so much resemble both of my parents, there would be questions, but get the three of us together and it's undeniable.

I can eat anything I want thanks to the physical workouts I keep up with being in this high-risk job. Every year, we have to pass a physical challenge course. They use the one down at the local army reserve site. I got to know some guys there, who would let me sneak in for an extra run from time to time.

That was my best benefit because I drink a lot of sweetened flavored coffees and I am addicted to dark chocolate, jelly donuts, and anything related to breakfast. That would be my diet if I could get away with it.

My jelly donut dependency is Michael's fault. He was briefed about me when he was assigned to my ambulance. Some people think I'm difficult to work with. I think some people are difficult to communicate with, so it's all about whose perspective you take.

Michael started our first shift together by asking if we could stop at Larry's Café. It was a little out of the way, but he assured me they had the best coffee in town, nagging until I gave in. I wasn't sure about Michael, and this was not a good start in my eyes. Realizing how annoying he could be, I drove there to shut him up.

He returned with our coffee and a half dozen jelly donuts. I thought it was odd that he only bought jelly donuts and not a variety. I mean he didn't even know me yet, and he only bought jelly donuts.

He opened the door, confidently twisting my coffee out from the disposable holder. With his eyebrow flexed and cocksure attitude, he handed over my coffee. I fixed the lid back just as I would with any coffee handed to me. Right then, the smooth aroma permeated my scent sensory awakening my curiosity. I sipped, looking for something to point out wrong, attempting to rip that confidence from his face. Okay, I had nothing. He had nailed it about the coffee.

Then he offered me a donut, adjusting in his seat, folding the cardboard/plastic lid back. Naturally, I resisted waving it off. I didn't give in until he was eating his second donut, and I had already had two sips of this delicious coffee he was right about.

This was the best coffee I have ever had from a shop. Now my curiosity got the better of me about the donuts. I could smell the grape jelly and the fresh dough. I glanced over to him. They looked delectably soft as he pulled the rest away from his mouth. I was ready to try one.

Michael peeked over, watching me watch him. He held the box up; I accepted as my hand pulled one out. The smell of the sweet sugar triggered a memory from my childhood. My mother would take me to Crawford's, our fancy bakery downtown, a few days before my birthday.

She called it a "pre tasting" of the birthday cake they allowed me to pick out. The sugar from this donut was already melting into my taste buds as I bit down on the cake like mixture, capturing a little grape jelly for the perfect bite.

The soft, fresh dough with the fine-sugar blend extracted a moan of satisfaction that I had no control over about how sinfully delicious this tasted.

That is how this son of a bitch hooked me on jelly donuts. We now stop there often. I know Larry personally.

My unappealing side, as some people have commented in the past, is that I have an attitude. I work hard, am self-supporting, and I am educated, giving me an advantage in knowing how situations should be dealt with; I am not afraid to call it.

I had a lot of practice being tough while growing up. Being bullied or talked down to from kindergarten all the way to the day I moved out of my parents' living quarters, in a life I did not fit into made me the woman I am.

The strong point which made me know that Michael would be a keeper was that on a few past occasions, he had my back.

He has saved me from my mouthy, hot-tempered lash-outs at Kyle during meetings twice now. I needed to tell him I appreciated it someday. Ugh, admitting that I went too far in the first place...

I am so bad at this...not one of my strong points.

Another change made from the first hijacking a month into my start here; they arm us not only to carry out in the open, but we also had a shotgun secured on the back wall behind my driver's seat. From that day forward, no one knew it, but I carried a knife...all this extra artillery in the ambulance, because some idiots sell body parts on the black market.

Organs were worth more than the money carried by armored trucks. I wish someone would finally realize this. I consistently argue for more training and better technology in our vehicles. The owners don't care; they are cheap. New recruits barely have a chance for surviving an attack these days. Hijackings are becoming more sophisticated and widespread.

We train a few times a year in mock setups, which are useless since we know about it and cannot react as we should. We use cap guns, and there's no contact other than a touch in designated areas; it's crap. I guess they're worried about the insurance risk of someone getting hurt, shot, or felt up.

Friday was the start of our rotation this week. My shift's schedule worked one first shift, one second shift, and two third shifts followed by two days off. Angel Wings has cornered the market, being the only private sector organ and blood transport service in the area. We were expanding. It would not surprise me, if they did this right, Angel Wings could cover the United States.

* * *

Kyle Webb is my biggest issue here at Angel Wings. He is the egotistical, second-in-command who runs the other truck on my shift. He is one arrogant bastard. He has been a thorn in my side ever since I started. He has one-year seniority on me and thinks he runs our shift. I have two degrees more in college than him so I outrank him in education on the tier structure here. He hates that I pull that card out every time he challenges me, which is often.

I could not stand him on most days. It's not exactly the power struggle between us. It's our personalities. He is oil; I am water. We will never blend. Kyle seems to be an expert at everything in his mind. He is one piece of work. Unfortunately, he was not born the god he thinks himself to be. It is also clear that people fell for this slick-talking mountebank.

I know many "Kyle Webb" types in my parent's social circle. Blake Montgomery comes to mind. I hated Blake. If there were one person, I could wipe off this planet and have it been forgiven, it would be him.

I had my suspicions that his family dabbled in illegal activities. Rumor had it that Blake had some serious charges brought up against him. It is still not clear if they convicted him; I never knew the whole outcome. The entire court case just went away.

This Kyle Webb didn't have the education or money to back up his own self-worth. The man was a joke in my eyes and I sometimes, occasionally, had enough of him and felt the need to set him straight.

I learned to taunt him just enough to make him look stupid. My upper-level education kept me in check on how to use his actions against him most of the time. I didn't have the training to deal with his pranks, but I was learning.

My physical side wanted one hour on the matts with that supercilious bastard. I've now had two years of training with my group, and I'm getting good at grappling. I feel confident I could leave him a crumpled mess.

Kyle was lucky that some of my ethics, drilled into me by my godmother, had such an impact because there were days, I just wanted to wring his neck.

At Angel Wings, we all have solid scheduled deliveries, mostly; hospital to hospital or the state's donation center to the hospital and state border-to-border hand offs. Those were the worst: the paperwork, the police details, the government officials; the time it took was crazy boring.

There was also a limit on how many containers they allowed us to transport. We didn't even know what we had on board for cargo. With cargo control, there was no way for us to track our inventory, along with two trucks running in our designated quadrants; it kept us on the go.

Last year we were up to seven hijack attempts, two just on our shift alone. Kyle and I seem to be targeted more than the others. I keep track.

With this job also comes a certain amount of people skills. I admit, Michael and I know more about peoples' lives than I care to. The medical specialists and nurses we hand our cargo to are the gabbiest bunch of gossipers I ever met. I thought my mother's social circle was bad... They could take pointers from these people. Believe it or not, I wasn't such a people person. I preferred hanging out with their frozen parts to being with the breathing versions.

Depending on the shift we worked, there were clearly disappointed looks on a few faces when I pulled in and backed up. To tell you the truth, I think Kyle was banging over six women on our combined routes. That was his business, though, not mine.

Today, we were midpoint deliveries as my phone alerted me to my selected "mother is calling" ring tone. I protested verbally while Michael offered to talk to her. I handed the phone to him as he answered.

Right away, he spoke, pleased that she called. "Hello, Priscilla, Tiff is driving; sorry, but you're stuck talking to me." Michael checked the mirrors observing, then switched it over to speaker. Just hearing my mother's enthusiastic voice on the phone that Michael answered made me give an involuntary eye roll.

"Michael, dearest! Since I have you don't let Tiffany hear."

We both turned to each other. My expression was a hard stare; his was amusement. "Go ahead, Priscilla; I'm moving to the back for privacy," he grinned.

"As you know, Tiffany turns twenty-seven in two weeks! I can't believe it myself. My little girl, where has the time gone!"

I'm crinkling my eyebrows down, pressing my lips and giving Michael the mad glare now! Michael's face was perfectly angular and when the left corner of his mouth turned up his dimple appeared.

I knew this look on him. He was about to have fun knowing I couldn't say anything. "Now that you mention this, Priscilla, I had a feeling something big was coming up... she's been so cranky lately."

I clenched my fist, ready to punch him as that full-blown, mischievous, naughty boy grin spread across his face.

I liked this grin. I've only seen it a few times since we've been together, but this look was appealing on him, brightening his whole persona. It was attractive.

At the same moment my mother laughed making me aware that I was staring at Michael. I turned my head immediately hoping he didn't see me linger. I ignored her voice and concentrated on the road.

"So, Priscilla, what is my part in your evil plan? I know you're plotting."

She laughed even harder, making me turn back toward Michael. He was enjoying himself as his eyes met mine for a moment. I felt exposed and quickly turned back, tuning out their conversation.

I had not realized Michael touched my phone to end the call. He paused a moment then asked. "I know when you zoned out; what do you want to know?"

I exhaled deeply. Michael has been with me awhile. He knows how to talk to my parents. He knows how to deal with Kyle around me, and most of all... he knows how to handle me!

He started with the facts. I had to come up with people to invite my birthday party since Mother had no clue about my social life beyond Hannah and Michael.

I shook my head, mumbling, "Whatever," then dismissed the idea.

I hated these parties...the fanfare, the fake good will gestures. Most would show out of society's obligation and to have a laugh about the fact that I drove an ambulance for a living, carrying organs. They didn't care about me. I was the black sheep, the rebel, the one that didn't fit in.

I remember Clarissa Montgomery once telling my mother she should just adopt and start over. I hated that witch and one of these days she would pay for that comment.

* * *

Pulling up to our next stop, I see... Oh boy, another disappointed wench from the Kyle fan club. Handing over my clipboard, I watched Jen as she flipped through the documents.

The idea hit me.

Michael was busy organizing the coolers, so I tried a conversation with her instead of just grunting and saying there were four coolers total for her delivery.

"Hey, Jen, I have a birthday coming up in a few weeks, and my mother lives for throwing parties."

I had her full attention. She stopped looking at my clipboard and met my eye. We never talked casually. The only reason I knew her name was the fact that her badge displayed the name Jen, even though she always signed her signature Jennifer.

I could tell that Jen was her preferred choice. "And when I say she's throwing a party, I mean open bar, best menu, five-star all the way. I bet you wouldn't have guessed that I came from money?"

Jen cracked a smile, with a little chuckle, giving me the once-over as if she would never have guessed. "It's been a while since I've been to one of those events."

"Well, Mother asked me to come up with a few people to invite."

Jen looked confused.

"Look, I know this sounds strange, but with all my training and working different shifts, you guys are about the only social circle I have these days."

She laughed. "I get that. I don't even remember the last time I went out with the girls. These double shifts have killed my social life."

"Me too. Unfortunately, I can only invite a few people so you would have to come solo."

She sighed because even I knew this was an odd request.

"I'm also inviting the crew I work with so that includes Kyle."

She lit up leaning into me. "Okay then, I will be there."

Michael studied us, waiting patiently, holding the cart packed with her delivery.

"This will be our secret." I winked, reassuring her it was strictly between us.

She nodded with a big grin, counted the boxes, pointing her laser reader on each tag, then signing the clipboard with a whole new level of ease between us already. She handed it back to me and thanked me for including her. Michael followed her in as I turned rubbing my hands together with the first success in securing my entertainment at my birthday party.

My new birthday plan was to invite Kyle and all of Kyle's women to my party to see what happens.

There, that's how I would fill my list and now I was looking forward to this birthday event. Michael was quicker than normal walking back out. We secured everything; then he handed me the new sheet to add to the next stop.

He instantly asked what the conversation with Jen was all about. I revealed my plan. His blank stare threw me off... I could see him thinking and then I felt a higher self-assurance in what I was scheming as he stretched up the corner of his mouth in a Grinch-like grin, adding a slow deliberate head shake.

He announced, straight forward inviting himself, "I'm riding shotgun for that show."

I laughed. "No one else I want in your seat, buddy."

CHAPTER THREE

My week followed suit. I had limited time to secure all the women I suspected Kyle fooled around with. Then I had to convince them to arrive solo to be Kyle's date. Now there was a new issue to think about: time this just right, inviting Kyle with enough bait to make him want to show up, given the fact that we hated each other.

This consumed me all week, while I continued to think about how I could do it without sounding like it was a setup. Kyle has a huge ego; this I could count on. How to tempt him though?

Poor Michael would try to start a conversation here and there, until I shut him down, explaining that I was thinking. Like the good partner he was, he kept quiet to let me plan the Kyle set up in my brain. By Sunday morning, our last stop and the end of our third day, my phone rang.

It was seven in the morning, and few people knew my shifts. I looked at the number, and the missing piece of my puzzle lit up my brain.

I grinned into the phone. "Jane Doe, you have perfect timing as always."

"Oh, good God, Tiff, I would see what you were doing for breakfast, but I don't think I need to bother. What are you up to now? You only call me that when you have a mission, that involves me, bad decisions and bail money. Somehow, I already know it will end badly. SINCE IT ALWAYS ENDS BADLY!" She paused, inhaling a breath to continue down memory lane, "Like when we were running from the cops, or that time we got SHOT AT!!!!! What about those damn dogs that were chasing us? No! No! No! I still jump every time I hear a dog."

I walked around to the front of the truck to let Michael finish up. "I promise this is easy peasy. Besides, we were kids back then, amateurs."

"The dogs were four years ago, Tiffany!"

I laughed. "Really, this is simple. I promise. I just need you to show up, down at my work, before my shift starts one day. It's that simple."

"Why!"

"Because Mother is throwing me a birthday party and I need you to do what you do best and aim it at Kyle Webb, I want him to show up at my party. You are so good at distracting men and making them do whatever you want."

"Oh right, I seem to recall that guy at that card table didn't think so. I am still traumatized that he pulled his gun out."

I softly snickered. "It was a baby gun, barely able to do anything. You were fine and in no danger."

She huffed and started to protest again.

"Hannah... Hannah?... Stop... Hannah ... Hannah calm down..." she grunted and there was silence for a few seconds. "So, will you do this for me? You don't even have to talk to him at the party; you can just hang out with me?"

"Why is this so important, Tiff? What's your angle? I thought you hated Kyle? Why is he invited to your party?"

Again, that smile creased my face as I turned into my ambulance resting my elbow on the hood. "As you know, Mother is throwing me an over the top birthday party that I don't want."

"Your mother is the party hosting queen. I don't know why you fight this. She is amazing with entertaining."

"Ya, ya, ya, anyway she asked me to come up with some people to invite, so I invited the women I think Kyle Webb is playing. They all said yes. None of them know each other and I promised that Kyle would be there alone."

She was quiet, too quiet, which made me glance at the phone to see if it still connected us. I heard her voice, so I brought it back to my ear. "You are naughty, very, very naughty. I can't believe you come up with stuff like this. Yes. I'm in. When do you want me there?"

Operation "Ho-down" was under-way. Michael sat listening and enjoying the new plan. I pulled away from the dock as we headed back.

When we rounded the corner to home base, there was a car blocking our way. It was still early in the morning and a Sunday, putting us on edge. We had the next shift's cargo to swap out so there was product in our freezers.

Immediately Michael's hand went into alert mode. He reached over pulling the release lock for the shotgun, and surveyed the area.

Both of us were scanning the area, my adrenaline pumping, heartbeat quickening, waking any idea of sleep away. My foot eased the ambulance to a stop. The quiet of the garage was adding another layer of stress as Michael calmly said "Ready."

I mimicked him, looking around and "ready." I didn't think there was any reason for a high jacking attempt right here at home base, but you never know. People are idiots.

I blew the horn in warning, not only to the car but to alert the people at the base that something was brewing outside the gate. A very distraught woman backed out from the rear seat holding some kind of plastic bag, waving paper towels, yelling something I couldn't understand.

I opened my door slowly, scanning the lot. Michael was in motion taking the next position. It was already bright out, making me squint from the direct solar glare coming off the mirrored glass in front of us. I adjusted my sunglasses trying to see.

I carefully watched for any movement, then hit the button to lower my window. I heard a small child crying as the woman apologized, trying to explain that her kid threw up and she would move in a minute. I felt no threat, but I knew better all the same.

I stepped away from my door, standing to reveal my gun with my hand on it, ready to pull it from my holster.

Chin up, loud and clear, I said, "Miss, the sign reads that under no condition, is this gate to be blocked. Now I suggest you find another area to conduct your business."

She dropped everything from her hands to the ground and shut the back door, scurrying to her driver's seat.

Michael and I surveyed the area.

We called all clear, hopping back in the ambulance and pulling up to the gate. Michael was watching in the direction that the car had gone. A small television screen popped on as I punched in my code. Barbara said hello to me and the screen shut off.

I grinned flipping my head up to Michael, "Bet she won't do that again."

He returned a smile. "Now, she probably has shit to clean up too."

I punched his arm playfully and nodded "Idiots."

The thing that I thought most annoying with this company was that before we left here, everything that just happened outside the gate; would be analyzed, talked over, and discussed to see if we had followed procedure or if this was a possible future set up, and dragged through every scenario Kyle could pick apart before we were dismissed. I hated that he had camera footage to pick apart. Kyle would be an ass, just to annoy me.

Now, this stranger was making me stay later which would make me late for my Sunday morning grappling class. Damn! I could already feel those extra pushups.

We were done, and it was twenty minutes past the end of our shift, only Kyle kept picking apart my angles, how I left myself open, making us watch over and over, pausing then rewinding. Michael being Michael and really observant, corrected him with the correct coordination my hips were at along with my footing.

We both watched Mr. Donovan and waited for him to have the final say.

"Kyle, I appreciate you caring for the safety of your co-workers, but Miss Chanler followed procedure and executed everything by our standards. This is a wrap. Good work everyone."

I shot up, ran out, signed my ambulance over to the detail department, and threw my bag in the back of my Lexus and scooted in.

This was my graduation gift three years ago. I immediately wanted to trade it in for the Jeep Wrangler I thought I wanted. I was convinced they would never get me.

When Father made me drive it home, I had to give in. Maybe they were coming around or maybe I needed to open my eyes a little more. I loved this car. I loved driving it; I loved the heated and air-conditioned seats; I loved the way it handled. Now I loved how fast it accelerated, getting me to my grappling class.

Okay, I was only ten minutes late. They were still in the middle of warm-ups. I rushed in and started stripping and re-dressing. My coach hollered at me, "For God sakes Tiff, drop your gun in the box, and go behind the screen to change! Dammit woman!"

Hell, I was almost done. If all the guys could change in the open, then so could I. I still covered up everything that mattered.

I fired back, "I'm sure you've seen more than your fair share of women's undergarments. Get over it."

Then I was done and joining the class. I've been training with my coach and a handful of these guys since I found this place two years ago, and every class he challenged me, which kept me coming here again and again. He was the only man I have ever known that would throw me to the ground, given the opportunity just as powerfully as an actual attacker would. There was no fluff between us.

Half the guys here still needed to get over my boobs. I learned to use this weakness to climb rank. If they were that stupid, then I would take full advantage.

Today my coach was especially tough on me because I changed in the open and sassing him with my comment. By the time class ended, the only thing I had strength for was to use two hands turning my hot water on, plugging the drain and climbing into my bathtub.

I was glad I had one day left in this work week. I had to regenerate because tonight seemed to be one of the riskier shifts for dealing with robbers. Something about Sunday nights increased the odds of a hijacking.

There was an extra layer with our company though... we had a contracted employee that worked undercover. I can only imagine where he had to hang out for the body-part black marketing and the people in it... Our guy is former trifecta special ops.

No one ever approached to ask what specialty unit he worked with when he showed up at meetings, because he was bat shit crazy. People commented that they could see it in his eyes.

He knew more about life and ending life than anyone I knew. He viewed most people as if they were a figure on a chessboard.

Not me though, Andy looked much different to me. I liked Andy. I had a strong attraction to him. He was older than me and I liked his maturity and wisdom.

There was something there that most people ignored. I could pick up on it, though. I was even intimate with him when we could hook up, which was not enough. I wanted more. Andy clearly showed a talent that no other man had in my opinion and I enjoyed his experience. I was free to date anyone I wanted, but it was him I desired.

* * *

Between Hannah and me, we thought three days' notice was the best scenario to invite Kyle Webb to my party. We set this up perfectly. It was the start to our second shift; I already had clearance for Hannah to update her information. She was my emergency contact and it just so happened that she had changed addresses a month ago.

I stopped at the gate. I announced myself and Hannah... she already knew to step out of her car. I looked back at the screen. Billy was probably muttering to himself and taking pictures of her. Hannah had to ask three times before stepping back into her car if they would allow her to enter.

She was buzzed in as Kyle pulled up in his pickup truck behind her car moving through the gate. He stopped and waited. I watched as the boys talked through the monitor. Kyle jerked his head at my friend's car and said something to Billy as he cleared him in.

He parked and waited. I signaled Hannah to wait as I walked into the booth, retrieving my schedule. This was Hannah's mark. She opened her door, swung out those long athletic legs and lifted herself from the driver's side of her sporty white Audi wearing an open cut sports shirt, a sports bra and sports skirt, ready to hit her tennis club. Kyle was a goner.

This was way too easy, almost unfair. I gave her a minute to talk to him before grabbing her and taking her to the office... I approached as Kyle was asking what she was doing this weekend. She grinned and ambitiously spoke about my party. Then she mentioned that he should come.

He glanced over to me. "I don't know. I'm not into crashing parties."

I shrugged my shoulder. "I don't mind if you show up. It's my mother's doing. Open bar, ridiculous amounts of food, a big crowd. She's invited half the city. Might even have the governor there? Besides, I am sure I won't even notice you."

He nodded because he was into Hannah. "Okay, sounds like fun."

Hook, line, and sinker... Hannah smiled, touching his arm. "Nice, I'll see you then?"

He looked her up and down again stepping backward with a stupid, smug grin. "Looking forward to it, Hannah."

She spun away on her tiptoes to follow me into the office.

Michael was walking in as we were walking out. Hannah burst into a smile throwing her arms around him. "Michael! Mmm, did you know you are the best hugger I know?"

He grinned holding her tight. "Hi Hannah, how goes the battle?"

He released her as she did a little swish of her body. "Good, you are coming to Tiffs party, right?"

He did a little head bob. "I wouldn't miss it for anything."

He cleared his throat looking at his clipboard and pointing to it. "I gotta go get additional paperwork."

His eyes meeting mine, he said, "Be right back." Then to Hannah, "Good to see you, Hannah."

He walked around us and through the doors. Hannah watched him until he disappeared. "Why are you not with him? I mean, seriously, Tiff, he is perfect for you."

"The only use I have for a man right now is sex, and Andy is doing a fine job with that."

She gripped my shirt, physically making me gravitate toward her as she gritted her teeth, "Andy! The unstable nut job? The guy that hangs out with people buying body parts Andy?"

I laughed as she let go. She was also another one of my favorite people to rile up.

"Are you insane? Doesn't he have some kind of mental syndrome?"

I smirked whispering, "Let me just tell you, when he says 'in coming' I am in for a treat."

Hannah narrowed her eyes and scowled me. "There is something wrong with you." Then she gasped, throwing her hands out, stopping my forward motion. "He's not coming to the party, is he?"

I paused, wouldn't that be interesting? I tilted my head slightly to the side thinking about what it would be like having Andy there. "Well, that could be fun?"

Hannah's eyes widened. "No! You cannot be serious, Tiffany? You'll already have half the party brawling please don't bring him. Besides, he's like your father's age. You will have enough people gossiping about you. No need to throw in that you have a daddy complex."

"Daddy complex? He's only ten years older than me. Not Father's age."

"Well, no one will believe it. Last time I saw him, he looked old and homeless. Please don't bring him."

The idea became incredibly amusing, but she was right; besides, I would not do that to Michael by choice.

Andy made him uncomfortable in our informational meetings. I didn't get it; I didn't get the discomforting vibe from him. Why was everyone else so edgy with his appearance at meetings? I was nearly giddy every time I saw him.

"I'll see," was my final answer. She knew I was messing with her, though she was not entirely convinced, because even I made some decisions and looked back and wondered what the hell I was thinking.

Michael walked back out, observing Hannah's expression along with my amusement. He continued walking right past us, announcing, "I don't even want to know what you two are up to. I'll be in the bus." That's what Michael occasionally called my ambulance.

I calmed my buddy down to keep peace in our kingdom for the time being; after all, if anything happened to me, it was all her decision on what to do with me. I had signed my life over to Hannah. She was my next of kin in my will, emergency contact, everything. I wish I could be gay because she was my perfect partner until I could trust a man as I trusted Hannah; she held my deck of cards.

Our shift was going especially well. One woman I interacted with tonight, coming to my party, was nice to me. They were all going to hate me next week. I better enjoy this while I can.

By the next night, I was almost feeling guilty. Almost... At least the girls would find out what a dirt bag Kyle was, so I was sort of doing them a favor.

What a difference a week would make. The ladies attending tomorrow, who we have seen all week, have been talking more casually with me. Inviting them felt like the right thing to do. How I was doing it was wrong. I almost caved over the last few days. I'll make it up to them at the party...have the waiters pay special attention to them or something.

Michael walked alongside my car, gently giving me orders to sleep late and have a nap in the afternoon. We had a long day ahead of us. He wished me a happy birthday, then lingered for a moment. It looked as if he wanted to say more. He hesitated, then said nothing. He turned, head hanging down, and walked away. I shrugged it off; if he couldn't say what he wanted to, then I didn't want to hear it.

CHAPTER FOUR

It was just past eight in the morning when I pulled into my parking lot. I lived in a gutted-out factory that Mildred had turned into condos. I knew when she renovated this place that I would live here.

My Fair Godmother was excellent at spotting buildings that would make her a lot of money. This building kept the open raw feel with brick and stucco hallways you could drive a car through. Mildred even placed seating areas around corners that welcomed neighbors to socialize or extra room for a visitor to hang out.

I moved those chairs as far away from my condo as I could and replaced them with fake trees. I liked my neighbors, but I didn't want them hanging out by my corner unit.

The car in my other parking spot instantly triggered a smile to my face. It looked like there was no need to make a call today as he exited the piece of crap Chevy, held together by duct tape, that he claimed was actually street legal. My heart raced just seeing him at my car door looking straight at me balancing a brown paper bag between his fingers then ordering me, "Grab your duffel Tiff and give it to me."

I did; he swung it over his shoulder, then swept me off my feet into his arms as if I were weightless.

My first reaction was to struggle against all this fuss, but I knew this man. He would just make it so I couldn't move at all. I've felt him restrain me with his body weight before in a playful wrestling match where I wanted to prove I could break free. I lost. Besides, strangely enough, this felt sort of nice. I even relaxed enough to put my arm around his shoulder while feeling the brown bag swishing under me.

"So, what's in the bag, Andy?"

Straight-faced, he looked down and ordered, "Keys."

I had them in my hand and fiddled with the door at this odd angle. I finally unlocked the entrance pushing it open. He stopped it with his foot and closed it behind him.

I studied him. "What's with all of this?"

He gave his signature slightly hard grin. "Stop your yappin', woman; just enjoy it."

I loved seeing his smile. He was up to something.

We arrived at my door with another command, "Keys?"

I was already opening it again at a difficult angle.

He caught it with his foot and closed it. He carried me right to my bedroom, let me drop the keys on the dresser, and tossed me on my bed. Yes, he definitely made me feel giddy. I sat up as he leaned into me with a proper kiss.

Looking into my eyes and straightening back up, he slowly removed his layers one at a time. I couldn't help watching him strip. This man was built like a fine marble sculpture. I knew he worked out intensely; I was the lucky one enjoying the view at the moment. Seeing him like this gave me pure admiration for the male gender.

I often fantasized what it would be like coming home to him. When we were together, it was like there was no one else in the world that mattered other than the two of us right then. He is complete satisfaction for me when we are together. He treated me well, and this relationship was working for both of us at the moment.

He picked up his brown bag and pulled out a baby blue, rectangular, small shoe box with a loose strap. Andy fed it through the side of the box. I watched not understanding what the heck he was doing. "What are you doing?"

He looked up, registering that I was watching, then back down to finish as he said, "Patience, woman."

Next thing I saw, he dropped his underwear and was adjusting himself through the back of the box, securing the strap around his waist. With everything in place, he turned to give me the full effect. "Happy Birthday, it's for Tiffany." He held on to both sides of the box walking toward me with his present.

Oh, my! My mouth fell open. I gasped out of shock, staring wide eyed, taking it all in. He was so clever. I looked at the box and noticed the scribbles in black marker saying Tiffany's.

I think he was trying to make it look like the box was actually from the department store that shared my name. I burst out laughing; he grinned, stepping closer to me. "Do you want to see what I got for the birthday girl?"

* * *

I woke up around one in the afternoon with Andy's arm draped around my shoulder as I was tucked against his body. He seldom stays; I was laying there as still as can be, thinking about my next move. Now what do I do with him? I shifted a little, waking him instantly; he pulled his arm away, checking the time which made him even more awake. "Hey, I got to go, sexy... Happy birthday."

He pulled me in, and kissed me like it was our last. He was superb at that last kiss, leaving me sitting there in complete bliss. He ordered, "Text me." With a wink of his eye, and a click sound from his mouth, just like that, he was gone.

I spotted the handmade Tiffany box and strap on my nightstand and grinned. Andy was something all right. Now I could add creative to my list of likes about him.

I spent the rest of my afternoon down at the garage. I knew my ambulance was due for an oil change, and Greg gave me the okay to do it. To him, it was like having an extra person on his shift. Not only did I do my oil change, but I did Kyle's and Jeff's. I wish Jeff was back on my shift. I enjoyed working with him. He used to tease the hell out of me and I loved every bit of it. Jeff mastered the art of playful banter and then he got married moving mostly to day shifts.

Looking at my phone to check the time, I noticed two missed calls and eleven texts displayed on my screen. Every text wishing me a happy birthday. My mother and Michael had called. I called him first. He warned me he would be late. It could not be helped. He had to help a friend with an emergency move. I was fine until he said that she had gotten herself in a real pickle this time, needing to be out of the guy's apartment quickly. I don't know why that bubbled a deep, pissed off reaction in me, but it did, oddly enough.

I focused on the time, just enough to grab a shower and be at the hotel for the 6:00 party. My attention immediately honed in on my hands. They were covered in grease, and oil stains. Mother was not going to like this at all.

I tried everything to clean them, including my dish pan scrubber. It removed a fair share, but you could still see the evidence that I had been playing at the garage this afternoon. I simply needed to let it go, accept it, and move on.

I grabbed my packed a bag for the night, grinned at my Tiffany box, then proceeded out of my condo, wearing my teal cocktail dress with the beige heels Mother brought back from Paris. Maybe, just maybe, she would overlook my hands and concentrate on these shoes. They felt expensive, and it would delight her that I was wearing them.

With my hair down, it was already tangling in my duffel strap as I heaved my bag into the back seat. I let out a heavy sigh, and glared at my hands wrapped around the steering wheel. "She is going to have a fit."

Hannah texted me the room number we had booked because I didn't want to leave my gun in the car. I knocked, hearing her excitement on the other side of the door, "Happy Birthday, Tiff!" she squealed, opening the door wide, then launched herself at me as she threw her arms around me and embraced me. She was the only other person I could relax with while being held in such a tight squeeze. That was until she started talking in a high-pitched, squeaky, mouth puckered tone to me like I was four.

She was so happy we were spending another birthday together. I'd had enough with the embracing. Hannah, on the other hand, didn't care as I made her walk backward entering the room. Finally, she let me break free. When she gave me some distance, all happiness vanished. "Your hands! What the hell have you been doing!"

I flipped my hair back so it wouldn't tangle in my duffel bag strap again. I pulled my gun secured it in the safe, then left everything else on the bed. "I worked at the garage this afternoon. My ambulance needed an oil change, and I had time to do it."

"All that from one oil change?"

"Um, no. I ended up doing three."

"Tiffany oil-stained hands do not go well with this dress. You look beautiful...except for your hands. Your mother... If you're looking to send her to the hospital, I think you may accomplish it."

I shrugged. "I got most of it off? Anyway, it won't be the first time I'll disappoint her nor will it be the last." With that said, and my firearm secured, we headed down to see the ballroom.

Mother was busy walking the final inspection with the hotel's event planner. I could peg her title from here. She was wearing a navy-blue tailored suit, and was tall and thin with the perfect shade of artificially colored blonde hair pinned up in a tight bun. They both turned toward us as we cleared the door.

"Tiffany!" Mother called, extending her hand in my direction. "There's my birthday girl. Don't you look lovely. Oh, to have a body like yours again, all the things I could do differently."

Hannah nudged me, giggling, "Like what?"

The party planner was smiling politely, extending her hand as we reached them. "Happy Birthday, Miss Chanler." Gasping, she pulled her hand away quickly, not daring to touch mine.

Mother's smile turned upside down as she reached for the clean part of my arm. "Tiffany! What is all over your hands?"

I looked down at the one she was examining. "I changed the oil in my ambulance this afternoon?"

"You could not have done that tomorrow or the next day? It had to be today?"

Oh, I hadn't thought about that. "Sorry Mother, it's just how my day has gone. I wasn't thinking about the effects of an oil change relating to this over the top party." Turning my head in both directions, taking in most of this room. I exclaimed, "Mother, this is a bit much for my birthday!"

She released my arm, countering my comment, "No, it's not. This is perfect because these are the best years of your life. I was pregnant with you at twenty-seven changing my whole life."

Hannah giggled, stepping away to give me a little privacy.

Slowly releasing a heavy breath, I asked the dreaded question, "So, how many are expected?"

By the time my mother finished giving me the rundown, I wanted to walk right out the doors and drive away. If it weren't for my pre-arranged entertainment, I would have left.

From behind me, I heard the raspy older voice calling my name like a truant officer yelling at a runaway kid, "Tiffany! Tiffany!" making me burst into a huge grin.

Mildred Jones, my Fairy Godmother, has arrived. She stopped halfway through the room, gesturing with her arms spread wide. "Priscilla, you have outdone yourself again. This child does not deserve all this fuss!" Dropping her arms, she broadened her smile, walking toward us.

I glanced back to Mother who radiated with pride. Mildred knew exactly how to compliment her. For decades, she had tried to teach me. There were a few skills that stuck, but mostly, I didn't really care enough to immerse myself into people pleasing, especially with the cut throat society I grew up in.

Mildred is the strongest, most independent woman I know, taking her role as my godmother seriously. And now, Fairy Godmother homed in on my hands scolding me. "Tiffany! Go to the kitchen and soak those hands in bleach. Right now!"

Mother gently argued that I shouldn't. This could be over looked. Bur Mildred was even more pissed at my careless decision, displaying fury in her eyes, signaling me to scoot right by her, and find the kitchen.

Hannah called for me to wait up, complaining that she couldn't run with the heels she had on. I slowed my mission march, letting her catch up as she latched onto my arm. "You should have known better," she snickered.

Answering with a huff signaling that she was right, we found the kitchen. I pushed the door open, stepping right in, scanning the setup, spotting the dish washing area in the back.

There were a lot of employees watching as I rummaged through the supplies finding the bleach. Hannah gently poured it over my hands as I scrubbed them together first, then soaked then in a bowl we had found. The smell was intoxicating, backing Hannah away a few steps. She suggested adding hot water. It was working... hmmm, well, would you look at that.

Hannah pointed, "This will probably poison you, but your hands are clean."

I soaped them up good then dried them on the towel she found. A manager approached, chastising us that we could not be in here.

Hannah apologized explaining that the big party in the ballroom was for my birthday and I needed to remove the ink that had spilled on my hands because it didn't go with my dress. He bought her little white lie and backed down, waiting to escort us out.

We made our way back to the ballroom with my hands now nearly the same color as the rest of my skin. It amazed Mother turning them over and commenting on the difference as Mildred nodded, satisfied by the outcome.

Now, she handed me an envelope. "Go tuck this someplace safe. Happy Birthday, my dear godchild. Twenty-seven... and you are still alive. That is a milestone in itself." Mildred grinned as if she had done her part in keeping me alive until now, then sent me away again...

Hannah and I headed back to the room to put my envelope in the safe. Her curiosity suggested I open it, but I couldn't. I knew it would be something spectacular, and if I opened it, I would lose my edge for the whole evening. I would open it later when the party was over.

As we returned down to the ballroom, the guests had started to arrive while we made our way in. The first one to approach cleared her throat behind me. I turned, losing my smile.

"Hello, Tiffany."

Hannah was facing Clarissa.

"Hello."

"I see your mother has gone overboard for you once again."

"She really nailed it. I keep telling her to open her own business, but she is happy being a wife and mother." I commented admiring the event, just to piss this woman off. I recently learned that Clarissa had to take a job somewhere.

Clarissa raised her right eyebrow. "Keep encouraging her to spread her wings. Change comes quickly. All is not what it appears to be."

I laughed. "Oh, are we in the mood for riddles tonight?"

She switched the conversation directed to me. "Still a delivery driver, Tiffany?"

I knew this game of hers. Hannah cupped my elbow to walk away. She too knew this woman all too well. I remember a few times Hannah telling me that she and her husband had left the restaurant without paying. That's the woman Clarissa was. Too good for everyone, and the world owed her.

I tapped Hannah's hand to let her know I wasn't going anywhere. Clarissa's perfume vaped off of her in an invisible cloud. That alone was a reason to leave; she smelled like regret. I refused to let her have the upper hand at my party. I had no problem referring to her by her first name. I was an adult, and she was rotten.

"You know, Clarissa, there may come a time that your alcohol-soaked body gives out, or that cold heart of yours wants to quit. I pray, trust I am not a praying type of woman, but I pray that it's me carrying the cargo you need. And with that knowledge I'll make sure I will be late."

Clarissa narrowed her eyes. "Do you remember my niece, Mandy?"

"No. There is not a day that goes by that I think of you or anyone associated with you. Why on Earth would you think I would waste brain cells like that? Oh, wait. I think I remember Blake going to jail, though?"

She smiled. "No, you're wrong. Blake is managing our expansion project."

"I had no intention to actually ask about him. I don't care."

"Why should you? He is out of your league."

"Oh Clarissa, I could not agree with you more."

"Mandy has moved to town, and landed a wealthy benefactor; she is such a beautiful girl. It shocks me to think she has settled so quickly on this man."

"I don't care, Clarissa, not about you or any member of your corrupt family."

I went to end this conversation, starting to turn away from her. She reached out touching my shoulder.

"Tiffany? I'm certain you'll cross paths soon; be a dear and try to be hospitable. She doesn't know many people around here."

This woman was nuts. On what planet did she ever think I would be social to anyone in her family? I uttered me closing my sentence, summing up our entire conversation,

"Enjoy the bar, Clarissa. Drink up. It's on me tonight."

Hannah now grabbed my elbow to lead me away, hunching toward me and scrunching her face before snickering, "I can't believe you said that to her! Sweetie, that was perfect!"

I noticed my father for the first time, walking toward me. A few guests tried for his attention. He reached us leaning in to kiss me on the cheek, flattering me by saying that I looked lovely. He commented on what a dynamic job mother had done with her arrangements.

Clarissa homed in on my father, making me search for Mother, so I could compliment her about all this fanfare again. I thanked her making sure she knew I meant it. This brought a tear to her eye as she forced it back, wishing me a happy birthday. Mildred nodded that I had done the right thing.

Mother seized this moment, announcing she was planning my next day off which included the beauty salon. Apparently, my hair needed highlights, and I was due for a manicure and pedicure.

I laughed. "What nails?"

Mildred gave me "the look" as I was about to protest. I stopped, and cleared my throat, committing to Mother's plan. A long time ago, Mildred explained that sometimes I just needed to sacrifice a little for the greater good. That much I remembered and applied when necessary.

Mildred loved my mother as much as she loved me, so this would be my sacrifice until I could hide again for a few months.

CHAPTER FIVE

The party was not really for me. I was the theme, and the intentions were there, but this was a power play for my mother in her social circle. Most of these people I could not stand. And once I spotted, Mitzy Wellington, I knew my mother was digging deep.

Hannah could play this game well; Mildred played this game well, and I now thought I should have brought Andy as my date to add another layer.

It wasn't until nearly an hour later, when Michael finally showed up, that I could relax. We were working tonight so my only alcoholic drink could be a sip for the birthday toast, which was no big deal. I didn't drink.

My mother greeted him first as I watched from a slight distance away. He was smiling, and holding her arms; she was his mirror image suddenly laughing, and tossing her head back. She reached up, patting his face with endearment.

My father walked over to Michael, shaking his hand as Mother's arm moved back down by her side. Michael was now searching the room as Hannah intercepted him. She pointed in my direction, and his head followed. When he spotted me, our eyes met, I smiled, and he blankly stared.

What? Why did he look like that? I lost my smile while marching over to him.

Bringing a fist to his mouth he cleared his throat. "Ha...hhh."

He cleared his throat again. "Happy birthday."

I grabbed him by the arm moving us off to the side. "Thanks. So, four girls are already here."

I pointed them out. "Kyle should be here any minute. What kept you so long?"

"Sorry, there was a scene. My friend's roommate showed up and tried to be a problem."

"You should have called me; you know I am looking for any excuse to leave."

"And that is exactly why I didn't. I dealt with it. You look twenty-seven tonight."

I frowned and smacked his arm, leaving him grinning and rubbing where the back of my hand had landed.

"I am just saying Tiff, you look beautiful, savvy, and in control."

I smacked him again, same spot, and he grunted on impact collapsing, then regaining his posture.

"You can shut the hell up now."

He rubbed harder. "Point taken, birthday girl."

I swung, but he moved making me miss which made him grin again. "Let me buy you a water, slugger."

Michael walked away as another Kyle fan walked in looking around with amazement. None of them were approaching me though. Why?

I made sure the waiters greeted every single woman walking through these doors tonight. They had wine and food immediately when they stepped in. I was wondering if this was too much for them to take in.

I discussed this with Michael. He said that they probably didn't recognize me in street clothes. Well, lo and behold, he was right. The transformation on their faces when I greeted them individually was pure shock.

There was no way I believed I looked so different in uniform than in a dress. It was as if I were a different person to them. I now had all of them here, easing them in, introducing them around individually as Kyle entered the fully swinging party.

I had planted Michael so that Kyle would see him first. My plan was executing right on cue. Slowly, one by one, Michael walked with Kyle around the room as the ladies spotted him. He was happy to receive the first one. He even kissed her cheek upon greeting her. He kind of latched onto her when Hannah made her way to being seen.

Kyle excused himself from the first woman and followed to where Hannah was walking in the crowd, only to bump into his next play toy. The look on his face was classic as he searched the room probably looking to see where the first one was. He swung his head around releasing number two-gal and spotting Hannah again.

Now, the tables were turning while I observed he knew that two of his ladies were here. He did not greet the second one the same way as the first. She received a quick hug as he continued focusing on Hannah.

Next came number three, and oh, my gosh, was this getting good. Number four spotted him, excusing herself to greet him. He lost Hannah, now staying in the company of number four. Michael and Hannah joined me on the sidelines watching.

This was better than any reality show as Kyle tried desperately to jockey among all the women. It was time to mix up the game again. Hannah went in for the greeting as Michael laughed, which made me laugh as I tried to calm both of us down. Just as it was getting really good, the evening proved that I had no control over tonight; all my entertainment came to a halt.

Someone had given my parents a microphone, and they proceeded to give a brief history, along with pictures, of my twenty-seven years on this planet. Karma was kicking my ass right now with a full slide-show for all the guests.

I wanted to drink, but I couldn't. They asked me to come forward and stand with them. Everyone sang happy birthday to me, we toasted, and this concluded any obligation I had to stay here.

No one was leaving; there was an open bar, good food, and the DJ was playing all the popular party songs. This was turning into a showcase party. The dance floor was getting crowded mostly with women my age. All of them had extensive dance lessons through all of their primary and teen years, proving that a fifty-thousand-dollar dance investment was only worthy of the best high-end strip club.

Michael looked entertained. "Hey, can you dance like that?" He pointed into the crowd.

"No, I only learned the classics. I protested learning Burlesque."

"Wow, um. Wow, that one's got some moves."

"Michael, do you need a napkin?"

He turned his head slowly to me. "Um, why?"

"You're drooling."

"Not my fault. Men pay good money to see this kind of performance. Now if I could only have a beer life would be perfect."

I sarcastically shook my head, men!

With more of the crowd on the dance floor, I could single people out better. I noticed that two hospital women were talking with each other. There was no way anything good could come of this. Half the women had already approached, thanking me for including them. They left as happy as they arrived. Those ladies were on the same shift as us tonight, so a little food, and a little joy went a long way.

Then there was the other half. Kyle was scrambling to keep his operation going trying to juggle them one by one and give equal attention without alerting the others.

I have to admit; he was smooth, and his multitasking was very impressive. The entrance caught my attention; another two women arrived who I did not know. One looked like I had seen her somewhere, but I could not place it. The other just looked smug grabbing a glass of wine from a waiter. She had a big attitude and there was something about her I instantly did not like.

It was my father approaching these females that gave me an uneasy feeling. I watched the one I already had a problem with. She was having words with him. Maybe she worked at his company?

She had issues, and there was something not right with this whole situation. Father stood in front of them so I couldn't see exactly what was going on. The brunette looked irritated standing there drinking.

Hannah distracted me and was pointing at Kyle, who had abandoned the women that were left at this point. He was now talking to Clarissa Montgomery's daughter, Reese.

I turned to look for Mother, who was laughing and being led to the dance floor by Uncle Dan. This became Michael's cue, grabbing my hand while the DJ started to play the older favorites, blaring through the speakers. Hannah screamed excitedly at the song, following us onto the dance floor. I would kill Michael later, but he didn't care as I got into the moment following along with my party people.

I couldn't help but keep an eye on my father. He was escorting the women out into the hotel. I tried to move off the dance floor, only to have Kyle block me.

"Don't think I didn't catch on to your little game tonight, Chanler. There is no way these women are random friends of yours. I found out many interesting facts about you tonight. Little girls who play with fire get their fingers burned. Game on, bitch!" he gritted through his teeth.

I watched for any sudden movement from him. He relaxed. "Oh, and thanks for the invite, food was good."

Michael and Hannah were now by my side.

Hannah asked, "Oh, are you leaving so soon Kyle?" He didn't even look back, just flipped his middle finger in the air as he walked out.

Hannah turned to me. "Okay then. Guess you accomplished your goal."

My father walked back in alone. From his expression, I knew all too well that, someone had frustrated him, and he was mad. I was a pro at conjuring that look out of him.

Mildred interrupted us announcing she would like a word with me. I followed her away from the crowd to a table where we could talk.

The first thing out of her mouth was that I should make more time for my mother. I rolled my eyes. Free time was better spent away from my parents.

Her response was pounding her fist on the table. She got my attention. I knew this side of Mildred. This was not a good place to be with her. She could rip the carpet right out from under anyone. I did not have immunity, no matter how much she treated me as her own. I have seen Mildred in business not thinking twice about any lives she destroyed.

I answered her quickly. "Yes, Ma'am. I will fit in more time with Mother."

She released the tight grip of her fist and splayed her hand out smoothing the tablecloth. "Tiffany, your mother needs you. There are things going on that they have not informed you of."

My eyes widened. "What is going on? Is she sick?"

Mildred now touched my arm as panic washed through me. "No child, nothing like that. She needs you."

Like I said, I knew Mildred more than I knew my mother and now she was not telling me something I needed to know. "This is crap. What are you not telling me?"

Mildred softened. "This is a conversation that needed to happen between you and Priscilla, but not here, not tonight."

She patted my arm standing up. "Make time for her Tiffany. I expect to see you at the salon appointment. No excuses."

I nodded. Damn it! What the hell was this about?

Michael and I had about an hour before we had to leave for work. I said good night to all my key people. I observed my mother as I thanked her, trying to figure out the mystery Mildred just dumped in my lap.

Mother confirmed that she would make the appointment on one of the next two Saturdays, which ever opened first. She knew my schedule just like Hannah did. I noted that I had those off now.

Just as I was about to argue to keep my Saturdays to myself because those were the best garage days, Mildred caught my eye and walked up to us. I gave up on the idea of arguing to keep the peace between both my mothers.

"I'll make sure I'm there."

Her face lit up as she leaned in, holding me close to her. She cupped her right hand at the base of my neck, softly embracing, while I had to control every knee jerking sensation to break free. My heart rate raced. I could feel it beating in my chest. This was a terrible position to be in for me. It was all I could do to control my breath and wiggle back out of her hands.

She released me while her fingers now touched down my cheek. It was painful to let her. I wanted to slap her hand away as I clenched my fist to endure it. This was my mother. She was not Blake. Sincerely, she spoke, "Happy birthday, my beautiful daughter. Be careful tonight and call me tomorrow."

I nodded looking around. "I will." I had to get out of here. Michael approached for his turn to say goodbye.

Michael went right in for a big hug. He had no issues with affection and my mother. He even kissed her on the cheek, telling her she had outdone herself and what a great party this was. He then thanked her for including him. Mother ran her fingers through his hair and commented that he needed a haircut and he should join us for salon day.

He just laughed, "No, no, no. That's a chick thing. You're not baiting that trap for me."

Mother laughed, tossing her head playfully and touching his arm. "I'll get you there with us one of these days, Michael. Now, you just gave me a challenge."

He leaned in patting her upper arm. "Good luck with that, Priscilla."

He politely nodded in a head bow to Mildred, acknowledging her, as Father was walking toward us.

"Good night, Tiffany, it was lovely to see you enjoying yourself tonight. Happy Birthday, Dearest."

A wide charismatic grin showed off his dashing, vibrant side. Everyone said I had Father's smile when it was genuine and not forced.

"Thank you; this was a lot of fun. Mother, you outdid yourself, as usual. I told you that party planning is your calling. You should do this as a living and not just as a hobby."

Mother smiled proudly. "I'm getting too old. Thank you, though. I enjoy watching you having fun. It warms my heart, Tiffany."

Father nodded in agreement, and angled his body toward my mother as he stepped in closer to her, stretching his arm around her waist.

She stepped forward away from him, removing his hand politely. She pointed between Michael and me. "Well, I know you two have to get ready."

Hannah was bouncing over. She hugged both my parents telling them this party was a hole in one, a home run, touchdown, goal... I stopped her with the sports references because she would go all the way to ping pong.

Michael looked at his watch and announced he would meet me at base. He wanted to check in on his friend first.

I narrowed my eyes feeling a twitch of irritation.

Hannah reminded me that I had to clean out the safe so back to the room we went. I changed first then knelt down to collect what I had in there holstering my gun and picking up Mildred's envelope. She was eyeing it as I almost got to toss it in my bag. "Hey, I want to see even if you don't. What did Fairy Godmother get you?"

I protested with a sigh. "Fine!"

I opened her card and there was a thousand-dollar gift card to a trendy clothing store downtown and a paper-wrapped square. I opened it. It was a lapel pin in the shape of little golden wings. On the paper she wrote, my dearest godchild, each year I have with you is a gift. Here is your first set of wings. I am proud of you, making it on your own. Consider thinking bigger, broader. See where your wings can take you from here.

I smiled and fixed the pin to my collar.

"Aw, she is so thoughtful. We will expand your wardrobe. Want me to hold on to that?"

I handed her my gift card.

"Okay, what time do you want me to drop off the rest of the cards?"

I grinned. "Just burn them."

She stomped her foot like a five-year-old. "I will call you at 2:00."

I nodded.

She hugged me and said, "Happy Birthday Tiff."

I turned and walked out, wearing my first set of golden wings and feeling empowered.

CHAPTER SIX

I drove straight to work. Kyle was there to greet me with affectionate birthday wishes such as, "Fucking bitch, you will pay for that." I love it when we come together like a family.

"You know, Kyle, I don't know if I should laugh at you, or feel bad for you. I'd laugh because you thought I would include you in anything to do with my life; I'd be sad that you thought you could play so many women at the same time and get away with it. See, I was only guessing and karma marched right in with a big HA! ASSWIPE!"

Kyle threw his work orders down. I dropped my bag, immediately reacting in a crouching stance. Michael and Jason came out of nowhere, intercepting Kyle. "What the fuck?" I yelled. "It's my goddamn birthday! Let him up!" I was trembling slightly from anger; they were interfering with my opportunity to go one-on-one with Kyle.

Now we were in lockdown. I stood erect, pissed that I didn't get to hit him or at least grapple him to the ground. They ordered everyone into the conference room.

No one left without their hands being slapped. All of us got our first written warnings. Let's just say it was a quiet shift until the morning.

My five dock transfers had nothing to do with my party gals tonight. Michael and I were in the rural areas, an hour away from the city limits. There were a lot of roads traveled tonight in darkness.

Kyle got the route with his ladies, so that made it even more boring on my end. Michael was exceptionally quiet. I wanted to ask why his mood was so somber, but I was thinking it had to do with his "friend," the other female.

I did not want to know anything about her, so it left us not to talk at all. Michael was texting a lot. He even answered a call walking away from me on one dock. Super, another great ending to the start of my twenty-seventh birthday.

Andy's piece of shit car was in my other space waiting for me. The morning sunlight illuminated the only new pieces of duct tape holding that crap car together. I slightly chuckled in amusement as it glimmered catching the light. Two days in a row? Hmm, something must be up?

I slammed on my brakes at this black cat darted out in front of me. That would have sucked if I had hit it. I looked and didn't see it anywhere, so I pulled into my space. Andy was out of his car in a flash, opening my door, lifting my body out by my hand so fast I could feel the anxious energy now radiating from him.

He growled through his teeth, "What the fuck happened back at headquarters?" Oh, Oh, Oh, Oh! That's why he was here?

"You know Kyle and I loathe each other, right? Well, tonight it came out." Andy seized my duffel bag from me. He walked in silence holding onto my left arm until we were in my condo.

He dropped my bag on a chair and went straight to the kitchen to make coffee. I knew another solid fact about Andy. He made the most perfect cup of coffee I have ever tasted in my life. If this was the only other thing, I had to bank on with him, I would take it. I would consider taking him on as a boyfriend. Fantastic lover and perfect at making coffee; he was a keeper. He was also moving around too fast. This was the end of my shift and I was tired.

Andy was clearly waiting for details. He also expected that I would just automatically give them. This annoyed me. I was supposed to tell him everything while he offered nothing? Screw this, not happening this morning no matter how good his coffee was. I didn't say a thing and pulled my guns out. They needed cleaning.

He started "What the fuck Tiff? The entire organization now knows there is a bigger issue between you and Kyle. You are now the weakest target. It's everywhere outside the company. You just increased your probable hits by sixty percent. You want to fight? You just opened yourself up for trouble."

I knew there could always be a leak in the company. The black market paid well for any information it could get. Everything Andy just said was true. I had to keep this to myself. I had to keep Michael safe and away from my careless mistakes. Kyle could die for all I cared. To hell with him. Michael was my only concern right now. I placed the guns on my counter and walked around it picking up the cup Andy had put down for me and I sipped. Damn, this would go well with a jelly donut right now.

Andy was waiting for an answer. "Tiffany!" I narrowed my eyes irritated with him. He wasn't my lover right now he was playing my parent. I didn't like him in that role. I dismissed the potential boyfriend status and answered him, "Okay, I didn't think of the repercussions. Andy, I can take care of myself. I don't need you as a watchdog."

He sarcastically grunted and then purposely pointed at me. "A watch dog couldn't handle you. You need a fucking small army." I narrowed my eyes. There was a moment of silence between us as I blew across my coffee, cooling it down some, to take another sip. I glanced up. Andy was watching my every move. "What?" my irritation got the better of me.

He stepped closer. "Do you know a woman by the name of Audrey Lanski?"

I shook my head, not recognizing the name at all. "No." I readied my lips to take another tiny sip. This was good coffee. No matter how I tried, I just couldn't nail this same taste. "No, never heard that name. Why?"

"Just asking."

"Who is she?"

"Someone in need of a new organ."

"Which part?"

"Does it matter? You don't even know what you carry."

"You know what Andy? I don't know if that is a blessing or a curse. I mean, if we knew at least we could judge the risk factor better."

He chuckled. "Or you could stage a hijacking better and split the profit."

"What the fuck! Seriously!" I straightened up, and flipped my palm upward.

"Tiffany, not everyone thinks like you."

"Andy is there a way to know what I'm carrying so I can better protect Michael?"

"You're worried about protecting Michael? And why is that?" Andy placed his cup down meticulously.

"Oh, fuck off. It's not like that."

He stepped into me. "Tiff, we don't have an agreement between us. You can see and be with anyone you want." He paused in front of me. "I just don't want him to compromise your safety. You mean a lot to me, babe."

WHAT! Was he serious right now? "What does that mean?"

"It means that I know my limitations. I know I can't be here for you, in any normal, come home to each other relationship. But it also means you are the only woman who has made it this far in my life. The way we are is how I can be with you. Yes, I take it for granted that you come home alone. But if your second parking space is open when I come around, then I am claiming it."

I grinned trying to fight it. Okay, maybe he was back on the boyfriend list.

I woke up again with Andy's arm around me; he spooned my body. It was two in the afternoon. I had to get down to the garage. Andy was still in bed when I was ready to leave. I touched his foot, and he shot up and out of my bed quicker than I thought was humanly possible. I was already in a crouch stance extending my hand with no sudden movements. "Hey, Andy. Hey, it's all right. Just me here, I did that. I wanted to tell you I'll be down at the garage. Stay if you want? I'm good with you hanging out here."

He was already dressing. "I'll leave with you."

I straightened, relaxing because he was slowing down. His pants were on and that's all he made it to as I continued talking, enjoying the shirtless view. "Well, if you make me a cup of coffee to go, you don't have to rush out of here. Clean my guns, have a shower, shave. Please shave?" I made light of his appearance and playfully laughed. He was super scruffy undercover man. It still looked sexy to me.

He made my coffee and took me up on my offer. This was the first time he has ever been in my condo alone... that I know of. For all I know he could have broken in and been here before as much as he wanted. I didn't want to think of him that way, though.

I walked past the eyesore of his car. Damn it looked worse in full daylight. I contemplated asking him to park elsewhere, but this old crap Chevy kind of warmed my heart.

Hannah was texting me, asking when a good time was to meet up. She was in charge of holding all my birthday cards when I left and now wanted to pass them off to me. I replied that Andy was at the house, and she could drop them there. I laughed as my phone immediately rang. "Are you kidding! I will not be left alone with him. He freaks me out, Tiffany!"

I stopped laughing. "I don't know why. He has done nothing to earn that mistrust with you."

"Tiffany! The only thing missing is black eyeliner, and he would fit the perfect serial killer image."

I grinned again. "I'll have to try that out and ask if he will let me put some on him, to see if you're right."

"Tiffany!"

"Personally, I think he would look like a bad ass rock star wearing black eyeliner."

"Okay enough about Mr. Unstable. Where can I drop this stuff off to you?"

"I'll be at the garage in about forty minutes and I'm staying there until around seven."

"Okay, I'll be there in an hour. Don't get too dirty before I drop these."

"No promises Hannah." I smirked and hung up.

I pulled up and Calvin wouldn't let me through. Apparently, they were slapping my hand harder and hitting me where it hurt. I didn't care. I shut my car off and walked past the gate calling to Greg. They didn't dare lock it down this time. Calvin puffed himself up and tried his best to be authoritative in front of me, only doing the opposite delivering amusement for me. I really tried to keep a straight face.

Greg was wiping his hands and calling to Calvin. He finally turned as Greg said, "Okay, Cal, good practice-run son; now let her the fuck in. I'm down two men and I have to replace an engine gasket." I tapped Calvin's chest with encouragement. "You're getting better, buddy, but useless words next time. Mystery is the key, so they don't know what you're thinking."

Oh, that got me a whole sentence of profanity giving away exactly what he was thinking. I grinned wider knowing how easily I could crush his ego as I make my way back to my car. I waited for the gate to open. I called Hannah and told her to text me when she was close and I would have to meet her outside.

Greg was a man of few words. He knew how to swear, though and when that bolt broke, he lost it, throwing his spanner on the ground and calling that bolt every name in the book. When he was done with his rant, he looked at me. "What the fuck were you thinking last night?"

What? Where was this coming from? And why was I under fire right now?

Hannah was calling me. "Hold that thought." I answered Hannah's call and told her, "Okay," repeating, "Just outside the back gate, ten minutes." I hung up.

I turned back to Greg. "Sorry, what was the question?" He grumbled, knowing I was being a smartass. I answered, "I was thinking it was time Kyle had a tune-up." Greg shook his head. "You know, one of these days, that smart mouth of yours is going to just go too far."

I smiled. "I know, but it isn't today. Thanks for letting me in. I see they're trying to make an example out of me?"

Greg's mouth turned up in the left corner. "Yeah, punish you for not letting you work on top of never getting paid while you're in this garage. You have to appreciate their reasoning. I mean that thinking must go straight to the top."

I wiped my hands and snickered. "I know, they're just downright mean. I got to go meet Hannah for a minute; be right back."

Greg straightened up and walked to his tool box as I scurried to meet Hannah outside.

She stepped out and said, "Yuck, you're already messy." She reached behind her seat and pulled out the long slender, sparkly, bag. "Priscilla has the boxy presents, but here are all the cards from last night. I opened a few. All gift cards so far."

I laughed. Only Hannah would be so bold as to open my birthday cards and scout out what was inside. "The good news is, the ones I opened were denominations of at least fifty dollars. Good places too. Look, I have to run. Call me when you get home later." She paused, looking at me holding the bag and smiling away. She quickly air kissed my cheek and hopped back in her car as I stepped away. She held her hand up to her face, gesturing for me to call later as the smile spread across her face again. I nodded and made my way back in carrying my shiny pink and silver glitter bag; I tossed it in the back of my car. I bet she bought that bag just to see me carry it. Good grief.

It took Greg and me three hours to get this motor back together. It wasn't until six that Jeff showed up "Get 'r' done, Gregory? Or am I in the spare?"

I peeked my head around; he laughed clapping, rubbing his hands together, grinning ear to ear "Ha. There's the troublemaker. Frame that warning slip yet, Tiff?"

I missed Jeff. He knew how to rile me playfully. "Tomorrow I'll go down to the framers."

"Happy Birthday, kid."

"Thanks, Jeff."

Greg walked around. "We got it done."

Jeff peeked around the quiet, deserted shop. "What? Did everyone bag work today? It's only Sunday?"

Greg nodded. "Yeah, you just can't get good help anymore."

"Well, lucky you got this one who doesn't have a life."

I tossed my rag at him as he quickly dodged it. "Okay, I got the wife in the car; just swung by to see if someone fixed her. I'll be back in a few hours."

I turned to Greg. "Anything else, boss?"

"That's it, kiddo; thank you for your help today. Just so you know, if there are any more write-ups against you, I won't be able to let you in here."

Grabbing a new rag, I wiped my hands a little better. "I see nothing more happening in the future unless they make Kyle and me ride together. If that happens, I'm pretty sure I will go to jail for his murder."

I scrubbed as best I could before leaving. Thank goodness my car was all black. Inserting my key into the ignition, my blue tooth alerted me to all my messages and missed calls. The only one I returned was to my mother. Now I had to go there tomorrow. She made me promise to stay long enough to have tea together.

Tea meant; she would bake her famous madeleines. I loved those darn things. I used to sneak into the kitchen before her company would come over and raid the plate, leaving only a few for her guest. It was years until she smartened up and made double batches; one for me, and one for her guests. If she made those every day, I would visit more often.

There was no sign of Andy when I arrived back, which brought me to thinking about leaving him here alone. I kind of liked the idea of him staying and hanging around. Maybe I would have liked him here, seeing his face when I walked through the door. I daydreamed a little about it as I poured a big glass of orange juice.

Picking it up, walking around my counter and placing it on my coffee table, I plunked myself on the couch flipping through the channels until I came to the home shopping channel. They were showing a new kitchen gadget that could open any bottle. Well, it caught my attention. This would be perfect for Mother and Mildred for Christmas. I reached over pulling my credit card from the pouch attached to the back of my phone and placed my order. They were always so cheerful on the phone taking my money, leaving only two minutes before this deal was gone forever.

This business had it down with, introducing products, limiting availability, and how they handled customer service.

Shortly after, I hung up and the next product was being introduced. Hannah's glitter bag was vying for my attention. I would have to burn it later. I dumped the contents out and texted her. Bag your idea?

She sent a smiley face, :)Yes! Don't you LOVE it!

I shook my head: *I think you could have found one with more sparkle.*

I got back: *No! I tried. This was the keeper.*

I laughed; she was the complete opposite of me. She had said she opened a few cards, but she had opened most of them. She made a point system drawing a one-to three-star rating on the back flap for good, better, or jackpot.

I texted her: *Did you get tired of opening these or drawing the stars?*

She replied: *LOL both!*

Well, I got a lot of gift cards. I placed the fresh stack in my fancy box on my coffee table and noticed that I had forgotten about the ones I put in there from the past Christmas. Well, now, I had added to my collection.

CHAPTER SEVEN

It wasn't until I went to pour the water into my coffee maker that I noticed it was already full. Coffee filter full, ready to go. Andy must have set this up for me before he left. I was thinking more about us in this relationship I have with him. Turning around, leaning against the counter, I texted him: *Thank You.*

He replied immediately: *K.* That was it, one simple letter.

I was appreciating just how uncomplicated this relationship actually was.

* * *

Not only did Mother have those special butter cakes, but she made me a batch to take home. If this was all she gave me for my birthday, then she would have succeeded. The party was over the top and a huge waste of money. Pissing Kyle off was worth it though.

Now she handed me one of the three boxes of wrapped gifts from the party. Glancing at the other two, shaking my head, I placed the one I was holding on top of the coffee table in front of me.

She looked a little awkward; something was up. Then she smiled big, handing me an envelope. I tried to refuse; this was getting ridiculous, but she insisted. I tossed it on top of the present.

She watched it on top of the pile, as if it would move on its own. "Please open that, Tiffany. I think you will approve of this one."

She was sitting across from me, with her posture leaning forward; I picked it up slowly. "Approve?"

She inhaled an emotional breath, touching her fingertips to her chest. We were now eye to eye. "I'm trying, Tiffany; Mildred helped me with this. To tell you the truth, I never even knew about this part of your childhood."

She had really sparked my curiosity as I straightened up and opened the envelope. My mother had picked out a joke card. It had a dog with googly eyes holding a martini glass. She was pointing, instructing me to wiggle the eyes. Okay, who was this woman, and what did she do with my mother?

I played along, wiggling them for her, making her laugh, while my eyes widened from the involuntarily uplift of my eyebrows. What was this new mood in my mother all about? Her hands relaxed around her knees as she leaned closer into me. "Looks like your father after your party."

Um okay? I opened the card as little bits of paper confetti fell onto my lap. She laughed again, pointing to my lap. "That was Mary's idea."

Mary was the other friend of my mother's that I liked. She had married her hometown sweetheart, who was a brilliant finance wizard and partner in one of the biggest firms here. This city never changed her. She was still a small-town misfit multi-millionaire; whom my mother had fostered under her wing fifteen years ago.

Mother's introduction into society left scars from a few women who wanted her out upon her arrival. She was not born into this level of money. Although her parents were wealthy, it was a working class earning.

My father was born into this level of old wealth. She had met him in college at an event. Mother was seeking a hospitality degree, and Father's track was business. Neither set of their parents approved of the marriage. This was why I was only close to Mother's family.

Regardless of their start, they made rank on their own here. Mother vowed that would never happen to another outsider if she could help it. She took it upon herself to coach Mary in this high society life, just as Mildred had done for my mother. It was looking like Mary was rubbing off on Mother now with back to the basics on how to have simple fun. Good for her.

I picked up the gold embossed white slip resting inside. It was a donation made in my name for five hundred dollars to the local West Side Girls' Club. West Side I knew well. It was far away from this neighborhood, where I experienced most of my street education. This section of town had improved over the last fifteen years and was nothing like when I dragged Hannah down there on my spontaneous adventures. This was also where my current grappling classes were held.

I loved this surprise gift. My mother had made me happy. I was genuinely smiling. "This is perfect. Thank you, Mother." Her eyes started to gloss over, and she cleared her throat. She looked up to the right of the ceiling, patting her chest lightly. I waited until she was back under control.

She gently cleared her throat a second time. "I think I understand you."

I nodded, holding up the paper, and waving it. "Very much, now if the money you spent on that party went to them, I would be over the moon happy."

She scowled. "Baby steps, Tiffany! Don't expect changes like that overnight. I am who I am." I stood making the first move, leaning in to hug her. I was genuinely pleased.

"Yes, you are. Thank you again, Mother."

Embracing her this time, my brain red flagged me. I could feel less than her normal slender frame. I could feel bone structure. Now, I paused a second to look her over. "Did you lose weight?"

She shook it off. "I have a lot of stress at present."

"What is going on?"

"Nothing, Tiffany, nothing that concerns you. Oh, and we have an appointment for the salon in two weeks."

I was about to let it go when the conversation Mildred had with me repeated in my brain.

I would get my answer. "Are you sick?"

My mother, standing from my release, looked a little anxious as I bent to pick up the box of gifts. Being the woman, I had grown myself into, I felt free to mention Mildred's little talk she had with me on Saturday night.

I just put it out there that Mildred was concerned about her. She abruptly placed her hand on her hip and huffed out a most irritated breath, swinging her other hand to shake her finger.

Well, I didn't expect that reaction. I thought this would be a simple talk. "That's the last time I ever confide in that woman."

I could feel my eyebrows stretching up. I had never seen this strong of a reaction from her when it came to Mildred.

"What is going on, Mom?"

We were both in shock. This was the first time I had ever called her Mom. She was not a casual mom. She was a formal mother. I stood there holding my box of wrapped gifts. She regained her composure by looking up, taking in a deep breath, and looking me square in the eyes.

"Your father is having an affair."

I dropped the box. Something definitely broke in there. She stared at me and I didn't know what to say. Talking was useless as only vowels came out. Then I waited a few seconds, wrapping my brain around her words, clearing my throat as if it would help, and asking her with doubt "Are you sure?"

I wasn't sure I had even heard her correctly. Father was the one man in their social group that didn't fool around.

"That brazen tart showed up at your party. That's why your father looked like that dog on your card coming home. I told him if he didn't end it, I was filing for divorce."

"Ah. Are you sure?"

"Stop asking that Tiffany. Yes, I am sure. This isn't the first time he has had an indiscretion."

"What?"

"Years ago, while you were away at college, he took up a relationship with a coworker."

"And you never told me?"

"No, and why should I have? They were discreet about it. I even like her. Look at all the world-class traveling I did at your father's expense. That was a fair trade in my eyes. I loved traveling. That French cooking school was one of the most memorable experiences I have had. The people I met, the food I tasted; it was incredible."

I had forgotten about all her excursions to Europe. Now I remembered that she was always traveling. I had thought little about it then. I was dumbfounded as I dropped into the chair. My father has been cheating on my mother and she was okay with this? She even likes the woman.

"Wow. Wait; hang on. You like the woman? Is she still around?"

"Yes, we're friends."

"You're friends?"

"Yes, I see her often."

"WHAT? Wait, the first one? What sets her apart from this one?"

"Different circumstances."

"Are you kidding me? How can you justify that?"

Then, I remembered the two women I spotted well into the party that my father had rushed over to. I think that is what I had suspected.

Mother walked over to the liquor cabinet. "Join me?" It was very early still, but I nodded to agree. This conversation was far from over right now. I didn't care what she was mixing, but whatever it was, she was doing it with purpose. Vodka and orange juice were a far cry from tea. Thank goodness for the tea cakes because I was feeling the effects from the booze on the first sip.

Not once did she ask if I was okay with all this information? Father sleeping around, Mother sitting here calm, me in shock. For a long moment, we sat in silence.

I didn't want to push her into talking because I wanted to know everything, right down to the last detail. I couldn't take it any longer. How could she still be married to him? Waiting was not a strong trait in me. The alcohol and tea cakes kept me occupied as she watched me eat one after the other.

"Tiffany! You are not supposed to clear the plate like that."

Taking a sip of spiked orange juice to wash down my mouthful of cake, I finally replied "I'm sitting here waiting for you to speak, and you are not talking."

Mother knew this day would come. She sounded like she had rehearsed this talk, explaining to me about marriage admitting that she and my father had hit a rough patch when I left for college.

She was almost relieved that the other woman who came into play was outside their social circle. At first, she explained, she thought that was her way out. She had thought it was a good way to separate and move on.

Only my father came home to her every night she was in town, confusing her thoughts about getting a divorce. They were even civil toward one another. They talked more about what was going on in my father's company, and she called him every day when she was away. They started to become friends when they were apart.

They made social commitments just as the power couple they had become. No one knew what was going on other than Mildred.

My mother confessed, looking back, how grateful she was they were so discreet about their affair. Then, Mother said Audrey by accident, speaking kindly of her character.

I nearly had to hold my head from separating off my shoulders. I shot up so fast demanding. "Audrey? Audrey, who? What's her last name?"

Mother sat as far back in her seat as she could, holding her fingers to her chest. I had startled her. She studied me, holding her answer until she was ready.

"It's not important Tiff. Don't you go after her; besides she is sick and only doing independent consulting work for us now. Your father and I made sure she was well taken care of by the company when she left her senior position at Henshaw."

"I don't care about all of that. What is her last name Mother!"

She put her drink down carefully but with a purpose. "Why do you want to know?"

"I can't tell you."

"Well, you had better tell me Tiffany, because this is not your call."

I had to rein my bossiness back in; otherwise, the two of us would be back and forth like this all day, all week, all year.

This was us for the past twenty-five years. Mildred's voice played in my head, flashing back on "how to deal with mother" lectures.

I scaled it back a few notches, and sat myself down in the chair. I drank what I had left of my cocktail and apologized to her.

"Sorry, Mother. I just heard confidentially from a friend; that a local woman named Audrey Lanski was on the donor list."

That's all I could tell her and prayed she would not put the need for an organ and my companies' risk of being hijacked together.

"That's her. Do they tell you names like that? Do you know all the patients who are on the list?"

Dammit! "No, not usually. She must be special."

"Audrey is special. I stay in touch with her. She is doing well for being so sick. The doctors moved her to high priority now, but she is in a difficult circumstance."

"Difficult circumstance? How so?"

"They are having trouble matching her."

I bent down, gathering all my presents that I had scattered about. Some were much louder now as broken pieces rattled in the wrapping. I stuck them back in the box wherever they fit.

"I don't mean to run out on you like this, but I have to go. I love you. I'm sorry you are going through this and I'm sorry I'm leaving. Mother, I am here for you. Call me anytime. Oh, and this donation was the best gift ever. Thank you, but I have to run."

She stood along with me. "Tiffany do not be upset with your father. He is a man. This is for me to settle."

I stopping in my tracks. Who was this woman? "Are you serious? He's a dick to have cheated on you, especially with the image he so badly pretends to have. I know all the dirty facts about men. Don't you worry about that Mother. I agree with your decision pertaining to the new whore. If you want me to have a conversation with her, I will gladly interfere."

Mother quickly responded because I was opening the door. "I told your father to take care of it. He assured me he would. If it continues, then he has more to lose than just me. Give him a chance to make it right."

I quickly turned. "Okay, it's your call."

"What about the other two boxes?"

"I'll be back for those later. Not sure when."

The second I was in my car, I texted Andy. My place right now!

When I rounded the corner to my parking lot, there was his car. I hopped out with a purpose "Inside right now." Andy took the box from me and followed. I held the door open. Once inside, he waited to follow again. I shoved the key into my door and opened it with more force than I should have. He calmly walked into my condo, waiting for me to start.

Neither one of us spoke.

He watched me and waited. I didn't want to attack him verbally because he could just walk out and I wouldn't get the information I needed to know right now. I was feeling warm from that cocktail. Heated. I think my face was blushing.

He spoke first. "Well, I can tell this isn't what I was hoping this emergency was for. What's up cupcake? Do you feel okay? Your face is red."

"Tell me you throwing out Audrey Lanski's name had nothing to do with her being the ex-mistress to my father." I couldn't read a goddamn thing on this man. I think he could actually play dead and fool anyone. "Andy! Tell me!" I took the box from him and dropped it on my table. He was as cool as ice speaking with facts.

"A lot of money has been put on the table for what she needs."

"Apparently she left my father's company with a lot of money."

"To pay her medical bills and private care."

"You think the money is gone? She still consults for his company."

"I think she does not have what is being offered."

Oh, damn it! I turned to get a glass of non-alcohol added orange juice. "Do you think my father is funding it?"

"No."

Well, what the fuck? I stopped in my tracks. "Who then?"

He shook his head. "I don't know Tiff. No kids, she never married."

"So, she must have the money. She was the top manager at his company and my mother said he took care of her financially when she left?"

"She is not the only player who needs this organ," was his solid answer.

I poured him a glass, and now he was walking over to me. "How did your mother come to tell you about her?"

I slapped the counter sarcastically. "Funny you should ask. I went over to see mother to have tea. She gave me my official birthday gift, which was a card that had a picture of a dog with googly eyes holding a martini glass. She made the comment that was my father coming home Saturday night."

He stood still, trying to follow where I was going with this. I rambled, "She made a donation in my name to the local girls' club, which is the perfect gift in my eyes. I loved that she did that. Then she drops the bomb of my father having an affair with some whore that showed up at my party. You know what? The moment I saw her, that was what I thought. How crazy is that?"

He studied me because now my hands were in full animation. "Then we had booze and she told me this is not his first indiscretion, and that he had an affair with one of his co-workers named Audrey when I left for college. I asked, no, I demanded to know her last name, but yes, yes, yes. For the first time in my life, I admit that I have my mother's temperament. There I said it!" I inhaled agitated all over again from what I had learned.

I could see a slight grin creeping along Andy's jaw-line. "Oh, no! No, No, No. You do not get to be amused right now because you knew all this yesterday morning and didn't say a goddamn thing to me!"

I drank some juice while Andy remained silent and patient. I exhaled, deep yet controlled. "This sucks!" I conceded.

"Are you done?" he questioned, not sure.

I nodded, agreeing I was done for the moment.

"It was not my place to tell you. It would not have mattered one bit if you did or didn't find out the connection. Your father is not the benefactor. What is important is that you put yourself at risk with your pissing match against Kyle. I can guarantee they will target you and the only thing I can say is to be prepared."

Okay. I got that message. I nodded. "I hope Kyle gets shot. Not a life-threatening shot, but just enough to get him out of the game."

"I don't think you should be concerned about Kyle. Watch your six."

I put the orange juice away. "Andy, can I learn those codes?"

"I can't do that, Tiffany. If you learn how to decode, you will be worse off because you will know what you are carrying."

"How can that possibly be? If I know what I am carrying, it will be better because I can assess the risk factor."

"Listen, if you know, your whole-body posture will change, and you will act differently. People can pick up on stuff like that."

I turned to him. "You can be a real asshole sometimes."

He grinned. "I know."

He grabbed the sponge, washing out his glass, and placing it in my dish rack. "I have to go." He turned to me "I'll figure something out to even the odds for you." He touched under my chin, tilted my mouth upward, and gently pressed his lips to mine. It was only a moment of lingering. He looked into my eyes. I felt there was so much more to us than just this lame seeing each other here and there. He turned and walked out.

CHAPTER EIGHT

I texted Michael and asked if he could meet me at the gym. He replied apologetically that he couldn't. I worked out one hour to burn the alcohol off, then went straight to my grappling class. I took no prisoners, which made me sloppy and showed that I wasn't concentrating. Everyone asked what was wrong with me and who pissed me off. My answer was "the world." They told me to sit out and wait to get back on my game. My instructor gave me a time out! I was not a child. Who did he think he was?

I was in a foul mood. When I got home, I assumed Andy had been back. There was a sheet of paper slipped under my door. I squatted down, picking it up and looking for a moment, at what seemed to be a bar code. Well, this made no sense. I tossed the paper on my coffee table and went to clean up.

I thought more about that paper as the hot water cascaded down on my head, making me think more clearly and less agitatedly. Curiosity needled my brain as I sulked on my couch, I leaned over dragging the corner of the paper across my table, inching it to me. I studied the barcode. The numbers below the vertical lines did not match up. I studied and noticed that the lines were different heights; some had breaks and their thickness varied.

This must have been something to point me toward what I had asked him about. What did it mean, though?

Tonight, I grabbed a blanket and pillow and slept on my couch with the television on. I woke up two hours before I had to be at work and I was still moody. I needed a plan to deal with what most likely would happen this week. We started off with coffee and jelly donuts. That set me straight. The bad mood was passing.

I peeled back the lid of my coffee, realizing it was the simple things I took for granted. "Hey Michael?"

"Yeah?"

"Thanks for being there for me?"

He did not expect me to say this. "What?"

"Hey, I mean it. I've dragged you into my conflicts. You just pick up the pieces and still make me come out smelling like roses. Thank you."

"Tiffany? Is this where you tell me you have three weeks left to live?"

I knew I sucked at this. "NO! Fucking thank you for having my back, damn it!"

He was enjoying this moment at my awkward emotional expense, chuckling. "Okay then, you are welcome, crabby."

Today was not the day we were hit. Today was the day I made new friends that had attended my party. For the first time in this company, my dock nurses were happy it was me showing up. Wow, new spin on my job. No wonder Kyle enjoyed coming to work. Heck, I wasn't even sleeping with them, and they were happy to see me. None of these women blamed me for what happened or what they found out. I saved the day, so to speak. I was the hero? Oh, this is so going to bite me in the ass someday.

They called us into a brief meeting before we ended for the day. It was all about hiring another four new recruits starting next week. We would each have an extra passenger for the following two weeks. Michael's group was the last hired in this company and before his was mine. I knew there was some overtime, but I didn't think enough to hire four additional people. It looked like we were expanding.

The meeting went silent when Donovan pointed out, "Do you two have anything to say?"

Slowly shaking my head side to side, I said, "Nope."

"Kyle, you always have something to say?"

He stared at the paper. "No, we done here?"

He looked from me to Kyle. "You two better get your heads out of your asses. Do I make myself clear?"

I shrugged. "I'm fine, sir."

He narrowed his eyes at me. "Dismissed."

Kyle shot up and exited the room first. I looked down at my watch. There was plenty of time to hit the gym and my subconscious wanted to check in on Mother. But first, I had a very special errand.

I pulled up to the valet and told them to hold my car. I would be twenty minutes tops. Still in uniform with my gun belt on, I carried in the thick legal-sized envelope, walking right to the kitchen. It was Tuesday afternoon. Several employees stopped and stared. I smiled. "Excuse me! Excuse me!" I had the attention of more than half of them and whispers spread, getting others' attention. "Hello, I'll be brief. You hosted my party on Saturday night."

A lot of nods and smiles spread across their faces. "I just wanted to thank you personally. Every one of you did an amazing job pulling that party off to perfection." I reached my hand in the envelope and grabbed a handful of gift cards. "This is my personal thank you. I have gift cards for every one of you."

Then their smiles grew larger as applause broke out. I went around handing the cards from my birthday to the staff. The dishwashers got near the largest denominations as the hotel manager burst through the door. He spotted me. "You cannot be in here!"

I grinned. "You said that to me once already."

He scowled ready to reprimand me again. I intercepted with a $200 card to Hannah's Family Restaurants. "I saved this one for you. Thank you very much for making my party such a success. I just wanted to show my appreciation to you and your staff." Applause echoed through the kitchen again.

He cleared his throat, half grinning and telling everyone to get back to work as he escorted me toward the hall. We stopped in the corridor. "This is very nice, Miss Chanler. I thank you and they thank you. But next time, come to me first." He half scolded and half grinned, handing me his business card. I nodded, looking down at his name.

"Will do, Peter. Thank you again. Oh, and if there was anyone who worked at the party and I missed them, please distribute these."

He bowed his head. "I'll check the schedule. What if there are extras? What do you want me to do with those?"

I thought about that "Maids"

He nodded again, grinning, "Pleasure doing business Miss Chanler. Please come visit and allow me to buy you a drink."

I touched his arm. "How's your nonalcoholic sangria?"

He nodded. "I think you will enjoy it."

"Then, I'll take you up on that."

My car was right there as I handed the valet my last gift card. He looked down amazed. "Thank you, miss!"

* * *

I spent my next morning down at the garage. I needed a little tool time. The boys harassed me playfully as I learned to replace my first timing belt on Kyles ambulance. I was learning new tricks to take him out of the game by messing with his transportation. Oh, the possibilities.

Second shift meant I would see Jen tonight.

She also raved about the party, looking at me differently. "Tiffany, you clean up well. I am sorry I misjudged you."

I raised an eyebrow, not understanding where she was going with this. "Misjudged?"

"Yeah, you kind of portray a bad ass bitch. You had me fooled."

I laughed saying, "You were right. That's who I am!"

She shook her head. "No, sorry, Tiffany. You're pretty cool. Thanks for extending the invitation. I had a great time." She was now scanning the coolers Michael had stacked.

I was watching intently. "Hey, Jen?"

She pocketed her scanner when she was finished. "What?"

"What does that reader do?"

"Shows the name of the hospital, so we know it belongs here. There is a bunch of code that follows. I'm not sure what it stands for. The correct hospital is all I'm concerned about. I'll get my ass handed to me back there if I check in something that doesn't belong here. Here's a little story for you to envision: Before someone started this new system, details in transportation were relaxed back then. We accidentally received an organ they were waiting for downtown. The hospital was in an uproar when their organ didn't arrive. We didn't even know it was sitting here for two days. A few people lost their jobs over that fiasco."

I played it as casually as I could. "Wow, I remember that. Can you imagine having to tell your boss? 'Um sorry, we misplaced your organ. It's here somewhere but we don't know where yet.'"

She laughed. "Tell me about it. They also added an extra layer internally last year. When Michael wheels this cart through the doors, he is greeted by a hospital guard waiting on the other side. Sometimes, I imagine this job as being part of some Secret Service project, and we are all pawns as they decide who gets to live and who must die." She laughed harder, touching my arm. "Sorry, I read political thrillers."

I grinned. "We should give ourselves spy names."

She lit up. "Yes! I love it! I'm naming you Armored Angel."

I smiled. "I kind of like that."

"It's true; look at you." She winked trying to compliment me.

"Okay, how about Joan?"

"Joan?" her face slightly twisted.

"Joan of Arc. Hello? Who else comes to mind when you say Joan?" I added, "It should flatter you. I'm a big fan of Joan."

"I was about to tell you that's a lame spy name, but that's really nice, Tiffany. Thank you."

Michael's face scrunched and tilted slightly toward his right shoulder. He was keeping his opinion to himself, but I caught the head shake over our conversation. I could play nice with others, and I just proved it. Jen waved goodbye to me while Michael followed her with the cart. Jen included him in our moment. "Michael, I'll think of a name for you. Nothing is coming to me at the moment, though."

"Great, can't wait to hear it." They disappeared behind the door.

I had more interest in timing, so I set my stopwatch on my phone, to record how long Michael was in there. His delivery:19 minutes.

Next stop we were switching. I was going in and he was doing the paperwork. We secured the coolers back in the new spots for our next delivery. Michael usually does this with me leaning against the cooler, watching social media videos of cats terrorizing people, but this time, I helped, giving me an opportunity to study the bar codes a little.

Michael looked down at his phone asking me if I had this. I looked over at him. "Of course." He answered the incoming call. His first words were, "Is everything okay?"

I was securing a cooler and half listening to him. He turned away just as I caught a female voice telling him that Mark called four times and she doesn't know what to do. "I hope you didn't answer."

He was stepping too far away for me to hear her reply. "Look, Rachael, I know you're having a hard time adjusting. I'm at work right now. If you need me to swing by after. I will, but you have to move on from this."

I stared at Michael for a moment, standing at the doors facing the dock, then turned back to the bar code. This code third line in was thicker than the others and the seventh line had a separation in the middle.

He was saying goodbye.

I stood up. "Everything okay?"

He let out a weak chuckle. "I'm not used to being the hero."

My eyebrows flexed. "Then stop rescuing damsels in distress."

"I'll make a mental note of that."

We were in route to the next hospital when Michael let out a chuckle. I glanced over; he couldn't help himself grinning like an idiot.

"What?"

He laughed again in a mocking tone. "We should give ourselves spy names?"

I held myself back from hitting him out of reflex. I know what I said was corny and out of character, but it worked.

CHAPTER NINE

It was a typical Wednesday afternoon, and everything was going smoothly. I did a few more deliveries inside, and there was a guard on the other side of every hospital door.

They all expected Michael so I was asked a lot of questions. I told them we were bored tonight and swapped jobs. I looked around as much as I could. There was a young person in scrubs waiting with the guard inside who also scanned the bar codes. I was standing above her in perfect view while we all engaged in small talk. The number across the bar code, three coolers down, caught my eye this time.

It displayed a serial number across it that looked familiar. Was this the number Andy had given me? Why would he have given me only one serial number?

I asked the guard how this operation worked, and he was all too happy to tell me anything I wanted to know. He spoke with the animation of a storyteller informing me this was checkpoint two, of the four-part process, with this hospital.

There were only three hospitals in this county that accommodated these types of deliveries. He assumed I knew what he was talking about. I didn't stop him to ask questions on what I didn't know. He had a flow going, so I let him keep explaining.

Everything gets scanned right until the last checkpoint which he called the meat locker. That's where they do basic tests to see if there is an immediate match at nearby hospitals.

If there is, they notify the recipient and prep for surgery. I nodded playing dumb and matter of fact as best I could. I now knew I was carrying an organ. This guard confirmed that, and now I knew this was one of the three hospitals that did this in our district. I spoke up, unfazed "I would hate to be on that list right now?"

The guard nodded. "Sometimes they're already here waiting on life support."

"Geez, could you imagine?"

He grinned. "See, bet you didn't know your job was so important, did you?"

"Nope, never looked at it from this point of view."

"It's all in the name of your company, Angel Wings. You are delivering a gift from the big wig above, for a second chance for someone's life."

I changed my stance to a more relaxed pose, bringing my feet closer together and brushing my ponytail back, waiting for my cart to circulate back to us.

I was a good thirty minutes into waiting. I first asked if I could go back and talk with Michael. They laughed and said no. I was stuck waiting with them. Now, I decided that was enough to break the ice even further, and I down-right got chatty with the crew, learning this operation behind the scenes a little better.

Megan explained more of the process also relaxing. She reiterated that their hospital, and she named the two others, were the only ones in the county that matched organs. I thanked her. She was a nurse here, asking if Michael was single. I laughed telling her that I think he had a new girlfriend. She snapped her fingers. "Darn it, just my luck."

The guard laughed and gave her some dating advice.

I switched the topic back to the hospitals. "So, that's why when we stop at those, it takes so much longer. Thanks, guys. Now, I can prepare better, bring a magazine or something. Or make sure Michael does these."

Megan requested, "Yes please, send Michael in," making us all laugh.

Five more minutes went by when another medical staff member came bursting through the door. Bumping Megan as she caught the door in her shoulder. The guard and I reached for her, helping her to her feet. This medical representative was in a panic, misjudging her grip on the stack of paperwork she threw at Megan, while the guard was now jostling the cooler cart.

"We have a match! Get this over to Burbank STAT." Megan's scanner had fallen to the ground. I swiped it while gathering her paperwork. I tried to take the cooler, but Megan intercepted, stopping me and telling me the guard had to secure it. She felt around in her pocket, then looked around the floor for her scanner I had stuffed down my shirt, now holding my clipboard in front. The other woman gave her scanner to Megan, telling us to, "Move, Move, Move!"

Both the guard and Megan ran out the door with me, while the other medical assistant caught the door, barking orders to hurry.

Michael stood ready, witnessing our commotion. We secured this one cooler; I asked about the others. This was apparently the only thing that mattered right now with her ordering us to come back after to collect the rest.

Now, Michael and I were hustling; she scribbled her signature on our paperwork, but Michael was too slow signing her paperwork, so she pulled it out of his hands before he was finished. They sealed our back doors. The guard tapped the ambulance with the all clear as we jumped in.

I knew about this kind of call. Never have I experienced this urgency in my time working for Angel Wings. My heartbeats sped up like a machine gun; adrenaline was kicking in as I half-listened to Michael's comments on how grabby Megan was with the clipboard.

They have trained us using mock transports with this type of emergency, but none of it came close to what this feels like. This was the real deal. There must have been someone high on the list and waiting.

We were headed to the main hospital, battling the evening commute. Michael flipped the emergency lights on; we were ready for action, going all in. I lived for these types of moments, making me feel like there was a purpose. I would save someone's life today.

Our siren wailed through intersections as cars and trucks pulled over or parted for us to clear through as if we were actually carrying a live person. We were five miles out from our destination; Michael was calling base giving them our range as Julie confirmed the update.

Three miles out, we were coming up to another intersection when all the lights changed to red, and we heard cruiser sirens blaring in the distance. All the traffic came to a halt. Base was alerting us to a high-speed chase coming through the city not too far away, but not in our path of traffic. There weren't many vehicles at this intersection, but the ones that were here all seemed to be in front of us.

Julie confirmed again that we were clear, and the hospital was ready and waiting. Michael and I watched both directions assessing the surroundings. I attempted to pull around since no one was moving. Our flashing lights were not enough.

They boxed us in. Michael flipped the sirens, blaring as cars finally parted away from the center aisle making room for us to pass.

Michael called the all clear as the final front two vehicles pulled to the side, making room for us to go through the intersection. Just as I was taking the turn, a pickup truck came out of nowhere jumping the curb and colliding into the backside of my ambulance. It took a second to feel the hit after I saw it happen in my side mirror. I shouted to Michael to hold on as my hands gripped the steering wheel, stiffening my body for impact, trying to control the motion as both feet pressed down on the brake pedal attempting to stop the jarring forward motion, spinning us in the opposite direction. With one final rock of the ambulance, my body went stiff, pressing as hard as I could against the brake pedal.

Michael grabbed my arm to see if I was okay. His touch triggered me to relax now. It was over.

The unexpected smash from the impact of a second vehicle without warning bounced my head off my driver's door while my body tested the restraints from my seatbelt. My vision loss immediately only registered white as specks of color started to fill the blank canvas.

I was coming back into focus now trying to look around. Michael was groaning. The second hit had compromised our back end as the ambulance stopped rocking. Cracks of light were flooding our cab. Flashing blue lights were streaming in, so it must have been a cop car that was the second impact.

My ambulance finally stopped moving as instinct kicked in, finally letting me shift the gears into park, taking a second to wrap my head around what had just happened. I swear it could not have been to the count of three from when the second vehicle hit us to what I was seeing right now.

Another cruiser screeched toward us as I tried to brace for the third impact screaming out for Michael to hold on as I white-knuckled the steering wheel and scrunched my body to the far right of my seat, holding on for this hit. My window exploded, pelting my face with razor-sharp glass pieces as my hands flew up too late to protect what was left. Michael shielded himself with the clipboard.

I felt liquid dripping down my cheek as sudden pain blinded my left eye. The heat and the sharp sting in my eye made me scream out as I cupped it with both hands. I heard and felt the rip of my seatbelt with a hand gripping my shirt, pulling my shoulders through the jagged broken window opening. I was yelling to Michael, who was not responding.

My hands left the protection of my eye as I focused on who was pulling me. My right eye registered that cops were trying to pull me out of the window.

I needed to make sure Michael wasn't hurt as I resisted them and the hold they had. The jagged edge of the window tore through my shirt, cutting my abdomen. It looked like a war zone out here.

A gun went off; people were screaming and running for cover. I kicked into survival mode, feeling the hands on my arms of who was pulling me. I quickly located their grip and bent fingers back, bracing my legs against my door so they could not pull me out any further. I could hear the reaction I was looking for as swearing started and grips loosened.

I could squirm and wiggle in enough to reach for my gun. The pain searing my brain from my left eye was unavoidable. I could only see out of my right eye, and I saw two uniformed cops trying for a different angle as they reached for me again pulling at me.

My left hand gripped the jagged part of the window, letting go quickly as I felt instant pain in my palm. Spectators were out of their cars and running toward us.

I heard Michael calling into the radio that we were being hijacked. "CODE RED! CODE RED!" he yelled as I now understood we were being ambushed. I fought to be free from the hold. I heard screaming and, "Get down," and two more rounds were fired.

I couldn't tell if they came from inside the ambulance or outside. I wasn't sure at the moment what was happening or who was who while I punched and grabbed at the only person trying to pull me out. Everything sounded like I was underwater. I heard a muffled scream. "Keep pulling her; it's going to blow!"

Then more hands from plain-clothed people tugged at me, ripping me back through the window. I focused on a woman with red hair, crying and pointing at me, "Please, save, her!" She was so upset.

It looked like cops were trying to pull me out again. I kept yelling at them to identify themselves and I felt a punch to my cheek that the glass had already pelted. The pain disabled me. I was seeing stars as my eyesight completely left for a moment. I was in motion not sure what direction I was moving. The scraping glass on my abdomen gave me a hint that I was moving back into the cab.

"I got you Tiffany." Michael grabbed my belt, and one yank from him, pulled me back almost entirely in as I slipped through their holds.

Michael's knuckles from his left hand dug into my backside beltline. I heard "Cover."

He shot past my ear, deafening me further. Smoke billowed from the left side of my ambulance, building thick, turning black, as the anti-cyclone twisted furiously from the hood of the truck smashed against my ambulance.

The dense smog gravitated in my direction, weaving around me like the devil's hands trying to finish what the others could not accomplish. I choked, coughing and trying to breathe.

In a flash, fire engulfed the rear of the pickup truck releasing its demonic hold of the pollutant strangling me shooting it upward to revenge the sky.

My last vision was everyone scattering or hitting the ground. I was jerked in the cab hard, hearing the explosion and feeling the heat of the fire as I fell backward on top of Michael.

The screams in the background started to fade as the sound of my ambulance's siren vanished completely. Feeling Michael hitting me, I blacked out.

* * *

I heard Hannah's voice. "She's coming to. Okay see you soon." I opened my eyes. I adjusted because I could only see out of my right eye.

Damn, my head hurt! My hand immediately shot up to my face as my heart raced. I smelled a sharp tar-like odor. Yuck, that was disgusting and it made my stomach uneasy.

Hannah was by my side as I felt a lot of bandages on my head. "Tiff, don't pull at it. They had to remove glass from your left eye and that whole side of your head. Your cornea has a good scratch. You're very lucky. Tiff, Tiff leave it alone, please."

She pulled at my hand, and I flinched batting her hand away. "Tiffany, stop touching the bandage."

I froze my arm, letting her guide my hand back down.

It was Hannah, and she was scolding me. Okay, I was all right. Hannah was here. Holy mother of headaches! The pain coursed everywhere in my brain and my body.

My last memory was of Michael, "Michael!"

I heard his calm voice to my right. "Right here, Tiff." I turned my head in his direction, but something was in the way. I now felt the stabilizer preventing me from turning too much to the right.

"What the fuck is this?" I tried to pull it away.

"Nurse she's awake!" I heard Hannah shouting. "Tiffany! Stop pulling at that! Just lay still. Your nurse will be right in."

I wanted to sit up and find out what the hell was going on. Everything hurt; my neck, my torso; I moved my toes; yes, they hurt too. Michael was now above me standing at the side of the hospital bed and holding my shoulder down. "Ouch! Ouch! Ouch!" I complained.

He lightened his hold. "Hey, it's okay, lay still; you're pretty banged up." My one eye scanned him over, taking in all his cuts and scrapes; he looked like he had a black eye. There was a pillow under his left arm.

I looked down my body to the end of my bed as Hannah was now making room for the nurse carrying a white tray. She spoke. "Well, hello there. Can you tell me your name and date of birth?"

I focused on her as she held my wrist loosely, looking at my plastic hospital bracelet. I repeated the information she wanted, and she smiled.

"I am happy to hear that, Miss Chanler. I will give you something to take the edge off the discomfort that is probably setting in right now. Your head must feel like it's under a lot of pressure."

She was right; it did. There was a constant high-toned ringing, piercing my ears with a vise grip sensation through my entire skull. I watched her slowly inject whatever medicine into my IV with my one eye. It hurt to concentrate with my only working eye. "Can you make that a double, please?"

She grinned. "Doctor Paris is on his way. Minimal talking, please until he clears you."

She finished up. Hannah announced, "Priscilla is on her way, Tiff." I responded with a thumbs-up. The nurse noticed.

"Now that is a great sign, Miss Chanler, already able to follow directions. I will tell Doctor Paris."

Raising my thumb was the only thing that didn't hurt right now. I thought as I accidentally spoke, "Okay."

She grinned. "Well, you almost got a gold star."

Damn, my head hurt. I smelled burnt hair now mixed with the tar scent as I touched the right side that had fewer bandages, grabbing a few strands of hair of what was left.

Hannah looked puzzled as she cocked her head left, pointing a finger palm up, squinting to me. I knew this look of puzzlement, and I was calculating how she would say this. "Umm, about that? You'll need a new hairstyle a shorter style. I brought you in a magazine with all the latest shorter cuts. I picked out a few that will look adorable; I promise. We can go over them later, sweetie."

I dropped my hand. "Great. What happened?"

Wow, this medicine was already helping and so quickly. My eye adjusted better to the brightness in here.

"We can't talk about it yet. You need to be cleared by the doc and then talk to this officer."

"What officer?"

Michael moved to reveal a cop now standing behind him.

"Oh."

The officer spoke. "It's Detective; I earned my stripes."

Michael apologized for the mistake and looked back to me and mouthed "detective" in a mocking way. I smiled, even that hurt.

Michael touched my shoulder. "I'll be right over there so you can see me better." He pointed to the right corner of the room down by my feet.

"Okay."

In walked the doc. He was good looking. Hannah smiled at him. "She's awake Doctor Paris."

He returned a smile to her. "This is a good sign. Thank you, Hannah."

He looked down at his chart. "Miss Chanler, hello, I'm Doctor Paris. They assigned me to you on your arrival. Let's start by saying you woke up earlier than expected. I see this as a positive sign. Before I fill you in, how are you feeling?"

I chuckled, setting off pain throughout my torso and ribs. "Damn it! Oh, fuck, that hurt. Well, like hammered shit, actually." I cradled myself out of pure reaction to the pain.

He gave a sympathetic sigh. "I bet. Nasty accident you had." He turned addressing everyone in the room. "Could everyone please leave the room for a bit?"

He made everyone wait outside my room, then he began my examination, explaining everything he was doing as the nurse was taking my vital signs. He went over play-by-play of what had happened since I arrived in the emergency room.

The good news was there was nothing broken. The bad news was I had some pretty ugly surface wounds and two patched up burns on my left shoulder and just above my left breast where my clothing had caught fire before Michael could put me out.

Nothing that needed skin grafts, but the pain right now was messing with my central nervous system. Clothing melting to skin was not a good outcome. Doc said there would be scaring and could recommend cosmetic avenues if I wanted.

Shoot I didn't care about scarring, and I knew from my psychology elective taken back in college, that this feeling would probably stay with me for quite some time; I would have to learn to live with it and make sure this was the one thing that would not keep me from returning to work.

My nurse was lifting the tape off my skin on the wrapped left arm. She pulled back the bandage as Doc observed. "Make sure you apply a generous amount of the salve with the next bandage change."

She nodded, saying, "I will," and re-securing the tape.

"Miss Chanler, your body is in super healing mode. This is a good thing." She smiled down at me typing notes on her computer.

Doc now switched focus to my face, continuing his examination. The cornea scratch was one heck of a good one, and I will be in this bandage for a few days. I had a lens put on, so that was probably what I was feeling. He recommended the use of an eye patch for an additional time until I completed my eye medication.

Doctor Paris made a few notes on his chart. "Miss Chanler, you were lucky. This could have been so much worse."

"When can I get out of here?"

He shook his head. "Let's talk about that tomorrow. I suggest your new motto is one day at a time. We have more tests to run. You get to relax in the meantime, so take advantage."

Well, I suppose I was stuck here for a few days. He added, "I am giving you permission to talk. I think you are responsive enough to verbalize coherent thoughts to be recorded."

I shook my head to thank him. Damn it! That hurt! "Ouch. Ouch, thanks." My hand was already in route to touch my head. Never have I felt this level of pain. It was like someone was stretching me in every direction, with my head in a vise with someone pulling my hair as tight as they could, while nails dug in, clawing over my body.

Doctor Paris allowed everyone back in, pausing the cop. "You can take your report, Officer. Be patient with her. Ask your questions clearly and simply. Do not mislead any information. I don't want her to strain to think. If she slurs or says to stop, all of you, or any of you, let us know immediately."

Detective Craig corrected his title again.

Doctor Paris apologized as he turned back touching my good arm. "I will check in on you before I leave. If you need stronger medication, just ask. Only you can judge your pain tolerance level."

"Whatever she just gave me is good enough. Thank you, Doc."

He smiled, "Certainly, Miss Chanler." Briefly turning, he said something to Hannah.

She answered, "I will," and, giving her a quick smile, he exited my room.

CHAPTER TEN

It turns out Detective Craig was one of my grappling partner's cousins. He already knew who I was from Steve. It also turns out I didn't remember a lot about the accident; the accident that was a staged hijacking. A professionally staged hijacking from what they told me.

There were fake cops mixed with real cops showing up at the end. The real cops didn't know about the fake ones. The hijackers stole the organ and got away. Detective Craig commented off the record how professionally they had executed this job, adding it surprised him that we were alive.

He was on the scene when I was being taken to the hospital. He and Michael talked about the truck blowing up.

This is where my burns came in as the flames engulfed the inside of the ambulance momentarily. I was what the flames grabbed onto until Michael could snuff them out.

My mother arrived quietly with Mildred in tow. I could see she had put her best brave face on. After all, this was the life I chose. She knew this was my passion. She asked with the same concern as if I had just tripped and scraped my knee. "Are you all right, Tiffany?"

I knew that tone, and her words were ripping her apart inside. I tried to make light of it.

"Of course, Mother, hell, bullets bounce off of me. Sorry, you gave birth to a superwoman. It's time you just accepted that."

"Superwoman would not be laying in a hospital bed recovering like this."

Mildred agreed, "That's right Priscilla; you tell this stubborn child."

She turned away from me for a moment. We both spotted my father approaching, turning the corner; she squared her shoulders as my father entered. Mother stepped closer, stating, "When they release you, Tiffany, I want you to stay with us until you are strong enough to go back to your condo."

There was no sense in protesting; everyone was willing me to say yes from the looks on their faces. I simply answered, "Okay." I would let her do this for one day.

For one day I could handle being taken care of.

One day would be the limit for me to keep the peace and let her mother me.

That single day was all I needed to corner my father to ask him what the hell he was doing with the bimbo and whether it was worth it.

Father was all over the place, demanding to find out who did this. He talked about a bounty and reward for any information.

Mother spoke up, "Richard, please, shut up."

He was just as taken aback as the rest of us. He stopped his rant.

The expression in his eyes as he observed my condition, resonated failure. He was reacting like he had failed me, slumping his shoulders, exhaling deeply. Well, right now he absolutely had failed me, by cheating on Mother, but now was not the time to get into that.

My head hurt, my body hurt, and I was stuck in this bed. It was very difficult to concentrate on anyone for more than a few seconds with my one eye. I was grateful Mother had stopped him.

I would stay there for one whole day. He would know exactly what my stand was on his cheating ass.

I looked up at him, exhausted but I still had my wits about me. "Hey, Father, my company is so much cooler than yours. Never could I have had this adventure working for you."

He shook his head. "Tiffany, you are your mother's great, great grandmother."

My Mother's great, great grandmother, Tilly Romee, had alleged connections to the actual Joan of Arc legend. I loved believing this fact to bring some normalcy to the constant fight I had in me, rejections against my high society upbringing and my love of strength and determination in all I thought was good and pure in this world.

I was far from a saint, but I still believed in fighting against evil. Joan was always the super hero I thought of first. The fight I fought to save the organ we had lost. I needed to find out who I failed. I wanted to make this personal. I needed to learn more about the black market. I needed to speak with Andy.

Well, it turned out I was stuck in here until Tuesday.

As soon as the head bandage came off, my mother arranged for her personal hairdresser to come to the hospital and work her magic.

Hannah's enthusiasm and reactions were infectious as I watched most of my hair fall to the floor. Hannah insisted on making my one exposed eye as pretty as she could, covering my partially healing blackened eye, applying make-up from the pallet she brought with her.

My mother and Mildred watched, as the hair stylist handed me a mirror. Oh, my God! I would never grow my hair long again. I was one bad-ass, take-charge-looking woman in this superior pixie haircut. Mother suggested I go very blonde and our official appointment at the salon was still on the calendar. I turned my head side to side, looking in the mirror, and agreed.

Doctor Paris was entering the room as the hair dresser swept up all my damaged hair. He greeted all the ladies and halted, looking right at me. "Miss Chanler? Wow...Wow... Excuse me?"

He looked down at his chart then back at me. "Wow. Am I in the right room?"

He walked out to check, then came back in. He was trying to be funny. Mother gushed over his reaction. The nurse now followed with her cart.

"Tiffany!" She stopped her forward motion.

"Oh, my gosh!" She pointed to the hairdresser. "Can you turn me into that?"

We laughed as Mother spoke up. "Tiffany can never hide her beauty. As much as she wants to; the more she tries, the more she fails."

She waved a hand over me. Mildred confirmed that my new style just might keep my ego in balance, or at least people would know immediately what to expect.

Everyone finally left, and I was tired. It didn't matter that it was only two in the afternoon; I fell sound asleep.

*　*　*

I woke up to Andy sitting in the comfy chair, pulled up to my bed, with his boots resting against my right hip. He was reading the hair magazine, waiting for me to awaken. I felt his boots first as my eye followed his body to the open magazine, he held that covered most of his face.

I cupped my hand softly to his shin.

"Hey." I turned up a little smile, happy he was here. He lowered the magazine. Andy had cleaned up. He had shaved right down to his skin revealing the scars and pit marks those scruffy whiskers concealed from his battle days.

I wanted to trace those marks with my finger while listening to their stories. This was the shortest hair I had ever seen on him. Our hair styles came close to matching. I grinned wider, tightening my hand around his shin. "Are you trying to copy me?"

He flashed a quick smile, bringing his mouth back to an even line. "Tiff, the new style suits you, very appealing look, even more so now. I might have to buy another car and dump it in your extra spot just to claim dibs."

I laughed. For the first time in a few days, my ribs didn't hurt when I laughed. "I like your look too. I may even be attracted to you now."

"Your swelling went down."

I sat up straighter; obviously, this was not his first visit here. "I'm fine. Did you find anything out about my hijacking?"

No response, so I nudged him, "Well?"

He finally spoke. "Jury is still out. I have my suspicions."

That was it. I knew there would be no more discussion on this topic. I wanted him to stay, so I did not press my questioning.

I changed topics. "Hey, they're releasing me tomorrow, but I will spend a day at Mothers."

He placed the magazine on his lap. "Good. Saves me guard duty for another day." I grinned. "No one forces you to come over, you know."

"I know, which pisses me off even more. I don't even have you demanding me to be there to hold on to."

Was I playing this relationship too casual? For the first time, I could read conflict in him. I think he wanted more. He was staring hard at me. I wanted more. I really wanted more with him. I wanted him to be my boyfriend.

I didn't know what to do about that. He should be the one committing to me. He should be the one to start it. I waited another moment, and we said nothing more, so I lightened the mood. "You can come visit me at my folks' house if you're around?"

"Okay."

That's all I got as we broke eye contact.

He did have a lot to say about my ambulance, giving me his full report. Looks like the parts were coming at the end of this week. Andy disclosed that Greg would not release my ambulance to the auto body shop. He insisted that he could do all the work there.

Greg had a nephew who was a body shop tech and was well-qualified to help. I figured he knew I would be around and looking for something to do until they cleared me to go back to driving.

That man knew me too well. Michael was already back to work. He was running our shift with Calvin. Calvin upgraded to a temporary promotion while I was recovering.

My physical therapist signed me off yesterday with her first evaluation. I did twice as much to prove I was fine. I only needed the okay from the shrink to return to work. In my mind that was two days away.

Andy tossed me a small brown bag. Catching it, I inquired, "What is this?"

He was moving his legs to stand up. "Just open it, woman."

I unfolded the flap and out slid a pirate patch. It displayed a sword piercing a skull straight through the top. I laughed. "I love it."

He took it out of my hands and put it in place. He tilted my chin up while raising the left corner of his mouth, taking in the whole picture. "Perfect, babe."

It was seven in the evening when Michael entered my quiet room. He looked at me flipping through the TV stations, backed out, checked the room number and meandered over to me.

I frowned. "Okay, it's not that much different?"

"Yes, yes, it is. I like the eye accessory, by the way."

"Thanks. Suits me, doesn't it?"

"It suits you. I really like the new cut."

"Bleaching it out to maximum blonde, so get ready."

"Thanks for the warning." He made himself comfortable in Andy's chair that was still in place.

Nothing, not a damn thing on the television. "Why don't they allow the Home Shopping Network in hospitals?"

Michael's left eyebrow shot up. "What?"

"Home Shopping Network, you know? They display products and deals, usually offer an easy payment plan over three months on the big items."

"Tiffany, you watch the Home Shopping Network?"

He was asking me this, quite surprised by this fact. "Yeah? Don't you?"

He laughed, "No."

I was now surprised "How do you shop then?"

Still chuckling. "I go into stores?"

My hands shot up, waving a halt gesture. "Yuck. I try to avoid stores."

Michael repeated, "Home Shopping Network? Never would have guessed you were a fan. So, what's the plan tomorrow?" He leaned in with his hands folded.

"I think my discharge is at 11:00. Hannah is picking me up and bringing me to my mother's."

"Want me to get you?"

Now, my left eyebrow was raised, "Do you want to discuss that with Hannah?"

He thought for a moment, "Um, no." He knew better.

This was Hannah's role in my life, and no one would take that from her without a fight. Hannah and I had been a team since the age of six. No one was worthy of changing that right now.

It opened up an opportunity to poke fun at Michael. "Besides you've already done enough with rescuing me. I just might turn needy like the other one."

I laughed at the possibility.

Michael went quiet then stated, "I kind of like you leaning on me and wanting my help, Tiff.".

No, no, no. I could not have this conversation with him. This was not possible. This could never be.

I asked without thinking, "How's your first damsel?"

He shook his head because he knew me. Michael knew more of me than I ever wanted any man to.

"She will be just fine on her own."

Damn it! I turned to business for the second distraction. "I read over the reports. How did you know it was a setup?"

He sat back. "The cruiser color was off by a shade."

"What?"

"Their color was just a little lighter than what it was supposed to be."

Are you kidding me? Michael knew the exact color of the city police departments police cars and could judge the difference that quickly and under that pressure?

"Seriously, Michael?"

"It's one of my things. Their uniform patches were off as well. They used black instead of navy for the border. It was very obvious."

I looked at this man for the first time all over again. "I don't get it, Michael? How can you distinguish that level of preciseness in colors?"

He turned matter of fact. "Here is your one fun fact about me Tiff. Now that I know you watch the Home Shopping Network. I can let you know this about me; I can tell you how old a bruise is by one look."

"What? Why? How do you know that?"

He glanced down. "Personal experience from my early years."

I smiled, thinking he was just like me, rebelling against the world as a teenager. "Did you get into a lot of fights with kids? Heck, I used to sneak down to the West Side at the age of fourteen, looking for trouble. I always found it."

Michael was serious. "No, my old man talked with his fists a lot. When my mother couldn't take the hits anymore, he went after us kids."

I cracked inside; part of me just broke.

I didn't know what to say. Rage began to seep through the place that snapped when I learned that Michael was an abused child.

I asked in a low, slow growl. "What age were you when it started?"

He shrugged his shoulders. "Honestly, I don't know. Three maybe four? It got worse after my mother gave birth to my little sister. I heard my mom screaming one night, begging him to stop. I tapped open the door and saw what he was doing. He had my mother's hair gripped in one fist as she was holding her hands in front of her face, pleading." I clenched my fists with fury, remembering the night that Blake had me pinned, holding my hair in his fist, immobilized. Michael leaned his head back, remembering, and pausing. He inhaled a breath and looked out the window, continuing.

"I didn't understand what was happening. I'll never forget the anger in his face. He turned to me, shouting, asking if I was a man. Next thing I realized was being knocked to the floor, listening to my baby sister crying in the corner. He threw something at my mother telling her to shut the baby up. I remember looking down to the puddle of blood below me. I don't even know what it felt like. I don't remember if it even hurt."

A flame ignited inside of me a feeling of solid fury, heating hatred, coursing through my veins; picturing him a small, scrawny, innocent child being struck with brute force from a grown man. I have seen my fair share of abused kids.

I bit my words out through clenched teeth. "Is he still alive?"

Michael looked at me. "Only the good die young."

I assumed his mother was dead. I wanted to hunt that piece of shit down. Michael watched my reaction. He knew I was furious, "Tiff, what doesn't kill you makes you stronger right? It was years ago."

"He deserves to be removed."

"Well, I can tell you all his parts are no good. He's a raging alcoholic. It's just a matter of time."

He focused in on my chest because I was heaving mad. My bandages were finally off.

"Tiff, it looks kind of like a bird spreading its wings." I looked down; he was looking at my chest.

"What? What does?"

"The burn mark from your shirt and hair." He stood up close to me and snapped a picture. I slapped his hand away.

"What the hell are you doing, Michael? I mean for real?"

"No, seriously, Tiff. Look at this...your burn."

He handed his phone over. I wanted to slap it away.

"Stop that, Tiff, Look!"

Snapping his phone up I narrowed my exposed eye at him, and then examined the photo he took of my chest.

It looked like a bird spreading its wings. It looked like a phoenix.

"Wow! Hey, this is kind of cool." I was struggling to look down at it with my chin tucked as much as I could get it.

He shrugged his shoulders. "Maybe you're some kind of prophet?"

I handed him back his phone and grabbed mine looking at the burn image through my camera. "A profit that now has a mission: to hunt down that piece of shit parent of yours."

"Tiffany, let it go. He is nothing to me. I haven't seen him in twenty years."

My nurse came in, and I waved her over. "Hey Barb, look at this. Michael just spotted it. What do you think?" I showed her the image we saw.

She walked closer, examining then standing straight again. "Well, will you look at that? Isn't that interesting?"

Michael waited until she was done checking my vitals. He moved on to Taylor, our newbie, who had her first ride along today. Another chick, great. Actually, there were two new women hired. He had not met Chris yet. She was a newly retired state trooper, and she was just looking for per diem work.

Michael remarked that his first impression of Taylor was a younger, chatty version of me. I asked him how so. He pointed out that she already knew everything about everything on her first day.

Reaching for my tissue box, I threw it at his torso as he playfully caught it having himself a laugh.

"Hey, do you have your stress evaluation date yet?"

"I think they set it up here and give me my appointment tomorrow. How did yours go?"

"I hope they don't send you to the same place. The guy that did mine had an ego issue."

"What happened?"

Michael turned to see Doctor Paris was walking in, giving a little knock on the door. I looked up, and that seemed to be the end of Michaels and my conversation. "Tiffany?"

I waved him in. "Hey, Doc. I have something to show you. Look what Michael spotted."

I pulled down my hospital gown as he came over and I pointed. "What do you see?"

He glanced at me, then down. "I see I am being baited for a lawsuit."

I laughed. "No, ha, ha, ha. You're funny. Look, what do you see?" I pointed right at my burn mark.

He now took me seriously, looking to where my finger rested. He leaned in a little closer. "Wow, would you look at that? Out of the ashes arises the mighty phoenix."

He grinned. "Tiffany Chanler rises once again. I think this is a good sign if you believe in stuff like that."

I nodded. "I am better and stronger than before."

He added, "I like the patch."

I grinned. "Thanks."

"Did your girlfriend buy you that?"

"No, a guy that knows me all too well."

He glanced at Michael who answered quickly in a monotone. "Wasn't me."

Michael's whole persona changed with the flip of a switch. He looked at his phone. "I have to be somewhere. See you, Tiff, bye, Doc." And just like that he left. I couldn't even get a "wait" in as he was clearing the door.

Doctor Paris turned back to me. "Wasn't the guy here in the black T-shirt wearing green camo pants, was it?" I was curious that he knew what Andy was wearing. "Ah, yes? Why?"

"Nurses were talking about him at the desk earlier. Apparently, he made them feel uneasy." I laughed.

I just didn't get it. Why did he make so many people feel like that? "He's harmless."

Doc nodded. "Tell me about Hannah?"

Now I was serious, "Tell you what about Hannah?"

"Is she single?"

Oh, so this is why he was asking. "Yes, she is, but just so you know, she is the single most important person to me. If anyone were to mistreat her or break her heart, I would hunt them down."

He grinned and shook his head. "Friends like you are scarce. I think, if it's okay with you, I would like to ask her out on a date." He was asking me permission to take Hannah out.

She would kill me if I said no. "Well, you know where I stand, and I just rose from the ashes better and stronger, so I give you my permission."

He laughed. "Oh, interesting words. I have permission but not your blessing?"

I nodded that he got that correct. "That you have to earn."

He smiled. "I like you, Tiffany Chanler. Who is picking you up tomorrow?"

"Your future date."

He peeked up from my chart. "Good. I will see you tomorrow then."

I scrolled through my phone and texted Hannah, warning her about the doctor. She called me, squeaking with joy. Oh, good Lord. She was definitely girly enough for the both of us.

The way Michael left bothered me. I wanted to ask what that was all about. He was on our shift right now, driving, so I didn't bother texting him. My body clock was right there with him, though. Sleep was out of the question unless the nurse gave me one of those pills I was trying to avoid.

With nothing good on the television, and sick of watching funny cat videos, I picked up the copy of the accident report and read it in detail. I still couldn't believe Michael knew those police car colors were off by a shade.

Resting the report on my lap, I stared straight ahead, thinking about Michael getting beat up by his father. My emotions were all over the place. My thoughts jumped from my father to Andy to my mother and back to Michael. I needed to do something.

Heading to the nurses' station in my bathrobe and slippers, I informed the ladies I was going for a walk. Connie made sure I had my phone on, me reminding me I needed to be back during the shift change.

Oddly enough, I was at Burbank, the hospital where we were delivering the organ. For five hours, I explored and made friends with one of the security guards. He walked with me for a private tour of this place. We had to check in once during the shift roll-over, but they knew Charlie well, and allowed my adventure to continue until I was tired. Charlie's hair was thin, the most handsome shade of silver-gray I had ever seen on a man. He retired from here ten years ago and informed me that retirement wasn't as glorious as everyone claimed.

He admitted he was bored out of his mind, so he came back and worked three shifts a week. That was unless someone went on vacation, then he'd cover one extra shift. Charlie made me smile; he was adorable. If I grew up with a grandfather, I imagined my mother's father would be like Charlie.

I had one surviving pair of grandparents. I have never met them. I knew my father's side disowned him when he married my mother. Mother's parents died when I was two.

Around 9:00 a.m., I was back in bed and ready to fall asleep. Michael came strolling in with coffee and jelly donuts. He saved me. I asked why he left so abruptly the day before, and he answered by shrugging his shoulders, "Just one of those things."

He would not tell me.

Hannah walked in minutes past ten o'clock. She was ready to be asked out for a date by the dreamy, hot doc.

She wore a blue pencil skirt, and a light beige silk sleeveless blouse with matching shoes. Michael stood up. "Wow Hannah, where are you coming from?"

She smiled, kissing the air at his cheek and going in for the Michael hug. I watched him as he closed his eyes, bending his body and wrapping his arms around her.

No wonder she enjoyed hugging him. He put his full body into it. He released her just as quickly as she answered, "You know, Michael, you should teach men how to hug. You are so good at it, but to answer your question, I'm just coming from home. Why?"

"You look impressive."

She lost her smile. "Impressive? How so? I'm just here to take Tiffany to her parents' house."

Doctor Paris walked in, stopped, scanned Hannah, and cleared his throat and smiled. "Hello, Hannah?"

She returned a flirty look, tossing her hair a little and reaching out her hand. "Yes, Hannah James. Doctor Paris, thank you for taking such good care of my best friend."

Doctor Paris held her hand a moment longer than he should have. She asked with concern. "Do I get to take Tiffany home this morning?"

His chin lowered as he looked at my chart and spoke, "On one condition."

She touched her hand to her chest. "Which is?"

He glanced at me and then at Michael. "Will you step out into the hall so I may have a word with you?"

"I hope everything is okay Doctor?" She walked past him, and he followed, looking back at me.

"Excuse us a moment Miss Chanler." He smiled big and winked. Michael stepped closer. "What the hell is that about?"

"Doc is going to ask Hannah for a date."

The light bulb went off in his head. "Oh, that's why she dressed up."

"Yup." They were only outside the door for a minute. Doctor Paris finished up my paperwork and stated if I needed anything not to hesitate to reach out to him. He wished me good luck, gave a small goodbye to Michael and personally told Hannah he would see her soon. She played it casual.

CHAPTER ELEVEN

We waited another hour for my release. I insisted on walking out on my own, but that was against hospital procedure. I at least tried to convince Michael to go home; Hannah and I could handle this alone. Michael was just as stubborn as the hospital staff, insisting on me leaving via wheelchair.

He answered with a big fat, "No," following me to Hannah's car, then to my parents' house, and carried my bags into the Chanler residence while he made himself part of the package plan.

We delighted Mother. She adored Michael. After an hour, I noticed he was fading. He said he traded his shift this afternoon with Jeff, giving him an extra midnight shift tonight.

If he was staying, he at least needed to get some sleep. I set him up with a pillow and blanket on the couch to the right. I sat on the opposite one, folding my legs to the side and angling toward the chair where Mother was sitting.

We talked, including Michael in the conversation. He lasted twenty minutes, then was out cold.

She glanced over at him, "He is very fond of you, Tiffany. Are you...?"

"No, he's my partner."

"Partner? There are many kinds of partners." She grinned.

"Work, Mother. Strictly work."

That's when I confessed that I was already in a relationship, telling her only what I wanted to about Andy.

She frowned. "You never share about what is going on in your life. How long have you been dating this man?"

"Do you really want to go there about sharing? Mistresses'... Hello!"

She didn't like that at all, and she pressed her lips together. She was thinking.

The only sound in the room was Michael softly snoring.

My phone vibrated to Hannah's text, asking if there was anything else, I needed from my condo because she was about to leave.

I remembered the serial code paper. I called her, telling where to look, hanging up after she confirmed that she had found it.

Mother was looking at me as I was looking back at her. She finally called a truce. "I guess you are more like me than I would like to admit. I miss the days I could blame your father for your strong disposition and opinionated traits."

We started with small steps, opening up, trusting each other a little, trading information.

I listened about my parents' marriage, and she listened more about my life. She didn't like my job at all. She did not like that I was exposed to so much danger.

I countered the feeling; I did not like her exposed to so much gossip. That's when she cut me a look. "Tiffany, you really have that Chanler trait. I hope your fellow is worthy of good debates."

"He can hold his own Mother. No need to concern yourself about him."

"What about Michael, though; he is fantastic to you?"

"Once again Mother, he is a friend, just a friend. I will not jeopardize our work relationship."

"He is sleeping on my couch, because he wants to be near you. It's jeopardized. You need to open your eyes, dear."

"Mother, would you like for Hannah to take me back to my place when she arrives back here?"

Her expression changed to insulted "Why? Why would you leave like that? I want to help you."

"Then drop the Michael match-up. I have Andy and I am not going there with Michael. Got it?

She flipped her hand in a twist from inside to outside. "Fine, but I am rooting for Michael."

"You can root for anyone you want; just keep it to yourself."

Hannah arrived back and handed over my bag with everything I had asked her to pack. She glanced at Michael sleeping on the sofa then right back to me.

"I love you, Tiffany, but you are an idiot."

Mother gasped. "Hannah!"

Hannah turned. "Well, she is. Look; Michael is here for her. Asleep, but he's here."

I growled, "Hannah."

Mother tried to smooth it over. "They're just friends. She has Andy."

Which segued me right into telling Mother about Doctor Paris, and how he had approached me, asking about Hannah.

That did the trick until they were done.

Mother stated, trying to do me a favor by keeping the man stories equal, and bringing Andy back on topic, that she looked forward to meeting him soon.

Hannah stomped her foot as her whole mood changed. "You are not bringing that psychopath over here to meet your parents! Are you?"

My mother's attitude changed, she had known Hannah since she was just a little girl, and Hannah was just as much family as Mildred was. "Psychopath? Why did you call him that Hannah?"

My eye hardened. It was not her call to influence my mother's opinion before she met him. "Hannah!" She knew something had angered me, and my mother suspected that something was wrong.

My best friend didn't like the fact that I just shut her down. Her lips pressed tight in a scowl; briefly readjusting her opinion, she replied. "Fine!"

My mother looked from Hannah to me. Neither one of us said anything further. She was not letting this end. "Hannah, why did you make that reference about Andy?"

She inhaled a deep breath and slowly let it out. I narrowed my eye at her so she got the warning.

"I just think Tiffany could do much better... especially with that one right there." She pointed to Michael "I mean we all know he would do anything for her and we already love him."

I intercepted, "Not happening. He is my co-worker."

"So is Andy?"

"Not the same, different departments. I don't work directly with him."

"Thank God for that."

"Hannah!"

"Okay, okay. I like Michael better."

"Then you date him."

"I just might if Doctor Paris doesn't work out."

Mother had enough of the sparring between us. She stood, "Okay enough, you two. Tiffany, you look like you could use some rest."

I was tired. This is when I should be sleeping. Hannah looked down at her watch.

"I should head to work anyway. Are you all set, Tiff?"

"Yes, thanks for picking me up then going back to get this stuff."

She smiled genuinely at me. "Any time, sister, get some rest. I'll call you later." Mother walked in with another pillow and blanket, this time from my old room, placing them on the couch. I fixed my couch into a temporary bed and watched Michael sleeping peacefully.

It was the conversation between Father and Michael that alerted me I must have fallen asleep. They were having dinner as Mother asked him why he did this for a living.

I called over. "You don't have to answer that!"

They all turned just as my head pounded. Medication time, I needed to save Michael from my parents' inquisition. "Ouch, Michael... Mother, where is my bag?"

Michael stood, already walking toward me. "Right here, Tiff."

"Damn, ouch. Argh. Not liking this at all."

He pulled my bag up and placed it in front of me on the solid coffee table. Then he went through it pulling three prescription bottles out. He read each one.

As he tried to pronounce the second drug, I stopped him. "Yes, that's the one. Grab my eye drops too. I need to put those in."

I expected him to hand me the bottles; instead, he opened one, handing me a pill, followed by the bottle of water on the coffee table. Taking the water back, he held his hand out to help me up. Ugh! Just sitting up made me a little dizzy.

I accepted, letting him help me up. My ripped-up abdomen and the burns on my shoulder were the most sensitive from the effects of the hijacking. I rubbed my hand gently over my abs. I clearly remembered those idiots trying to pull me through the window. I stood there for a moment, looking at my parents watching me in silence. I ignored them as Michael stepped back to let me pass in front of him. Definitely only sticking to the twenty-four hours here and then back to my place. I didn't like all these eyes on me.

Michael followed close behind, right into the bathroom, where I stopped him. "I got this?"

He deflated. "Are you sure? I know how to administer eye drops. I'm a pro."

Okay, I'll bite. "How hard is it to drop liquid in your eye, and why do you think you know how to do this so well?"

He didn't want to say. I could see it in him. He spoke quietly, opening up another memory from his past. "My mother had her fair share of eye injuries. She couldn't handle much movement near her head, particularly when it came to her face. I learned to be so quick she didn't even have time to flinch when I approached with the medicine. I'm that good."

My heart sank. His mother was so traumatized from her monster of a husband, and Michael was standing here proud; remembering a skill he gained, bringing her comfort in the saddest, most desperate of circumstances.

I didn't want Michael taking care of me, but I couldn't help but let him in right now.

"Okay, Michael, let's see what you got."

I removed my awesome eye patch that Andy had bought for me. He peeled back the eye bandage, the sudden light exposure made me squint from the discomfort, and all I heard was, "Ready?"

I felt the slight sting that let me know the medicine was in. I can honestly say I didn't even see him do it. I don't think I even blinked. I blinked every time they put the meds in my eye at the hospital.

"Oh, you're good," I congratulated him.

He smiled, proudly, "One of these days, you'll trust me on my first words."

I humbled myself. "I do trust you, Michael. I'm just complicated."

He grinned, "And stubborn."

Okay, this was enough for tonight. "I think you should head out. You have a long night. Thank you for all your help and thanks for this." I wagged my finger in front of my eye, showing the talent he had.

He nodded looking at the time. "You're right; I have to swing home and change. Call me if you have any problems or just want to talk."

I gently backed him out to send him on his way. "Okay, I'll let you know if I need you. Thanks, Michael."

* * *

My mother was running interference with me having any conversation alone with Father tonight. She would not let it happen and I was puzzled why. This would have been the perfect opportunity to just get it out there for all of us to move on and know what one another knows.

She kept telling me to rest and saying we could talk about it tomorrow. Another oddity that was going on was that I should have been wide awake.

It was my second shift night. I think she drugged me with meds hidden in the orange juice to make me fall asleep. She was really eager for me to drink that juice.

I know they gave me pain pills that make me sleepy, but I was staying far away from them. I wanted nothing to do with those. Buy it was eight o'clock, right when I would be driving well into my shift, and my eyes felt heavy, very, very heavy. As I attempted to pick up my phone off the coffee table, I was down for the count.

Giving in and closing my eyes, I was back at my birthday party talking with Mildred.

This time, I heard it right from her that my father was having an affair.

This time I walked up to the two women and asked who they were. Oh, that little witch told me who she was straight away. She didn't care why I was asking or give a thought about crashing my party. She was here to make herself known. My father was nowhere in sight, and I caught the look on my mother's face. She nodded, waving her fingers to sweep the trash, giving me full permission to remove this unwanted guest.

Michael was by my right side. Hannah showed up on my left. I automatically stepped slightly back, shifting my weight on my right. That is the side where I carried my gun, and I was in my work uniform now and not my dress. I even had my holster on and my finger snapped the safety buckle off. I leaned in toward that tramp telling her she was not welcome here. She tossed her head back, laughing. That's when I stepped in and removed her wine from her hand, passing it to Hannah to hold. Then I was close enough for her to feel my breath. "Get the fuck out!"

Her companion tugged at her arm. "Come on; let's go." She pulled out of her companion's hold, a sense of entitlement all over her face. "I will leave... for now. Richard will hear how badly you behaved toward me. You had better get used to me being around because I intend to become your stepmother."

That's when I pulled my fist back, landing a blow that sent her sprawling to the ground.

I jolted awake, sitting upright. Geez my abs were not expecting that. With one hand rubbing my stomach, I looked around not sure where I was for a second. I focused in on my mother asleep on the opposite couch, where Michael had been resting.

I remembered as a kid, whenever I was sick this was our set up. Maybe my childhood wasn't as terrible as I remembered. I could hear my father in the distance down the hall already on the phone. My head wasn't too bad, but I was groggy. Mother had definitely drugged me.

Reaching and pulling my phone toward me. I saw that it was just five in the morning. I had slept the longest I can ever remember. I heard my father clearly arguing with someone. It's been a few years since I have slept over here. I remembered he was usually up by four and on his computer before he left for work. I heard him angrily scolding "For God's sake, my daughter was hijacked; she could have been killed. I have to be around. She needs me."

The pounding that was starting in my head now reminded me that it was medication time.

Today, I had to wean myself from my eye patch. I could only wear it for six hours this much I remembered. I stood up and went to the bathroom. I heard Father moving about from his office to their bedroom. "Stop this right now. Crying does not work on me."

Curiosity got the best of me as I navigated toward his voice. Crying didn't work on any of us. Whoever he was speaking to was doing a good job of making him angry. They were getting his clenched-jaw talk. It happened when Father was disgruntled.

Anyone that knew him knew this was a final warning. I knew exactly what he looked like, teeth clamped tight, a slight angle to his head, with those fierce eyes boring through the poor soul if they were present. He was just as effective over the phone though.

This fury from him was not conjured by a small mistake; this tone derived from a major fuckup, something which had a personal effect on him. I have only heard it twice over a phone conversation, but witnessed it once. So, I knew it was bad. I touched the wall to steady myself. That darn medication she slipped in my orange juice. I would hide those pills. I needed water.

I was listening closer, leaning toward his voice, and there was a pause. I peeked in scanning my parents' bedroom. Mother's side of the bed was still perfectly made, but his shone with evidence of the blankets tossed back in place with clumsiness; he was in his walk-in closet. I stood in the doorway, leaning as far forward as I could without making the official step to enter. I strained to hear between the growls what he was saying. I almost fell in as I grabbed the doorframe to steady myself.

"I pay your rent. I give you an allowance. All of this can end today... stop it...stop. Mandy, stop this!"

Mandy? The tramps name was Mandy? How cliché. I knew a few college girls that had this set-up married men paying for their classes and off-campus housing. I never thought my father would be that guy.

He was walking out jaw clamped, demanding that she stop in a final snarl. He halted in the middle of his and my mother's bedroom looking up to see me in the doorway.

"Tiffany." He hung up, looking immediately into my eyes softening, standing still.

I knew all about this. I knew about his first affair and this affair. I had seen the tramp myself at my party. I would have confronted him about this bullshit last night. I would have had words with him last night; I already knew about this. I did already know about this.

"Mandy?" She now had a name.

He looked like he had ten spotlights on him. He softened, giving in like he had just lost the fight.

He didn't have to say a word. His look confirmed it.

I also didn't know he was paying for everything for her; she was a kept mistress.

I snapped, and everything I felt towards him destroyed. We stood there staring at each other; neither one of us moving. This was the worst offense in my eyes.

He spoke with a heavy heart. He said my name as an apology. "Tiffany."

I couldn't move. I couldn't talk. His next words were said with honest regret of what had just happened. "Tiffany, I am sorry."

I could only return my look of despondency. All my life, I had fought against this spoiled rich life. I have seen people behave badly, and abuse money and privilege in the worst of ways.

I had resisted for as long as I could remember against my parents and their ideal way of living, but deep down, I always thought they were in this together. This was their life. They made my father's empire together with no help.

Everything I knew of our family, was now broken. He turned out to be just like the rest. This ridiculous money had empowered society crumbling down around me for the last time.

We were never going to really be a normal family together. Father was just as selfish as the rest of the men I knew in power, and he was using it for sexual pleasure just like the rest.

He stepped toward me. My hand shot out in defense as I command, "NO." I stepped back, turned, and there was Mother looking worried as she spoke my father's name, asking what was going on.

I needed to get out of here right now. I felt like I couldn't breathe the air in their house. I threw everything lying around my bag back into it as my mother pleaded with me to wait. She offered to send the car around.

I thought of Father doing that for his mistress. I didn't want any part of this life anymore. I stopped her with a firm, "No." as I jammed my feet into my sneakers and rushed past her. I could hear her calling my name anxiously when I opened the front door, then heard her voice turn to anger as she called my father's name upon me shutting it.

I called Hannah as I exited the elevator, walking out the lobby entrance of their sky rise.

She sleepily spoke, "This better be good."

"I need you. Pick me up the corner of 42nd and State Street."

Panic resonated in Hannah's voice. "What happened? Are you okay?"

I stopped walking and turned into my reflection from their modern multi-billion-dollar structure looking at myself in the glass mirrored window. I looked like hell. I answered, "No."

I could hear her shuffling about saying, "Be right there," and I hung up.

I was trying to blend in and not look like I was homeless in my sweatpants, braless T-shirt, and halfway on sneakers. This required changing my clothes right now as passersby noticed me.

I ducked into a coffee shop a few blocks down and took over their bathroom. I was now ignoring the seventh call from my mother. She switched over to text. Your medicines are here Tiffany. Please, come back. Your father is leaving; we can talk.

I didn't want to go back. I never wanted to step foot in that place again. It was my past, and I was detaching every memory of it with each blink of my eye.

Hannah pulled up to the curb where I was leaning against a post. I was never so grateful as I was right now that she had found my aviator sunglasses in my condo and tucked them in my overnight bag. They covered my eye patch and brought a look of normalcy. She was quiet for a whole three blocks. Then it ended. "What is going on?"

"I don't want to talk about it." Another three blocks went by.

"The last time you ran away was because you didn't like the college they made you go to." I frowned. "I never ran away. It's not like that. I just need distance from them." Another three blocks of silence then she spoke again.

I asked, "What's with the three blocks?"

She looked at me, confused. "I don't understand that question, Tiffany?" I pointed it out telling her every three blocks she allowed quiet, and that was it.

She smiled, "I didn't realize I did that. But here is some good news. My doctor made our date. He said he would take care of all the arrangements; wanted to take me to his favorite restaurant. We had a Doctor Paris book a premium seating in our steakhouse restaurant last night. He specifically asked if there were any extra perks he could pay for, to make tonight special."

I looked at her, forgetting all my issues and gave her a genuine smile as I touched her arm. "Oh, Hannah, I am thrilled for you."

She slammed on her brakes causing both of us to test the limits of the seatbelts because both our heads were not paying attention to the new road work going on with a sudden right lane closure. Damn, that hurt my body, which also caused me to overreact immediately crossing my arms to protect my face.

She looked but didn't say a thing as she merged with our seatbelts still sealed against us. Panic washed over me as I had to breathe through it not to show a reaction. I was over feeling this. My emotions were all over the chart. What the hell was happening to me? I needed to unclip my belt from the restraint. Again, she didn't say a word...only watched what I was doing.

"Tiffany, how am I going to tell him my family owns that restaurant? That we own four restaurants and I am head of marketing, but, hey, wait... it's a family business, and sometimes I am a bartender, a hostess, a cook, or sometimes I am even the cleaning service?" She sighed. "This sucks! Put your seat belt back on."

Focusing on Hannah, I could see she needed reassurance. "I think you are over thinking. And I think Doc will realize he hit the jackpot with his new girlfriend able to feed all his culinary cravings, especially with his crazy shifts. You know what Hannah?" Her eyebrows were scrunched, and I could see that she was trying to think of the possibilities that I was right.

"What?"

"I think you and the doctor are perfect for each other."

She smiled, reaching for and gripping my hand. "I hope so because he is all I can think about."

I was truly happy for her through my own misery.

She put both hands on her steering wheel. "Why am I picking you up from only six hours of sleep? What happened over the eighteen hours I left you?"

I now allowed myself three blocks of silence. This was our pattern. I stared at my hands in my lap. "Well, I found out Michael has a talent for administering eye drops. And I found out my father is completely funding the life of his current mistress."

Hannah swerved the car over to the right and stopped, shifting it into park. "What!"

"Yes."

"Current?"

"Yup, but crazy as this sounds? The first one I don't have a problem with. This one he pays for."

Hannah looked at my phone. "Want me to answer that?"

I shook my head no. "I cannot speak to him or listen to what he has to say right now. I will say something I'll regret and I need the dust to settle before I address this."

"Well, I have plenty to say to him that I have no regrets about saying."

"I just want distance from them right now. There is something else."

"What?"

"He is completely funding her. This is serious."

Hannah squeezed my hand again. "That money belongs to your mother!"

"I know."

"I have plenty to say to your father now. Let me call him."

"No, I need to think about this."

CHAPTER TWELVE

Hannah pulled into my second parking space and started to get out of her car. "Hannah, I'm all set. Thank you for the ride. Go home and get some sleep. I am sorry I had to pull you out of bed. I know you were up late."

She looked concerned. "Are you sure sweetie? I don't mind hanging out with you. I can grab some sleep here as well?"

I loved this woman. "I just want to be alone. Thank you, though. You are the best." She knew me better than anyone. "All right, as you wish. Call me later, okay?"

I agreed that I would as I closed her car door and headed into my condo. Michael was calling me. It surprised me, but I answered, "Hello?"

"Priscilla phoned me; you left your meds behind. I'm on my way to pick them up. You had better answer your buzzer and let me in when I get there."

If I was stubborn at times, Michael was ten times worse when he wanted to be, and I knew this tone he was using with me right now. I also knew that if I didn't let him in, he would be outside pushing that damn thing until I couldn't take it anymore. I huffed out, "Fine," then hung up the phone.

I could tell Michael was tired. He pushed my bag of prescriptions into me as he walked right past not looking for an invitation to come in.

Michael went straight to my couch that already had a blanket and pillow on it from where I slept the morning of the hijacking. He made himself at home, removed his shoes, put his gun belt on my coffee table, and ordered me to wake him up in six hours.

When you trade a shift plus your next regular shift was a midnight shift, it threw your whole sleep schedule off. I knew that feeling, and that is why I didn't work overtime or trade anymore. I let him stay. I wasn't expecting Andy to come around, and if he did, he would see Michael's car that he was over and he'd come back another time. Michael would be asleep in a few minutes anyway. He did save me a trip back to my parents to pick these up.

I took three attempts to get the damn eye drops in. I tucked my eye patch in my pocket, grabbed my wallet, and car keys, and headed over to Mildred's office. I needed a dose of Fairy Godmother right now.

Damn the light made my left eye sensitive. I had to cover it with my hand a few times. Mildred was expecting me because I had called ahead. There she was, standing, looking irate. She obviously knew all about what happened this morning. She stood with one hand on her hip, head tilted down to the right, looking over her reading glasses without one ounce of sympathy or compassion for me.

"In my office, now!" she pointed.

I obeyed, walking past her and her secretary. Mildred dropped the packet of papers she was holding with a free fall onto the table, telling Jules to start at the first document and work her way down; she would be back before the last page.

I didn't care much for Jules. She has been working for Mildred for the last fifteen years as far as I can remember. Every time I interact with her, my mind pulls up the day Mildred had sent her to pick me up one night when I had gotten myself caught in a scuffle downtown. I should have been in my bedroom asleep that night.

Jules is Latino; she did not particularly enjoy being sent to pick me up that night or any other for that matter. All the way home, she ranted at me, up one side of me and down the other, and I was trapped in Mildred's car.

"Your godmother doesn't pay me enough to pick up spoiled little rich white girls who can't appreciate the privilege you were born into."

I can't remember the rest, but she didn't end it until we were back in front of Mildred, and I was handed off to her. When I say she didn't stop, I mean she didn't stop voicing her opinion until Mildred told her that was enough.

I could see Michael had that in him; that's why I was weary about testing his limits. He was not Latino, but he could pick apart anything just as good as Jules could. That car ride home, with Jules that night was enough to make me pay attention to that personality trait.

Mildred closed the door behind her. "Sit, Tiffany."

I knew this drill and waited until she said it was okay for me to sit; She walked behind her desk. Mildred had the most beautiful color of gray hair I had ever seen on anyone.

It was a trend now to mimic this shade that she achieved naturally. The sunlight reflecting off it right now illuminated some specks of silver and white, making it shine.

Mildred's motto was "Never cover up who you really are unless those changes improve the soul of the original model."

"So, child, explain to me how you managed to make your poor mother's situation all about you?"

I shrunk in my seat. How could she ask me that? I didn't make it all about me; it upset me. That's how it came out. I thought about her accusation. She had the ability to use her tone to make it feel like her words were stones, chastising me.

"I?"

Looking at her, I suddenly felt shame. Or was I just embarrassed? No, I had bailed on my mother. She was trying to take care of me on my release from the hospital. I knew about my father's affair.

She was right; I had made this morning all about me. "Tiffany, you are an adult. You have your own relationships. You have grown into a beautiful, strong woman. You are self-supporting. Your mother comes from a different generation."

"She was married with a child at your age. She raised you with little support from her family and in this society that tried to ruin her right from the start. Your mother has always fallen in the shadow of your father, even though she played an equal part in his success." Mildred sat back, thinking. "Tiffany, relationships take a lot of work in normal circumstances. Add money, power, and good looks to the mix and it becomes a battle. Women have been throwing themselves at your father for as long as I can remember. Half the females your mother knows have tried to come between your parents. After a while it becomes tiring. They grew apart; taking a break. Priscilla ventured off to explore Europe. It was the second-best decision she ever made after marrying Richard."

I didn't dare interrupt. I knew none of this and I wanted her to keep talking. My shoulders dropped into a more relaxed frame; she slowed her story taking notice. "When your mother returned, Richard realized how much he had missed her and they reconciled."

I sat taller now. "So much for that? Now there's Mandy?"

Mildred narrowed her eyes. "She is just a minor distraction to bring the three of you closer." Mildred could not be that crass right now. She was sounding down right delusional.

"Tiffany, believe it or not your father is trying to hold onto his youth. He is approaching a challenging age. Younger men are looking to push him out; younger women are looking to replace your mother and he wants to hold on to his youth. Your father has not figured out how to trust himself. I also know he loves Priscilla."

She waited for a comment from me. I had nothing to add. "He had it easy with Audrey. She didn't need or want his wealth. She had respect for your mother."

My throat was feeling a little tight.

"This new one is power-hungry, though. She has an ego to feed. She wants the reality-show profile of being rich. This little temptress has shown him how to lose everything.

"She is living off of my father!"

Mildred leaned forward, placing her hands spread apart on her desk in front of her. "Yes, I suspect someone has strategically set this up from the start."

It confused me, making me scrunch in my eyebrows, "What? What does that mean?"

"Your father has seventy percent of the business to lose."

"You think he is being set up with this whore? Why seventy percent?"

Mildred smiled her signature flat-line grin with only a slight raise on each corner of her lips. "They would reveal this on your thirtieth birthday. I think you can use this information now. Although with that tantrum you displayed this morning, I am doubting what you can handle."

What the hell was going on? She had lost me by justifying my father's indiscretions. "I don't have time for this nonsense. "These riddles are stupid. Tell me in three years. I'm going now."

Mildred stood to tower over me angrily. "Sit down!"

I let out an aggravated, deep breath. She even made me growl in frustration. She didn't sit until I was ass in chair. I knew this tactic of hers. It used to scare the hell out of me when I was younger. I grew out of that feeling for the most part, but she still had the effect she wanted over me. I waited and waited some more. Finally, she spoke. "You own twenty percent of your father's company."

I don't know why I tilted my head. "What?" I was a business major. I knew about stocks. I knew if I was a twenty-percent-shareholder, they should include me in the business, and I should go to the board meetings. Hell, I should be on the board.

"Well, not yours yet. The agreement was that your mother would turn the stocks over to you at the mature age of thirty."

I thought for a moment. They were bringing me into the business whether or not I wanted to be there. "Well, that's great. How much is the stock going for right now? I'll sell it and donate it to the underprivileged."

And now here was Mildred slamming that fist down like a hammer. "You, stupid girl! You will not sell that stock. You will take your part in your parents' company that was intended."

So that was how this was going. "Nope!" I pressed my lips together.

Mildred narrowed her eyes. "All your life, you have been barking against our social status all wrong. Look at the opportunities that have been handed to you. You would not have your current employment if it weren't for what your parents provided."

"Not true."

"I have spent a half years' worth of working hours taking you to all your martial arts classes, and picking you up on the streets when you should have been home. All those nights I bailed you out when you were in trouble. All the times I never spoke a word of what you have been up to behind your parents' backs. Tiffany, your current employment you love comes with a high risk for injury. If something goes wrong again, and you suffer worse damage than this last one, you will at least have the means to live in the manner of which you choose. It's all your own money, on your own two feet, and your stock in your father's business that your parents built will see you will be comfortable. Tiffany, this is your safety net." She had my attention now. She was right. I could look at it as my retirement plan.

"I will think about this. You made a good argument. What am I going to do about Mandy?"

"When she finds out, his worth, if it comes to a divorce; you will have nothing to be concerned with. He may even have to move into that condo he is funding for her. Tell me, dear, how attractive is she going to be then living on a tight budget? And how attractive will your father be with a limited income?"

Now how did Mildred know her last name? I had the tramps full name now.

Mildred sat back. "Tiffany, your parents love each other. This is just something men go through to realize the grass is not greener on the other side."

"I am not one to sit idle Mildred. This tramp is breaking apart my family."

"No need to worry about the New Jersey girl. She will ruin her arrangements all on her own. You should ask yourself, what are you going to do to support your mother? And second, what are you going to do to forgive your father and open up to him so the three of you can grow stronger?"

I looked down at my watch. "Where would Mother be right now?"

* * *

My mother didn't bother to greet me; she graciously filled in the blank spaces where information was missing. She sounded both wise and forgiving.

"Tiffany, I would like to go for a walk in the park. Will you join me?" It was now ten in the morning and the sun was revving up the brightness. I pulled my eye patch out and secured it in place. The light still hurt, giving me an instant headache. I had to wear my sunglasses.

Strolling through the park, she pointed out different landmarks of my favorite spots to play when I was younger.

I never gave it much thought, but this park and I spent a lot of time together. There was the fountain's ledge. I learned how to balance on my tip-toes and balance on my heels. I only fell in a few times, and they asked me to leave more than a dozen. Mildred was fantastic at talking to the park security, making up stories for them to turn the other cheek, to let me practice.

I tried to learn how to ride a horse here. Being the great descendant of Joan of Arc. I thought I had the need to ride my steed. I was afraid of horses as it turned out. I liked having my feet on the ground not around a one-ton animal that I had no control over.

Thank goodness I was born in a much later century where our transportation was mostly man made and not livestock.

Mother stopped and pointed, "I still have that Buffalo Blue picnic blanket."

"You mean it is still in one piece?"

She grinned, folding her hands together in front of her body. "I would like to give it to you, when you have children someday."

I cut her a look. I never thought of myself as being a mother. "Don't hold your breath. Speaking of kids though, why didn't you have any more children?"

She chuckled, tossing her head over to look me in the eyes. "You were enough, Tiffany. Besides, it would have been unfair with the long hours your father and I had to work. I am forever grateful to Mildred. She truly is family."

"Really? I thought it would have been kind of nice having a sibling to get in trouble with?"

"Hannah is your sibling."

"This is true."

We both laughed. She turned to me. "I have to admit; I dislike your choice of employment. I am frightened, especially by what happened recently." She touched my arm gently. It didn't hurt, but she made me flinch. "Mother, it was just a reaction. It doesn't hurt. See?" I squeezed my arm to show her. She sighed. "Tiffany, I've been thinking. I understand your attraction to what you do. You are in power; you have control; you look risk right in the face, and those are all traits of a successful businessperson. You calculate your probabilities and you adjust. You are every bit your father just as much as he would argue that you are just like me. You still express the strong traits you were born with to your more acceptable setting. You have such a strong core."

"I enjoy being in control."

Mother's right lip-line turned up. "Well, I guess I should retire the idea I will throw some extravagant white and pink wedding for you one day, and accept that it might be by a campfire with...beer."

I laughed, a belly-shaking laugh that hurt my abdomen. Not only did it sound funny hearing her say the word beer, but the look of disgust she was trying to cover up was hysterical. I calmed down enough to answer while holding my stomach. "Yes, throw out the white wedding part. Throw out the whole wedding idea. I'm not sure I will ever want that kind of commitment."

Mother stopped walking and turned to me. "Tiffany, marriage is still a wonderful union. It takes a lot of work, dedication, and compromise by both parties involved. Marriage has many good benefits."

"Well, I know from looking at the examples before me, that I am not a fan."

Mother stepped back. "I'm sorry I wasn't a better example."

Then I realized it had come out; not as I intended. "That was not directed toward you. It's just your whole fucked up society people sleeping with other people's spouses; everyone trying to ruin or take away what others have. And look at how badly Father is behaving? I thought he was the one man who was better than all of that."

"Tiffany, I know there have been a lot of bad influences, but don't disregard marriage. You would shortchange yourself of an amazing experience. It truly is a wonderful feeling to be with someone who loves you and has the same goals in life as you do. What about your guy, Andy?"

I nearly choked on my saliva. "Um, no. Too complicated."

"How so?"

"Andy is not the marrying type."

"Everyone has the potential for marriage."

"I like the freedom of not being in a commitment. Besides, I have Hannah. She won't put up with a guy taking over best friend status."

"Tiffany, are you gay?"

OH MY GOSH! Did she really ask me that! My eyebrows shot up with a simultaneous jaw drop "NO! Why would you ask that?"

Mother shrugged as if it was a common question. "Well, I've never seen you with a man except for Michael and you keep him at bay saying it is only friendship. I was just wondering. It's perfectly okay if you were. I'm just giving you my support if you are. Being gay is quite in now. I think it's chic."

I cleared my throat. "Well, thank you, I guess, Mother. I am not gay. I like men. I like Andy. I was thinking about giving him a key." Why did I feel the need to tell her that? I liked keeping this stuff to myself. I didn't even know I wanted that kind of relationship with him, but I guess I kind of do.

"When do we get to meet him?"

I shook my head; so, she wanted to meet Andy. I think that is a brilliant idea. "Let me see what his schedule is, and I'll get back to you. He is a very busy man."

"Good. I look forward to meeting him. Why doesn't Hannah approve of your Andy?"

Ugh... "He has a strong personality."

"Well, I know a lot of men who have strong personalities."

"You'll see when you meet him."

"I look forward to it."

We walked on before we turned to head back. I was wondering about why she only had me.

"Is the reason you didn't have more kids really because of me?"

She laughed and patted my arm turning toward me. "No, Tiffany, women were always coming onto your father. I had to make my presence known. That doesn't work when you are pregnant or having to take care of multiple children. That decision was my own. Your father wanted more, but I decided that you were enough."

"Seriously?"

"Money is a powerful motivator. The more you have, the more people want to take it from you."

I took a slow deep breath, filling my nostrils with the sweet smell from the pine trees and freshly cut grass. I slowly released it looking around. "Where is this first mistress, Audrey?"

My mother dropped her head some, then raised it back. "She is in town here living at the hospital you were in."

I could feel my eyebrows had shot up. "Are you kidding me?"

We stopped walking. "The liver you were transporting last week...It was meant for her."

My face scrunched up. "WHAT!" My mother shook her head and looked away for a moment then back. "That was hers."

I stepped back and circled. "I was carrying her liver? I bet this is how karma is getting even with me!"

Mother narrowed her eyes. "Karma? Tiffany, with all your education, do not tell me you believe in all that hocus pocus?"

I would not get into our beliefs right now. "How do you know all of this?"

"When I wasn't down visiting with you, I was upstairs visiting with her. She and I are close. It devastates her that they hurt you because of her."

"She knows about me?"

"Yes, she does." My mother looked away from me.

"What else is going on, Mother?"

She sighed, turning back as a tear glossed her eye. "Unless she gets that transplant, she will die."

I was a little confused. "Why do you care so much about her?"

Mother looked up, blinking a few times as she adjusted her body, stood straighter, and looked me right in the eyes "Because I think she deserves a long life. I like her very much and have the utmost respect for her. She helped build your father's company and took no credit for it. I think if she was better, your father would realize that the women in his life are strong enough to get him over this phase he is going through. He would get rid of this contemptuous, social climbing, money-grubbing, little whore and our lives would be in balance again. Audrey was superb at keeping him on track. Her lack of presence has affected the company and your father's morale."

I felt bad for all of them right now. In my eyes, they lived in such a delusion. "Why don't you just divorce him Mother?"

She let out a breath, setting her shoulders. "Your father is the only man I have ever been with. When I married him, I meant it to be forever. When you arrived, I vowed to keep us together no matter what. I have failed you."

I shook my head. "No, you haven't. You would be a better example if you showed me you will not put up with his crap. I give you my full support to divorce him."

She turned to walk again. "I don't want to divorce him, Tiffany. He's just going through a rough patch in his life. We are getting older. I am through menopause, and we are approaching our retirement days. Men go through something similar. They want to feel attractive, want to feel that power they had when they were younger."

I rolled my eyes. "What do we know about this Mandy bitch?"

Mother stopped walking. She became tight-lipped. I probed. "How did Father meet her?"

Oh, I knew she didn't want to say anything now. I guessed, "At work? Through friends? Who is she Mom!" I called her mom again.

That made her speak. "She is the niece of Clarissa Montgomery."

I could feel my blood pressure rise. Rage filled my veins. I said her name through my teeth just like my father did this morning, talking to Mandy. "Clarissa Montgomery's niece? The stuck-up bitch Reese always complained about from Jersey?"

Mother looked away and answered, "That's the one."

"He's a fucking asshole! Divorce that prick! Shit, I think I'll divorce him."

Mother touched my arm. "No one is getting a divorce. He needs to see what she really is and I need Audrey to get better."

I could not get past the fact that my father was messing around with and supporting Clarissa's niece. This was the perfect revenge for Clarissa. She hated my mother. She was jealous of her, from what I understand at their first meeting thirty years ago. Clarissa was the woman who had to be the center of attention.

When Mildred fostered my mother in society, she became spiteful. Mildred was the one woman who could take down Clarissa, and she knew it. This must be like Christmas Day for her. Now, she had something to sink her teeth into and use against my mother forever. No wonder she was so cheerful at my party. She knew. She was gloating! I bet she even told that little gutter-slut to show up. I hated that woman even more now! What a bitch!

I stomped into my condo and slammed the door louder than I meant to. Michael sat up from a deep sleep, looking around. I forgot that he was here. "Sorry Michael. I didn't mean to wake you." He turned to me sleepily asking. "What time is it?"

I picked up his gun belt. "Not time for you to wake up. I'll clean these for you. I need something to do. Go back to sleep."

He looked up at me. "Are you okay Tiff?"

"I'm fine. I'll clean these; then I'm going to the garage." He pulled the blanket off, bunching it up next to him. "You can't until you get cleared from the evaluation."

My eyebrows instantly shot up. "What?"

He stretched up then slumped forward, looking up at me in my standing squared-off posture. He stretched again and yawned. "Tiffany, they won't allow you on the property until you get the all-clear from the psychological evaluation."

"But it's the garage? They don't even pay me for that?"

He shrugged. "Doesn't matter. They will escort you off if you show up. When is your appointment?"

"This is crap, it's a total pissing contest to govern me. One thing has nothing to do with the other."

"Tiffany... When is your scheduled appointment?"

"It's in my discharge papers but only if I clear the physical appointment with my regular doc. I think they scheduled it for Friday because my physical is tomorrow."

He waved his hand over for me to sit. "Come here, let me walk you through what will happen and what they're allowed to ask."

Great, he said the guy who did his clearance must have been new at it. He was looking for a reason to red flag Michael. Michael confessed he knew more about psychiatry evaluations than he ever wanted to, because of growing up in an abusive household. He coached me on how to answer if I got the same guy.

Michael claimed this guy was power hungry and a danger. I retrieved my discharge papers. Michael pulled the one out that contained my scheduled appointments. Yes, it was the same agency, and they only had this one evaluator.

I already had a bad feeling about this. If this guy thought for one minute, he had any say over me, then they may as well lock me up right now.

It was eye med time. I mentioned out loud that it was time for me to put in my stupid eye drops, with the hopes that he would volunteer. He did, and, damn, was he good at that.

I looked at my phone and it was almost three in the afternoon. I asked Michael what he was doing the rest of the day and said I would buy him an early dinner if he wanted to hang around before his shift tonight. He accepted and then I asked him if we could take his car. Now he grew suspicious and tested me. "That's fine, but I'm driving."

I held it together as best I could. He said the one thing he knew would let me know that he knew why we were taking his car. I pulled from deep inside to let it go. I still needed to play nice, and I needed to play this to my advantage with my eye injury. The sunlight still hurt my eye without the patch and driving was more of a challenge than I expected. "Fine, but we have one stop to make first."

Michael walked past me, slipping his black work boots on as a text from Andy lit up my phone: *How goes the battle?*

I smiled and replied: *I am home, just on my way out with Michael to do a little surveillance and buy him dinner after.*

Andy replied: *why are you not at your parents' house?*

Long story.

K

I thought about this little exchange and I was kind of missing him. I extended an invitation: *Want to come over after?*

There was an instant response: *K.*

This man made me happy: *I will be back around five.*

I waited a moment. There was that single letter response again *K*, making me smile bigger.

CHAPTER THIRTEEN

There were benefits to being the passenger, especially when going to stake out the pushy tramps living accommodations.

We pulled up to the address my mother had given me. She had already sent a private detective for her own record keeping. Oh my! There she was on the phone exiting a Lincoln Town Car with the driver setting all her designer store bags on the curb. She was giving him orders that he was not carrying out.

When his trunk was empty, he closed it and nodded to her with her shouting and waving her hands over all her bags in anger, pointing at him and saying they would fire him. She sounded like the gutter trash she was while he drove away.

She was on her phone, ranting to someone about what had just happened. There were too many bags for her to carry in one trip. I was cringing at the thought that my father had paid for all of that.

Michael couldn't take it anymore. "Why are we here looking at this stupid woman and watching this ridiculous display?"

I turned to him. "That stupid woman is my father's mistress, and he is paying for all of that."

Michael's lips separated in shock. He didn't say another word. Ten minutes passed; another car pulled up. This stupid cow didn't bother to move one step. A guy our age got out, wearing a Hawaiian shirt with a few layers of gold chains around his neck, smiling as he greeted her with a big lip-to-lip kiss.

I was filming this with my camera. Not a relative since he smacked her ass, scooping up as many of her bags as he could carry. She picked up the last two he couldn't carry and walked behind him as they disappeared into the building.

Michael turned toward me. "Well, this is simple."

I flexed my right eyebrow. "How so?"

"You just need to buy some hunting cameras, set one up in that tree and one in that tree and let the evidence collect. Shoot, I bet you could set one outside her door, and she wouldn't know."

"Really?"

"Oh, fuck yeah. She's a city chick; she won't have a clue what a hunting camera is, this is easy."

"Okay, wilderness man, where do I get a hunting camera?"

Oh my, the world of outdoors. I never enjoyed shopping, but this was like entering Santa's Village for a four-year-old. It enchanted me. I have never been to a store like this. Pro sports, pro wilderness, I was coming back here for sure with a couple grand in my pocket to spend.

My new stock inheritance was looking fantastic to me now. Michael found what I needed and my homework was to read up on the directions. We were planting them in the next few days.

Hannah was working the bar tonight. It was perfect because I made us late because I didn't want to leave that store. Michael was currently going through a root beer phase that kicked me into a root beer phase, making Hannah remember she used to love root beer when she was younger.

We ate at the bar and I filled my gal in on what we were up to this afternoon. She liked the idea of the camera's, but asked, why hunting cameras? I let Michael explain.

Michael dropped me off an hour and a half later than the time I told Andy that I would be back. As Michael rounded the corner there was Andy's car parked in my second space. Instant happiness spread through me as Michael commented, "Did someone take your space?" I told him to stop as a black cat darted out of nowhere in front of us. That cat would be a pancake one of these days.

I unbuckled, "That's Andy's car; he's allowed. Hey, thanks for today; I really appreciate everything. I truly mean that Michael. You are my second-best friend." He rolled his car a little further up just before mine. Michael flicked his chin in my direction. "Good luck at the doctor." He pushed his unlock button to release my door.

That was it; as soon as I stepped away from his car and closed the door, he reversed, speeding away in the opposite direction. I watched as Andy was standing casually leaning his backside against the trunk of the crap mobile and watching Michael's exit.

"Hey, babe." He turned my head to kiss me. We were in the open and never has he done that before. He took my shopping bag, reading the store's name out loud and peeking in. I asked how long he had been waiting. Oh, gosh. He has been here since 6:00 and I never thought to call him and tell him that I was running late.

I apologized telling him I would fix that in the future. He didn't seem to care. He had one thing on his mind and he was making sure we were both on the same page.

* * *

Andy volunteered to set up my hunting cameras. I knew how experienced he was living under the radar, and this would be perfect.

97

We were still under the covers; he was laying on his right side up on his elbow; I was tucked against his warm smooth body, as he traced a circle repeatedly, softly with a kiss to my shoulder every so often.

I muttered about my evaluation coming up. He assured me he would have a talk with the guy if I didn't clear. The vision of Andy confronting someone on my behalf sparked a little joy in me. Then he announced he would hold me long enough so that I was in my second stage of sleep then he had to go.

This was both a feeling of security and invading my space at the same time. This was not the Andy I had been with for the past few years. This was Andy playing the role of a boyfriend. A role he clearly could not commit to, but here he was trying.

At some point I nodded off. I woke up feeling snug; something felt tight around my body while I rocked slightly and half sat up. I looked down at the blankets; he had swaddled me in a cocoon, pillows tucked against my body both at my back and front. I looked and then sat up higher, grinning. He tucked me in. Now, I was debating getting up or laying here for another hour.

I looked around for my phone. I couldn't find it. Now I had to get up. I couldn't remember where I left it? There it was right next to the coffeepot ready to go. There was a missed call from my mother and one text from her asking if I needed a ride to my doctor's appointment. It was only six in the morning, but I was sure she was awake. I answered her text that I was all set.

Next, I texted Andy: *You are just full of surprises.*

He answered: *Good morning, babe.*

I asked him what he was doing this morning.

At the gun range.

Hmm, I think I would like to go shooting with him sometime.

Now, I was getting antsy. I looked at the time. I could go to my grappling class, then have plenty of time to come home and get ready for my doctor's appointment.

Well, it was plain that I was the last person they expected to see walking through the door. I wasn't sure if it was the new haircut and they didn't recognize me or that it shocked them that I was back so soon. After the surprised looks faded, I was asked how I was feeling. I answered that I was fine and started to change.

My instructor stopped me right there. After a five-minute argument, he led me to the matt. The agreement was, if I could take him to the mat, they'd allowed me to join them.

The angry mood I'd developed with his attitude, questioning me about my right to be here, made me all too happy to accept. I wanted to make this simple. I went for his knee, only my eye was not a hundred percent healed, throwing my perception off, making me graze to the left of where I should have landed.

He swept my feet out from under me, making me land right on my back, knocking the wind out of me.

Steve rushed over pulling me up as I gasped and gasped trying to breathe. Sensei squatted in front of me. "Come back in two weeks, Chanler."

I slowly got my breath back as the class started. They ignored me mostly. Steve kept peeking over, though. I wanted to scream, punch something, and cry all at once, but I did none of those. I stood up, walked over to my bag and left.

I don't know why I drove to Burbank Hospital, but here I was in a parking space turning my engine off.

I found, Audrey Lanski easily. I was sitting outside of the ICU, waiting for permission to enter. The nurse came out, "Tiffany Chanler?"

I stood up. "Yes?"

"You are on the visitation list; you can come in. Audrey is very pleased you are here; she's just fixing her hair. Let's walk slowly so she can finish."

It confused me. "I'm on the visitation list?"

She grinned. "Yes? Your mother told us she would bring you by next week, but this is just what Audrey needs right now. Great timing, I must say. I heard you were the organ donor driver that carried Audrey's match."

I had not taken into consideration that it would single me out like that. This must have been the gossip of every hospital. Great, just what I needed. I answered with an abrupt, "We never know what our cargo is when we transport."

She nodded. "I bet that is a tough job. I hear there have been several attempts of hijacking this year?"

Okay, I was done with this conversation. "All rumors. This was a singled incident. My job is pretty boring day to day."

We stopped in front of a door, the nurse knocked, walking through first, and announcing us. I passed the hospital curtain not exactly ready for what I saw.

There she rested, a plain, petite, slender-looking woman; her skin tone was yellowish, a clear sign of her liver failure. Her dark hair was thick and styled in a sensible pageboy cut that suited her. She sat up tall, wrapped in a cobalt blue satin bathrobe over her hospital gown; her eyes were a deep brown, and their shaped suggested an Asian influence about them. Her smile, exhilarated the drab overcast feeling of this sanitary cell that they referred to as a hospital room. Happy, she displayed genuine joy to see me. The nurse grinned. "I love that smile. I will leave you two to visit."

"Thank you, Jessica." Audrey's toothy grin shifted from the nurse back to me.

I stood there, not sure what to do. She spoke confidently. "Tiffany, I am happy that you are here. Please, sit."

She gestured to the chair with her eyes and a full, palm up, arm extension. I sat looking across at the woman I had not too long ago pictured as the enemy.

She may have been frail, body wise, only right now she masked any form of discomfort as she sat there enjoying this moment I was here.

I didn't know what to say as the silence grew between us. She took control, only waiting a respectful moment, and then formally introduced herself. "Tiffany, I'm Audrey. First, I want to say I am relieved you are okay, that nothing more serious or crippling happened to you last week. It would have devastated me if you had permanent injuries from that transport. I am sorry that my organ caused you such a danger."

I wasn't sure if she wanted me to answer or if that was rhetorical. "That's my employment, nothing personal. It didn't matter who I was transporting for. From the moment I step into my ambulance until the moment I turn it over at the end of my shift, I have a big target on me. It's kind of the reason I like my job so much. It's unpredictable; anything goes."

I was having a hard time getting past her Asian features with a name like Audrey Lanski. It just didn't match up.

She joked, "You would be an excellent stockbroker."

I chuckled. "You are not the first to tell me that."

She spoke in confession, "Well, I must admit that I know a great deal more about you than you do about me, so let's even the score; shall we? Tiffany, you may ask me anything."

Stupid woman, wrong thing to stay to me. "Why did you have an affair with my father?"

She went straight-faced for a second, then a little smile crept back in. "Boy, your mother warned me you were tough, but fair enough. Staring death in the face has advantages. You may know that. Richard and I worked closely for twenty-five years. Being a woman in a powerful position came with many sacrifices that I made for the love of my career. I always kept my respectful distance. I knew your mother well. She was the silent partner in your father's success."

She wasn't stopping. This could have been a PowerPoint presentation.

"There came a time when you went off to college; they grew apart. Richard was spending more time in the office. He was working the long nights I was used to working alone at the company. I didn't have the care, nor desire for the flashy lifestyle that came with making money. I loved the competition of the business game. I wanted that next contract and the next and the next. The only thing that would shut my brain down for the night was Vodka."

She glanced down at her stomach. "See where that got me! My dad would have a drink now and then. Only Vodka, He was a good Polish man. Anyway, Richard would join me time to time on our late nights for a cocktail to close the end of our workday. He often remarked that, for all the money I made, I was lousy at picking a decent brand of alcohol. He said the Vodka I bought was gut rot. He was right again."

I moved in my chair slightly to ease my posture. I didn't want to act like this was an interrogation. She was being open with me and the least I could do was appear more relaxed. She continued observing what I was trying to achieve. "This is the part you probably don't want to hear."

She waited for any change of my decision. I was not wavering. I wanted to hear it from the source. "I can handle it."

She nodded. "I thought a sexual relationship with your father would be uncomplicated. We didn't love each other, and there was mutual respect. I asked your mother's permission first and when she granted it, I proceeded with the affair. We kept it very discreet."

WHAT!!!! She asked permission! My mother granted it to her! I was about to stand up and leave when she recognized what I was about to do.

"Tiffany, please don't go. You asked a very difficult question. I apologize for the blunt answer. It was a convenient arrangement at the time. I would never have done so without her consent. It never interfered with the company, and never interfered with Richards or my work ethics. There was no jealousy, no revenge; I had no intention of taking him away from your mother. It was an arrangement. I have always cared for your family with the utmost respect."

Wow, could there be such a thing? I cooled off some. Mandy wants to take everything and ruin my family. I sat thinking about this for a moment.

Geez, her name and appearance really got to me. "I have a curious question for you. Your name is Audrey Lanski, yet your features are Asian. Were you adopted?"

I don't know why I needed to know this, but it was bothering me, and she said I could ask her anything.

She lowered her head with a slight grin, paused, and then elegantly lifted her chin to answer looking right into my eyes.

"You are not the first person to inquire. No, I am not adopted. My father, the good Polish man, married my mother, who is Cambodian. They met in Vietnam during the war. My mother is... quirky, to say the least. She is a huge fan of Audrey Hepburn, the actress. She can recite line by line every movie she starred in. I would classify her as an obsessed fan. She owns every movie poster of the actress, has her hair cut the same way from the movie Sabrina, and has a shrine dedicated to the actress. You can only imagine what it was like growing up with that. It was an excellent motivation to be successful in business."

"Does your mother live around here?"

"No, when dad passed away, she moved in with my sister, Heppie."

My head tilted, "Heppie? Is that a Cambodian name?"

There was a serious look about Audrey now. "Good God, gracious no! That's the only play on Hepburn that my father would allow. Let's just say it relieved me to be their firstborn."

I broke into a grin, Audrey and Heppie. Suddenly I didn't mind my name, Tiffany, so much.

Turned out, I enjoyed learning about Audrey. She even shared her embarrassing moments growing up with her mother. I laughed out loud several times. This woman had a clever sense of humor for sure.

I also learned more about the liver than I ever cared to. Audrey was having more difficulty because of her Asian heritage. I learned that most Asian Americans were not organ donors. No one even considered a partial donation.

I ended up staying for a whole two hours talking to this amazing woman, and I could have stayed longer. I liked Audrey more than I thought I would. She was not an enemy. I felt compassion for her situation and I wanted to help her live a longer life. I understood Mother's feelings toward Audrey.

Maybe Mandy's liver was a match. I wouldn't mind getting rid of her, but on that same thought Mandy is not good enough to live in Audrey's body. She just needed to be taken out and dumped in the trash.

CHAPTER FOURTEEN

I entered a few minutes late to my doctor's checkup. Thank goodness they were also running behind. They checked me from head to toe, and I received the all clear from this doc.

Tomorrow, I had to see the one person who could stop me from returning to work. I already didn't like him having that power. I called Michael upon his request for my update. Then I called my mother and planned to meet her at the edge of town.

We met at my favorite coffee shop that made the best jelly donuts in the world, Larry's Café; the staff greeted me. Mother looked around, commenting that this was a charming little place.

She said that wiping the table in front of her with a linen handkerchief. She was out of her element here. This was not the high rollers club she was used to. I ignored her and told her all about my visit with Audrey.

She waited, remarking a few times that I should not have asked her that or brought up this...Blah, Blah, Blah. I think my bluntness brought Audrey and me together. She was honest, sharing, and most certainly, not intimidated to tell me what I wanted to know.

Mother finally sipped her coffee. Her expression was a pleasant surprise as she looked into the cup taking another sip. "What are we going to do about saving that poor woman? She has become a friend... one I value."

Now I had to know more than ever as I asked her. "I've wanted to ask this, but I wasn't sure how to bring it up."

Mother stared curiously at me. "What is it, Tiffany?"

I drew a swig from my coffee, pondering for a moment whether I wanted to know the answer.

"How could you have given Audrey permission to sleep with Father?"

Her long slow inhale gave me the idea that she was not expecting me to ask this. She looked down for a moment, then sat straighter, exhaled abruptly and told me the whole story. By the time she was done, I regretted asking her.

What a messed-up life they pretended to lead from my perspective. I could completely understand her reasoning though. It was all just odd, and they were my parents. I tried to be non-judgmental. This was their life. They would still be my parents, no matter what the outcome was from here on out.

Three things were clear to me about my future. I needed to get back to work. We needed to save Audrey. Mandy had to go.

* * *

My psych evaluation was the only thing that could delay me from my first goal. I called Michael again to go over what I needed to do to pass this test.

It wasn't until ten in the evening that I started to get antsy. I looked at the cameras still in their sealed packaging and opened one of them reading the directions from start to finish. This accident had messed up my body clock and I didn't know when to sleep anymore. I texted Andy to come over.

I should have known something was up when he arrived. This was an instant booty call; he had no intention of staying the night. I delayed him a little as we made coffee at one o'clock in the morning.

I told him I was concerned about the psychiatrist. He gave a slight grin reminding me, "It won't be any trouble for me to have a chat with him."

I liked that idea much more right now. "Yes, well maybe? Let's see what happens first. Michael said this guy is a prick. He's the type to abuse his powers."

That piqued Andy's curiosity. "What does he know about that?"

"He saw him last week, and the guy was looking for a reason not to clear him."

"Oh? Who is he? Name?"

I walked past him to my table that had all the paperwork. I retrieved the packet with this guy's name and address, handing it over. He held it, looked at the name, then dropped it on the counter like it was insignificant. "You'll be fine. Don't worry about him."

Something confused me. "Do you know this guy?"

"No, but I know he doesn't have enough capital letters abbreviated after his name to hold you out of work."

"What does that mean?"

"It means he can only do an evaluation. If you need further psych care, he is not qualified to treat you. He has to follow a questionnaire. If you answer any that you are afraid, depressed, or spend more time alone than usual, then he can alert your employer. They decide if they want to pay to have you professionally tested. This is just to cover your employer's ass. If this guy gives you a hard time, let me know."

Oh, this was good news. Why was Michael so worried about this guy if he couldn't do a damn thing to keep me from returning to work? Michael said this guy was trouble, though.

Andy finished his coffee, kissed me as if it was our last and told me to get some rest. I was catching my breath from that kiss. He did that so well. We walked toward my door; He warned me that he had a busy day ahead, but to text him about how my appointment went.

He winked, giving me a click noise from his mouth. "Good luck, babe."

"Thanks."

I closed the door when he turned the corner. I decided it was time that Andy met my parents. I would make that happen soon.

I woke up at seven and started my day just as I usually do. It was time for me to fall back into my routine. I hit the gym since they had banned me from grappling class.

My phone was blowing up by eight thirty from Michael asking where I was. I texted him and told him I was just finishing my workout. He texted back that he would meet me at my house to grab those hunting cameras and volunteered to install them himself.

I wasn't sure if Mandy had seen him at my party or not, but I knew Michael was good at blending in. I originally wanted Andy to install them, but since Michael could do it today, I agreed.

I wanted them up and functioning sooner rather than later. I needed surveillance on that bitch right now. Michael came over giving me one last piece of advice for the evaluation appointment.

I wasn't worried about him anymore and I told Michael what Andy said. For the first time, I saw anger in Michael's eyes. "That fucking head case is wrong, Tiffany. This guy can become a thorn in your side. You need to listen and trust me. I am right about this. I wish I could go with you but ethically I can't. Where is Hannah? You need someone there in the waiting room."

I couldn't figure out why Michael was so bothered by this. "Hannah has her hot date with her doctor tonight. There is no way I will make this day all about me. I'm fine. I got this. Why are you so worried, anyway?"

I could read conflict in him. He didn't want to say. He paced some, then stopped, and picked up the cameras. "You're right. I'm overreacting. Call me when you're out."

If there was one thing I knew about Michael, it was this. He was withholding information right now. "No, no, and no. What is going on? You are a terrible liar. Spill it, now!"

He conceded, "Kyle made a phone call to the guy who is doing the evaluation about you."

I didn't understand what he was saying. "What? How? Why? How do you know this?"

His shoulders sank. "Our new candidate, the retired state trooper. She knows this game all too well, and the dumbass put a call into Reardon in front of her. She knows the politics' and gave me the heads up."

Fucker! Andy would hear all about this. I calmed my emotions. I needed to have a plan to use this to my advantage. I needed to think. "He wants you out of work longer. I don't know why yet, outside of the fact that you two hate each other. Something else is up."

"He is such an ass. That is totally illegal."

"Doesn't matter, Tiff, I'm telling you. This guy is a power-hungry quack. There was something not right about him. I couldn't put my finger on it, but Kyle just gave him more incentive to interfere."

My hand was on my hip. I looked at my phone. Damn, I did not want to make this call. I wanted to do this alone today, but the only other person I knew, that had any kind of experience with therapists was probably already waiting and willing me to call.

I huffed out putting the phone to my ear. "Hello, Mother."

She was waiting in her Mercedes sedan when I parked. Mother had a new driver today. He was younger than her regular driver and definitely more handsome. He exited the car as I approached. "Miss Chanler?"

I nodded. "Yes?"

"I'm just checking. Your photographs do not do you justice."

Seriously! I rolled my eyes as he walked past me and opened the door for her. He held out his hand as her brown glove slid into his hold helping her from the back seat; she genuinely smiled at him. He bowed his head, telling her he was parking over there, lifting his arm, and giving a directional point, then requested that she text him when she was leaving the appointment.

"Thank you, Jordan."

"Where is Driver Tim?"

"Vacation. I might give him an additional week." She grinned wiggling her eyebrows.

"Stop that." I shook my head.

I located Reardon Services on the second floor. This was a professional screening service all right. My mother instantly pointed out the fact that this person was not a doctor, and this was just a service.

The fake wood paneling dated this building at least thirty years back. The entrance door was hollow wood. I pushed it open with more force than needed as I didn't expect it to be so light. It flew open to a small waiting area.

We were the only visitors here. A young woman sat behind the counter on the phone, turned away from the seating area. She continued laughing and gossiping about who she was meeting up with tonight. Whoever it was sounded like she had a mission to get him to commit to her once and for all.

Mother looked at me, standing there. She had enough with waiting and being polite. She knocked on the window that separated us. startling the lady to screech into the phone and end the call abruptly. She was a little peeved from being startled, sliding the glass door over and asking with attitude, "Can I help you?"

I smiled. "Tiffany Chanler for my ten o'clock screening."

She looked down. "Have a seat. I will let him know you are here."

Mother walked over to the seating area and looked at each chair. She finally decided on the best one to sit on and pulled out a small can of disinfectant spraying her seat, then mine. I smirked as she frowned, implying how much this place needed a makeover.

He made us wait a good five minutes. His secretary sat behind her desk again when a brown hallway door pulled open. Mother stood up with me.

"Miss Chandler?" There he stood, in the doorway, no taller than five foot three, drab brown shoulder-length wavy hair. He looked like he was still trying to hold onto his youth rather than a naturalist look. The first thing out of his mouth was to mispronounce my last name.

Mother corrected him before I did. "It's Chanler. There is no 'D' in our last name."

Instead of innocently making light of a simple mistake, he narrowed his eyes at her. Oh boy, this will be fun. "I assume it is your daughter I am seeing today?"

"Yes, Mr. Reardon. I understand her employer requires this standardized, routine questionnaire before she returns to work. About how long will you be?"

He looked away from her for a moment to glimpse at me, then back to her, "That will depend on your daughter. Usually, my patient's appointments are around an hour."

My mother straightened up, switching her handbag from her right arm to her left. "Did you say your patients? Mr. Reardon, do you have additional credentials above a consultant? This is a standardized questionnaire. It should allow her to fill the paperwork out in this waiting room."

"Mrs. Chandler, please sit. She will be out when we are finished." My mother held her gloved finger up, about to give him more than a simple correction this time. I intercepted gently, lowering her hand. "I will be right out."

Mother watched me with a tense jaw. I knew where she had learned that from, my father. After living with the same man for thirty-two years, they had adopted habits from one another. Still neither one of us could beat my father's clenched jaw look.

I knew where she wanted to go with this, but I needed to get back to work. I had already summed up what this was all about. Mother had succeeded in giving me what I needed to know about this guy in their brief exchange.

I nodded to her, patting her forearm holding the purse. "I've got this."

I walked into the hall ahead of Reardon as he closed the door a little more forcefully than he should have. My mother had riled him up, without a doubt. He commanded me, "Second door on your right."

I looked inside the first door that was open. It was an office, and there was a very interesting simply framed copy of *The Punishment of Marsyas* hanging on the wall.

I had taken an elective in college about mythology and the fine arts. I remember this picture and the class's opinions about it. The picture was about being flayed alive for winning a challenge over Apollo.

I remember the class discussion on this painting that ended in a heated debate. Best class I had ever taken in an elective. It almost made me change my major. Now I really knew what I was in for.

I turned right and stood just inside the doorway. I softly settled into my shoulders. Now was not the time to show any sign of weakness or have a direct confrontation.

Mr. Reardon picked up a clipboard that must have been in his office and, upon walking in, he motioned with the clipboard to where he wanted me to sit. The chair he guided me to looked like a dental chair in its upright position, while his seat was a plush leather wingback chair. Oddly enough, he sat taller than me in his seat.

"Miss Chandler, before we start, I would like to ask you how you are feeling? From what I understand, that was quite an incident you went through."

I cleared my throat, ignoring the mispronunciation of my name again, replying calmly and matter of fact, "Just another day at the office."

He looked down at his clipboard, pulled the pen from the top and flipped open a lined notebook. He made a hmm sound and wrote something down. I waited, looking around the busily decorated room. It was a little chilly in here and maybe I should have worn a sweatshirt.

He continued, "Well, your world must be hostile if you think it's normal to hijack."

TRAP! That's all that went through my mind. I didn't respond to him as I waited for his next question. Again, I heard a hmm, and he continued "Miss Chandler, tell me what happened that day." I looked at his clipboard that had the sheet of the questions covered up by his note pad. I continued with my matter-of-fact attitude. "Is that a question on the evaluation?"

"Miss Chandler, I need to understand what your current state of mental health is. That is all."

"That is not your job, from my understanding."

"If I do not know that you can objectively answer these, then I can only suggest to your employer that you need further testing and became uncooperative, leaving you out of work for an extended period."

"About a mile out from the hospital they ambushed us. I ended up in the hospital. I received excellent care."

He waited for more. I was done. Hmm he wrote in his notes.

He looked up. "Is that it?"

"Yes, no, I was cleared by the company's physician yesterday to return to work." I waited.

"From my understanding, you seem not to want to talk about what happened."

"I talked about what happened."

"From my understanding, there is a lot you are leaving out. Have you forgotten, maybe blocking it out?"

Now, I could understand why Michael was red flagging this guy. Wow, it felt even cooler in here. "Mr. Reardon, I know the risks of the work I do. We all train to keep ourselves safe. Practice is key. The more I train, the better I am at the task at hand. I have been cleared by the medical exam, and I would like to return to my employer. I do not hold on to situations that I have no control over. I learn, I accept and I let go."

He glanced at my chest that was now reacting to the temperature in this room. Then he glanced back to his notepad, making his notes. I knew my breasts were reacting from the room temperature.

"Hey, can you turn the temperature up a little? It's uncomfortably cold in here. I didn't bring a sweater."

"No, the air conditioner is on a timer."

I looked around the room. There were a few magazines on top of a bookcase against the wall. I stood up as he announced, "We are not done."

I flashed a grin. "Yes, I know that, but if you will do nothing about the temperature, then I need to cover my chest. It clearly seems to distract you."

I picked up the magazine and opened it. I sat back down with it covering my chest. "Now, as you can see, I am completely in a good place to give an open answer to the standard questions that my company pre-selected, or have you modified this evaluation?"

He looked angry. "Miss Chandler, I will be right back. I will see what I can do about the temperature of this room. Excuse me a moment."

Stupid man. I looked around the room and studied the wall opposite my chair. My other favorite hobby was reading true crime books. The wall directly across from my chair had a rather busy art picture. Almost too much to stare at.

I got up quickly and tried to tip it. They had fixed it to the wall. I scanned over the artwork. There was a camera sticking out a few centimeters from the original canvas with what looked like a silver melted mirror covering it as camouflage. This picture was so busy that it hurt to look at it for too long.

There was definitely a camera behind this. This guy was a predator. There was no way it was legal to film anything that happened in this room. I was done. I pulled open the door; he was on the other side, looking down at his phone.

I grabbed it and saw it was showing surveillance of the room. I gripped onto it as tightly as I could and knocked his hand out of the way as he reached for it.

"You have to the count of ten to okay and sign that evaluation clearing me to return to work. One."

"Give me my phone back!"

"Three."

"You are a psychopath."

"Five, six."

He looked at the phone. "I will call the police."

"Nine, ten."

"Give me that phone!"

"No need to call the police; I will."

I pushed past him as he tried to grab my hand. I ran my heel down the inside of his ankle and shoved his shoulder back, knocking him onto his ass.

"You are a predator. I am not a victim. Wrong woman to pull this on."

He sat there, wide-eyed that I had done that so easily.

"This is my insurance. If you do not clear me, I will take this to the cops. I expect my employer to call me this afternoon with my clearance to return to work." I turned and walked on.

His secretary was in the hall, seeing her boss on the floor. She must have heard our confrontation.

"Doctor Reardon! Are you okay?" She brushed past me

"He's not a doctor. He's a predator." She was reaching to help him up as she was asking if she should call the police. He was telling her no as I cleared the door. "Come on, Mother. My appointment is over. We need to go. Now!"

Mother stood up and asked, "Is everything okay, Tiffany?"

"Yup, come on. Let's get out of here."

I grabbed ahold of her elbow and opened the door with his phone still in my grip. Mother asked why we were in such a hurry. I answered that the guy was a creeper. She asked what that was. I didn't want to explain, so I brushed it off and said that I passed the test and the guy was full of himself. I waved to Jordan since we left in such a hurry. When he stopped the car at the curb, I opened the door for her, thanked my mother for coming, and assured her that I would call her later. She knew this was me getting rid of her. "Tiffany! What is going on?"

"I need to get us out of here; something happened in there. I'll tell you later."
She was between mad and concerned.

"Mom, please, trust me on this. I promise I will tell you soon. I have to go."

She nodded, pointing her finger. "You had better call me."

I shut her door scurrying to my car, leaving the parking lot as quickly as I could.

CHAPTER FIFTEEN

All I could think about was calling Andy. I texted him instead, telling him I needed to see him ASAP. He replied it would be a few hours. I answered Okay.

I waited until I was back in my condo before I called Michael. He was just finishing up installing the cameras and said he would be back in an hour. I called Hannah next. I needed to tell someone, but then I remembered her big night tonight with her doctor.

I shut up about what happened and made the conversation all about her, asking if she was ready. My squeaky girlfriend gushed over her excitement, doubt, fear, and insecurities as I reassured her it would be just fine. She calmed me down as I listened to all the normal things that happen to a woman... like going out on a date.

Hearing her talk made me a little sad that I would never experience the emotions of being a woman like she could. That had me thinking of my teens and Blake. I needed to let it go. Why was he still getting to me?

I really was denying myself the chance of a house with a white picket fence, children, and a husband.

My buzzer was ringing. I looked at the time. It had to be Michael. Hannah and I had been talking for almost an hour. I hung up and let him in. He gave me the confirmation that the cameras were set up and asked for my laptop.

I gave it to him and he loaded the codes and set up my passwords. All three cameras were officially up and working. They were motion detected and single frame shots, but they were still effective.

Michael asked me how my appointment went. I hesitated to tell him. Michael's calm expression contorted into concern the longer I remained silent. He was asking too many questions. He wanted to know, and he was right on track with his questions.

I'm sure my frustration showed that he was correct. He demanded to know right now. I knew this would go badly, so I went right for the gut; I told him everything in plain detail.

It was strange. Michael's face altered. I could see the hard lines forming. He was trying to become expressionless. I could feel the angry energy around him though. One look into his eyes said it all. They burned with rage.

I made my next mistake by pointing to Reardon's phone. I was telling him that I needed to find evidence that Kyle had contacted him. Michael was about to grab it. I stopped him in his tracks, blocking his reach with my body. I reminded about fingerprints.

I made it clear; only mine were on it so far. Michael pressed his lips together as he clenched his fists tight. I've never witnessed this anger in him before.

My door buzzer sounded. We both turned at exactly the same time. It must be Andy. I relayed this to Michael as I stood straighter, seeing that Reardon's phone would be left alone. His only reply was, "I'm fucking staying."

I opened the door as Andy was rounding the corner. He glimpsed Michael over my shoulder, standing in my kitchen. Andy paused in front of me, pulling me in with a kiss upon greeting. He released me and quietly asked, "What's going on, babe?"

I shut the door behind him and told him about my appointment. Andy handled the news much differently. He was calm. He didn't display any emotion like Michael did. He asked me for a plastic bag, turning it inside out and picking up the phone, pulling the baggie over it to contain it as evidence.

Michael asked him what he thought he was doing with that.

Andy rebuked him, "I'm taking it."

"Like hell you are. We are taking it to the police. This guy needs to be arrested."

"I need to see what he has on it first."

"We got this. I don't need you to bring this guy down."

Andy's expression altered slightly like he was dealing with a child. "Listen kid; when you can run a special ops mission from your basement, then we'll compare whose balls are bigger. My girlfriend needs information extracted correctly on a first attempt, without all your fanfare, sloppy investigations, and pulling the cops into mess it all up."

They were now locked in a staring match. I jumped between them before the first fist flew. "Hey! Come on. Stop this. The guy is a predator. We need to work together."

My phone rang. Michael broke away from Andy's glare first, glancing down. "It's the office Tiff."

I scooped it up. "Hello."

I had my clearance to return to work. Now, this situation was in my control. "Andy, can you really break into this easily and retrieve what I need?"

"This is child's play, sexy. I'm guessing there is more on this phone to bargain with. Especially if you have your clearance after what you said happened."

I knew he said that on purpose to taunt Michael, and it was working. I needed to run interference; I don't know why this was becoming a pissing match between them. I turned toward Michael with my back to Andy, acknowledging Michael's good deed. "Hey, thanks for setting up the cameras."

Michael's grin caused a counter reaction as Andy stepped in closer to my backside leaning over my shoulder, cupping my upper arm adding, "Hey, I appreciate it, man. I wouldn't have been able to get to it until Sunday. Thanks for helping my woman."

Oh crap. Michael was fuming. I needed to get him out of here before they started swinging. "Hey, um yes, thank you again. I'll see you tonight on our shift. You better get some rest, because I'm ready to jump back in the game."

Michael stormed past me. "See you in a few hours, Tiff. I'm here for you anytime."

I turned to Andy when Michael pulled my door harder than necessary when shutting it. "Could you have been just a little nicer to him?"

Andy re-adjusted, "No."

I asked, "What's with the girlfriend comment?"

He placed his hands on my shoulders. "I want to try."

This made me happy. "Good, then it's time for you to meet my parents."

Andy left with Reardon's phone, and I made the phone call I had promised to make earlier.

"Hello, Mother." I didn't get into what happened in Reardon's office. I confessed my uneasy feeling about the guy; then I proceeded to lie to her about finishing the questions I could have done in the waiting room. I gave her the update that they had cleared me, and I was returning to work tonight for the last day of my work rotation. I promised I would meet her in the morning at the hairdressers.

That satisfied her enough, but she said she knew I was holding something back, promising to get it out of me tomorrow. Well now, I had to think up something else to say to her. I knew it had to be good enough to warrant such a strong reaction from me getting us out of there. I needed to think smart about this.

I texted Hannah to tell her I was returning to work tonight and would see her in the morning, wanting details on how her date went. She texted back with an emoji of a thumping heart.

Pulling up to the gate made me think back on that car a few weeks ago with the woman in the back seat, taking care of her crying baby. Could it have been a setup to get me out of the ambulance for someone to size me up?

I needed to talk to Andy about this. Maybe that was more than we brushed it off to be.

Well, Pam was delighted I was back. She requested I stop by before her shift ended. She wanted to hear about the hijacking straight from me. I wanted to visit my ambulance first, see what kind of shape it was in.

Since it was Friday night, no one was in the garage by the time I got there. I flipped the lights on and spotted that Greg had tucked my rig in the back corner.

I approached slowly, a sudden shiver coming on without warning. I adjusted my jacket, wrapping it tighter as my arms folded in front of me.

Flashbacks popped into my memory of the ambulance spinning from the first hit.

Wow, the damage on the driver's side door was worse than I imagined. No wonder they were trying to pull me from the window. I walked on, examining every inch.

My memories were only of the people right outside my cab, noise from the sirens, people screaming and being tossed around like a rag doll. Looking at the exterior put everything in a whole new perspective.

They smashed my driver door in with the pickup truck's impact, which caused it to be in operable. I automatically moved my hands down over my stomach, still tender from the cuts healing.

I remembered how it felt being pulled and dragged across the jagged glass. The scene played in my mind as I stood where they were trying to abduct me. Another involuntary shiver seized my torso, as I pictured how they were yanking at me while I fought them off.

I walked on, touching the black paint from the pickup embedded into the side. I glanced upward, seeing where the paint was a bubbled mess on the corner of the rooftop.

I followed carefully looking at each dent and impression from the impacts. I halted at the back corner where they had gained access.

My back-driver's side door had unhinged at the top. They broke the door and it no longer lined up with the other. Anyone could pull it open easily. I did just that, gently opening so it wouldn't fall off still attached bottom hinge.

I slid in, climbing up through the back. I wasn't worried about contaminating it with my fingerprints. They had already collected all the evidence, and now it was ready for rebuild.

I stood up, surveying the back compartment. It was obvious that the robbers didn't care about my ambulance as I assessed the damage they had caused.

I touched a bullet hole. "Sorry, old girl. Good news, though, we are a lot alike. We can both take a good hit and come back better than before."

I ran my fingers over every place they had scratched and destroyed her. "I will fix you, no worries."

Slowly, I walked through and made my way to the front cabin. Glass was still shattered about. I grabbed a rag and brushed off my driver seat from side window pieces.

I climbed over to take my position behind the wheel. I glanced at Michael's hanging watch. I reached to touch it.

That was his contribution to our cab. He always said nothing beat the reliability of a good wrist watch. I read the time, 9:30. Quickly turning my head to the lights flickering, there was Michael, standing at the light switch.

"Tiffany?"

I leaned further into the window. "Right here, Michael." He made his way toward me.

"I knew I would find you here."

He stood at my driver's side window. "She took a good hit, didn't she?"

I nodded. "Yup."

He walked in front of the bus and opened the passenger side. "Do you mind if I hop in?"

I put my hands on the steering wheel. "It's your side. Come on in."

He stepped up and slid into his seat, just like he always did. We sat there in silence for a minute. He looked around the inside. "So, do you remember much of what happened, Tiff?"

I nodded, turning my head toward him. "Yes, some of it. Most of it, I think. I remember right up to the part of choking on the smoke."

Michael stared into my eyes. "That's when you collapsed. I had to drop my gun to grab your shoulder and yanked you back in. I fell backward, with you following on top of me, as the cabin engulfed in flames."

Michael's eyes searched mine. He slowed his speech, regretting having to relive the memory. "Tiff, the only thing the flames could attach to was you. I grabbed the emergency blanket and covered you. I was so busy trying to smother the flames that I didn't even realize they had pried the coolers open and left. I distinctly remember the smell of your hair burning. You were my only priority."

I was peering into his eyes, envisioning what must have been going through his head when he pulled me in. He saved me.

I could now read the pain, the hurt he must have felt as he witnessed my limp body on fire. I know I would have done anything I could to save Michael if the situation was reversed. I softened, feeling compassion and gratitude for what he did for me.

He leaned in slowly, the pain in his eyes seized now, overtaken by the smolder of desire and I realized we were kissing, passionately kissing. My head was spinning. He felt so right. His energy radiating heat as our mouths touched and our tongues swirled and danced, gliding over one another. I could taste Michael for the first time.

He moaned as I snapped into consciousness after being lost in the moment. This is what I have been fighting to avoid as Andy's kiss reminded me of Michael's amateur status as I compared the two right now. He stopped, drawing back for a moment, looking for any signal for permission to continue as he softly spoke my name as a question.

I wanted to give him permission, but I couldn't. We both heard a voice from the doorway.

"Hey, who's in here?" It was Calvin.

I stopped Michael softly, "No."

He leaned back, chest heaving. He wanted more, and I nearly gave it up to him. Calvin called out again, "Anyone in here?"

I turned away.

The moment was over. I leaned closer to my open window. "I'm in my ambulance, Calvin."

Calvin walked toward me. "Tiffany? Is that you?"

I leaned forward more so he could see me. "Yes, in here."

"You back now?"

"Yes, and thank you for stepping in while I was out."

"How are you feeling?" He was nearly at my door.

"I'm good. Ready to jump back in."

"I heard that was a well-orchestrated heist." He was at my window now. "Oh, hey, Michael."

"Hey." Michael adjusted to sit taller in his seat.

Calvin peeked in. "It held up pretty good taking the hits." He was referring to my transport.

"Wow, Tiffany, a new haircut?" he'd just noticed my hair.

I nodded my head, chin heavy. "I kind of didn't have a choice with my hair catching on fire. New hairdo, I am coming back with attitude, buddy."

Calvin laughed. "Like you need more of that? Speaking of attitude, have you met Taylor yet?" Now, he directed the conversation toward Michael. "Did you warn her about Taylor? She riding with you guys tonight, right?"

Michael shot Calvin a disapproving scowl. "No, she will meet her soon. I don't want to pass judgment onto Tiff."

Calvin snickered. "Do you have earplugs Tiff?"

I looked from Calvin to Michael. "Why do I need earplugs?"

Calvin chuckled again. "Junior talks a lot?"

It puzzled me, "Who is Junior?"

Michael glared harder at Calvin. "Hey Cal? Zip it!"

Calvin shrugged with an ear-to-ear grin. "Okay, I'm clocking out for the night. Glad to see you are okay Tiff. This last week has taught me I am happier keeping an eye on this place than on the road." He double-tapped my driver side mirror, turned and walked out.

Michael broke the ice. "I will murder him later."

I cracked a smile. "I better get ready."

* * *

I was in the locker room, buttoning my shirt when Taylor walked in. She's taller than me, about five years younger, brown hair, on the plus size of the scale, and clearly a know it all college student. She immediately asked, "Who are you?"

I kept my expression rigid. I was the boss of my ambulance, and I needed her to learn this right here, right now. "Taylor?"

She dropped her bag in front of a locker. She answered with a raised lip and eyebrow, "Ya?"

"I'm your boss tonight."

I caught her by surprise with my abrupt answer. "Oh, you must be Tiffany? I heard about you," she answered in a snippy tone.

"Nothing good, I hope. Otherwise it's all lies." I tightened the notch on my gun belt mimicking her reply.

She watched. "Hey, I'm taking classes for my license to carry right now. Was it hard getting your license?"

I picked up my duffel and secured it in my locker. "I don't remember it was so long ago."

"Have you ever shot anyone?" She was confident with her body now changing in the open here. I'll give her that much; a lot of women hide behind a curtain to change.

"I have, yes."

"Kyle said you were in a heist? That you ended up in the hospital because of it. He said you choked and couldn't defend yourself?"

"Hmm, Kyle said that, did he?"

"Ya? Isn't that what happened?" She was asking with some attitude now.

"Are you sleeping with Kyle?" I nearly laughed with the horrid look on her face. This was priceless.

"He has a girlfriend! I would never do that to her." Her mouth was still open surprised I even asked.

"He has about ten girlfriends," I chuckled subtly.

"No, he doesn't, just Reese. They just started dating, I believe. I got to meet her. She is so pretty and polished. She comes from a very wealthy family."

Great. I rolled my eyes and shook my head. Kyle and Reese. They deserve each other. I shut my locker and walked past her. "Ambulance leaves in fifteen minutes; make sure you are in it. I don't wait for anyone."

"I'm riding with you tonight?"

I didn't bother to answer as I cleared the door. Pam stopped me in the hall, complimenting my new haircut while we walked and talked. I rounded the corner to the boardroom and heard Michael's voice talking with Donovan, who commented that he was leaving right after this meeting. I walked in to our briefing. Donovan also mentioned my hair cut before welcoming me back.

Michael observed my attitude. "Did you meet Taylor in the locker room?" I nodded that I had, tight-lipped closing my eyes slowly for dramatic effect. He chuckled. Kyle walked in next, surprised I was here as his eyes locked on my short haircut. I didn't say a thing. He was up to something and I needed to collect evidence. Reardon's phone would be my start.

Chris was the next one to clear the door. Michael introduced us. I immediately liked her. She definitely came from the state troopers. She had a stocky build, and she too was taller than me, with a short haircut like mine with streaks of gray throughout. She smiled and shook my hand like a team player.

She had heard I was out on injury and expressed some concern but lifted her arm sleeve a little and pointed, "Bullet went in through here and clean out the back."

She understood this game and remarked that she looked forward to working with me soon. Chris reminded me of Mildred on my first impression.

She was exactly who she was standing in front of me now and who she would be five years from now. I thanked her for her concern regarding my recovery and returned the compliment.

Then there was Taylor entering. She smiled at Michael, "Hey, Mike," she greeted him while he corrected her, "Michael." She lost her grin, "Oh, sorry, Michael; I forgot."

Then she greeted Mr. Donovan and walked over to Kyle, standing next to him and starting a conversation. Mr. Donovan asked us to take a seat. He announced that Jason had called out sick tonight and Chris would ride alone with Kyle.

Then he assigned Taylor to us, which we already knew was scheduled. She interrupted him and requested to ride with Kyle and Chris. Mr. Donovan's straight face looked over to her. "I don't take requests. You are on observation only." His final words ended our briefing. They adjourned our meeting.

Michael waited for me to go through the door first, then followed behind me, not waiting for Taylor to catch up. He stopped in the office, picking up our route. I checked over my temporary ambulance. Taylor caught up and asked what I was doing. I told her I was doing my pre-check for our deliveries tonight. She made a face, announcing she would wait in the ambulance.

I was done before Michael made it back. I hopped in, and she was already sitting in Michael's passenger seat. I motioned for her to take the jump seat in the back, and she replied, "But I want to sit here?"

I shook my head. "No, you are back there."

And she dared to protest. "But Kyle let me sit in this seat when I rode with him?"

I frowned. "Then he broke the rules. You are unarmed, and you are not my copilot. Back Seat Now!"

Michael opened his door. "Taylor, get in the back. You know the rules."

She muttered with annoyance as she unstrapped awkwardly making her way to the jump seat.

"Ouch." I turned to see her rubbing her ankle "Strap in, Taylor. Rules are rules."

If this girl wasn't talking, she was singing. It was hard enough trying to have a quiet conversation with Michael without Taylor constantly including herself.

It was bothering me that I had kissed Michael. I had let myself get caught up in the moment and I could not talk to him about it with Taylor here. I needed to clear the air with him about the kiss. I excused every reason in my head; it was just one of those spontaneous moments. It was nothing more than just a kiss.

As my best efforts failed, I knew this conversation would not happen tonight. Aside from Taylor's ability to talk about absolutely nothing, it was an uneventful long night.

When we returned, Michael tried to make arrangements to see me today. I wanted to nip the kissing moment in the bud, but I had plans at the salon with Mother, Mildred and Hannah. I also wanted to run my new surveillance on Mandy. I confessed that I had a lot going on and was busy. I wasn't brushing him off; I just had my priorities and then fit in sleep.

I think Michael took it wrong because he started to turn a little pissy. I got a "whatever" from him. Presently, I did not have time for this. I would not chase him and apologize for my busy day.

I clocked out, then made my way to the garage to speak with Greg. He stared at me for a quick moment, then smiled. "Oh, Tiff? How are you, kid? Are you back?" I grinned. "Not much can keep me away. I don't recommend a scratched cornea. That sucked."

He scrunched up his face. "I don't want details. Come here. I got something for you."

I followed him to his office curiously. He picked up a brown paper bag from on top of one of his file cabinets. He smiled in his grumpy way that only I could tell was a real show of his happier emotion, despite the lopsided alignment of his lips. "Happy Birthday, a little late, but it was on back order."

I had no problem showing my toothy grin. "You didn't have to get me anything."

"Just open the bag."

I did, and I unfolded a mechanics jump suit. It was gray like the rest of the guys. I loved it! "Wow, thank you, Greg. I take that back. Yes, you needed to order this for me. I love it!"

He threw his chin up in my direction. "It will save your clothes some. We have our work cut out putting your ambulance back together." He leaned over and opened his top drawer.

He tossed me a do rag. "Here this will save your hair." I laughed. "Speaking of hair, I have an appointment to bleach it out. I have to go."

He stopped me. "One last thing, I cleaned out Sully's locker. Here, this is yours now." He walked over and opened the third locker over. I wanted to hug this guy. Best presents so far. "Wow, this is perfect, really Greg. Thank you."

I hung up my jumpsuit and placed my headscarf on the top shelf. I shut the door and laid my palm against it for a few seconds.

"Mine." I turned my head to Greg. "I will keep earning this. Thanks."

Greg was a man of few words. "I expect ten hours a week, or I am demoting you."

I laughed. "I think that's fair." He waved his rag from his back pocket. "Your parts won't arrive for a little while. Go home and get some rest. Your ten hours start next week."

"Next week starts tomorrow?"

He turned toward his calendar. "The week after."

I grinned. "I'll check in on Monday. I have some stuff I need to take care of this weekend. I am sure I can find time this week to help in here."

He nodded, "Okay" and that was it.

I had three hours until I had to meet my mother. I grabbed a quick nap. When my alarm sounded, I saw that I had missed a text from Andy. Text me when you are up.

I did just that. My phone rang as we discussed the rest of the day. I went over the commitments I had; I mentioned Greg this morning and my new locker at the shop. We planned to meet back at my house at seven. He wanted to go over what he found on Reardon's phone.

I asked him if that time was too late to eat. He said no. Now I had to figure out for the first time in my life, how I would feed the one man who was an official candidate for the boyfriend role.

I was over thinking. I was getting myself worked up. Never had I felt this emotion in my life. I was contemplating all my options, opening all the kitchen cabinets.

I was worrying about food. I stared into the sparsely filled refrigerator to see what I could serve him. I closed all the cabinet doors. Canned Spam was probably good enough for this guy. Only it wasn't good enough for me to feed him. I needed Hannah. She was so much better at this than I was.

I hadn't realized this was distracting me to the level that, when we were getting our pedicures Hannah couldn't take it any longer. "Tiffany! What is going on with you!"

My mother lowered her magazine. "Finally, someone is asking. I didn't want to pry because you have been dealing with enough on your plate. Tiffany, I have never seen you this way. Is everything all right?"

Mildred reached over from my left, touching my hand. "You are acting out of character. We are all here for you. You know you can tell us anything."

I looked from Hannah to Mildred to my mother. I lifted my chin and inhaled as much air in as I could and tightened both my fists as I exhaled evenly. "Andy is coming over for dinner, and I have no idea what to make him. I have never cooked for a boyfriend before."

My mother tried to hold back a smile. Hannah's eyebrows went up in horror at the mention of boyfriend and Mildred patted my clenched fist, alerting me to relax. She spoke first. "Men are easy. Put on something sexy and give him a sandwich. That's all it takes, Tiffany."

My mother protested, "Mildred! This is important; do not downplay the importance of planning a perfect first meal. Tiffany, do you want to cook for him or order some nice take out?"

Hannah changed her initial look. "Looks like I'm outnumbered. I can have anything delivered from our restaurants if you want? I will make sure it's perfect for you." I actually didn't know what to do. Mildred's idea was the best so far. I could handle that.

CHAPTER SIXTEEN

My hair dresser had turned my chair while blow drying, adding the finishing touches. She smiled leaning down against my ear. "Ready?"

I nodded, and she swiveled my chair for the first peek. She made me look like the woman I had always strived to be. I bored my eyes into the mirror. I knew who this woman in my reflection was for the first time in my life. I would become the fantasy I have been feeling in me forever.

I was the great descendant of Joan of Arc and evil was prevailing here. I would be the best warrior I have been training to be. I would find Audrey what she needed and make sure it was delivered to her this time.

Hannah entered from around the corner. She gasped. "Tiffany! I love it!" This cued my mother, who was walking toward my hair dresser's station.

"Perfect. It will not matter what you feed Andy tonight. He will not be able to take his eyes off of you."

I liked this look; I felt powerful. Hannah offered. "Do you want me to do your makeup?" I grinned. "I'm not putting makeup on. Thank you for the offer, though."

She frowned. "How about a little colored lip gloss then?"

I agreed to that, and she walked away to retrieve her bag. Mildred was still on the phone when Hannah returned with four completely different colors. I laughed. "Do you carry these everywhere?"

She looked at me like everyone does. "Yes, why?"

My right shoulder automatically shrugged up and down. "Oh? I don't, that's why I asked."

"Tiffany, you don't even carry a purse. How could you know the essentials on what to fill it with?"

She was right. I had no use for them. I wasn't a purse carrying "type of woman." I had my duffel bag that held my wallet, gun, my gun belt, my knife, a towel, and an extra change of workout clothes.

My mother sounded hopeful though. "Tiffany, maybe we could go shopping one of these days and see if a purse or handbag might be of use to you?"

I knew this trap. I hated shopping. I liked that hunting and fishing store Michael took me to and I had noticed they had a lady's department. Maybe they would have a purse I would consider? I set down my restrictions. "Only if I get to pick the store."

She smiled like she had won. "I'll agree to that."

Mildred was returning in as she called out to my mother. When she turned the corner she paused, taking a moment to look me over, and grinned proudly.

"Now, that suits you. Tiffany, you are beautiful. I'm sure you could open a can of pet food tonight and your fellow would not complain. He will take one look at you, and nothing else will matter."

My mother questioned, "Pet food?"

Hannah commented, "I'm sure it wouldn't be the first time he has eaten it."

Mother turned to Hannah sharply. "Really? No, you must be joking?"

Hannah shrugged her shoulders commenting, as she could believe it, "I wouldn't be surprised."

I stopped at the local grocery store. Well, my local grocery store which was actually my go to gas station that had an impressive mart attached to it.

I could walk this store blind-folded and know where everything was. I texted Hannah as I walked the aisles: *Help I am at the grocery store.*

She replied: *Oh good which one?*

I looked on the shelves for something to pop out: *Quick Stop.*

My phone rang. "Tiffany, Quick Stop is not a grocery store; that is a gas station."

"Well, it's where I shop. I can't decide on anything."

Hannah huffed out. "That's because they don't carry much. You shop there if you run out of milk, not to stock your refrigerator."

I looked around, puzzled why she had said that. "I shop here all the time. They have everything I need."

I could hear the frustration in her voice. "Buy breakfast stuff. You can't go wrong with bacon and eggs."

What a brilliant choice! Now I had a vision and a plan. "Thank you; you know no one will ever take your place, right?"

"I know, but I'm thinking maybe Andy is the perfect guy for you after all. He probably shops at your same favorite grocery store."

I bought breakfast for dinner. When I arrived home, a motion in the shrubs caught my eye. I waited a moment, stretching my head to see nothing. I pulled my plastic bag from the back seat, and I heard a growling sound. I don't know why I made a kissing sound; it sounded like a cat. Maybe one of my neighbors' cats got out and was looking to get back in. A very cautious scruffy-looking black cat stepped out from the bushes. It was the cat that ran in front of my car a few times and Michael's a few days ago.

"Well, damn, look at you, buddy?" He was dirty and had some fur missing from scars on his ears. He growled at me.

He looked hungry, and all I had were eggs and a package of bacon. Well, he would have to settle for a raw egg. I rested the bag on my trunk and reached in for an egg.

"It's all I have, but pure protein if you're willing to try."

124

I cracked open the egg and slowly walked toward him. He hissed, so I stopped. I lowered down calling him, and placed the cracked egg, shells and all, on the ground.

He sniffed. I stepped back to give him room as he approached and immediately licked it up. He looked like he was starving. I pulled the bacon open and tore off a few strips into little bits. I tossed them near the egg, and he watched me as he chomped down on the raw bacon.

"Okay, if you are here tomorrow. I will cook an egg and bring it out to you. If not, then good luck, buddy. I hope you find your home."

He was devouring the food as I walked away.

I glanced at my phone. There was a missed text from Michael. He asked for a picture of my new hair color. I snapped a selfie in my kitchen and sent it off to him, already ignoring the kiss, thinking we were back to normal.

My mind clouded as I thought ahead to Andy coming over for our first pre-arranged dinner; I placed my phone next to my keys and sort of forgot about it.

I had enough time to take a nap or check out the surveillance camera. I went for the cameras. A little over an hour into basic traffic patterns, I picked up on Kyle's truck pulling to the curb in front of Mandy's apartment. I saw another camera pick up on Reese exiting Mandy's apartment.

Kyle was there to pick up Reese. He never got out, but I saw the way Reese was laughing, then holding one finger up while she continued to talk to Mandy, who was now in the hall wearing a silk robe and holding a half full Champagne flute, as she grinned, moving toward Kyle's vehicle. Reese followed right after her, laughing and bringing her hand to cover her mouth. Mandy leaned into the passenger side window, having a conversation with Kyle as Reese waited to open the car door. She finally stepped back and spun hugging her cousin and walked back in. It was painful looking at each still shot. I wanted motion.

I wondered if she was drunk. The camera picked up on this at two this afternoon. I didn't like Kyle as it was. I really didn't like him in Clarissa's circle. The good news was there was no sign of my father anywhere on the cameras.

My door buzzer alerted me to the fact that my dinner date had arrived. I watched him round the corner. He was officially my boyfriend now, and I still didn't know how this all worked.

He stared at the top of my head, softening his expression. "I am a fan."

He leaned in to kiss me, and I quickly noticed that he was cleanly shaven. As his lips touched mine, I was no longer ignoring Michael's kiss, guilt washed through me.

"Did I say something wrong?"

I stepped back. "No, come in. I need to tell you something right away."

His whole expression altered as the emotionless mask slid across his face. I shut the door, not sure how to say this. He deserved to know. I know I would expect the same respect from him. "Tiffany?"

I blew out a nervous breath. "I went in early last night and checked out the ambulance before my shift started."

"I thought you might?"

"I am actually surprised they didn't total it."

"There's no frame damage; it'll surprise you what a dent puller can do. She's still got a lot of life in her. It's good to have a few battle scars. Keeps you remembering you are still top side."

I drew my eyebrows together. "Top side?"

"Above ground, not below."

"Is that why your car is still alive?"

"My car is perfectly fine."

"That's debatable. Anyway, I was going through what I remembered. Michael found me inside as I was trying to replay what happened the day we got hit. He climbed in his passenger seat. He told me in detail what happened."

"Did you fuck him?"

I couldn't believe he went right to that. "NO!" Even though I had a fleeting moment of wanting to have sex with him.

Andy relaxed slightly. "Then you need not tell me anything else. I understand an emotional flood. It's okay, Tiffany. I get it. I'm glad you didn't take it to the extreme."

"But?"

"Tiff, let it go. I'm good. Your answer and the way you responded is all I need."

"But?"

He stepped closer and slowly tipped my chin up for the kiss he wanted out of me when he walked in. I felt right about us. He was who I wanted to be with.

"Okay," I whispered against his lips.

Breakfast for dinner turned out to be the perfect choice. I learned that we both like our eggs scrambled, but the bacon would be an issue between us. We had cooked the whole package. I let him have the last piece when he offered to make the coffee.

Now, it was time to see what was on Reardon's phone. Andy pulled out an extension cable and hooked one end to a small square device, the other to my computer. I pointed to it. "What's that?"

He answered in a low, hushed tone, "Untraceable."

He typed in some code, then another, and a file came up; pictures started to load. I could see there were lots of women. Some nearly naked and some looked like they were not out of high school yet.

My skin started to crawl all over with goose bumps. I already had a bad feeling about this guy even before I met him.

"Andy, what is this guy?" The photos loading got stuck on one of a young woman being touched by a hand against her panties, as it now moved on and loaded the next batch.

"Well, the first thing I can tell you is that he is a porn addict."

I could feel my blood boil smoothing out the goose-bumps as the pictures loading finally slowed. They were not look of pleasure on these women's faces. They looked scared, desperate, and forced. I thought about the art in his office. He was absolutely a predator.

"It seems your evaluator has abused his powers."

I scrolled through a dozen more. "You think?"

This man made me sick. It looked as if he sexually touched them for his sign off and taped them secretly on top of it. Andy confirmed exactly that assumption.

I asked him what we would do about it now. Andy answered that he would take care of Reardon; I was not to do anything or go anywhere near him.

I wasn't sure what that meant. I didn't want him to do anything illegal, especially since I was the one to take his phone, knock him on his ass, and was now potentially the one to expose him.

At the same time, I wanted justice. I wanted Andy to remove this guy's scrotum and see if he could sell it and donate the money to a rape crisis center.

These poor women were forced into something they didn't want to do. I kept flipping through the images. I saw nothing more than inappropriate touching against their undergarments, nor did I see evidence beyond these photos of actual rape or intercourse. Reardon had to be stopped, though.

Andy assured me that nothing would come back on me. He had a few ideas about how to deal with Reardon that would be executed promptly. None he would share.

I stopped clicking through the photos. I had had enough. I turned into him now asking how long he could stay tonight. He leaned toward the computer and closed the program out.

He reported, "Until you fall asleep." I thought about the last time he did that; I was wrapped like I was in a cocoon.

Still curious about having this boyfriend-girlfriend relationship, I asked what he was doing tomorrow. Maybe I could adjust my day and spend some time with him. He informed me he was at the gun range for most of the day.

Hey, I wanted to go to the range. I wanted to do stuff like that with him, so I asked about joining him. He was not into me tagging along at all. His lips separated from the side of his mouth, and he drew in a slow breath through clenched teeth showing an automatic frown as he shook his head slightly, suggesting it was a bad idea.

I stood up, insulted. "You know what? I'm good; I have my own stuff to do. As a matter of fact, I don't think it will be long before I fall asleep, so you can go. Now." This was not a good place for me to be in. I did not take rejection well. All my life, I have been underestimated, and if he didn't think I was good enough for the gun range with him, then he could go alone. He could do everything alone.

He looked a little confused. "Are you asking me to leave?"

I folded my arms "Um no, I am kind of telling you to go. Thanks for coming over for dinner. That was fun."

He stood up from the couch, disconnected his thing from my computer, and the file disappeared. "Tiffany, did I say something wrong?"

"Nope, not a thing. I am tired and I have a busy day tomorrow. I will text you at some point."

He hesitated, not sure what was going on. He conceded, "Okay?"

Again, he hesitated at the door. "I'm not sure what I said or did. I warned you I wasn't good at this relationship thing. Maybe someday you will tell me what I did wrong. Well, good night Tiff." He leaned in to kiss me and I turned slightly in the opposite direction. He stopped trying. "Okay, I'll talk to you tomorrow at some point. Thanks for dinner." I nodded and closed the door just as he cleared it. Boyfriends suck!

Sunday morning, I woke up too early, and started out monitoring the surveillance from last night. Another night with no pictures of my father. I saw this as a good sign. Mandy left her apartment all dressed up Saturday night. They picked her up in Reese's car.

I packed for the gym and called Mother. Andy was texting me but I ignored it. She and Father were going to a brunch later this morning. They were meeting with a few key managers informally to go over some changes in the company's structure.

Mother asked if I was interested in joining them. As a matter of fact, I was interested. I wanted to see my father. The last time we were together was the day I ran out on him. I haven't returned his calls or attempted to talk to him. I needed to move past that day. I needed my family back to the messed-up way I was used to.

Maybe this was just a fling with Mandy. Heck, my new track record showed that I had started a relationship, and I already kissed someone else before our first official date. Maybe there was a cheater chromosome I had inherited from Father. No wonder I hadn't seriously dated before. Genetic flaw doomed me.

I needed to focus back on Henshaw Logistics. I wanted to learn about the empire they created, Now that I knew I would inherit a good chunk of the company in a few years, I wanted to see their vision.

Mildred had me thinking about the bigger picture. I wanted to know my options beyond my current work status. She was right. She was always right.

My mother's enthusiastic response, informing my father I was joining them while still on the phone, made me think about what to wear. This was a rare moment for me. I decided to join them. I knew these were power house brunches. Something must have been changing for them to get together informally and on a Sunday.

I owned one business style jumper. It was one piece and a pain in the ass when I needed to use the bathroom. It had spaghetti straps, and of course I had the matching sweater wrap to hide those. Hannah had picked this out for my graduation.

I thought it was too much of a statement for the after-party, so no one has seen it on me. I was always cautious about wearing black because of how much it contrasted with my eyes. It was like I had lights shining behind them when I wore anything black.

People had a hard time not staring at me, which was why I didn't wear black. I went to my closet and pulled it out. I put the jumper against my body and looked in the mirror. My hair pulled some attention away from my eyes now. Well, black jumper it is.

My cat friend was near my car. I had brought a piece of chicken I cut up to spread out for him. He growled at first then I got a meow. I placed it in front of my second spot because I didn't want my car scaring him when I started it. Cat was too busy eating to notice me driving away.

Andy left another text while I was at the gym. I ignored that one as well. Michael texted me asking if I wanted to get a bite to eat later and asking if I had found out anything about Reardon's phone.

I decided on a yes to Michael. I asked him to meet me at Hannah's restaurant after my brunch meeting. He was in. Hannah was in and told me she was wearing her bartender hat. We were meeting at the bar. Andy tried again with a hello. I finally replied with the same hello.

Now, he wanted to know how my morning was and what I was doing this afternoon. I replied that I was having a business brunch with my parents and then meeting Michael and Hannah after.

He asked where. I texted him where I was meeting my parents. He asked specifically where I was meeting Michael and Hannah. I didn't want to answer. I was still furious about the gun range insult.

I purposely left my phone in my car when I pulled up to the valet. If he didn't want to be with me on the range, then I did not want him to be with me at this brunch. Adjusting my sweater to cover up my healing burns from the accident, while I ignored the nagging vibes about leaving my phone behind. I confidently walked into the hotel. Mother was not hard to locate.

She stood out with natural grace and beauty. I slowed my pace, watching how she carried herself. She and my father knew how to play this game. They were here for a statement as she tossed her head back, playfully reaching to touch my father's arm as he turned his cheek, genuinely smiling, appreciating her reaction.

I stepped forward almost bumping into another gentleman, whose arms flung out to steady me. I was quicker than he expected at halting myself, holding my hand out to stop him from touching me.

The bit of commotion drew attention as Mother gushed upon my entrance. Waving her hand for me to join them she stated, "Oh, that color is divine on you, Tiffany. I never understood why you don't wear black more often. The color brings out your eyes so dramatically."

"That's why I stay away from this color Mother. I don't like the attention."

She reached to fix a blonde strand of hair out of place. "Well, you can't hide your beauty, darling. Every color brings attention to you. Thank you for dressing up. I know it's not your favorite thing to do."

I whispered, "You're welcome." She winked at me.

The four men my father was conversing with turned and focused on me. This alerted my father to do the same. There was a fraction of a moment that sparked humbleness in his eyes. "Gentlemen, let me introduce my daughter, Tiffany."

I politely said hello not knowing any of these men. They each greeted me with a hello except for Frank. He walked over and tried to kiss my hand. My mother interjected that it was unnecessary, smoothing over my refusal to give him my hand. I did not play this game well. I would not let him touch me.

Someone suddenly tapped my shoulder. I flinched from being surprised abruptly turning, seeing it was Andy with my phone in his hand.

"Tiffany, you forgot this."

Here he was in a black T-shirt, camo multi-color gray cargo pants, black boots, arm extended, handing me my phone. He looked like a bad ass mercenary. Now, everyone in our party and passers-bye were staring at him. My shoulders pressed together, and I narrowed my eyes, grabbing at the phone and growling, "Thank you."

Mother stepped closer. "Excuse me? and you are? Why do you have her cell phone?"

He now addressed my mother. "Hello, Mrs. Chanler; I am Tiff's boyfriend, Andy."

Mother's surprised smile said it all, as she reached out to touch his shoulder "Oh! Well, I pictured us meeting in a more casual setting, but this is a lovely surprise. Will you be joining us?"

My mother's eyes were admiring him top to bottom. I have never seen her like this. It shocked me. She was checking him out.

I interjected, "Um no, Andy has to be at the gun range all day, training. I am surprised you left to bring me my phone!" I said that last bit through my teeth.

He lingered a counter-stare, then addressed Mother, "Yes, Mrs. Chanler, this is true. I am training today. Tiffany forgot to bring her phone and I wanted to make sure I could get ahold of her if anything should happen. I like to keep in touch, even when we cannot be together." He countered my snippy remark.

Mother crossed her hands, touching her chest smitten by his openness about his feelings toward me. I rolled my eyes, then quickly introduced him to my father, who shook Andy's hand.

Andy addressed both my parents. "My apologies for interrupting. Can I just borrow Tiffany for a moment?"

Mother practically pushed me in his direction. "Of course, Andy. Nice to meet you. I look forward to having you over soon."

Andy nodded and took hold of my upper arm, leading me out of ear-shot.

"Tiffany, I really don't understand what is going on with you? And now you won't tell me where you're going this afternoon?"

He just wanted to know where I was meeting Michael. Clearly, he would stay until I told him. Eager to get this over with and back to my business brunch, watching mother watch us, I confessed about the way I interpreted his reaction to taking me to the range.

"Dammit, woman. You read that all wrong. I look forward to taking you to the range. Just not around the people I'm with today. I'm getting to know this new group that is a clear threat. I want to see what they know and how they act around weapons."

I was so stupid. I bet my expression revealed just how much I knew of my stupidity right now. I should have talked to him last night when he reacted like that. I took it personally. I suddenly felt like I had screwed that up; I wasted an evening and my morning being ticked off over something that was not even there.

He quickly changed the subject. "You look beautiful, babe. Can I see you later?"

I nodded, "Yes."

He pulled me in for a kiss, telling me he would be finished around four and to text him.

I watched my ruggedly handsome, confident boyfriend adjust his aviator sunglasses to cover his eyes, nodding to me that he was expecting me to communicate for the rest of the afternoon. I flipped my palm up and showed him my phone I understood.

I followed Andy with my eyes as he walked out of the hotel, catching many people's attention.

CHAPTER SEVENTEEN

Our business brunch was very informative. The ideas they were presenting opened up new avenues for clean energy transportation. It was actually very interesting.

One guy talked about a new engine that burns cleaner, uses less energy, and is overall better for the environment. The cost to replace a fleet of transport vehicles would recover in three years and be far ahead of emissions laws a decade from now.

I was pretty good when it came to talking about motor parts. Greg made sure I had learned the proper terminology along with new ways I could swear. I had a few of my own questions about these new green motors. The first was about the added electronics and cost to maintain.

My ambulance had the latest version of a comparably sized diesel engine. I knew all about what he was getting at, better than he did apparently. When they found out, I actually had a brain and knew about how engines worked, it made them step up their game when speaking to me.

No, I was not the princess they were expecting to sit at the table. I was the future queen; even Father sat back listening to my inquiries.

Mother leaned in commenting a few times about the raw, masculine look Andy had about him. She admitted she could see why I was attracted to him. Then she mentioned she could picture him living amongst a wolf pack, or wrestling bears in the wild.

"Stop with the visuals, Mother."

She laughed elegantly, tossing back her mimosa.

I didn't get to spend the time I wanted talking to Father. We made up, and I let him hold my arm as he claimed he was proud of me today. He asked if we could have lunch alone some time. I thought this to be a good idea. I accepted and informed him I would call later.

* * *

Walking into Hannah's restaurant, I witnessed a rare moment that her mother, Florence, was at the podium, seating guests. I had just cleared the door calling out a hello. She quickly glanced at me, still talking on the phone. She covered the mouthpiece with her hand. "Tiffany!" she spoke, grinning happily. She sped up her conversation and hung up the phone.

"My God, Hannah told me you went with a shorter style. I love it."

She checked me over. "She also told me about the accident. When are you going to quit that hazardous job and come work for us?"

I laughed. "Working one week with Albert would make me slit my wrist. You think I'm in danger now at my employer's. If I worked for Albert, it would be far worse."

"Oh, he's not that bad, darling."

I nodded. "Yes, he is."

"He's calming down in his old age. Not like when you two were younger. Although he blames you for the premature graying of his hair."

I grinned. "I bet he does."

"You look beautiful. You should come visit more. I miss seeing my girls together. You two have grown up too fast."

"Well, if you didn't own the top five restaurants in town, maybe you would see us together more."

"So true. We have been blessed."

"I don't know about blessed. I know this family has worked hard for every bit of success you achieved."

She smiled. "Hard work is all we know. I have a few new employees coming in this afternoon. Margo needs to take it easy. She is already six months along, and I know she won't complain or say anything."

"Gee, I wonder who she takes after?"

Mrs. James laughed. "I know, cut right from my cloth. I met Hannah's doctor friend. What a nice fellow."

"He better be. I have my eye on him."

Florence patted my arm. "I am so glad you and Hannah have each other. Listen, I have to get ready for my new recruits. Enjoy your afternoon. Good to see you, dear. That color looks fantastic on you. You should wear black more often." She pulled me in for a hug just like Hannah does all the time.

"Thank you."

I cleared the opening entrance to the bar. I heard an immediate complaint from the bartender. "Seriously? You would not wear that to your big graduation party, but today for lunch it's okay!"

Hannah was giving out to me as Michael turned. "I attended my parent's power brunch; with the new team that is spearheading the future of his business. This was all I had besides my work uniforms, a few cocktail dresses, and my gym clothes."

"I need to take you shopping. I mean it Tiff; get ready. It's in your future."

I shook off a quiver at the thought of that shopping disaster. "I'll think about it. Hey Michael."

He stared. "Hi, Tiff."

Hannah plunked a few menus down in front of us. I waved them away. "Just came from The Summit. I think I ate enough for the entire week."

Hannah gushed. "They have the best glazed pecan rolls. Oh, that's where I'll take George next. Coffee, Tiff?"

"Yes, please, so Doc has no issues about you being in the restaurant business?" She huffed. She knew this conversation would eventually come up. "Fine! You were right. He sees this as a perfect match. Hey, how was your dinner last night?"

"Breakfast for dinner is always a winner." I grinned at my cheesy rhyme.

Michael wanted to know what was going on. "I had breakfast for dinner too. We should have met up."

Hannah interrupted. "Andy went to Tiffany's last night. See, I told you. The guy is simple. No stressing over what to feed him."

Michael's already slightly miffed attitude changed immediately; he was now acting pissy. "You cooked for Andy?"

Hannah answered for me. "Are you okay, Michael?"

He turned to her. "Why?"

"Because you just flipped, like a switch?"

"I'll take a Bloody Mary please, Hannah."

"Okay, you want one Tiff?"

"No, thank you."

Michael adjusted his neck stretching up, and twisting until a few pops sounded on each side.

Hannah placed his drink in front of him. "This is a new recipe. Tell me if you like it."

He drank a few good swigs and placed it back on the coaster. "It's a keeper. Good one, Hannah." She explained the ingredients and how she came up with this new concoction.

Michael attempted to scale back whatever his problem was, turning to me, he said, "Find out what was on that phone yet?"

I placed my coffee mug back down. "Yup. Sure did."

Hannah froze us from talking. She wanted to hear, and there was a party of four taking seats at the bar. Michael continued to drain his Bloody Mary. He didn't speak.

I tried to bring up my impression of Taylor only Michael remarked with a quick grunt.

Hannah was back. I dove right into what was on that phone. Michael ordered another drink. He knew exactly the type of guy Reardon was and began a rant.

"It should be a simple, standardized test to see if an employee actually needs professional help with dealing from a traumatic situation. Some people asking the questions think they are qualified to actually judge another person's stability when something significantly bad happens in their life. Then they use it to manipulate the individual, because they are already in a weakened mental state, and some of these predators take it a step further and use it to maneuver their own sick pleasure."

Hannah had to ask Michael to quiet down; he was getting himself worked up and other people were glancing toward us. He demanded that the police had to get involved now.

My last psychology professor would be proud of me right now; even though I had mixed feelings about the idea of EQ, I understood the positive effects it had with employees. Removing the chip, I tended to carry, I answered in the emotional intelligence structure, which was fist fighting with my normal tendencies inside me right now.

I validated Michael's opinion. He always had my best interest at heart; I knew that deep down. I also thanked him for giving me the heads up, trusting his strong instincts about Reardon. I calmly explained that Andy would take care of Reardon.

Which got me a, "What the fuck do you see in that guy!" from Michael.

I was about to say something far from being emotionally intelligent...something my quick temper would have made me regret.

This was Michael, though. He had a few drinks in him at this point and we had first shift together in the morning.

Hannah answered for me on Michael's side. "We may never know Michael, but it's something neither one of us can see. It's Tiff's decision."

I decided it was time to exit this meeting. I threw down a twenty-dollar bill, half ordered Hannah to call me later and turned to Michael who was now staring at the red burn blotches exposed by my displaced sweater. I covered them back up. "I will see you in the morning, Michael."

He stood up, "Tiff, wait. I'm sorry. Please, stay."

"I have some stuff to do. I really can't. See you in the morning." I turned, not giving him another chance to recover, and walked out.

I texted Andy to tell him I was on my way home.

He replied: *Good.*

There was my scraggly cat waiting for me. Damn it; I didn't think to take any food for leftovers. I got the growl and told him I had to go get something inside. He meowed a sweet little soft meow. He started to follow me, but stopped at the corner. I turned back. "I'll be right back; I promise."

I looked in my fridge beef tips from a few days ago. I cut them into smaller pieces and went out by my car. I called and called Cat, but he was nowhere in sight. Okay, I put them down where I have been feeding him and gave one more kiss-kiss call. Nothing. I walked back in.

Andy would be by in a few hours, so it was time to check the computer and bring up today's surveillance on Mandy.

Clarissa had paid her a visit. It was a good two hours long, which reminded me of the lunch offer with father. I picked up the phone and planned it for Thursday since it was the last day of the work week for me.

He acknowledged my input at the brunch today, sharing how proud he was of how I handled myself. Then he asked me to consider working for him.

I was staring at his mistress on my screen, who was standing out in her hallway, no idea she was being taped, when he said my name for a second time. I thanked him for letting me attend as I now focused on another guy walking toward Mandy's building. I ignored the offer, stating I would see him on Thursday, and hung up.

This guy was clearly looking down, he wore a branded baseball cap I did not recognize, and his chin was tucked so I could only see his nose, mouth and chin. The resolution on these still shots was not that good, but I had a feeling I had seen this guy before.

I just wish he would have looked up as he stood in front of the building. Mandy walked toward the doors, letting him in. When they were in front of her door, she was laughing as she pushed him inside. No luck, he never looked up.

Andy was buzzing to be let in. I greeted him in my comfortable clothes. He had dirt stains on his belly and commented that he had a long day, explaining that the guys he was working with were a bunch of cowboys. I wanted to hear all about it, especially since I was banned from going today.

I have to say, the little bit he would share made me realize I didn't understand what Andy's job was. My eighth question to him, trying to figure it out, partnered with his now standard replied of, "I can't answer that" really started to annoy me.

My phone lit up on the coffee table. Michael was texting with another apology. Andy had seen it again.

We were silent for a minute.

He came right out and asked why Michael was apologizing now twice. I used his go-to response. "I can't answer that."

My tough guy mercenary did not like it coming back to bite him. He went quiet again. I changed subjects and asked him if there was any way to make the surveillance photos clearer.

Naturally, he knew I was asking because I had seen something I wanted to identify better. I brought up the part with the guy walking into Mandy's apartment.

Andy looked at the pictures over and over finally commenting, "I've seen him before."

My eyes widened. "Him? Are you sure? How can you even tell? There's no clear picture?"

"I think we need to swap out one of those cameras for a higher resolution one."

"Okay, do you happen to have one lying around?"

"Yes."

"Do you really think you've seen this guy before?"

"I know I have, Tiff."

"I cannot imagine where."

"I have some stuff to take care of. I will swap that camera out tonight okay?"

"Okay. Do you want to do something tomorrow after work?"

"I have a lot going on the next few days. I'll keep in touch; don't leave your phone behind again, okay?" He stood, holding his hand out to help me off the couch.

I let him help me, even though I was far from needing assistance. Not sure what to say I went over my appointments this week. "I have plans with my father on Thursday. Probably going to do something with Hannah at some point and I guess I'll be at the garage the rest of my free time if you're looking for me."

"I will see you before Thursday."

I wasn't used to having a boyfriend and now I was confused with not having him around. He kissed me as if it were our last. Before he left, he made sure my coffee maker was set up for the morning. I could get used to this, appreciating the little things he was doing to take care of me as I walked him out the door.

My messed-up sleep pattern was even more annoying as I reached for my cell phone displaying 4:12 this morning. There were two missed text messages. Andy had swapped out the camera.

He texted me a new link to where I needed to download the viewing options. The other was from Michael warning me that they had hired Taylor and she was going to the training academy today. I threw off my down comforter and slipped on my sweatpants, gravitating toward the kitchen to start my Andy-prepared coffee.

The link Andy sent was in real time, and I clicked on the feature that was labeled Library.

This feature stored past motions from when he had it up and running. I wondered how many days it could hold of past clips. This looked like a pretty sophisticated system he had going on now. He had installed this just after eleven last night as the time displayed in the corner. He looked directly into the camera and gave me a quick wink, making me grin slightly.

I scrolled through the clips and at 12:42, there was a movement on the camera right outside her door. Someone was leaving her apartment. It was a male figure. This image was very clear, but I could only see the back of him. He exited her building entrance to the right, facing away from the hunting cameras.

The way he carried himself looked familiar. After my seventh rewind and agonizing single flip through of the still shots, I gave up.

I picked up my phone and texted the boyfriend that I had seen a male figure leave close to 1:00 this morning. Now, those hunting cameras are driving me nuts. I can't see shit.

I waited a few moments to see if he answered before jumping into the shower. There was my cat walking out from the bushes, meowing at me. I smiled. "You silly cat, you took off on me. I hope you got your beef tips. Here you go buddy, breakfast."

He walked right to me. No hissing and no growling, just sat and waited. I squatted and poured out a cooked egg with what I had left of the beef tips. He was bent over, eating and purring. I waited not moving at first, telling him, "Good kitty." I slowly reached over to pet him and he growled while he ate.

I retracted my hand and nodded, "Okay, but at least you're not running away. I get it. We will take it slow."

I stood up and told him I was going. He purred loudly while eating his breakfast.

CHAPTER EIGHTEEN

Kyle was walking in ahead of me. I don't know why I assumed he would hold the door open; this man hated me, but I also didn't expect to walk into the door like I did. My depth perception was still off. I rubbed my healing burned shoulder that had caught the edge closing on me.

That hurt more than it should have. Doc told me the nerve damage would be the hardest to recover from. I think I needed to go to the range after this shift ended to make sure I hadn't compromised my shooting ability. I hadn't thought that could be an issue until right now.

I walked by dispatch and noticed Chris at the computer station. I paused in the doorway entrance. "Well, looks like you get to override the academy and jump right in."

She clasped her hands behind her head. "Apparently, twenty-two years on the force gave me some advantage. Although I'm not a huge fan of dispatch, but whatever." Nodding, I tapped the door frame. "They know better than to ask me to sit in here."

"I heard you were tough to ride along with?"

Hah! That made me crack a smile. "I have a low tolerance for stupidity." Chris shot a finger at me. "We will get along just fine, Chanler."

I stepped back. "I think so, too."

Michael started out all business-like, looking at our schedule and commenting that we would have Taylor for a month when she returned. I would not worry about the future much. I needed to get the feel of my replacement ambulance. I let too much slip by on my Friday shift, forgetting what I needed to pay attention to.

I was driving an older model, much different from what I was used to. The weight of it alone was heavier as I adjusted my acceleration pressure to compensate. I could feel the pull around corners and the deviation in the braking distance.

Her creaks and noises handling the road were also contrastive. These factors were supremely important, especially in a compromising circumstance, when I relied solely on instincts. This old gal would be ours for a good six months until we reassembled my bus. I had better adapt to the way she handles the streets.

It took a full cup of coffee and two jelly donuts to begin to ease the tension in our cabin. Michael was sorting our papers and slapped everything down on his lap. Out of nowhere he confessed, "Look, I know I came on a little strong yesterday; I apologize. Tiff, you are not the same person around him."

"Him? Do you mean Andy?"

"Ya... him."

"Well, Michael, I've never really had a boyfriend before. I'm not exactly sure what to do. Give me some time to adjust."

"You shouldn't need time to adjust in a relationship. Tiff, you and I have been together for a while. It's been pretty natural right from the beginning."

"Not the same, Michael."

"I disagree."

"We have never been intimate."

"I sleep on your couch."

"Michael! Not the same."

"Tiffany, I know just about everything about you. I get along with your friends, your family, even your scary godmother."

I snickered. "You mean Fairy Godmother."

"No, I mean scary godmother. Mildred Jones scares the hell out of me. I think she snacks on the bones of tenants who can't pay her rent."

That statement made me tilt my head. "You're just not used to being around strong and independent women. Mildred practically raised me."

"I know; it shows."

I laughed. "What does that mean?"

"You can be an Uber bitch when you want to be."

Snorting my laughter, I said, "Well, thank you, Michael."

"Tiffany, I know you felt it when we kissed. We make sense."

I lost my amusement with this conversation. "Michael, you are my co-worker."

We were still a few minutes out from our next stop. "So is he. How did you even hook up with him?"

That memory was easy to retrieve with the first time I laid eyes on Andy. "Well, he helped stop some bad guys one night who were attempting to steal my cargo."

"Stop them or plant them?"

"Seriously, Michael? Do you think he would put our company employees in danger?"

"I think he is capable of having his own agenda."

"Then you need not hear anymore."

"Tiff, wait, sorry. I don't trust him. But I will try to keep my opinion to myself."

I waited a moment, not really sure if I wanted to tell him now.

"Tiffany, I'm an ass. Maybe hearing your story will make more sense to me."

I'll give Michael that much. He knows how to talk to me. "Fine, but one negative word about Andy and I am done."

"Not saying a thing."

"I must have been on the job a month. Mechanical failure with my ambulance. All those damn new electronics I knew nothing about crippled me on the side of the road. Jason Neeves was riding shotgun."

"Who is Jason Neeves?"

"Someone who retired after that night. He argued I was bad luck right from the start. He claimed, in his ten years working at Angel Wings, not once had he been in a dangerous situation. My first ten days working, we'd already had a mishap at one dock."

"What happened at the dock?"

"Wrong shipment delivery. Papers were missing. Stock was missing."

"Oh, that's not good."

"They let it go. No way was I going to be blamed for any of that. I looked into how many jumbled deliveries there were. I am the reason the whole system got revamped."

"Figures."

"My college degree ended up being very useful."

"Ha! So, why didn't that guy Jason just ask to be transferred?"

"He did; they denied him."

"Oh, what made him quit?"

"Well, my new ambulance died on the side of the road, computer failure. We were waiting for a tow and replacement transport to arrive. I started the generators to keep the cargo cold when a van pulled over in front of us."

"Sounds like a classic B movie plot."

"That's what I was thinking. These two guys get out trying to act helpful. I called for them to get back in their vehicle; I said we were all set. By the way, this is why we have a shotgun now. Back when I started, we only carried tasers."

"Already knew you had something to do with that."

"Ha, ha, ha. Anyway, one guy goes missing from view. I locked the back, since I was there. There was no use listening; the generators were too noisy. Keeping my voice down, I warned Jason to look around. Just as he turned, his window shattered. I watched the end of the club make contact with Jason who was already shielding himself from the shards of glass.

It was like slow motion watching the hand open his door, and pull him out. Like a taser would help in that situation. They were beating him good when I caught another guy jumping out of the van. The first guy was now climbing in through Jason's side and coming for me."

I turned the wheel a little tighter than I was used to in order to clear the corner.

"I could hear Jason swearing, yelling for me. This guy entering assumed I was fresh meat. I saw the look in his eyes as he glanced over my body, stopping too long to look at my chest. He grinned and advanced enough for me to take a clear shot, so I punched him in the ear, then shoved my finger up his nose, gripping onto his face to hold my finger in place."

Michael reached up to cover his nose. "You did what?!"

"You should have heard the blood-curdling screams coming from this guy as he tried to pull my hand away, collapsing on the floor while I latched onto his face. He was twice the size and strength of me. I had nowhere to go, trapped in there; I was lucky to get the ear hit in. It bought me enough time to reach for my stupid taser as the third guy was climbing in. Just as I pulled my finger out of the guy's nose, blood spurting everywhere, hoping this new guy would back down, this invader halts me, hands showing and repeats our code word."

"That's how you fucking met him? He was the third guy?"

"Yup, he was undercover, and I was just hired out of college. They thought I was the weakest link."

"They thought? Or Andy thought."

"What do you mean? Andy was undercover. He was there to help."

"Or there to see if they could get away with it?"

"Look. You asked me how we met. That's how we met, and that's when we started to hook up."

"You're telling me you've been with him for three years?"

I hadn't thought about that. I shrugged. "I guess? Yes, we have been. See; it makes sense for us to be dating now."

Michael was acting pissy again.

"Michael, you're the one who asked. I could have said nothing. I like Andy, and there is nothing anyone can say to change my mind. He wants to try this relationship thing, and I'll give it a shot. I may screw up; he may screw up, but at the end of the day, I want to be with him."

Michael picked up his papers and sorted them with more energy than necessary.

"Hey, Michael, you will always be my friend unless you turn into an ass so deal with it."

I pulled the clipboard out of his hand, flipping the page over and studying the bar codes. From what I was learning, I think we were carrying a body part and if this was true, we would be here ten extra minutes at least. I let Michael go in while I started the stopwatch on my phone.

I texted Andy: *Hey, how's it going?*

I poked around the back of the ambulance. This was a bigger space than my other ambulance. I had to shuffle over an extra step to touch wall to wall. It was wider on the inside. My cooler space could have fit all the varieties of a well-stocked ice cream truck.

My phone vibrated as I dropped my hands picking it up.

Andy replied: *Hi babe, I just got word that something big is brewing. Be aware of your surroundings. Make a plan.*

Plan? Plan for what? Another hijacking?

I didn't like that text, but it clearly put Audrey front and center in my mind. I failed her once; I would not do it a second time. Michael was an additional ten minutes just like I thought. When we were both back in the ambulance, I asked him for the clipboard. Burbank was our third stop. Good. I needed to see Audrey.

Michael asked about the Mandy surveillance. This was a safe subject between us so I gave him a full report. I also told him that Andy swapped out one of the cameras for a higher resolution that was live action. He didn't comment. That was a good thing.

We were so comfortable talking right now that, I also shared the fact that I was going to lunch with my father on Thursday.

Michael smiled, "Good. I know it's shitty that he is having an affair. I'm not making excuses for him, but he cares about you. Even I can see that."

"It is shitty that he is banging a bimbo my age and paying for her apartment and giving her an allowance. It's even more shitty because of who it is."

"Tiff, I didn't mean to bring it up like that."

"It is what it is. Good news though, he has not been over there since we installed the cameras. Maybe he is realizing that it wasn't such a good idea. He and Mother seemed to get along yesterday and it felt like we were a family again. I can't even remember when I felt that last."

"I like your mother."

"She adores you, Michael."

"Well, at least one of you does."

"Michael, stop that. I like you too, just not the way you want it to be."

"Great."

"Michael!"

I followed my boyfriend's advice until we reached Burbank hospital. I lied to Michael telling him I was locking the truck to go find a bathroom. He went into the delivery and I snuck upstairs for a quick visit with Audrey.

She was perky as ever as she set aside her laptop. I informed her I was working and could only stay for a moment. I asked if I could come by on Wednesday. She delightfully agreed, but halted me a moment and checked her laptop.

Then she quickly swore out loud. "Shit, what time?"

Umm, "Ten o'clock?"

"I have a treatment at 11:00."

"How about 8:30?"

"Yes, good. See you then." She waved me out along with a big smile that made me feel good about coming up here.

I picked up the marker on her message board and wrote my cell phone number. "You can call me Audrey."

She nodded. "Okay, thank you for stopping. See you Wednesday, Tiffany Chanler."

I was back before Michael returned. One thing that quick visit proved to me is that I was winded from rushing time to get my butt back to my regular gym schedule. Being out of shape was not allowed anymore. Time for me to get my priorities straight.

I texted Andy for my first priority: *Going to the range after work. I banged my shoulder this morning, and it hurt more than it should have. I want to make sure I can still shoot steady.*

He answered: *The academy range?*

Well, duh? That was the only one I could use through work. *Yes? What other one would I use?*

He asked: *Are you going alone?*

I thought about that. This might be a good opportunity to show Michael that we really were just friends and nothing had changed between us.

I texted Andy: *Inviting Michael.*

His reply: *K.* This was the simplest guy ever. I loved that about him.

Michael arrived back, and I mentioned I was going to the gun range after our shift asking if he wanted to join me. His smile lit up his eyes as he tilted his head and informed me he was in. "Lead therapy is just what we need. I'm in."

Perfect. This will put us back on track.

CHAPTER NINETEEN

I knew Taylor was a current resident here. She was Monday through Friday for the pathetic two weeks' mandatory training. I also knew I was hard on her at our first meeting. I remembered starting here myself, Angel Wings, first female delivery guard. Before me women were hired for office duty only.

I knew my company's hiring decisions. They must have seen something special in Taylor. It was time for me to open up and use my business degree without my own damn opinion involved.

Andy now texted, informing me the next few days would be limited communication between us. I understood this, but since he was stepping up his game to official boyfriend status, it bothered me.

I liked knowing I had twenty-four-hour access to him. This was not sitting well right now as Mother's call came through.

"Hello, Mother."

"Hello, darling, I will make this short. I know you are trying to get back into your routine. I just wanted to remind you that Mildred's "Giving back to the community" charity gala is in two weeks. I bought our table as usual, but she has a special surprise for you that I need to disclose. I think you have had your fill of suspense lately."

"I completely forgot. I don't know why I'm so absentminded lately. Thank you. I really appreciate you reminding me. Can we include Hannah and her Doc? I think I would also like to bring a date?"

"Of course, Tiffany, will you be bringing Andrew?"

"Call him Andy, and yes, I would like to invite him."

"I will make sure our head table is seated together; there will be an overflow though. Four tables might be more appropriate this year; I can ask Mildred to rearrange. You, too, might want to visit her and see the seating arrangements. She will have them displayed in her office, darling. Do I need to hint anymore?"

"No, I read you loud and clear. I will stop by and figure out the seating arrangements. What's the surprise I am in for?"

"Your Girls' Club will be center stage for the fundraising. Would you be willing to say a few words on the history and importance of the club?"

I froze. This was personal. This was my life away from this exploited money-grubbing society. Everyone would know where I spent my time. I wasn't sure I wanted my childhood exposed to these people.

Mother waited long enough, listening from the silence on my end. "Tiffany, I understand. I just had an idea that you could speak from personal experience. I will speak on your behalf. We will work on the points you want to include, and I will deliver the message for you."

My eyes glossed with wetness, and my throat was hot and scratchy. I tried to clear my throat of nothing, excusing my sudden clearing noises, while wiping the moisture from my eyes with this sudden emotional outburst.

I never thought in a million years that she would be my ally, on something I frequently used as a tool, to push her away.

"Mom."

"Not another word, my darling Tiffany."

I wiped at the tears over flowing steadily.

Okay enough of this! I don't cry; what voodoo was causing this?

"Tiffany, you need to find time in the next ten days so we can make this speech as good as you want me to deliver it."

"I will."

I heard her broken tone as well. "I will talk to you tomorrow."

"Bye." I hung up.

We both choked. We were so bad at this.

I called Hannah to reminder her and to tell her to invite Doctor hot stuff. Why did she tell me she already had, and they had both blocked the evening off work?

I knew my girl was way better at all this stuff. I needed my mother to remind me. I had to be more socially aware of the responsibilities I had to my family. It was time for me to accept my roots.

* * *

I was eight inches off center to the left. My left arm was comprising my shot. Michael didn't say a thing as I lined up my next shot and swore at the results. This was crap. I would not stand for this.

We were leaving, and I needed to hit the gym to work out my left side with strength training. Michael tried to reason with me, chalking it up to the injuries, and saying I needed time to heal. Screw that. I would fix this my way, and that included the gym right now.

I dropped Michael at his car and arrived at the gym in my range clothes. I didn't care I was heading to the free weights. That was my new plan.

I texted Andy about my location change and explained why.

No response.

Whatever.

It just added fuel to my fire that was burning inside of me right now.

I was tough on myself. It focused me, and I had a mission. I didn't bother with any cardio. Besides, I hated running in boots. If I was on an outdoor course that would be one thing, but I was in the gym and I didn't want to draw any more attention to myself. Michael never followed me so I guess this was a good thing. I let myself relax even more since he and I were back on track.

*   *   *

There was my cat waiting for me in my parking spot. I forgot to bring food. He actually followed me to the door this time. We were making progress. I needed to maybe invest in a litter box and cat food.

I had never had a pet in my life. I hope they sell that stuff at my store. I came back out with a can of tuna fish. He would have followed me in. I needed to think about this. Did I want a cat?

I placed the can in front of my bumper and had a talk with him. I told him he had to use a litter box if I was going to invest in him. He purred, then growled when I tried to pet him. "And you have to lose the attitude. I'm the only one allowed to have an attitude, understand?"

I sent another text to my boyfriend telling him I was home and that maybe I adopted a cat. Still no response.

I would not get moody over what I didn't know. Before we became official, there would be days, even weeks, that I didn't hear from him. I knew he was trying to make a stronger relationship out of what we had. The least I could do was to be patient. I logged onto my spy programs instead.

Well, well, well. Mandy Stone was a busy little whore today. No sign of Father over there; that was a plus. Only Kyle and Reese's visits are a little disturbing, especially when Clarissa arrived with a briefcase and left without one. What the hell was this woman up to!

That Reese also left with her mother leaving Kyle behind was another red flag. I fast forwarded through another hour of nothing; then Mandy walked out of her apartment to open the lobby door. I could see Kyle's right shoulder waiting in the door frame.

Mandy was arm-in-arm with Mr. Baseball cap. Maybe I should be more grateful to Kyle, because him standing in the doorway made Mr. Baseball cap tilt his head up just enough for me to see his eyes.

I knew this face; I knew this guy. As soon as they were back in Mandy's apartment, I replayed his entrance. Damn it! That's Frank! I met him at my parents' brunch; he was the creep who tried to kiss my hand.

* * *

Not hearing from Andy was not an option right now. I did whatever I could to let him know this was an emergency. I texted an SOS. I called and left messages. I texted what I had discovered.

Nothing came back.

No return message...no nothing.

I thought about Michael; I really wanted to call Michael right now. Staring at my phone didn't help one bit. I was weak, and I wanted support.

I knew he would drop everything and come right over to figure this out with me.

I knew Michael wanted the chance to solve everything with me.

I knew Michael wanted more. He wanted me and I couldn't break my rule about no dating my coworker.

I wanted Andy.

I wanted him even more so in my crazy world with my parents, Mildred, Hannah, and Michael.

I wanted to hang out with him.

I wanted to eat meals together.

I wanted to lay next to him on the couch, flipping through the channels, watching the shopping network together.

I was falling for him. I may not express myself as well as Hannah around men, but I think he knew I was all in.

Two hours into watching my shop on the home cable channel, I was desperate. I had already spent three hundred dollars. I did thirty minutes of cardio with the jump rope and still no text back from my boyfriend. Over the next hour, I obsessed about the cameras. Enough!

I did something that I was against my whole life. I was struggling between Andy and Michael. I looked at my phone one last time.

I walked into my bathroom, pulled the mirror cabinet, and watched my reflection until the door opened all the way.

There it was, that one medicine bottle that was guaranteed to knock my ass out. I reached for the bottle, twisted the cap, and jiggled one small white pill out into the palm of my hand.

My mother had drugged me the first night I was at their house recovering. I knew what to expect and how I would react to this medication. I don't know why I broke the tablet in half. I dropped the other half back in the bottle and twisted the lid back on.

I needed to shut my brain down before I called Michael and dragged him into this. I stared at the half pill. It looked harmless enough. Was taking a half tablet any better than the whole?

My psychology right now was reasoning yes. I placed the half pill on my tongue and filled my water glass. Yuck, the bitter taste from the broken end made me cringe. I glanced one second to look at myself in the mirror. I brought the glass to my lips as I watched myself giving in.

* * *

I woke up with a warm body spooning mine. My eyes flew open just as his scent caught my nose. Andy was slightly snoring in my left ear. He was here. He was here? He was here! I jockeyed to sit up with him releasing his hold to posture up as quickly as I was, looking around for danger as he shoved me behind him. He toppled me over so fast and with unnatural strength.

The first words out of my mouth were, "Andy, it's okay. You startled me. How did you get in?" He relaxed some and helped me back to my original sitting position.

"I used my key?"

"You don't have a key yet?"

"I always have a key."

"That is breaking and entering?"

"Tomatoes, tamahtoes. You told me it was an emergency. I was getting in, no matter what."

I rubbed my face, scrubbing away the minor side effects from the pill.

He rubbed one hand over the right side of his scruff "I have never seen you this unresponsive. I tried several times to wake you, all of which failed."

"I broke down when I couldn't get a hold of you. I took one of my knocks out pain pills last night, well, half a pill. I needed to shut down my brain. I needed you, and I didn't want to reach out to anyone else but you. So, I drugged myself. I am not great at this. I'm sure this was a poor decision. I don't drink, and I spent three hundred dollars on crap shopping on TV. I was going to call Michael, but I rely on him too much as it is."

"Damn right, you do."

I felt ashamed, "When spending money plus a half hour with the jump rope didn't cure my anxiety, I remembered I had those pills. I broke one in half and took it."

We sat there staring at one another. Nothing awkward... just looking into each other's eyes.

"Tiffany, you spent three hundred dollars because you couldn't reach me?"

"Um, yes?"

"Shopping on television is your distraction?"

"Did you hear that I did cardio with the jump rope for thirty minutes?"

"Yes, I did, but what did you spend three hundred dollars on?"

My shoulders shrugged; this was not the issue. My drugging myself was the issue. "On stuff? From the Home Shopping Network. I purchased a scarf that I can use multiple ways, so it wasn't all crap."

"Wow?"

"Wow what? Are you really stuck on the fact that I spent three hundred dollars?"

"Yes?"

"Don't you ever order stuff on line?"

"No."

I thought about that for a moment. "Okay, so it's just about the way I shop that you are hung up on? To tell you the truth, I hate shopping in stores. When I found this channel, it opened a whole new world for me. Maybe some night when we can hang out on the couch, I can show you my world."

He nodded. "Oh, okay."

He was checking me out in my camisole. "Did you get this on your shopping channel?"

I looked down. "No, this was a gift from Hannah last year. She also likes to shop for me."

"Well, I like the Hannah shopping club much more than I like whatever crap you buy on the television."

He crouched on top of me, forcing me back onto my pillows, making me grin. He leaned in kissing me with all the feverish talent he possessed. I said it between breaths. "I love you."

He stopped, pulling back and staring at me. I didn't know if this was the right time to tell him. I was falling in love with him. I waited with his long gaze searching my eyes. I was about to apologize when he stopped me with, "I want you always to be mine."

I nodded relieved. "I will."

He pressed his lips back against mine and gently forced me back onto my pillow.

* * *

Andy made the coffee, and I toasted English muffins. I spread peanut butter over them and offered him two. He accepted. "Baby, you would not believe the stories I could tell you on peanut butter alone."

I was hoping I made the right choice, thinking about the carb to protein ratio. "I'm sorry. I didn't even ask if you liked peanut butter or if you were allergic."

"I have no allergies."

"Phew, that's good to know. I don't either, well maybe to a few people."

One swift kiss landed on my lips, followed by his large bite out of a half muffin.

He declared, "Big fan of peanut butter. Most people in America don't realize that this simple jar," he lifted my 16 oz processed jar that I had purchased from my grocery store, "this is worth the price of gold in some countries."

My eyes widened. "Really?"

"We consider this simple jar comfort food; it's nutrition and can save people from starvation."

"Starvation? Really?"

"Tiffany, there is a distinct look in people's eyes who have gone without food for days... its pure survival instinct. Three things are embedded in all of us; The need for food, breeding, and fight or flight.

When it comes to food, people will do anything for one more day."

I went silent, unable to look at Andy right now. Never have I felt so ashamed as I did right now.

Me and my petty display last night. Blowing money on crap, drugging myself. I did everything that everyone in my parents' social status regularly does. I was a classic product of this environment. I was just like them.

"In the society I grew up in, what I did last night is a common way to deal with stress. That's not me. I'm better than that."

"You have no idea babe, how third world countries live. I hope you never do. Look, you were born with more opportunities that's all. Personally, I think you turned out pretty damn fine. I also like the fact that you initiated action against giving in, and calling that bozo. Big deal, you drugged yourself, so what? I've gone on whiskey benders and other stuff. I am far from perfect."

"What other stuff?"

"Nope, not going there today; leave that one alone for now."

"Well, Audrey needs a new liver because of alcohol, just saying."

"Don't worry about me. Okay enough of that, what was with the SOS?"

"The camera got a clear shot of Mr. Baseball Cap. I know who he is."

I turned to go pick up my computer off the coffee table.

"I went through it. He was one of the guys standing with your father at the hotel when you left your phone in the car."

"How do you know that? You were just there for a minute."

"I pay attention to detail."

"Wow, you are good."

"But you already know that."

"Did you see the whole briefcase thing?"

"Yes."

"And? What do you think?"

"They are setting your father up; it looks like blackmail."

"Do you think Mandy Stone was a setup?"

"Of course. What's the easiest way to get to a man?"

I narrowed my eyes. He grinned.

"Look, if she has him by the balls, everything else follows."

I growled. I did not want to hear this. It was my father we were talking about, and everything Andy just said was true, but it was still my father. "Well, he hasn't been following her lately that I know."

"Then that's good, right? He must see she is bait."

"I'm seeing him Thursday."

"Are you telling him?"

"I don't know?"

"Tiffany, you know he's being set up. Your buddy Kyle is now in on it. You struggled not to call dipshit because I wasn't around. Don't you think your order of importance is a little messed up?"

"I don't want him to fly off the handle and get himself in deeper if this is not really what it is."

"Well, here is my advice, tell him, tell him everything you know. Tell him about your surveillance and what has come up from the cameras. Your father is a smart man. He didn't get where he is today without dealing with problems along the way. Give the guy some credit. I know you want to protect him, but let him do what he does best because honestly, this is way over your head. It's up to you sexy, but if that were my old man, I would tell him everything and I would sit back and learn."

I knew he was right. This was a way to bring my parents and me closer.

"Okay, you made good points. You're right."

"I don't care about being right. I just want you to see the bigger picture. You are focusing in too narrowly, too singular. Does that make sense?"

I inhaled deeply. "Yes."

"Good, I gotta get back."

"Oh, one more thing."

He stopped his approach to kiss me. "What?"

"In a week and a half, Mildred is throwing her big charity event, and this year it's the Girls' Club I used to sneak out to. Will you be my date?"

"I will try my best to be there. I want to be the one walking your ass through the doors. Maybe I will even take you on the dance floor."

My smile lit up, surprised. "You dance?"

He pulled me into a dance frame so quickly that, I squealed astounded by his talent as Andy moved us into a perfectly coordinated box step, ending with a kiss, relaxing his dance posture and releasing me.

"Remember, the next few days will be tough. Text me; call me. Be patient with my return reply."

I nodded okay as I walked him to the door and watched until he rounded the corner. I remembered my cat. "Wait!"

He backed up. "What?"

"I have my cat. He needs breakfast."

"Are you referring to that scraggly furball hanging around your car?"

I grinned, cutting up chicken. "Yes, he's been hanging around. I think I'm going to let him in. Can you give him this? He's waiting for breakfast. Just dump it out in front of my car. He'll eat it up."

I handed Andy the zip-lock bag of cut up chicken.

"Okay, but this could be my lunch." He took the bag.

"Do you want me to make you lunch to go?"

I had never thought of the idea. Should I consider making him food to go? Is that what girlfriends do? I know Hannah has taken Doc a few meals. I totally sucked at being in a relationship.

He was being sarcastic and grinned about me falling for it.

"Just kidding. I'm all set."

Now, I was as confused as ever. I needed to go over relationship etiquette with Hannah. He slid his arm around my waist and said, "I was kidding." Hegave me a quick kiss, slapped my butt with a click sound and a wink and left for the second time.

CHAPTER TWENTY

It was just past nine when I showed up ready to do my time in the garage. Greg had a list for me this week. I met his nephew, who pulled the damaged parts off my ambulance. Every so often I would go work with him and if I was spending too much time there, Greg would ask me how much was finished from the list. Michael arrived an hour early checking to see the details of what was going on.

Looking at the grease stains on my hands and arms, he asked if I had been here all day.

"Of course, You know me." I smiled, wiping my hands.

"Well, you better find a stopping point; you have an hour before our shift starts." I had lost track of time.

"Thanks, Michael."

He grinned, "No problem, Tiff." He continued walking toward our ambulance to see the deconstruction.

I signaled to Greg that I was finished for the day with him shouting over for me to put the list back on his desk and he would see me tomorrow. I gave him a thumbs up and proceeded to my locker to get out of this jump-suit.

I texted Andy that I was finished at the garage and heading to the showers to wash up before my shift. No return messages.

I felt that Michael and I were back on track; the highlight of my evening is that I could see Jennifer tonight. I liked her more and more. I felt like I still needed to apologize for setting her up at my party.

My mother had reserved two tables for Mildred's function. I bet I could buy one toward the back and put all my new nurse friends together there with each bringing a guest.

Screw it. I was making this happen. I mentioned it to Jen; she was on board. I already had the table half filled by our third stop. I called Mildred to make sure this could happen, and it delighted her. She was glad I was coming out of my shell.

Next, I called Mother to let her know. She, too, was looking forward to meeting my extended group. Then I called Hannah, who also agreed that it was a good idea.

Suddenly I felt like an ass. Here I was talking to everyone about the party in front of Michael and I hadn't invited him yet. I asked Hannah to hold on as I turned to him, while he was securing his seatbelt. "Hey, Mildred has that big charity event in a week and a half, want to come?"

He grinned. "Absolutely. The cause is your Girls' Club. I wouldn't miss it for anything."

It relieved me. "Oh well, I just secured a table and I am inviting all my nurses; do you want to sit with them, or do you want me to ask Mother about sitting at our table? I have to warn you; Andy will be there as my date."

"Of course, he is your boyfriend after all. I guess you haven't talked to your mother about who is at your table. I'll be sitting there too, Tiff. Priscilla already called me to get the head count and asked me if I was bringing a date. I told her I would bring a date. She didn't mention it?"

I tried not to react to what was going on in my head. I still had Hannah on hold. "That's settled then."

I pulled the phone back to my ear. "Sorry, Hannah, just trying to work out the logistics of the charity ball. Between you, and Michael, and me bringing dates I'm sure we can squeeze everyone in."

She said, rather unsettlingly. "You are bringing Andy?"

"Yes? Boyfriend, hello?"

"Oh, good Lord. I want full access to the seating charts."

I knew Michael was listening and the blow he just delivered deserved a counter jab. "Well, I have another secret to reveal. He is an accomplished ballroom dancer."

Out of the corner of my eye, I could see that hit home with Michael.

Hannah gasped. "Are you freaking serious? He probably had to learn it at spy camp."

She made me laugh as my heart beat quickened, thinking about being in his arms. "I don't care where he learned it; the man knows the classics."

Our last stop had my nurses table officially filled. Each of Kyle's ex flings was attending, bringing their own plus one. I felt good giving this to them.

I glanced at my phone on the way back to base, still no return message from Andy.

I watched Kyle carefully. He was looking around; it also looked like he was hiding something in his left pocket...the way he kept grabbing the outline; as if he was checking to see if it was still there.

I leaned into Michael, "Does it seem like Kyle is acting out of character tonight, or is it just me?"

Michael watched him. "What do you think he is up to?"

"I don't know, but he is acting odd."

"I agree."

I followed him until he went into the men's locker room. I asked Michael if I could turn in all the paperwork and he could keep an eye on Kyle. He agreed handing me over our packet and heading into the locker area.

Twenty minutes I waited, lingering around dispatch and talking with Pam. Michael surfaced and nodded his head for me to walk out and meet him at our cars.

I tossed my duffel bag in my back seat as he looked around suspiciously. "He is definitely up to something. When I walked into the locker room, he was on the phone. I got to hear part of his conversation. He was saying he will corner her at the function. Calvin walked in shortly after, loudly greeting a hello to me. Kyle ended his call abruptly."

I thought about it, "Function? What do you think he meant? Any functions coming up?"

"Mildred's fund raiser, perhaps?"

"NO! That turd cannot be going. Damn it, Clarissa must have a table?"

We both watched Kyle walk directly to his pickup truck and race out of the garage.

"Something is up. I'll view the cameras when I get home."

Michael nodded "Want some company?" He quickly retracted, asking, "Oh, your boyfriend is probably waiting. Some other time."

Before I could get a word out, he was walking away and putting his phone to his ear. "Hey, how's it going? Just getting out."

Whatever, I shook it off. I was tired after a full day at the garage plus a full shift.

I had my "welcome to my home" kitty bag. I called Cat, but he didn't appear. I opened the dry cat food and left a pile in front of my car. I hoped I had picked out the right flavor. He seemed to like chicken and I couldn't imagine the cat food company screwing up that flavor too much.

I ran through the cameras, and it looked like Reese and Mandy were having a spat. Reese looked mad as she was pointing her finger and yelling at Mandy. I think Mandy slammed the door on her from the distorted interruption on the camera and Reese stepping backward with a surprised look on her face.

I had enough, and it was late. I walked out one last time to see if Cat was out here. The food was gone, but he didn't answer when I called. Okay, I tried.

I texted Andy: *Good Night.*

Having a boyfriend was frustrating. No return text was pissing me off even though he warned me that communication would be scarce the next few days. Tomorrow was my visit with Audrey, and I had to ask her about Frank.

My alarm went off at 6:00 a.m. I wanted to chuck my phone against the wall. I tapped it to shut it up and dropped back onto my pillows. Pulling my left hand up, I looked at the screen to see if there were any messages. Nothing. Fine!

That motivated me to get my butt up and start the day, forgetting about Andy. If he wanted to be a ghost, then I would treat him like a ghost. Since I was going back to the garage after I visited with Audrey, I wore my college T shirt and jeans. After packing my duffel, I headed out the door.

There was my kitty sitting at the curb. "Hello Cat, do you want to try this? I can let you in, but I will be gone all day. You can spend the time getting used to the place? What do you say?"

He meowed at me. I kiss called him toward the building's entrance; he followed. This was a good sign. I opened the door, and he bolted in, running up the stairs instead of down the hallway.

"No Cat! This way, come down here." I heard a deep gruff meow on the third floor.

"Cat!"

I smacked my lips together. "Here, kitty. Come here kitty, kitty, kitty." Damn it! I sounded like Hannah.

I ran up the stairs and saw him sniffing and walking deeper into the building. A neighbor was leaving her condo, watching me cautiously. "I adopted a new cat. He's roaming the halls. If you see a black cat, just let him out. He knows my parking spot."

"Okay?" she answered warily.

"Kitty!" I hurried after him.

He followed me to the front entrance door and ran out. That's all I could do today. I didn't have time to chase cats. "Bad Kitty. We live on the first floor. Not upstairs. You will have to wait until I have something for you to follow." He followed me to my car, though.

"I'll be back later. Maybe we can try this again." I climbed into my car as he was rubbing himself on the bushes next to my empty parking spot.

I stopped at Larry's Café thinking a dozen donuts in hand would cheer Audrey up. I believed you have not truly lived without trying a jelly donut from Larry's.

When Larry questioned why I was picking up a whole dozen, I told him a little about where I was going with these. Big old Larry, with a heart of gold, told me to hang on and boxed up another dozen ordering me to give them to the nurses.

"Larry, I will tell them these are directly from you."

He scowled. "You can tell them where they came from, but I'm not looking for any credit."

I understood, "I get it, Larry, thank you."

Then he pulled a rag out of his pocket to wipe the counter. "Okay, you can go away now, Tiffany."

I laughed. "You don't have me fooled for a minute, mister. See you tomorrow you big ole softy."

I arrived with a dozen donuts for the nurses' station. I gave Larry full credit over his disapproval. I also told them the second dozen was going into Audrey's room. I winked to encourage more visits for her.

She was ready for me. Audrey was so slender; she couldn't be over one hundred pounds soaking wet. She had even arranged the room, adding three adjustable hospital tray stations ready for business.

One for her, one for me to put a computer or anything I wanted on, and one in the middle. Jelly donuts, and a black coffee with a cup filled with various creams and sugar on the side went on the middle tray. This woman drank her coffee straight up black. She moaned, letting the first sip slide down her throat. "This is the best coffee I have ever tasted. Where is it from?"

I told her, watching and a little confused that she was drinking unflavored black coffee. Nothing, absolutely nothing, added. "Try the donuts; they're famous for them." She nodded, taking a bite, then spitting it in a napkin, "Blech, too much sugar."

Okay, this woman loved her bitters. "You can probably hold an auction for the rest of those. They are very desired amongst individuals who thrive on sugar."

She closed the lid and set them to the side. "Thank you. I will take that into consideration."

First person on my mind, Frank and the three other clowns at the brunch. Audrey didn't know Frank existed. He was a recent hire. She adjusted her glasses, tilting her head down, and typed.

This woman could type crazy fast. All I could hear were her fingers tapping the keys and grunts and groans every few seconds. I couldn't stand it any longer, demanding to know what the heck she was doing "Audrey!"

She looked up. "Sorry, come here. Sit next to me. I am in Henshaw's database."

My posture straightened. "Are you allowed to be?"

She cut me a look. "Of course, I am. I still work for your father; I never left my job completely. I am a private contractor now, consulting for him. I still have top security clearance. I helped take this company to where we are today. It's still my child to the day I die. I have been suspicious over a few of our new accounts."

I leaned in. "I didn't mean to offend you. I just didn't know you were still on the payroll. I'm sorry, Audrey. I know you put your heart and soul into Henshaw."

"No offense taken. Now, cut the apology and let's get down to business."

I was trying to be sympathetic. Not one of my strong points I know. But geesh, let me practice at least.

Audrey pointed to the computer. "Look at this account right here, Montego Bay. I did a little poking around. I can't find any stats on this company. We were supposed to be using it as private transportation. The payouts have been low, under ten thousand. What caught my eye is that there have been seven payments made, totaling sixty-eight thousand, and I have no tracking invoices of them billing us."

I looked over the numbers. "Where are the payments going?"

"New York."

"Do we have a lot of transportation services in New York?"

She nodded, "Yes, about forty. It's one of our busier hubs."

"Is this unusual?"

"This is not, no. The smaller carriers come and go all the time. What is different is that I don't have a standard invoice. I get that smaller companies don't have the sophisticated billing we require. Most of these companies, for under twenty thousand hand-write an invoice, send the minimum insurance and it's good. They are usually an owner/driver one man show. I have nothing other than our payments to this company."

"Whose job is it to collect the info to issue payments?"

"Third floor. We have twenty-seven employees that strictly handle these contracts. Their job is to have all the complete documents signed, insurances met, and the contractor forms set and ready for billing. We pay the twentieth of each month with a five-day grace period. If contractors don't meet the deadline, then no payment for another month. Henshaw makes sure our contractors get paid. Seven of those employees get paid more to stay on top of who has not billed us. No one is supposed to get by without an invoice."

"Who issues payments?"

"Lizzy, Gail, Carole Ann, Joe, Matt, and Nick."

"Could one of them just have paid a contractor and not have filed the proper invoice?"

"Not likely, all of them have been with the company for a long time. Nick is the newest recruit, and he has been there for six years. They all know the drill."

"Is Nick bribable?"

"Anyone is bribable, but I know the benefits package your father and I put together a decade ago keeps those temptations to a minimum. Nick likes his Volvo too much to jeopardize all his extra's."

"Oh, you give the employee cars?"

"We have a great deal with Geely Holdings Group."

"Hmm, I didn't know that."

"You really should be more active in the company, Tiffany."

"Don't you start too."

"Just saying. Okay here we go, Frank Gallo."

My phone vibrated. There was a text from Andy: *Hi.*

Seriously? That's all?

"Hang on, Audrey, my boyfriend is texting me for the first time in a while. I need to answer."

"Boyfriend? What boyfriend? Is it the guy from work that your mother raves about? Um...Michael?"

I wasn't going there. "No, that's my coworker. This is Andy."

"She mentioned him too. Rugged guy, wrestles bears?"

I shook my head as a big smile spread across her face.

"I heard all about that one. I would like to see a picture of him."

I replied to my ghost: *long time no hear?*

He texted: *Sorry babe, been busy.*

He told me he would be busy. I asked with the slightest hope: *Want to meet up later?*

I need sleep, going to crash at my bunker for a bit. You on second shift tonight?

Interesting choice of words to describe his place. Bunker, is it? *Do I get to see your bunker someday?*

Sure, if you want. Nothing fancy, though.

Well, you know where I live. I would like to see where you live. Don't worry about impressing me I've already seen your car.

What's that supposed to mean?

Whoops, he didn't like that comment. *Nothing I was kidding. I'll be down at the garage soon. Just going over some stuff with Audrey.*

Audrey Lanski?

Yes.

Why are you there with her?

She's looking into Frank's info at my father's company.

K

Call me when you get up.

K

My simple guy. Audrey was all over it. "You're in love."

I shrugged, "I don't know. Never been in love before. I know that having a boyfriend around and then him not being around pisses me off."

She grinned, "That counts. I've never been in love; you are one up on me."

"Really?"

"If we count work, I am in love with my job."

"Never? You have never been in love? What about my father?"

"Richard! No! I have never been in love for a second with your father. It was an arrangement of convenience. Don't think of it as any more than that. Hey, I'm still a woman."

Bad territory to talk to the woman who my father slept with about cheating on my mother. "I shouldn't have brought it up. Let's not go there ever again, okay?"

"Agreed. So, not much on this guy Frank. He has an impressive resume, though."

"Really? What's it say?"

"Military guy, an engineering background, worked in Chicago, then transferred to New Jersey."

"New Jersey?"

"Yes. bounced around the state for a few years, then over to New York, and finally here."

"What branch of military?"

"Um, um, um, Army. Oh, he was an officer."

"So, he was educated going in?"

"Yes, that must be from his engineering degree."

"How old is this guy?"

"Thirty-seven."

"I would have pegged him younger."

"Men age so much better than we do. They suck."

I laughed. Hearing Audrey say the word suck must have been mimicked from my mother. She looked at me. "How long do I have you for, Tiffany?"

"For another half hour, I guess. I am going to the garage from here."

"Good, I have a favor to ask. Come, take a look at this."

CHAPTER TWENTY-ONE

I arrived at the garage, slipping on my already soiled jump suit and stashing my car keys in the locker. Instantly, I smiled, catching Danny out of the corner of my eye pulling the shell off my ambulance.

Greg walked over. "Had a big delivery this morning. Danny also found a salvage ambulance this make and model. Back end is perfect, so that should arrive in a week. That kid is a wiz at finding stuff."

"Oh, nice."

Greg and I walked over, stopping about fifteen feet from Danny. He was wearing headphones, average brown hair slicked back with over-use of hair gel. His beard was perfectly designed and cut, with a tattoo sleeve on his left arm drew my attention. There was some bling strategically placed that caught my attention. I leaned in to Greg. "Hey, are you seeing what I'm seeing?"

Greg knew exactly what I was talking about. "Yeah, I don't get it. New fad. Those are little stick-on sparkles. Probably stole them from his ten-year-old sister's doll collection."

I laughed out loud, and this caught the attention of Danny from his work mode zone. He pulled his earphones off, nodding his head. "Tiffany, that is such a prime name. Did Uncle Gregory tell you what I scored?"

I looked at Greg, who muttered, "Don't fucking say it."

My smile widened. "Yes, Gregory told me. Nice find, by the way. Thank you for doing such diligent research. Hey, I like your sleeve by the way. What's up with the sparkles? They caught my eye."

"Sweet. Friend of mine and I were at a party one night, and this high ender came over and dusted us in a glitter cloud. I saw how some flakes stuck to my arm, and it added to the beauty so I said to myself, "Why not." I started a trend. All my friends with tats do it, and it has just become a movement."

I asked, reaching for his arm. "Do you mind if I look closer?"

"No, not at all, Tiffany." He extended his arm in my direction.

He had seven well-placed tiny stick-on silver sparkle dots. "How long do they last?"

"A day? My bed has its fair share of renegades."

"I hope you don't sleep naked?"

He laughed. "Good one, Tiffany, that's how new ideas are born."

Dress Danny in a formal collared shirt with the sleeves rolled up wearing loose dress pants, and he could be on the cover of a men's magazine. Damn he would be eye candy and he was only a few years younger than me. Hannah had to see him. If for nothing else than for us to talk about and appreciate.

I texted her: *Something for you to admire. Arrived at the garage fixing my ambulance You won't regret stopping.* I snapped a selfie photo with Danny to mark the beginning of our fixing my ambulance journey and sent it to her.

Her reply was immediate. *I will be right there, you left your... hair tie here. I know you need it for tonight. Give me forty minutes.*

I replied: *you're welcome.* It was forty minutes on the dot. I walked out to clear her visit. When she parked, opening her door, she was wearing tennis gear. She had a lesson in an hour and had to make this quick.

I brought her over to my ambulance under construction. She stopped and grabbed onto my arm. "Are you kidding me! George, George, George, George."

I gave her a click and a wink, "Exactly."

I yelled over to Danny, "Hey!" He looked up at me, then Hannah, and stopped working.

"Sorry, Danny, before you pull more off, I want my friend to see it. I didn't take any photos."

"I have thirty photos of before. I do the before, during, and after documentation. Want me to send them to you?"

I nodded casually. "That would be great. Thank you."

Danny reached his hand out to shake Hannah's, "Hi, I'm Danny."

Hannah stared at his sleeve. "Do I see bling?"

He grinned. "Ah, yes, starting a movement."

"Well, you will be successful, nice touch."

"I didn't get your name?"

"Hannah, sorry about that."

"No, prob. I like knowing people's names."

I wanted to ask Hannah something alone. "Danny, will you excuse us for a moment?"

He wiped his hands on a rag from the ground. "Sure, but let those bad vibes go. She didn't mean to fail you."

"Fail me?"

"Your vessel, she took as much as she could. She tried to protect you."

Both Hannah and I had our eyebrows scrunched together. I gave him two head flips up. "Okay, we just need a minute."

We watched him walk away. Hannah said it first.

"Everything was going great, and then he spoke."

"I know, sorry."

"Okay sweetie, I have to go. Thank you for the view. I will try to erase what came out of his mouth, but it's highly unlikely."

"Well, at least you know George is front and center."

"Yes, he is. See me when you can. I know George is taking time away from us, but..."

"But nothing, stop it, woman. I already know you are the love of my life. Let's give George a chance at second best."

She reached up, patting my cheek. "Bye, I love you."

"Love you too, Sista."

She laughed at my best attempt with street slang.

* * *

Once again, Michael came in to give me the warning that I had to stop and get ready for our shift. He walked over to see the progress Danny had made this afternoon. Everyone was gone, and I was finishing the last item on my list from Greg, detailing his wife's car.

He warned me that she was riding in with him tomorrow morning, and it had better be done. I slipped out of my jumpsuit and put it in the pile that would go to the cleaners tomorrow. I wasn't planning on coming in. Tomorrow was my lunch date with Father and, hopefully, I'd see Andy in the morning.

Michael probed tonight asking whatever happened to Reardon, and what was on the camera's lately. Then he said his date was looking forward to the gala.

I knew this game better than him. I had learned this tactic in third grade the hard way. Power plays were well bred into those growing up in the city in families over fifty million in earnings. Poor Michael was using the basic levels. He would get nowhere testing these jabs.

I pulled deep from my education. "Michael, it will be a great evening and a cause I am passionate about. Let's focus on that."

He turned to me. "Okay, but she is very excited to be included."

We arrived at our first dock. Jen lowered her mask, and I cocked my head to the side. She knew exactly why.

"Nasty bug going around. We all have to wear these. Who is coming in with me?"

I pointed to Michael, "He is."

She handed him a mask. "Nothing to worry about, Michael; we're just being careful. Don't need the staff wiped out all at the same time. We haven't had this kind of outbreak since the Norwalk virus. Live and learn."

He glanced over, placing his mask on. "Well, isn't this just great."

Audrey came to mind. She couldn't afford to get sick, so I called my mother to let her know that even the nurses were taking extra precautionary steps not to spread this plague. Within two hours Audrey was phoning me. "Now, I'm under house arrest because of some virus?"

"Oh, sorry about that. When I arrived at my first stop, they were making us wear masks because of this contagious bug going around. I called Mother; she always knows what to do, and you have become...important."

I could hear her huff, "Okay just this once. I expect you to call me in the future when it is about me."

I was resigned because I should have called her, not my mother. "Okay, I will."

"Good. I expect a report on what I asked you about by tomorrow night."

I grinned into the phone. This woman was the definition of get it done. "Written or oral?" I asked.

"Both for being such a pain in my ass."

I grinned. "Yes, ma'am"

"I hate these damn masks! I don't enjoy the feeling of this against my face. These are the only reason I did not become a doctor," she protested again.

"You wanted to become a doctor?"

"Yes, Heppie and I used to play hospital. Then one day I was the surgeon. She made me wear a mask, and that was the end of my medical career."

I chuckled. "Sorry, until you get fixed, we will not risk anything happening to you that is preventable."

"Chanler women!"

She ended the call abruptly telling me she had to go. This poor woman was stuck with needles more often than I could imagine. I stopped at the convenience store and ran in to buy a spray bottle of disinfectant. Each time Michael came out I sprayed him for extra protection. By the third stop, he was getting annoyed with me.

"We can't afford to get sick. I don't care about anyone else. I have Mildred's fundraiser and Audrey to think about."

"Germs are afraid of you; stop worrying about it."

"I hope you're right. If I get sick, I'm blaming you."

"There's a surprise."

We were done for the night. They asked us at home base if anyone wanted overtime. Scott had called out sick for his day shift. It was already starting. I stopped in to see Greg before I left. He commented that I had pleased the wife and handed me my list for the week.

I stuck it in my locker and texted Andy to see if he was around. No reply had me thinking all the way home. That was until I spotted his crap Chevy in my extra parking space triggering an instant grin. As soon as I parked, he was out of his car and waiting for me to hand him my duffel. "Did you get some rest?"

He nodded, "Yes. Been thinking about you for the last few hours."

The cool morning air suddenly awakened my spirit. I breathed deeply, listening to the bird's chirp. They were chirping a lot. A lot, a lot, like they were warning about something. Andy turned at the same time I did. Out of the woods walked my mangy black cat.

"There you are, troublemaker."

Andy watched Cat rubbing against his pant leg.

I protested, "Hey, what's the deal, Cat? I'm the one that feeds you." Andy reached down to pet him, and Cat reared up to meet Andy's hand.

"What the hell?" I reached down, and Cat was just as affectionate to me, "Aw, good kitty."

And not even ten seconds went by before Cat changed his mind and hissed. He'd had enough and walked to the front of my car. Andy focused on me. "Come on; let's go in," he said nudging my shoulder. "That's not the pussy that needs attention."

My jaw dropped. I couldn't believe he just said that. He looked down at Cat. "You'll have to wait." He just swished his tail and sat cleaning his paw.

Andy closed my condo door, took my hand, and led me to my bedroom. I woke up to Andy reading a report.

"What time is it?" I sat up, looking for my phone.

"Eleven. What time are you meeting your dad?"

Dad, that sounded odd. "Two o'clock. He knows I worked third shift."

Lowering the report, he asked, "Want to get another hour in? I'll wake you at noon?"

I scrubbed my face. "Two hours is fine." I reached over to kiss him. "What-cha reading?"

"An old military case, the soldier got away with a civilian shooting. I'm looking for the loophole."

I raised my eyebrows. "That sounds exciting."

"Come on; I'll make the coffee." Andy slipped on his pants, picked up his report, and headed toward the kitchen.

I checked my phone and grabbed my uniform off the floor and slipped Andy's T shirt on. I walked out and into the kitchen.

He gave me an approving nod, "Good look on you."

"You're welcome to stock some clothes here. I'm kind of into wearing boyfriend clothes around the house."

"I might just have to do that. I like this on you." He handed me a cup of coffee.

"Do you want breakfast, Andy?"

"Sure, if you're offering?"

I leaned into him; I've never asked this of any man. For a fleeting moment, I braced for rejection. I whispered, much softer than I initially intended, "For a kiss?"

This man should have received a five-course meal for that kiss. I cooked our favorite breakfast plus a little extra for Cat.

My boyfriend left right before I got ready to meet Father. He instructed me, dead serious, to tell him he is being set up. I had such mixed feelings about this. I avoided eye contact until he swapped Cats baggy into his left hand and cupped my shoulder with his right. He forced me to make eye contact.

A few seconds went by in our staring contest. He made his point, softened, then asked what I was doing after. Besides killing any chance of meeting Father for a light, happy occasion, he said, depending on how his day went, he might be able to take me somewhere, when I was through with my lunch date.

He pressed on the time to make it a long meeting with Father. I would need it. Besides breaking the news of him being set up, I had Audrey's information to collect.

It would take some digging, and I had my list of who to start with. I briefly told him I had additional business there on top of my lunch date. He waited only a moment, then dismissed any further sharing. His hand went from my shoulder to cup the back of my head as he stepped in for our goodbye kiss. "Text me when you're leaving," he softly commanded into my gaze.

A shiver shot up my spine. "Yes, I will," I said as the heat radiating off of him followed him as he stepped away. I watched him leave with Cat's food in hand, making me grin a little.

I liked the sound of hanging out with Andy after, no matter what we did. Just the thought of spending time together filled me with excitement. Looking at my clothes selection, closet doors wide open, Hannah's mantra repeated in my head, "Expand your wardrobe; expand your wardrobe."

Scanning my options over the slim pickings that desperately screamed needing to "expand my wardrobe," I finally settling on jeans and a collared light blue dress shirt.

It was okay but not great. I went to check my mail, and I had a package. I had a few packages waiting for me. I looked at the return address and score! Just in time. My home shopping channel had shipped my scarves. I was saved. This was the perfect accessory to make my drab outfit special. Even Hannah would approve.

I texted my emergency contact: *I am ready to go shopping when we have time off together.*

She replied: *Halleluiah*

I chuckled.

There was Cat, half lying in the bushes in front of my car. I puckered and kissed to him making him raise his head lazily. "Well, I see you ate all your food. I hope you were nice to my boyfriend. You two might live together soon."

He gave me a little squeak of a meow. I bent down in front of him. He was too deep in the brush for me to pat him. I spoke to him from here. "Maybe we can try going in again when I get back? I think you will like the place. I set up an area just for you." I could hear him purring with his eyes closed, and he almost looked like he was smiling.

I smiled back. "Good. See you later, kitty."

* * *

I didn't have a clue what I was going to say to Father. If my mother just let me confront him weeks ago, this would be a lot easier.

Hannah was texting me: *Good luck, just be honest and it will all work itself out.*

I was screwed. Now there was no turning back in telling my father he was being blackmailed. I didn't know where to begin in telling him about my impromptu surveillance on the whore he had hooked up with.

Desperately wanting to call Mildred for some guidance, gripping my phone tight, I scrolled through my numbers, then hit send.

Andy made this sound so matter of fact and easy, only this was layered with complications. The voice on the other end answered enthusiastically, "Tiffany, is everything all right, sweetheart?"

"No, I am about to meet Father for lunch. I think you should be there too."

"On my way." My mother hung up without question.

Mother's car was parked out front. I knew I was staying later, so I pulled into the employee garage. When I walked up to her car, Jordan was lowering the window. "Good afternoon, Miss Chanler. Your mother is already inside."

I smiled, said, "Thank you," and I headed in.

I haven't stepped into this building in about a decade. They had updated the look with giant prints of the company's transport trucks in motion on the open scenic roads' nice shots, very appealing to the eyes.

They also had side-by-side diesel engines behind a glass case stuck right in the middle of the lobby showing the detailed advancement of technology comparison charts on how far they had come with clean energy. No matter what Frank's deal was, he was correct about bringing on cleaner burning engines.

I signed in and they gave me an all-access pass as the feeling of butterflies began to hit my stomach. I gripped my hand into a fist, down by my side, and walked to the elevators as I repeated in a mumble, "I can do this. I can do this." The elevator doors opened with Clair Young pressing the button to hold the doors. "Tiffany! My, my, my, what a beautiful woman you have turned into." I smiled, greeting my father's secretary. "Hi, Ms. Young. Thank you. Hey, I didn't see you at my birthday?"

She sighed out a disappointed breath. "Believe me; it was as much a disappointment to me to have missed it. All four of my kids are in sports, dance, or music. I seriously look forward to coming to this full-time job to get away from that full-time job. I need to be cloned, Tiffany."

I snickered. "How old are the kids now?"

"Sixteen, fifteen, twelve and seven. Charlie just got his permit. I can't wait for him to get his license. It's tough when Bill has to travel. Thank goodness the older two are so helpful. Your mother was smart to stop at one."

I thought about that. "I don't know, I always wished I had a sibling."

She smiled. "Well, I would probably be bitching even with one kid, so ignore me. I need a vacation."

We laughed as the doors opened. "Your mother and father are in the conference room. I just rode down to say hello. Crystal buzzed me when you arrived. It's been too long since I've seen you, dear. Don't let that amount of time lapse with your next visit." She leaned in to hug me.

"Okay," I agreed letting go, moving in the opposite direction from her, down the hall.

Both parents stopped talking and turned toward me as if I were up to something. Father spoke first. "Well, I was expecting a lunch with my daughter, but your mother is always welcome. I wish her arriving was not such a surprise, though."

I closed the door behind me. "Sorry, it was last minute. We all need to be together. I have some bad news."

The expressions on their faces altered dramatically. They were both on their feet trying to approach me at the same time. "Tiffany?" they spoke in unison.

I stopped them in their tracks. "No, sit, please. We need to talk."

They turned toward each other, desperate to know if either knew what this was about. They silently searched each other's reactions. Perhaps one of them would confess and give the other a signal that everything was okay.

"Please, sit."

They took the nearest seats abandoning their original, now sitting next to one another. I didn't know where to start. I huffed out a breath in frustration as Andy's simple declaration of, "Just say it," popped into my thoughts. Right. Not that simple. Mother tried to be patient, with her hands clasped together, finally pleading, "Tiffany!"

I quickly registered anxiety and desperation in her voice and facial expression. Then I glanced into Father's eyes, which mimicked hers, but his were colder.

I felt him ready to do whatever it took for whatever I was going to say. Only it was his safety I was concerned about right now.

"Father, Mandy Stone was a setup."

He relaxed considerably, bringing his hand to his forehead. "Jesus Christ, Tiffany." He went to say something else but I got it out first.

"They are setting you up for blackmail."

Both parents started in with how, what, why, how do I know this? The two of them were talking over one another.

I held my hands out in a stop gesture. "Frank, Clarissa, Reese, and even my line-guy at work, who I do not get along with at all, are in on this."

My mother asked who Frank was, and I pointed out that he works here, and we met him at the brunch.

My father asked how Clarissa knew Mandy. "She is her niece from New Jersey."

My father's face dropped. He quietly repeated, "Mandy Stone is Clarissa's niece?"

Father went stone cold, asking, "How do you know this?"

Mother looked at him. "You didn't know she was her niece?"

"Priscilla, I did not know."

Time to confess about the cameras. "Well, I set up surveillance at the condo you are housing her. I've been watching the cameras. It was the arrival of Frank stopping by several times that made me upgrade the camera outside her door, but we tagged that son of a bitch."

"We?" Father grew angrier.

"My boyfriend."

"The fella you work with?"

"No, Father! Michael is not my boyfriend. Andy, the guy who handed me my phone in the foyer of the hotel before brunch."

"The military guy?"

"Yes."

"He looks a little old for you, Tiffany."

Seriously? Father was pointing out my boyfriend's maturity right now?

"How old is Mandy?"

I really had to work on not challenging people back. That was wrong, and now it upset Mother even more.

"Stop it, both of you. This isn't the time for this kind of conversation. Your father didn't mean Andy's age is an issue. Tiffany, I didn't realize you were going to that extent with surveillance on her. I'm sure you are in violation of an abundance of privacy rights."

Mother had given my father enough time to recover from my retaliation.

"That is illegal, Tiffany. You had better remove those cameras."

"I don't care, Father. Those cameras have caught the group of them scheming against you. What possible reason would they all have to come together and not have it be about you?"

Mother was clearly having an internal battle. I knew that hard, focused stare. She fixed her eyes on one spot on the table, controlling her breathing. She was digging deep. I used to be good at making her this angry. She was trying to control what was going to happen next. It was on the verge of a blowout or taking a step back to regroup.

I, too, needed to stay on task, coming right out and asking him. "Are you still involved with her?"

He shot me a hard stare, trying to silence me in front of mother.

I narrowed my eyes, wanting answers myself right now impatiently waiting. "Well?" That came out a little too strong.

He expelled a displeased breath about me questioning him. "No."

"Really? She went on a shopping spree a few days after I left your house that day."

"I ended it the day you left that morning."

"She looked quite cozy, ordering the driver to carry them in."

"Tiffany, it took two hours to shut it all down. It's over. That was not my funding. Any money she has is not coming from me."

My eyes widened. What if that brief case was to pay her rent for a while? What if I was making a mistake? What if this is a whole misunderstanding! Heat coursed through my veins, making me doubt myself assuming what I viewed was a setup.

My mother cleared her throat, finding what she needed within. She turned to my father, addressing him in a polite but generic manner. Kind of like she would speak to a stranger.

There was a disconnection. Even I felt it. "Thank you for ending it, Richard."

He softened, ashamed. His shoulders slumped as he leaned forward, rubbing his fingers near his temples as if to soothe a headache.

"I truly regret her. I am sorry, Priscilla. I will do whatever it takes to fix this. I want my family. You both mean everything to me."

Now, both my mother and I were taken aback. My throat tightened, feeling itchy. I grabbed the bottle of water in the middle of the table. I had better be right about this because, if I am wrong this will turn into a disaster between us.

She spoke at him. "We will have that conversation later."

She turned to me. "Now, what about this blackmailing? If it is Mandy, we already know."

"Yes, but they don't know we know."

I felt sick. The only thing that got me through this was Andy's observation that it was blackmail.

I told them everything in detail, and by the time I was done it looked clear to all of us that I was right. I was the only one questioning my facts now.

Our next forward motion was deciding, how we would handle it. We divided to conquer. Mother announced she was bringing Mildred in on this. Father started to protest out of sheer embarrassment. He lost the two out of three votes to include her.

He also didn't like my suggestion to bring in Audrey. Again, he lost by majority rule.

Mother and I brainstormed for what Father could do about looking into Frank's background. Frank was the number one suspect since he worked here.

What access did he have to what files? What files or information could benefit him? What was his angle? What use could Clarissa have for him in this company?

We came up with a detailed list of motivation, gain, interest, and reason for revenge I could think of from watching my cop shows.

Impressed, Father asked how I had formulated the list. I told him it was from watching television. He insisted it was the education dollars he had spent on my degree. I let him roll with that theory. I'm sure some of it came from my education along with this back-stabbing society I grew up in. At this table we were Team Chanler. No one was going to mess with my family.

CHAPTER TWENTY-TWO

Lunch was going to be a rain check. I pulled my Audrey list out. First stop, Accounting.

Father ordered Clair to escort me through the building, making sure I had access to whatever information I needed.

She was happy as ever, telling me she didn't care what I was doing and said this was a refreshing change for an afternoon. She even caught up with the office gossip as I pulled files and made copies.

I had to call Audrey a few times to make sure some of these documents were what she needed. It looked like a lot of nonsense paperwork. She sternly pointed out that if I had started working there when I graduated, I would not be looking at this paperwork as if it were nothing.

I hung up on her. I didn't need to hear another team member giving me shit about my rightful responsibilities with my parents' company.

Three hours I was here collecting crap. I hope this was the time Andy needed when he said for me to make it a long visit.

I texted him that I was done here.

He replied with an address, telling me to meet him there in one hour. Clair and I went back to Father's office for me to say goodbye to him. He had me close the door and asked how Audrey was doing.

I looked at the time and my GPS. I had about ten minutes for this conversation. I gave him more information than just how she was doing.

I told him what a downright pain in the ass she is and that she now had a special place in my heart. I was going to do everything I could to get her the organ she needed.

He let out a little chuckle, shaking his head. "I also regret the intimate relationship with her. Although Audrey was different, it was just an act. She always showed professionalism, and she has been one of my greatest allies even to this day. I have stayed away from her, communicating via email. You're right to bring her in, Tiffany."

I did not have time to unpack this conversation right now.

"Listen, Father, I really like Audrey. I know she will be someone I hopefully know for a really long time. You should go see her." I looked at my phone again. "Look, I have to go. Sorry to cut out on you, but I have to go." Oh, I wanted to give him a dig about meeting my older boyfriend, but I let it go; I didn't have time to play right now.

He stood up. "Okay, but let's reschedule our lunch. I want to spend time with just my daughter." Oh, gosh, he was going to hug me.

"Got to go. I'll call you." I bolted out the door before he reached me. Our relationship was a long way from earning that privilege back, even if it was just a polite gesture most of the time. We would start with baby steps. I don't care if he was my father. He had to earn my trust again.

Seeing Andy's car as I turned the corner filled me with relief. This was an old, dilapidated warehouse. I parked next to him and texted that I was here.

He gave me instructions: though the door, second level, first door on the left. I squinted upward. The way the sun was reflecting off the windows, I couldn't see in.

I pushed the creaky door open, closing it snugly behind me. It only had the door handle with a separate deadbolt lock above it. I turned the deadbolt to lock it, just out of habit. I wasn't sure about this place, but only Andy's and my car were out front. I reached the second floor, and walked a few yards into the hall. The door was slightly ajar. I actually took a few steps to the left, cautiously pushing it open. Rose petals were scattered on the floor. There was a basic kitchen to the right, basic as in a stripped-down industrial look.

As I took my first step into the room, I heard music start. At the end of the room, there he was. Dressed in a tux walking past a free-standing pedestal of what looked like Champagne chilling. All this to take in... he pulled me into a dance frame. "You're late."

I grinned. "Only by a few minutes?"

He was serious. "Minutes could cost you your life."

Okay? Didn't understand that comment. "Um, okay?"

He swirled me into a waltz. Precise, fluid and with conviction. I was breathless when he kissed me at the end. I had trained in ballet. I had trained in martial arts. Every one of my muscles felt his intensity, his manipulation, placing me in the exact position where he wanted me to be. This man was in full control of himself and of me.

I stood there with a giddy grin, feeling like a feather could knock me over, waiting to see what was next. Andy looked so handsome... dressed up, clean shaven. I couldn't wait to show him off at the fundraiser.

He poured two half glasses of Champagne. It surprised me when he touched my glass to his and raised the alcohol to his lips, taking a sip. I smiled following suit as the aroma from the beverage tickled my nose.

I looked around. This was a beyond basic living quarters. A king-sized mattress with box spring was on the floor, covered with white sheets, a few grey wool blankets, and two pillows. That was it. No nightstand; no light. This must have been around sixteen-hundred-square-feet of empty.

The only thing this man had besides his bed were a heavy bag, some weights, and a jump rope on the floor. There was an outside deck table with two chairs and posters of outdoor scenes on the walls. There was a very sophisticated seven-monitor multi-tier structure, with multiple modems, connection towers, keyboards, a gaming mouse... wow, and what looked like an old gaming joy-stick.

He followed my gaze "Command central"

I turned back to him. "Obviously?"

He grinned, and I asked, "Is this where you live?"

"Yes, babe. This is all mine."

"All of it?"

"Yes, all of it." He gently pulled my drink from my hand; placing it on the counter, holding my other hand, he guided me up the stairs.

This was his weapons room. That hunting store had nothing on my boyfriend. This was the ultimate candy store. He grabbed a few selections, and sat me down at a window. I looked out.

Holy mother of set up shooting ranges! Right in his backyard. I couldn't even see imagine what he had set up out there. When he handed me my first long gun, he told me to count the second target down. I scoped it in and broke position. No way! This was out of range for my ability. Two-hundred and fifty yards, they do not teach you that in close combat training.

I am crap at long distance. "Andy, no. I can't do long distance."

He leaned down, mouth to my ear. "I will teach you, babe. You don't get better than my ol' man. I learned from the best. This is something I want to teach you. It will make a difference on where your mark is short or long range. Even if you're shooting a short with a long-range target. Your odds just jumped fifty percent in your favor. Especially since you are still healing, from the nerve damage to your shoulder."

I looked at my shoulder. "Hardly notice it anymore."

He pressed his finger on a spot. "Ouch!"

Grinning, he said, "But you noticed that?" I rubbed where he had touched, spotting an old photo of a man in camo, laying feet apart in sniper position.

"Really? Then why don't they train us this at the academy?"

"They don't want you to know this, gorgeous. At all."

I shook my head, disappointed. "Figures."

I pointed to the picture. "Is this your father?"

He confirmed with a head nod. Then with his fingers he raised my chin a little looking right into my eyes. "I want you to shoot a short distance gun long and a long-distance gun, well longer."

I grinned because I thought he was going to say long distance gun short. But I knew that would be stupid when I thought about it.

If this was his idea of a date, then he nailed it. The man was shooting guns with me in an army jacket over his tux, gently correcting and giving me breathing lessons. The way he had this table set up, one push and I would be headfirst out the window.

There was a lot of trust going on right now. So much so that my breathing was ratting me out. I wanted him like I have never wanted a man before in my life.

I woke up from a quick nap, in my boyfriend's bed, two hours before I had to be at work, his body entwined with mine. You could not shove me off of cloud nine without a bulldozer right now. I felt completely in love.

I had packed my uniform, just in case we were together until right before my shift started. I just needed to retrieve it from my car. Moving to exit the bed, Andy pulled me back down, making me laugh at his playfulness.

He offered to get my bag as I fished through my clothes on the floor, searching for my keys. One soul-melting, heavenly kiss later, I watched him slip on his tuxedo pants and head to my car.

I looked around, admiring the raw feel of this place. I would be thrilled to move in here.

Andy was back, placing my duffel on the counter and telling me he was starting the coffee. He said for me to feel free to take a shower or whatever else women do to get ready.

I laughed; he was being funny. All the same, I skipped the shower to spend more time with him. I was in a great mood when I pulled into work. Not even Kyle could rain on my sunshine right now.

Michael was very pleased that I was in such good spirits. He asked how my lunch with my father went. I nodded that it was good.

Our last shift of the week was smooth sailing. The next two days were all mine, and I wanted to spend them with my boyfriend. I texted him that I was heading home. Nothing. When I was a mile out from my condo, he answered that he was in the field. He would text me when he could and said good night to me.

Well, what the hell? I didn't like that at all. For a split second, I wanted to drive to his place and see if he was being truthful. Why would he lie to me? I dismissed my logic. He was in the field. He is always working.

I stopped at my gas station/grocery store and picked up a can of wet cat food. At least I was going home to someone that would be happy to see me. There was Cat meowing as soon as I opened my car door.

"Hey, buddy, miss me?" I opened the can and chopped the food up, so it was easier for him to eat. He purred and growled at the same time. Kind of reminded me of how I felt right now. Happy but pissed off all at the same time. I thought he was going to try to follow me in, but at the last moment, he looked toward the woods and took off in a running crouch. Second male to disappoint me today.

Hannah's name lit up my phone. "Hello."

"Good morning to you, crabby. Have a tough shift?"

"No, just in a bad mood suddenly."

"I hear you. Me, too. When you get up, do you want to go shopping? Maybe grab a late lunch? Gala is in eight days sweetie, and you need a dress."

Hannah got me to redirect my bad mood. I conceded. "Yes, Okay. Sounds like a date."

She squealed in delight. "I have the afternoon off. Let's do this."

Suddenly, I realized she just said she had the afternoon off. "Hey, what about George?"

A second of silence fell before she answered. "Girls' day. I am not worrying about men today."

Well, that sealed the deal for me. Neither was I. Screw them. "Sounds perfect, Hannah."

"Call me when you're up. I already know where we're starting."

"Will do."

And we hung up. Andy greeting me in his tux was the one memory playing like a movie in my head. I wanted to look good for him. I wanted us to look like a power couple. Maybe I should consider the color black to match. It was on my radar for possibilities.

I was still mad at him as a text came through that said: *sweet dreams.* Well, what was his game? How could he unravel the last hour of pissing me off in two words to set it all straight?

I grunted, kicking my door shut stronger than I intended. I stared at my phone then answered: *wish you were here.*

I read and reread it, then cringed and thought I might be acting needy as I hit send.

He replied: *So do I.*

Damn it! Damn it! Damn it! No wonder I avoided taking on a boyfriend. This sucked, and I hated being away from him. Nothing I could do about it now. I dropped my phone on my end table and connected the charger.

I stripped down to my underwear and climbed into bed. I grabbed the pillow he last slept on and it still smelled of faint traces of him. I cuddled into that pillow and fell asleep.

* * *

Dress shopping with my fashion consultant... When I mentioned I was open to a black gown, the whole atmospheric pressure dropped. Shit, just got real. Hannah reached for my hand and abandoned the shop we were in. She went right for the gut. Our city's highest fashion go-to boutique that no one thought to use. The bridal shop!

Hannah was barking out orders as four women scurried like rats through separate tunnels. The co-owner was grinning and carrying a bottle of Champagne and three glasses. Hannah introduced herself, mentioning her sister's wedding.

Megan grinned, and looked me over. She nodded to Hannah. Never in my life had I wanted to drink until now. Hand me the damn bottle.

It was like magic. I had twelve black ball worthy gowns hanging on a rack ready to fight for my purchase. Was it bad that I pictured Andy dancing with me around the ballroom floor in each dress? I spun the bejesus out of every dress, making Hannah giddy with pure girl power.

Final decision, I walked out carrying two dress purchases. I loved each in their particular style. Andy would have the final decision, but I was going to have to remove the price tags. I didn't want him complaining about how much I just spent. I sent him a picture of me in each one that Hannah insisted on taking. No response.

Over a late lunch, Hannah confessed that George was acting distant. She couldn't pinpoint it, but she suspected there was something amuck with a new nurse arriving. He kept telling her what a breath of fresh air Kelly was. And that Kelly displayed an enthusiastic mannerism with each task. "If I hear her name one more time, I will scream! Hey, can you go check her out?"

"Why don't you just show up with a delivery of food?"

"Honestly, I don't want to meet her."

"You guys haven't been dating long?"

"Time means nothing. He is the one."

"The one? George has ruined any future man for you?"

"Yes!"

I reached over to cover her hand with mine. "So soon? Are you sure?"

"Stop asking me that Tiff! I need to know about this Kelly chick."

I released her hand. "Is she working today? I have to go to Burbank and drop some stuff off to Audrey." Hannah slumped her shoulders and leaned in.

"Isn't it a little odd, spending time with your father's former mistress?"

I cocked my head to the side. She was an outsider looking in. I suppose she was right. "Yes, odd. I like Audrey. I like her a lot. She still works for my father, and my mother likes her too."

"You guys are freaks."

I laughed. "I know I can't explain it, but she is important to us. I think it's her love of the company. She is so passionate about work. Even on her deathbed. I think that is keeping her going."

Hannah sat back, lifting her coffee to her lips and mumbled, "Freaks," again.

I chuckled, sipping mine.

CHAPTER TWENTY-THREE

Well, that was an easy assignment for my new friendship circle, of best nursing staff ever. They went into detective mode to find out what they could about this new nurse, "Kelly." They thrived on gossip. The investigation was on.

I walked into Audrey's room. There she was on her computer wearing a face mask with a diamond shape cut out smack in the middle, exposing her nose and mouth. "You know, that defeats the purpose."

"I told you. I hate these damn things. If I could wear one, I would be a top surgeon right now."

"Okay, a surgeon sitting right where you are because you like cheap ass vodka, waiting for a new liver."

"No, I would already have my new liver. I would have just taken a perfect slice off someone that matched."

My mouth fell open. I didn't know whether to laugh or be scared. I could picture her doing it.

I plunked down the bag of paperwork files I had copied from the list she gave me. She quickly sorted through them, nodding and mumbling as I pulled the chair over. She looked up. "Good job, Watson."

"Ask, and you shall receive."

"Did anyone give you a hard time getting these?"

"No, Clair escorted me around to make sure I had access to what I needed."

Audrey sighed. "I miss seeing Clair. She shares the best stories of her children."

"She was very helpful. I enjoyed hanging out with her."

Audrey gathered a handful of papers and aligned them all with a quick rap and shake against her table.

"This can wait. I will call you with what I find."

Still no word from Andy. Looking up from my phone, I thought she was dismissing me.

"Do you want me to go?"

"No! No, Tiffany. I want to know why you have a long face. What is bothering you? Did everything go okay with your lunch yesterday?"

I couldn't look at her with that hole cut through her mask.

"Take that off, please. You look ridiculous."

"No, you made me wear it, so I have to wear it, until this flu epidemic dies down."

"But you're exposed with the cutout."

"I can breathe with my alteration."

"It's distracting."

"Good, see, not all ideas should be executed. Mask, bad idea with good intentions. Still a bad idea. Now, what is going on with you?"

"Well, I had a moment yesterday when I was telling my father that he was being blackmailed of feeling that I was wrong."

"No, Tiffany, I think you are correct."

"Well, he shut Mandy off financially and the briefcase could be money she needs to keep her going."

"What briefcase?"

Oops.

I backtracked and confessed about the surveillance. I have never seen a woman more enthusiastic about the idea of spying on someone in my life. She wanted to know if I could grant her access to the cameras. I informed her that Father ordered me to remove them.

Audrey counter argued to leave them. I brought up the codes on my phone that Andy had linked me to and together we figured out how to upload it on her computer.

Audrey navigated the site. She knew so much more about computers than I did. She typed and cursed at the keys, then smiled. "Now this is cool."

I had doubtful thoughts again about the first mistress, having spy options on the second mistress. "Are you sure you can handle this?"

She nodded, wide-eyed. "New reason to live."

She gasped. "Is that her?" She pointed to the image.

Yup, that was her. "Yes."

"Son of a bitch! Are you sure Richard ended it?"

"He said he did."

She pointed again. "Who is that?" I looked closer. Hmm. "That is my coworker Kyle."

"The one you don't get along with?"

"Yup."

"He's sleeping with her."

I looked again. "No, he's dating her cousin, who I know from growing up."

"Well, he is sleeping with her too."

That mask was annoying the hell out of me. "Either you take that mask off or I am leaving. I can't look at you with that hole cut out."

Audrey surrendered. "Fine."

"Thank you."

"It was your idea, remember."

"Okay enough about the stupid mask. Why do you say Kyle is sleeping with Mandy?"

"Look at them. He's hitting that booty big time."

I watched until they entered her condo. I don't know if it was the power of suggestion, but she was right. Kyle was flirting. She was flirting. What a dirt bag. Once a dog, always a dog. I kind of felt bad for Reese. Kyle was playing her too.

My phone vibrated. Andy was texting me thanks for the pictures. *Exactly what I need. I am stuck on a roof watching traffic. How are you doing, babe?*

And just like that, every insecurity melted away.

I am good. Sitting here with Audrey. I wish I was with you.

He replied: *Me too. Something has come up. I won't be around much over the next few weeks*

Immediately, I thought about the gala.

What about the fundraiser?

I will be there. No matter what.

I relaxed. At least I had that to hold on to.

You better. I bought a dress to match your tux.

His response took longer than a minute: *Looking forward to parading you around.*

Audrey had gone back to the beginning of the surveillance. She pointed to Andy, who was winking into the camera. "Who is that?"

I grinned. "My boyfriend."

She paused and watched it several times. "Military man?"

Still smiling. "Yes."

"Looks it. How old is he?"

"Why?" my brows knit together.

"No reason, just looks older, that's all."

"Not you too."

"Not me too what, Tiffany?"

"Father said he was too old for me."

"Oh? No, that was not why I was asking. He's rugged. Has that mature aura about him. I was just wondering."

"Andy is ten years older."

She paused, looking up from the computer. "That's nothing. Good for you. I think he'll teach you a lot. Everywoman needs a good experienced man in their life."

I wasn't sure where she was going with this. As she moved through the video library. "Is he going to be your date for the gala?"

"He better or I will haunt him."

She smiled. "Did you buy a dress yet?"

I pulled up the two dresses on my phone showing her the pictures.

Audrey had a favorite insisting I wear the black with silver trim. That was my first choice.

* * *

Well, there was Cat, laying half under the bushes. It was downright hot out today. I squatted in front of him "Hey buddy, found some shade, did you? Want to come in? It's nice and cool in the condo?"

He meowed rolling onto his back. Nope, not interested. That was fine. I noticed a dead chipmunk to the left.

"What? I'm not feeding you enough?"

He rolled upright again, purring away.

"Okay, I'll be out in a little while with dinner."

I scratched under his chin then headed to my condo. Sorting through my mail, I saw a postcard with a beach scene on the front. It was from my grappling instructor. The words written were: Vacation over. Time to get back to work.

I suppose he was right. I needed to get back in shape. I have no excuse anymore. I am well healed from the accident and I was just going to live with and push through the nerve damage to my shoulder. Andy had even improved my shooting with one lesson showing me how to control my breathing.

Time to toughen back up and keep my head straight and be ready to intercept Audrey's liver so she actually gets it this time. Tomorrow was Saturday. Perfect day to start back with grappling.

Someone was texting me. *Your list is waiting.* I should have called Greg to tell him I wasn't coming in.

I replied that I had some personal things to take care of the last few days and I would be in tomorrow after grappling.

He answered: *Good because I need your help. Kyle's truck is acting up. This will be a good learning lesson for you. Don't miss it.*

Looks like my Saturday was back on track; grappling then the garage. It was strange not to hear a word from Michael today. I texted him. We were still friends, and he asked me to coffee the other day. Instead of texting back, he called, "Hey, Tiff, how was your day?"

"It was good. Hannah dragged me dress shopping. I visited Audrey. I think I made a mistake today."

"Why? Did you see your boyfriend?"

"Ha, ha, ha! I set Audrey up to monitor the surveillance with Mandy."

"You did what!"

"I know; I know. Father told me to take it down. Something about legal issues. So, instead of watching it myself, Audrey will monitor it. She is having way too much fun. I think I gave her too much power."

"Well, that ought to be interesting. The first mistress spying on the second mistress. How is her health holding up?"

"Good, actually, I think becoming a spy gave her a new adventure to focus on."

"Well, that's good."

I heard traffic and people speaking. "Is this a bad time? You sound busy."

"No, it's all good. I grabbed another shift. Guys are dropping like flies around here with the flu going around."

"You better not get me sick. I have to be at the gala next week."

"Don't worry, Tiff; it won't be me getting you sick. I can't get close enough. You banished me."

"Michael!"

"What? It's true. You only need to worry about fleas off your boyfriend."

"Michael! Stop it." I knew he loathed Andy more than anything.

"Hey, I'm pulling in to our stop."

"Who are you riding with?"

"Our recruit, Chris."

"Oh, nice. Tell her that I say Hi."

"Will do; gotta go, Tiff." And he hung up.

Knowing I was starting back tomorrow morning for grappling, I jumped rope for twenty minutes, then did a few floor exercises. Not too many, because my shoulder was still on the mend.

It felt good to stretch. I looked in the mirror, examining the healing scars. The one that my hair and shirt scorched into me still resembled a phoenix... like a bird spreading its wings. "Out of the ashes rises the mighty phoenix," I repeated out loud.

It was dinnertime for Cat. I cut up chicken and as I was walking out, I saw the perfect opportunity to lure him into my condo. He was waiting and watching me already suspecting something was up.

I crouched down to him. "You know, I think you'll like the condo."

He groomed himself. I tore off a small piece of chicken and put it next to me. He looked at it and kept grooming. I tore off another little piece. "Come on handsome. I can't have both my fellas ignoring me."

He watched then began to purr. I hand fed him a little bite. He liked that, and now he was standing and walking toward me. I kissed at him to follow. He was good right until a couple came out of the building. He ran into the nearby bushes. I stood up as they greeted me with a hello. I nodded.

The coast was clear. "Come on, Cat, all clear."

I made more kissing sounds and he came out, purring and rubbing against the bush branches. I waited a few minutes; now he was halfway to me. I placed another piece of chicken down and he trotted over, sitting and eating.

Someone else came out and he went to run, but I put my hand on him while he was going for it and picked him up.

I carried him like a football, ducking into the building and patting his head. He growled once, and I told him we were almost home. Inside, I shut the door quickly and let him go. We were in.

Cat scurried to the left to my bedroom. I went to the kitchen while talking to him and retrieved a plate. I dumped the chicken out where I had put him down, then walked to the bedroom. I couldn't see him anywhere. I called then lifted the comforter that was half on the ground.

There he was. I tried to tell him this was his place now, but from the growl, I didn't think he approved.

On my hands and knees, I reasoned with my cat under my bed. "I know you'll love it. You can go out whenever you want. I promise. Just try it, okay?"

He gave a soft, high-pitched meow. Good, we had an understanding. I told him I was going to turn on the television and lay on the couch. "Explore around, buddy. I'm right here."

His legs were folded under him as he stared at me and then looked around. I dropped the blanket and walked out.

I texted Andy that Cat was in the house. Nothing.

By my third cop show, I spotted a movement to the right. Cat was finally exploring. I called to him; he ignored me, sniffing and looking around. Well, two can play at that game. I stood and went into the bathroom, ignoring him. When I came back, he was on my couch, sniffing the blanket and purring. I didn't touch him. I turned the television off and said good night.

I woke up and repositioned my legs, only to have something attack them. I shot up startled. Cat went leaping off the bed and into the condo. He must have slept with me last night.

I called after him, apologizing and stepping on grit. What the hell? He had kicked the kitty litter everywhere. Everywhere! Ouch, ouch, ouch! I made it to the kitchen to grab the broom and swept.

"Maybe you should be my outdoor pet? You're a slob."

He jumped up on the back of my sofa watching me. I started the coffee and put his food down so he could eat. He was lying on the back of the sofa now.

"I have to get ready. I have a long day today. You need to decide if you are in here all day or outside."

He gave me a purring meow. "If you're inside today, no more litter everywhere, okay?" He closed his eyes almost smiling.

Time to go. "Well, what do you think? In or out?"

He rested his head on his front paws. "Okay. It will be awhile. Don't tear the place apart."

I paused, looking for one more sign. He was staying. I texted Andy that Cat was in my condo and then my schedule for today. Nothing.

I got so much playful banter from the guys at grappling that it was almost fun to be back. My instructor reached for my arm. "Hey, Tiff, take it slow for the next month." He examined my burn scars.

"Yes, sir." I would not fight with him again.

After a good first day back, I headed to the garage. There was Greg, Danny and me. Danny was working on the back doors. It was coming along. What a difference a few days made.

I asked Greg where everyone was; the flu had wiped out half the crew, and now he was getting behind. Well, we worked on Kyles ambulance all day. There was a lot of line tracing to finally a broken connection. Greg was right. This was a good lesson day.

Michael walked in dressed for another shift. I joked "Geez, that will be a nice paycheck next week."

"I'm pulling a double tomorrow, too."

"We have first shift. Are you going to be sleeping between stops?"

"Most likely. Allen asked for one more day. But he sweetened the deal. He is swapping next Saturday with me."

"We have the day shift? The gala isn't until the evening?"

"I know; now I have the whole day off."

"Three days off in a row? Wow, that's like a vacation. So, I have Allen next Saturday?"

"Yup."

"That's fine. As long as he keeps his germs to himself."

Greg and I were done. Still no reply from Andy. I hated it when he didn't reply.

I walk into my condo, stopping in my tracks. My cat was a slob. Again, the litter was everywhere. I kept the door open to see if he wanted to go out. He just rubbed up against the kitchen stool, purring away. I fetched the broom to clean up after him; he watched while grooming himself with no interest in leaving. "I should call you pig pen." He purred very happily answering me.

Hannah was texting. George had canceled their date. He had to work late. It was time for me to be there for her. I insisted that she be ready in an hour and we would go to dinner.

She was upset when I picked her up. The first thing out of her mouth was that she wasn't going to the gala. This was beyond stupid. I pointed out that the hospitals were understaffed with people being admitted with this flu going around.

Hannah was convinced it was Kelly. For the first time in my life, I observed how vulnerable she was sitting here. My poor friend was in love, and this was killing her.

I wanted to pay the good doctor a visit to get the answer straight from him. Tomorrow I would see my dayshift nurses and see what information they had come up with.

Audrey was calling me. "You are right about foul play going on. Never would I have caught this. Just wait until you see what I found." I wanted to know. I asked Hannah if we could swing by the hospital.

She put her foot down with an absolute NO! There was no way she wanted to run into George after he had canceled on her.

I asked Audrey if I could come by in a few hours. The time was already approaching eight. She suggested tomorrow would be better when I left work, and she might have more to tell me from the videos.

She was only on episode nine of 62 Highland Ave. It took a minute to catch on, but she was naming each day an episode, and I realized that was Mandy's address. Audrey was quick-witted. That made me fight a grin in front of Hannah.

"Hey, do you want to spend the night at my house? I have to warn you though; I have a pet cat." The surprised look on her face at the fact that I had a pet showed that I had made her think. "Well, that's two for two. A boyfriend and a pet. Never thought I would see the day, Tiffany."

"I am surprised myself; believe me."

"Look, I know I haven't been open about the idea of Andy. Clearly, I'm wrong. I hope it works out for both of you. I'll try to shelve my opinion. He scares me, though."

"A lot of people say that. I don't get it?"

"Do you remember a few years ago when you met those army guys that invited you back for 'extra training'?"

I grinned. "Yes?"

"And you thought it would be a good idea to take me along in case their intentions were not pure?"

I chuckled, five big, burly rangers. We didn't have a chance if they had had intensions. "Yup, but again, you misjudged them. All nice guys. Just trying to help."

Hannah narrowed her eyes. "Do you remember Roy?"

I laughed again. "The guy that proposed to you within an hour?"

"Let's not talk about that. I want to tell you a story he shared. It freaked me out back then and the first time I saw Andy, that story was copied and pasted right to him."

"Really?"

"Look Tiff, while you were improving your target practice, he was bragging about being a sniper. I didn't even know what a sniper was. He explained! Mr. Big Shot just loved educating me. Roy said it was all about the long gun and distance with him. He talked with his hands, showing me how he held the imaginary gun; he said it was all about the feeling that overcomes you. You become disconnected from everything surrounding you. To a sniper, he said, your mind bends to what you see in the scope. Everything in it becomes a snap decision, live or die. He compared it to a prize. Target, prize, target, prize. The guy scared the heck out of me. Then he talked about the thousand-yard-stare, blank, emotionally detached. I couldn't wait to get out of there."

"Thousand-yard-stare?"

"Yes! Well, what I remember from looking in Roy's eyes when he was telling me about that is like looking at Andy. Your boyfriend reminded me of that story and the way Roy looked telling it. Andy has the thousand-yard stare; he looks emotionally detached and like he could snap someone's neck any second without conscious thought. I only know what one soldier explained, and I wanted to leave."

"I've never heard that expression. You couldn't be more wrong about Andy, though. He is kind, funny, jealous, protective, moody, loving, and honorable. The guy has my back. Ever since our first meeting, I felt we were connected. Deep down I wanted him to be the one. I know his life is complicated, so I didn't push. He needed to decide. He chose me. I am what he wants, and I want us just as bad."

"Tiffany, I am sorry. I will be open to him."

"Thanks, Hannah, just don't fear him, okay? Let's figure out what's going on in your relationship, because not showing up to that gala is not an option. Michael is bringing a date. We may need to do shots of tequila."

She sat back, examining me. "Why? You don't like Michael! He can bring whoever he wants."

"Not what I'm getting at! No one will ever be good enough for him."

"No one except, you?"

I crumpled up my napkin, tossing it at her. "Not what I am getting at!"

She caught it. "Interesting."

I narrowed my eyes. "Stop it."

I woke up to my alarm going off. Just as I moved, Cat attacked my feet, making me jump out of bed.

"Bad kitty." I shook my finger at him with his tail swishing slowly back and forth, waiting for another movement under the sheets. Two can play at this game. I crouched down, sticking my arm under the sheet and making scratching sounds.

Kitty went mental, making me laugh. This is definitely a new source of entertainment for me and a new way of distracting me and wasting time. I was running late, and kitty was waiting at the door wanting to go out.

"Okay buddy, here's the deal. I can't chase you today, so I'm carrying you out." Duffel over my shoulder, Cat tucked under my arm in a football hold, we exited the building. When he started to push against me, I crouched and let him jump.

He walked two steps and sat, bathing himself. "See you later, buddy, I'll be late tonight."

Michael was walking out with our paperwork. "You're late." He reached for my arm, making me stop. "Your side is covered in black hair."

I looked down. I never thought to check. Oh, I was covered in black hair, kitty sheds.

"Shoot! It's my cat. How do I get this off?"

"Tape."

"Thanks, Michael; I'll be right out."

I turned to head in and there was Kyle, walking toward us grinning wide as can be, "Morning, bitches."

"Morning ass wipe," I said returning as big of a grin as I could while walking past him. I vaguely heard Michael exchange words with him as I walked to the office, looking for tape.

I set us back a half hour in our start schedule. We had to skip morning coffee and donuts which threw both of us off. Alerts came over our phones, looking for second and third shift coverage. Michael made a call. "Fill me in for the second shift."

I glanced over at him. "You're burning the candle at both ends Michael. You'll get sick; we have Mildred's gala at the end of the week. I would hate for you to miss it?"

He was texting on his phone, not looking at me. "Not a chance. I will need to stop for caffeine soon."

"Me too."

There was a lot of new construction popping up. State elections were up in the fall typical political strategy. I was going to put my complaint in to the governor if he showed up on Saturday.

I kept looking at my phone. Nothing from Andy. Where was he that he could not respond? I know he told me to be patient, but that was hard to do when I had no information to hold onto.

I signed Michael and me out as he jumped shift to cover for Pete. I walked into the garage and informed Greg that I only had enough time for one oil change. He grumbled and muttered pointing to an ambulance. While I was adding the new oil, it occurred to me that my father's company had a whole IT department at my disposal.

I bet if I took that scanner in, they could tell me what it is programmed to do. I was going to ask Audrey who I should go to, with an IT problem.

When I arrived, her room had the entire window wall lined with moveable hospital bed stands. Each one was transformed into a portable desk, holding neat piles of stacked papers with a separate notepad on the end. She was hoarding six tray tables now.

Audrey instantly complained that I smelled like a garage, ordering me to go in the bathroom and spray myself with room freshener because she would not sit with me smelling like this for our visit.

I looked to the other wall. She had a printer setup.

"Well, you have been busy. Where did you get your own printer?"

"I called Richard; they installed it this morning."

"On a Sunday?"

"They would have come at midnight if I requested it."

"Well, aren't you the Boss Lady?"

"I save the company millions. I get what I want."

"But you are a consultant."

"Not any longer. He can't afford consulting fees; I'm back on the payroll, limited duty, full benefits. Come here, look what I found."

"Welcome back."

"Come sit." She scooched over to share her bed. "Blah, you still stink."

"Well, I can sit over there." I pointed to the chair in the corner.

"No, I will just have to endure it."

Audrey's theory was that there was not money in the briefcase. Frank had stolen paperwork.

Over the past two years of Audrey's absence, my father had slowly hired this new team that I met at the brunch. Frank was the last one in. Audrey pointed out missing billing, missing paperwork, and missing deliveries, all from companies in the New Jersey and New York area. She explained that they deduct for such mishaps.

These were port issues, and if you were not playing nice with the right people, you would get screwed no matter what. Then she brought Monty Technologies up on her computer. This company used a lot of the same carriers my father did. They were reporting gains, and they just went public on the market.

"Do you think they upped their capital using the missing stock from Henshaw?"

"That is exactly what I am thinking. Only not just from us; there has to be another source. They are a startup company, only had fifty thousand going in, and now they show four million in capital."

"But they're a technology company. Maybe they have the next best thing?"

"Maybe they are competing for the contract your father and I have been investing in the last four years. We've poured millions into Bravado Cummins Diesel. This is such a hush, hush operation. We want Henshaw to be the first in industry standards that could surpass emission regulations for the next two decades."

"But this other company only has four million. Surely, that is nothing to even worry about competing with?"

"Monty Technologies is now holding seventy million through stock and attracting investors."

"Oh, that's not good."

I left Audrey with my head spinning. She had to have told my father all of this. I texted Andy to please call. Nothing.

I called Hannah to see how she was holding up. I could hear her disappointment over the phone as she tried to act like it was fine. I offered to hang out, but she was working tonight.

I couldn't help myself. I drove to Andy's place. It looked as deserted as ever. Seeing that made me feel good that he wasn't here but awful that I was missing him.

Cat was happy to see me. He even voluntarily followed me to the building's door. I picked him up before opening the door.

When I opened the door inside my condo, I froze. Rose petals were scattered about and led a trail to my kitchen. Cat struggled to get down. I squatted to release him. "Andy?" I called out. No answer. I looked around, my heart racing and walked to the kitchen. The coffee pot was set up, and there was a note. Just be patient, babe; I can't wait to see you.

That was it. I searched the house. No Andy. I texted: Thank you. No response. Again, I was happy and pissed off all at once.

CHAPTER TWENTY-FOUR

Michael had grabbed double shifts all week. Mind you, I was in the garage helping Greg all week. At least Michael was getting overtime, but I was gaining engine knowledge.

I wanted to know why Monty Technologies was trying to compete so badly with my father's company. I texted Andy and gave him the name Blake Rivera with a little background on why I wanted to see if he could come up with any information.

Wednesday night, Michael was a zombie. I let him sleep between stops, even went in to Burbank and did the delivery myself so he could get a solid hour. I wanted to see if my nurse spies had any information.

Maggie confirmed it had been a nightmare here. They had to turn people away on Monday. She said it was slowing down, though; they were in between waves at the moment, and most likely next week would be the worst, then it would get better from there. I asked if she knew Doctor Paris. She brightened up. "He's a doll! Everyone loves him."

"Do you know about this new nurse, Kelly?"

She shook her head no.

"Do you know if he's seeing anyone new?"

"Do you know Doctor Paris?"

"I do. He was the doctor that fixed me up when I got into an accident. I heard he was in a relationship. I'm just checking. You never know." I winked and nudged her.

She grinned. "Get in line. He is the most eligible bachelor. I heard he was seeing someone new. Maybe that's her."

I could spit a nail right now.

"Are you okay, Tiffany?"

"Oh, sorry. I just forgot about something I should have done earlier. I hate that; don't you?"

"Story of my life. I even write stuff down and forget to bring my list. How pathetic is that?"

Poor Hannah. I wanted to confront him right now. Michael was snoring when I started the truck. We were halfway to the next stop when the night construction lights woke up sleeping beauty with a start.

"Where are we?" He lifted his arms to block out the brightness.

"Almost to Hannamon."

"How long have I been sleeping?"

I looked at his hanging watch. "Two hours."

"Tiffany!"

"What? You've been working ridiculous hours. I got this."

"Thanks," Michael straightened up checking his phone.

"So, why all the overtime? Planning a big purchase?"

"Something like that."

I laughed, asking sarcastically, "What a house?"

"Not far off, a condo. I'm looking for something bigger."

He's moving in with her. I did not want to know this. I'm shutting this conversation right down. I needed coffee, and these lights were blinding.

I preferred Michael when he was sleeping. He tried to bring up Hannah, and I answered vaguely; he brought up my parents' and I answered vaguely; then he brought up the gala.

I had no problem talking about what a wonderful time I was going to have with Andy and said that I couldn't wait to introduce him around. I brought up every perfect thing Andy did, and I couldn't wait!

Neither one of us needed coffee now. We were in a pissing match over whose date was better. By the time we got back, I stormed off to Greg's garage. After two hours of me stomping around, and breaking more things than I was fixing, he had enough with me. Greg kicked me out, told me to get some sleep and come back later when I was in a better mood. I did just that.

Cat was nowhere around. I walked into more petals scattered on the floor. My heart jumped. I called out, "Andy?"

He answered "Bedroom." I dropped my bag, closed the door, and ran to the bedroom. There was my boyfriend upper body naked, under my covers, reading something, while my cat stretched out alongside him purring loudly. I was so happy I didn't know what to do first.

"I would get up, but she's pinned me in here."

I grinned. "He."

"She."

"My cat is a she?"

"Yes."

"Well, I'll be damned. All this time, I thought it was he. Makes sense now that you say that. Did he come in with you? I mean she?"

"Yup, followed me right in."

I walked over and petted her. I think she was smiling. "Hey, I didn't see your car?"

"I'm not driving it."

That was it. Andy pulled me up. "Enough with her. I don't have a lot of time." He grabbed hold and flipped me to my side of the bed, making me laugh and squeal in delight, kissing me as if it was our last.

I woke up alone to the sound of digging, followed by the sound of kitty litter spraying across my floor. "Bad Kitty!"

I looked at my phone; I had a perfect four-hour nap. Andy was gone but my coffee pot was ready and I was in a much better mood.

I texted Hannah to see if she wanted to get an early dinner in, but she said she was meeting George. If he was breaking up with her, I was going to wring his neck.

I called Mother, who invited me to come over for dinner at seven. Hmm, two Thursdays in a row with them. Looked like a new tradition brewing.

Father showed up, pleased that I made the effort. Mother was cooking her vinegar glossed chicken. This was one of my favorite meals of hers. My mouth began to salivate. "Tiffany, would you like a drink, dear?"

"No, thank you, I don't like alcohol, Mother."

"Oh, well, that's good. We should all drink less."

My father picked up his martini. "Maybe next week. I have no intention of cutting back right now."

I cracked a smile. "So, how was your lunch yesterday, Mother?"

"Very civil actually, Quite out of character for them. The gala was all anyone could talk about."

"Do they know I used to hang out there?"

"Unfortunately, they do. Your name came up several times. Mildred spoke about how impressed she was with the programs, even back when you were growing up and how they have stayed true to their mission all these decades."

"Wow."

"Not a lot of back comments when she was through."

I grinned. "I bet."

"There will be a lot of the girls you trained with at the event. Mildred thought it would be a good idea to bring you back together. I think she has several tables filled. Some are bringing their daughters, who are enrolled in those same programs now. It will be such a lovely evening."

I haven't seen those girls in years. They were my people. I couldn't wait to catch up with them.

It was a nice evening spent with my parents. I don't remember the last time I enjoyed their company like this. I asked my father if I could borrow one of his IT guys to look at something in the morning.

Ishmal was the only person he said to go to. He praised him as one of the best programmers he had ever come across in the industry. If Ish couldn't help me, then no one could.

* * *

I had snagged some chicken for Cat. I shook the bag making kissing noises. It was a cool spring night. The moon was half full lighting up the night sky. I listen for a few moments, but she didn't respond.

Okay, she was probably out hunting. I'll just tempt her in the morning.

I had grappling class first; then I'd be off to my father's office to see what Ish could find out about the scanner, then to the garage. Another overtime second shift opened up. It was slowing down just like Maggie said it would. This was Taylors last day at the academy, and we had her to look forward to for two weeks, then she was being assigned a permanent position.

When I handed the scanner over to Ish, he started to dismantle it. I was horrified and tried to stop him. He assured me everything was going to be okay. He needed to see the core processor. He was pretty bored with the simple setup. Every organ had a separate bar code. I asked him what the one for liver was. He found it with ease and printed it out for me.

If my memory served me correctly, it looked similar to the print out Andy had stuck under my door. In no time, the scanner was back together, and I was thanking him. He held onto my scanner for just a minute longer. "So, how about coffee sometime or something?"

I smiled. "I don't think my boyfriend would like that too much."

"Oh sorry, figures. Well, okay, then. Anything I can help you with in the future just stop by."

"Thanks, Ish. I didn't mean to act so crazy when you disassembled it."

"That's nothing, Tiffany. It was nice to meet the boss's daughter."

I smiled and left.

Greg nearly had his full crew back, recovered from the plague. Marco was the only man down, so the shop was in full swing. Danny was doing a great job with my ambulance. He had replaced the entire shell of my driver's side, and it was looking good. When I went over to poke around, he was inside welding. I looked away, not having the proper eye-wear, as he shut it down.

"Tiffany, I'm pretty stoked about this. Uncle Gregory said I could play around a little bit, so I made some modifications. I didn't like how this crumpled on impact, so I added some cross hairs to reinforce it. Come here; let me show you."

He was making this thing as secure as an armored truck. I wanted to kiss him. Well, I wanted to kiss him regardless, but this was one more reason I wanted to. All of our trucks should be reinforced like this, not just my broken one.

"Hey, Danny, how long until I have her back on the road?"

"Things are going smoother than expected. If my next batch of parts is on time, I'm looking at ten days here, then send her off for some new skin and we are golden."

"New skin?"

"Paint job, Tiffany, the girl's gotta have a new wrap."

"Oh, I get it." Greg yelled over to me, asking if I was here to work or socialize.

I adored this grumpy old man, "Thanks Danny. She is looking great. And thank you for the extra's."

He slid his welding visor back down, firing up the flame.

I called Cat again when I arrived back. No sign of her. Now I was getting worried. My kitty has been here waiting for me every day. Did she run into the building when someone was entering or leaving?

I searched this entire structure, no sign of her. I walked out again with her bag of chicken. Nothing, no sign anywhere. Now, I was really worried that something had happened to her.

I texted Andy to let him know. No answer. This shit was getting old.

I woke up missing my cat and missing my boyfriend. The gala was tonight, and he had promised to be there. I just had my shift with Allen to get through, and then I could concentrate on my social activities.

Audrey sent me a good morning photo of her feet in the most rhinestone-covered silver shoes I have ever seen. *I may not be able to physically go tonight, but I will wear these all day. Priscilla dropped me off a dress as well. I will send you a picture of my virtual arrival.*

I knew my mother would include her somehow. I laughed over those shoes. Leave it to Audrey to be the brightest, shiniest, person here. *I do wish you were coming. I would have arranged spot lights to shine on your entrance to blind the crowd.*

You're just jealous. You know I would have upstaged you.

I loved this woman's wit: *Yes, because it's always about me.*

I will be with you tonight, even when I cannot physically be there.

I smiled: *Well, we'll get through this year and make sure you're my date next year.*

As long as Andy doesn't mind being the third wheel.

I sideways smiled. She was awesome.

My next text was to Mother: *Thank you for setting Audrey up with a dress and those blinding shoes.*

Mother replied that is not even the half of it. Just wait until later.

I could not imagine what they had planned for tonight but it was making Audrey happy. I was in.

Things were looking up. Kyle was out. I seriously hope he caught the flu. It wasn't until I was walking to my ambulance that Michael stood up, exiting a car I was not familiar with. He was buttoning his uniform shirt and striding toward the office. I turned, jogging after him. "Michael! Are you working today? I thought you traded with Allen?"

He glanced over his shoulder. "I did; Kyle bagged out. I wouldn't let them dump all of today on you."

"But we have Jason?"

"No one volunteered the shift. They won't send him alone."

"Oh? So, I'll swap out Allen then?"

"Like hell, you will."

I stepped back; my heart quickened, surprised at he had just said that. "What? What do you mean?"

I followed closely behind him to the entrance of the men's locker room. He stopped, spinning to me with a toothy grin. "I'm driving Kyle's ambulance. I'll finish ahead of your slow poke ass and be out of here in plenty of time to rest up for the gala."

I narrowed my eyes; so, this was his tactic. "Game on, partner." I turned, ramping up my march, leaving him at the door.

I heard behind me in his most sarcastic tone, "Don't be late, Cinderella."

Allen was talking to Julie, leaning against the door frame as I stormed by, "Come on, Allen, we don't have all day."

I was in my ambulance, watching him walk across the parking lot. Geez, he was slower than a turtle. I beeped the horn for him to pick it up a notch. He opened the passenger door. "Oh, I forgot my clipboard."

GRRR! "Just get in. I'll get it!" I bolted out and ran to the front desk, then ran back, tossing it on the dashboard as I saw Michael trotting to Kyles ambulance with Jason in tow. He knew I was looking at him as he was flipping his watch up and tapping it. I shifted her into drive and sped away.

Allen pulled the clipboard toward him. "What's the rush?" he asked concerned. I took the corner sharply squealing the tires. "I want to be done on time. I have plans tonight."

"So, do I, but let's slow it down so we make it back alive."

The construction was killing me. I didn't think they would be working today, but a few dump trucks were making my life miserable.

Michael was texting an update. *Just completed second drop. Where are you, Miss Daisy?* I gritted my teeth. Allen just walked in for the second drop. He was taking forever. He appeared to be casually walking and talking with the nurse. They smiled at one another as I pulled the hand truck out of his grasp and loaded the coolers myself. He was still talking to her as I was sealing the doors.

I turned tapping my pretend watch. "Come on, we got to go!"

I jumped in and blew the horn and he climbed in the passenger seat. "Tiffany, what is your problem? I've been trying to ask her for a date for weeks."

"Allen, were you in there flirting with her, when the cargo was ready for our next stop?"

"Well, for a few minutes? What's the big deal?"

"What's a few minutes?"

He shrugged. "I don't know five, ten?"

"Which is it?"

"Closer to ten, I guess?"

I slammed the brakes. "You were in there talking to a woman for ten minutes while I was waiting for you outside? Cargo was ready? And you were just talking?"

"Tiffany? What is your problem? Relax?"

"Get out!"

"What?"

"Get out of my truck."

"What?"

"I said, get the fuck out. I can do this on my own."

"That's against regulations."

"I don't care right now. I am not letting your hormonal urges mess up my schedule today. OUT!" I pointed.

"Is this how you treat Michael? Poor bastard. I'm not getting out, so you just better drive."

Michael was texting: *Stop number three. I bet you're just poking along.*

I shook my phone and growled.

"Did you forget to take your meds this morning?"

"Shut up. Look, I want to get through this day as quickly as we can. Just do your job and get it done as fast as you can."

"Fine by me, the quicker this shift is over, the sooner I can get away from you."

"Ditto."

I was back on the road and a solid stop behind Michael's pace. The slow references were starting to really annoy me. By our seventh stop, I was sure we were gaining ground.

Allen and I were dead silent in the ambulance. Michaels last dig was: *Come on slacker you're taking on your grandpa-boyfriend's habits, must be naptime for you.*

We were at our last stop. We were at least close to finishing at the same time when a dump truck cut me off. I blew my horn. I was so angry. Allen told me to calm down as another dump truck pulled up behind me. They boxed us in. Allen was telling me to lay off the horn as he was looking around. "Hey, Tiff, something is up. Knock off the horn." He was now on full alert.

"This isn't a situation; this is construction workers being assholes." I jumped out of my ambulance and told the guy behind me to back, the fuck up. He was laughing while he was on his hand-held talkie. It was all fun and games until I was in full view with my hand on my gun.

Mr. Dump Truck Driver lost the stupid grin and gestured his hands up and backed off. The guy in front was now moving ahead.

I hopped back in. Allen was all over it. "You just broke every protocol we are bound by."

"I got them to move the damn trucks."

"Every rule out the window."

"Allen, I see this playing out two ways. You make a big deal and we are stuck together for another two hours, or you shut your damn mouth and we leave on time and everything is quiet."

"You are dangerous."

"Let's keep that in mind too while you are deciding how this plays out."

Michael's next text was coming through: *Oh looks like I am the winner. See you at the ball Cinderella. I'll have them save two plates for you and Grandpa.*

Despite the time gained, those construction shenanigans cost us a half hour. Michael was gone when we pulled in.

Chris handed me a note that Michael had left. I opened it to a scribbled hand-drawn 2nd place winner ribbon. I crumpled it in my palm, tossing it in the trash.

It turned out that Allen and I were on the same page. He did not report me, letting us leave at a reasonable time. My boyfriend left a text ten minutes ago. I was so caught up in getting out of there that I didn't even feel the vibration.

Going to be late. See you there.

Damn it. Okay, it's just a time thing. I would not read into this. I called Hannah.

"He said he needs to talk to me."

"What? Are you okay?"

"No, he is coming over here in an hour and said he needs to talk to me about something. It can't be good. That's time cutting into getting ready."

"Look, Andy just texted he was going to be late. Want me to come over there?"

"No, if he breaks up with me, I'd rather he does it privately."

"Stop thinking the worst. Maybe he wants to get ready with you since you two haven't seen much of each other."

Hannah sighed. "Maybe, but I doubt it."

"I'll see you downtown. Think positive."

She snarked "Those words from the world's biggest cynic."

"Over the last few weeks, I've been seeing things differently."

"Tiffany, are you in love?"

"I think I am."

I could hear Hannah lighten. "Well, I'll be damned. See you at the gala. We might get drunk tonight."

I snickered because that could be a possibility.

CHAPTER TWENTY-FIVE

Pulling into my parking spot; I saw Cat lying in the bushes. I opened my door, talking to her, lecturing her that I didn't like her staying out all night and asking where she has been this whole time.

I walked over with my duffel over my shoulder. "Come on, naughty girl. You are staying in tonight."

Nothing, she didn't even move. I crouched down. She wasn't moving.

Panic red-flagged my brain, making me scramble down on all fours, pushing the branches up so I could get closer.

I pulled her stiff body from the bush. My hands knew immediately as she laid dead, eyes open and her tongue hung from her mouth.

Tears filled my eyes. "No! Cat, NO!"

I looked around, tears streaming down my face. I didn't even know what I was looking for.

I opened my bag and retrieved my gym towel. I wrapped her quickly, scooped her to me and carried her to my condo.

I didn't know what to do; I didn't know where to put her as I clutched her lifeless body to my chest. I couldn't see as tears flooded and streamed landing on the towel as I sobbed uncontrollably.

Never in my life have I experienced this pain. She was lifeless and I couldn't stop the tears. I whispered, "My kitty, my beautiful kitty." I softened my grip sliding down my door to sit on the floor. I rocked her a little. "I got you kitty."

Ten minutes went by. She wasn't coming back to me. I'd never had a pet before, so I didn't know what to do with her. I placed her in front of me and stared, wiping my tears away and staring at her. I lifted the towel. There was blood that had dried coming from her ear. I felt around. Her shoulder was caved in. She must have been hit by a car.

I petted her lifeless body. My cat was dead. She needed to be buried.

I couldn't do it now and I didn't know where to do it. I also needed to buy a shovel. I retrieved two bath towels and went to my closet to grab my spare duffel. I petted her one more time telling her she was the best kitty in the world.

My heart was broken as I wrapped her in the towels and tucked her in the bag. Audrey was texting me, showing a full picture of her with her makeup on. My heart sank.

I had to get ready. Well, I looked a wreck; I felt wrecked. I left Cat in the middle of the floor snugly tucked in the bag.

I pulled my dress from my closet and dragged it behind me to the bathroom. I kicked the other shoes aside and dragged my black heels forward. Then I pulled drawers open to collect my under garments. Wiping my nose on my forearm, I turned the shower on and sat on the edge of my bathtub. I felt numb.

Once the steam cleared, I looked at myself in the mirror. I felt pain. I was in pain. Someone killed my cat. Someone had robbed me of the one thing I was happy coming home to, ripping her away from me.

Audrey was now sending me an upper body shot of her in her dress.

Someone ripped my whole night of joy away from me. I couldn't even smile. I texted her I'm not dressed yet.

She texted back: *Get moving; you're going to be late.*

Get moving. I didn't even want to go now. I looked at my make-up bag that Hannah had supplied for me. I dumped everything out and surveyed the choices. I was feeling dark. Very Dark. The smoky look it would be.

There was nothing elegant about the way I was carrying myself. I was angry.

Deep, deep core-shattering angry. I don't even remember the drive to the gala. I pulled up in line to the red carpet. I wasn't waiting for the paparazzi. I slid out and grabbed my clutch, signaling an attendant to park it.

Well, they didn't like me jumping ship and someone tried to tell me to wait. I turned back giving my own orders. "Park it."

"Yes, Ma'am" was the quick reply.

I needed to tone this down, or I was going to defy the purpose of this evening. Audrey was sending me a full photo of her on the red carpet. Mother had arranged a rope and red carpet set up in her room.

The idea was sweet. Very, very sweet. I just could not appreciate it at this moment.

I walked in, giving my name. Damn, I forgot my invitation. I handed over my license instead. After a few security calls and me calling my mother, they let me in, giving my mother custody of me.

"Tiffany, I think your makeup is a little heavy dear."

"Bad day."

"Where is the handsome Andrew?"

"He will be late."

"Are you okay?"

"No, not really."

Mother was walking me to the nearest bathroom.

"We need to fix your makeup. This is a charity event not an underground rage." There was a full hospitality cart in each bathroom filled with every emergency item you could think of including makeup.

Hannah was texting: *Where are you?*

Bathroom left front entrance. Mother is fixing my makeup.

Be right there.

Hannah found us straight away. "Oh, good God Tiffany, the goth look is not appropriate for this event.

I intercepted her hand. "What is this?"

She grinned. "All the reasons he has been acting so off this week."

Her shiny new engagement ring was almost as bright as her energy.

My mother took over, telling her not to leave out any details.

Hannah's good news eased some pain in my heart over Cat's death. They were just about to start on my makeup when Michael was texting: *Stuck at work pokey?*

No, I'm here, girl talk in the bathroom. See you in a bit.

"Michael is here."

Hannah raised an eyebrow. "Are you going to play nice?"

"Of course, why wouldn't I?"

"What time is Andy getting here?"

"He didn't say; he just said he would be late."

"Well, that's not very helpful. There, much better."

Now Audrey was sending me a picture of her with a bunch of celebrity stand up cut outs behind her. "Mother, did you do all of this?"

Mother laughed. "Guilty, not even Audrey knows what's coming next. I have everything precisely timed."

"Wow, that's neat."

"I thought since she can't be with us, we should bring a little fun to her. I don't know if she will make it. She has been an amazing part of Henshaw. Your father has even reached out to unconventional sources looking for a solution to her failed liver."

"Unconventional?"

"Technology, experimentation. Something has to be out there."

"Enough of this. Let's celebrate Hannah's future wedding and the Girls' Club expansion."

I looked at myself in the mirror and nodded. Time to live in the here and now.

Here was Michael and now he was wrapping his arm around his beautiful date Rachael to introduce us. I grinned and put my hand up to stop him from talking. "Hi, excuse me for a moment. I'll be right back."

I turned and headed to the bar. The bartender smiled; his crooked name tag read Jerry. "Champagne Miss?"

"Got anything stronger?"

"Wine?"

"No, I was thinking a shot."

He twisted his lips to the side "My kind of gal. What's your poison?"

"I don't know. I don't drink."

He nodded again, then paused a moment and studied me.

"I've seen that look before." I couldn't answer him as he was on his tiptoes, grabbing a bottle from the back. "Normally, I would pour something smooth, something lady-like, but you look like you need to chase a few demons back, long enough to deal with them later. Here, I only share this sparingly. You need Louis."

He twisted the glass fleur-de-lis top, tipping the bottle to fill two shot glasses. He handed me one and raised his.

"A lady never drinks alone unless she is in trouble." He touched our glasses and said, "Cheers," then he nodded to me, "Cheers," I repeated touching the glass to my lips and pouring it down until it was gone. I cleared my throat of the slight sting, shaking my head slightly. "Thank you, how much do I owe you?"

He grinned. "Open bar, Miss."

"Oh, and thank you again..." I tilted my head to read his name tag, "Jerry and Louis."

Jerry looked concerned. "Try to have some fun. Your trouble isn't going anywhere. It will be there waiting when you leave."

This man was right. Everything would wait for me when I left here. My phone was vibrating. *I am not going to make it, sorry, babe. This cannot be helped. Have fun, but not too much fun.*

I looked at the text. I read it and reread it. Michael was approaching me alone. "Are you okay?"

I cleared my throat. "I'm fine. Why?"

"You just left abruptly when I was introducing you."

"I needed to find Louis right away. Sorry."

I stretched around looking for his date. "Um, where did she go?"

I spotted Kyle instead, "Son of a bitch!"

"Tiffany? What the hell is going on with you?"

"Kyle, Ten o'clock."

Michael turned. "Looks like he is miraculously better."

"Fuck!"

"What?"

I shook it off. "Nothing."

"That's pretty strong language for nothing."

"The guy behind Kyle."

Michael was looking, "Slicked back dark hair?"

"Yup."

Michael turned to me. "I couldn't stand here all night with one sentence clues. Or at least until Grandpa shows up."

"Stop calling him that. He's not that much older than me."

"Okay fine. What's with the wanna-be mob boss?"

"Hmm, that obvious? Blake Montgomery, kid I grew up with, Reese's brother. I thought he was still in jail."

Michael raised an eyebrow, "Jail?"

"Yup, no one knows for what, though. My guess is racketeering. His father is shady. His mother is right there." I pointed her out. "Clarissa Montgomery. Thinks she is top dog in this society. I really hate that woman."

"I remember Clarissa from your party. Why is she here?"

"Anyone who can pay ten thousand dollars a plate can be here."

Michael coughed. "Ten thousand a plate?"

I nodded like it was ten dollars. "Yeah, Mildred is trying to raise a million for the renovations. That's why everyone is so fancy."

"You look beautiful, by the way. Even for second place."

"Ha, ha."

He grinned. "So, when is Gran... your date arriving?"

"Something came up. He can't make it."

"Figures, um how many times has he bailed on you now?"

"Stop it, Michael. It's none of your business,"

"Are those our nurses?"

I stretched up. "Yes, I invited them."

"At ten thousand a plate?"

"I was allowed to fill a few tables for free."

"Oh."

"It's my way of making up to them for my birthday party."

"Wow, Chanler, you do have a heart."

"Yes, and it's pretty broken at the moment."

Michael became serious. "Tiffany, what happened? Are you okay? You just need to dump that asshole."

I was sorry for saying that out loud. "I don't want to talk about it."

He kept pressing.

"Michael, stop." I brushed by him before my demons could make cracks in Louis. I was far enough away from Michael when I bumped into his girlfriend.

"Oh, sorry, you're Tiffany." She stretched up like I do. "Have you seen Michael?"

I tried for another quick get-a-way tossing my head in his direction. "He's over there."

She blocked me. "Hey, it's finally nice to meet you. Michael talks about you all the time. To tell you the truth, I was getting a little jealous, but now I see I have nothing to worry about. Thanks for inviting us."

Umm. Did she just do that? There was nothing charming about my delivery right now. "I didn't invite you; my mother did. She is the one you should thank. She has such a fondness for Michael. I'm sorry he didn't warn you that this was a dress-up occasion. Just stand behind someone, when the camera comes around. You'll be fine." Bitch! I walked past her, making her move.

I nearly collided with Mildred, "Tiffany, is everything okay?"

"No, yes, I mean yes. Did you know Blake Montgomery was going to be here?"

She scowled, "No."

"I thought he was in jail?"

"Corporate detention, I believe, is the proper name."

"How can he be here? He's a disgrace."

"I heard he started a new company with one of the men he met in his 'Time out.'"

I sneered. "Who in their right mind would go into partnership with that crook?"

"I believe his name is Marcus Rivera. Equal crook. Runs the east side shipping ports."

"Figures. I can't be around him."

"Tiffany, only you can let someone have the upper hand on you. Forget the past. He is the same person as he was a decade ago; he will never change. You, on the other hand, have grown into a beautiful woman, and you, my dear, are so much stronger now."

Well, I didn't need that trip down memory lane right now. I was looking around to see what else this damn night was going to spring on me.

"Please, go welcome the women and children from the center. I'm sure seeing you again will put them at ease."

"Where did you seat them?"

"Left side of the stage."

"Okay."

Audrey sent me a photo of her sipping what looked like wine. And holding it like a flapper girl pose.

I found my parents, "Mother! Did you give Audrey alcohol?"

Mother laughed. "Of course not, that's sugar-free apple juice. I checked with her nutritionist. She is having a great time with the props, isn't she? I love this photo."

There was one with her kissing the card board celebrity Johnny Depp in his pirate costume. Okay, Audrey knew how to have fun. There was so much happening inside me right now. I think Louis was going to need reinforcements soon.

I was almost at the first table when I watched the woman I was approaching from behind, reach out, and touch the woman's arm who was facing me. They were clearly sharing a genuine moment. I almost hated interrupting.

The woman I was facing looked up and lost her smile. She said something to the woman now turning to see why.

"Thank you, Mandy. We'll see you on Monday." Both stood up. Mandy Stone! "Well, hello Tiffany, I'm not sure you know who I am?"

"Oh, you're the whore that my father just dumped."

She laughed. "He said; she said."

"What are you doing here?"

"I am the new mentor for the Girls' Club."

"Mentor? Are you going to train them, to sleep with married men, and ruin families while getting those men to pay for extravagant lifestyles, so they'll never know what it is to truly respect themselves?"

She grinned. "I wasn't trying to steal your father away. I was just having a little fun?"

"Now, you're having a little fun with Kyle? Does Reese know?"

"Leave my cousin out of this."

"Well, that answers that. What are you doing here?"

"I just told you. I am working for the Girls' Club."

"No, Mandy, I mean here. Right here. Why did you come here?"

"I had a calling, I suppose."

"You're a piece of work, Mandy. You won't last a week there."

"Well, I've been there for two weeks, so that's a week more that you predicted."

"I don't know what your game is. Stay away from that club."

"Why, because they are your people? You know, when your father talked about you growing up and how he used to sneak over to the community center to watch your classes, I never realized what an asset this place could be."

I nearly choked. I never knew my father watched my classes. I thought it was only Mildred. I gritted out, pulling deep to hold it together.

"They don't need trouble like you."

"Did you know they loathed you, Tiffany? All these women sitting at these five tables have their own stories about you being the spoiled rich kid and you never fitting in. They hated you, Tiffany, and now you and your rich godmother haves decided to tear their community center down and build a new, better building. They don't even want the new building."

I looked around. Each of the women gave me a hard stare. Did Mandy poison them against me? Was she right about this? Looking at their faces, I could see that Mandy was right. I thought they liked me over there. But these women hated me.

"So help you God, Mandy. If you fed these women a pack of your lies, I will hunt you down."

"And do what? It's you who should watch your back. Word has it you will lose everything." She knew more than I had figured out and she was slipping with information, letting her pride overcome her. I needed to keep her talking. She was the weak link. "I have nothing to lose whore."

She was getting mad at me calling her a whore. "I hope your condo is big enough for your parents to move in."

"Listen, slut; my parents will never have to move. The only thing my father lost was a bit of his reputation when he moved temporarily into your filthy crotch. He's moved out though. I don't know where you're whoring your next income from. Kyle can't afford you. I know the center can't pay for your lifestyle so good luck staying true to your job."

I leaned in. "Here's a tip, none of these woman's husbands can support you." I straightened back up.

Her eyes narrowed. "I can't wait to see Blake take you down." I grinned getting what I needed. These women did not want to talk to me, so I announced, "We don't have to do anything to the club. It can stay where it is and run on your budget. It's very easy to find an equal club that wants the funding. I don't care what you thought of me growing up; your community meant a lot to me when I was there. Please, enjoy your evening. This woman right here. Don't trust her and watch your husbands around her. Good luck and I will let Mildred know to seek another organization."

I turned to see Blake Montgomery coming toward us looking smug. "Tiffany, aren't you looking very fuckable in that dress?"

I flexed my hands because I was starting to shake. Louis could not hold the gates any longer. My father was marching toward me with two security guards behind him. He pointed at Mandy and said, "Remove her. Blake, I think it is best you leave on your own."

There was quite a commotion stirring in our corner. Michael was weaving his way over until he was freed from the crowd and could run to my side.

Blake looked me up and down. "You're trembling, just like you did that night I took your virginity. I can see you now as I did then; nothing has changed. You have the body, but you still don't know how to use it. Happy to give you lessons again, little girl."

Michael tried to put his arm around me. Wrong move. I didn't need his comfort; I was shaking because of the rage inside of me.

"No, Michael," I growled through my clenched teeth, jerking his release around my shoulder.

Blake laughed. "She wouldn't know what to do with you, anyway. She just lays there like a dead fish."

Michael saw it and tried to stop me, but I was too fast. There was Blake collapsing to the ground and now I wanted to finish the job. Rage coursed through my veins as I lost it.

Michael tackled me to the ground and the only thing I think saved him was my dress because I couldn't move in it very well.

He kept repeating, "Jail. He's not worth it. Police. Calm down. Breathe. Tiffany. Breathe. Come on. Come back. We are at a public function. Public. Public."

I looked around, and girls were screaming and crying. People were huddled around Blake; George was running to him, asking everyone to back up. George called out to call an ambulance. Clarissa was being held back by Kyle and Reese, who were shouting, "We are pressing charges."

Mildred pointed to security. I needed to breathe; Michael was smothering me. I started to hyperventilate. He eased up, and I scrambled out from under him. My dress tore. My mother had her hand over her mouth, looking at Blake in horror. I backed up, looking at Blake's limp body on the ground.

Hannah came over to me slowly hands in front. "Tiffany, he's alive, slow, slow, just breathe sweetie."

I had to get out of there. Michael handed me my clutch. "Tiffany."

I grabbed it and bolted.

When I reached the red carpet, cameras went off everywhere, blinding me. I ran to the right, pushing the valet out of the way and searching for my keys. Cameras were coming at me. I spotted my toy ambulance key chain. I grabbed my keys, then ran.

My car had better not be boxed in.

It wasn't. This was the only thing helping me today. I jumped in and sped away. I didn't know if I was going to be arrested, so I pulled into the posh liquor store down the street that I have never stepped foot in before.

My parents shopped here. I always waited in the car. Ripped dress, and all I walked in. I didn't even know where to begin, so I walked straight to the guy behind the counter. He took in the state of me with one eyebrow raised, "Can I help you, miss?"

"I certainly hope so. Do you have any Louis?"

He was confused, "Louis? I don't know what that is."

I snarked, "Neither do I. Um, at a function down the road. Having a tough time upon arrival. I'm not a drinker. I asked for a shot. Bartender said I have something to chase your demon away, pulled this reddish-brown liquor bottle out from behind the top shelf, called it Louis."

A gentleman from behind me finished. "Louis Xlll Remy Martin."

I turned, "Familiar story?"

The guy behind the counter said he would be right back.

He shrugged. "Been there once or twice."

The guy behind the counter came back with two boxes. "This stuff is expensive, Lady."

"How much?"

"This one is $600, and the bigger one is $3500."

I didn't react. I don't drink, so this is making up for it. Andy was going to blow a gasket, though. I handed over my credit card, "Bigger one, thank you."

He shook his head taking it. The guy behind me added, "That's just buying you time, you know?"

"That's all I want it to do, sir. I just need some time."

He grinned. "Then enjoy. You picked a good stop watch."

CHAPTER TWENTY-SIX

My phone was blowing up with calls, texts and voice messages. I didn't care one bit as I dragged my bottle of Louis closer to me.

I was sitting on the floor where I had held Cat last. My dress was tucked up around my waist, and my shoes kicked off across the floor.

I had pulled Cat's duffel bag between my legs, and Louis was securely in reach from the arm that had dropped Blake like a leaf.

I told Cat all about it while my prize-fighting fist picked up Louis for me to take another swig.

"Blake Montgomery," I lowered my eyes.

Then I told Cat all about the night he raped me.

* * *

There was a knock at my door. Then I heard Hannah say, "Tiff, are you there?"

Then I heard a key in the lock. I opened my eyes, seeing my apartment sideways, my cheek against the floor. I sat up, grabbing my now pounding head. "Tiffany? It's Hannah. I'm alone, sweetie."

"I'm here, Hannah."

She opened the door further. "Oh, my God, Tiffany. Sweetie?" She looked past me. "Louis Remy Martin?"

"Yup." I rubbed my head.

"And you complain about spending five hundred on clothes?"

"Yup."

She went to move my Cat.

I pointed. "Be careful with that bag."

"This?" she took the handles.

"Yes, my cat is in it."

"Your cat is in this bag?"

"Someone's car hit her; she's dead."

Hannah stopped herself and turned to fully face me. "Oh, Tiffany, I am so sorry."

I lifted myself upright, taking the bag and moving it to the side. "I have to find a place to bury her."

"They do pet cremations. My sister has her dog in an urn on her mantle."

"I think I would like that."

"When did you find her?"

"Yesterday before the gala."

"Oh, Tiffany! Why didn't you say something?"

"I don't know. I was just trying to get through it, I guess."

"I think you should call out from work today."

"No, I think the busier I am, the better I will be. What happened when I left?"

"Blake has a concussion."

"Good, at least I'm not going to jail for murder."

"Clarissa called out that she was hiring a lawyer."

"No surprises there."

"Come on. Let's get you cleaned up."

I looked down at her ring. I placed her hand in mine. "I am so happy for you, Hannah. I'm just in a bad place right now."

"I know. You have six months to snap out of it. You are my maid of honor. I already have the venue; George loves steak. My parents will close the steak house for the day. It's all mine. The only thing you have to worry about is what I pick for a dress and my bachelorette party."

"Deal."

"Have you told Andy about the last twenty-four hours?"

"No."

"Why?" she handed me my phone. "A lot of people care about you. Go through these and answer them, please."

Hannah made the coffee then made me breakfast. I showered and went through my phone, and I just couldn't bring myself to call anyone, especially Michael.

Audrey was calling me. "So, slugger, I thought I would have heard from you by now."

"Sorry, Audrey, I had a bad evening."

"Tiffany, get your head out of your ass and think. It's front page news; you solved the mystery."

"What are you talking about?"

"Blake Montgomery."

"Please, don't mention his name."

"Tiffany! Think! Blake Montgomery, he spent time in jail for corporate crime, met Marcus Rivera in the same jail, Monty Technologies."

"Are you Fucking Kidding me!!!"

"You didn't put that together? You just knocked him out cold for no reason?"

"I had ten years of pent up reasons to knock him out. He is the one that is trying to put us under?"

"Yes."

"Did you tell my father?"

"Yes, he is on it. Stock report comes out tomorrow."

* * *

Hannah dropped her cup, shattering it on the floor. She was so dramatic. I had never told anyone about Blake Montgomery raping me besides my dead Cat. Then I brought her up to this present day and all the bullshit his family is causing.

Hannah being Hannah, I endured her hugs, tears, hugs, tears, and her declaration that I should have killed him. It all came together for her why I had pushed everyone away ten years ago and acted recklessly. Then she repeated that I should have killed him.

That was my girl, and the reason I loved her like she was my twin.

I wasn't sure what to expect at work today from Kyle. He was in thick with the Montgomery clan.

What I didn't expect was Michael requesting a transfer. They assigned Chris to my shift. Michael worked the dispatch. I tried to talk to him, but he said talking was for last night and all day before we started. This was stupid. He was being a little brat.

On a positive note, Chris and I worked well together. I warned her that tomorrow we had Taylor in the jump seat. She announced that tonight was the end of her rotation. The next two days were hers for the taking. Shift three opened up. Two people were down. I put in for one, with my life so empty right now and up popped another opening; there were three shifts open. Chris looked at me. "Let's do this, more money to blow at the casino, right?"

They paired us up on the same route. This time, the overnight construction crew was playing their games again. I didn't like it. Chris didn't like it, and both of us exited the ambulance at the same time.

She took over dealing with them. I admired seeing her in action. She pointed, making sure they were understanding her.

There was no talk about breaking protocol. I mentioned yesterday with Allen. She shook her head. "Sometimes you just have to make your own judgment calls."

"Exactly!"

It was four in the morning and we had two more stops to cover. She brought up the paparazzi photos. I didn't see any of these. I knew Mildred had stopped the majority of the pictures because they were taken by people she had hired, but there were a few that went viral.

The headlines were horrible "Debutant Flattens Technology Start-Up." Chris was laughing so hard at some of them. I had to pull over, catching her contagious humor. I've never laughed so much in my life. My stomach muscles hurt. We must be overtired.

She shared a story about a website she was caught on when she pulled over a dignitary once. She never again underestimated the power of persuasion or how camera angles could tell a completely different story if it was suggested in the right way.

I was grateful that she shared this. It was perfect evidence that video and pictures could be tampered and mis construed. We had a case against the Montgomery's. Especially with Mandy and the Girls' Club set up.

Pulling into my parking spot, I looked at the bush that Cat always waited under or near; I thought this was a good place to bury her. I tracked down our maintenance guy, Joe, and told him what had happened. He didn't think there was enough room to bury her there with all the roots from the bushes. He suggested a spot in the woods across the lot, but I wanted her closer. Maybe her ashes were the best idea.

Entering my condo, I was so angry with Andy. Nothing since his canceling the gala. I blasted him with both barrels. *Someone killed my cat. I sent Blake Montgomery ass over teakettle to the hospital. I was waiting to be arrested for his death. I drank a half liter of Louis Vlll Remy something, much to your happiness my best partner ever, quit me and is requesting a shift transfer.*

Just like always, Nothing.

I needed sleep.

Audrey was calling. "Their stock is pulled. The company is under investigation."

"How?"

"Bradley Steinbeck."

"Who is he?"

"A man your father is forbidden to converse with, but Lanski Consultants is allowed."

"I thought you were back working at Henshaw?"

"I am, but I am keeping the consulting business as my own. It will come in handy for reasons such as this."

"So, who is this guy?"

"An old college rival... we hated each other opposite debate teams and now he is the lead investigator in accounting crimes with the IRS."

"Nice guy to have in your back pocket."

"I don't know about that. I spent an hour arguing with him. It was kind of nice, like old times."

"So, what did he do?"

"I gave him enough facts to investigate. He found enough to stop any sales of stock until further examinations are made."

"He must have found something then?"

"That would be my guess."

"Okay, thanks, Audrey. I'm just coming off a double. I need sleep."

"Call me later."

"I will."

Mother was now calling. "I am just coming off a double shift, Mother."

"That's it? You couldn't call me yesterday to tell me you were all right? Do you know who I heard from? Hannah! Hannah reported to me because she knew I was worried. You... Nothing. Not a single word."

"I'm sorry. I had a terrible weekend. I'm not ready to deal with it yet."

"We have a lot of news about our company. Your father is investigating eleven employees. There is more going on than we were expecting."

"More than Frank and Blake?"

"Much more. Audrey and your father connected everything after she found out that Blake Montgomery was the Blake in Blake Rivera Monty Technologies."

"She just called me about shutting their stock sales for today."

"I think Blake is going back to jail."

"Good, listen... I'll call you later. I need sleep."

"Promise me."

"I promise, Mother."

She ended the call. I checked my texts. Still nothing from Andy.

CHAPTER TWENTY-SEVEN

I woke up groggy feeling something at my feet. I smiled, Cat.

I leaped out of bed. Cat was dead. There was a flak jacket with a note. I picked up the note. It was in Andy's writing, "Wear this every time you leave this condo. EVERY TIME YOU LEAVE THIS CONDO!"

My stomach knotted up. I was a target. My mind flooded to the number of people who wanted me dead right now. Every curtain was drawn in my condo. I walked to my kitchen; there was a set of keys and the word "bathroom" written on the key tag. I walked into my bathroom, and there was a note written on both mirrors.

Take only what fits in your duffel as if you're going to work. Act as if you are going to work. Go to work. There will be a car in the main garage; here is the plate number. These are the keys. Park your car, switch vehicles and leave with this car. Park this car and arrive to your work in your car. What you have been waiting for is coming. I took Cat. I will bury her on the range. Stay at your parents for a few days until further notice. Wash these mirrors.

I bolted out of the bathroom to see that she was gone.

He took my cat?

He took my CAT!

He had no right to take her. Who does he think he is!

I don't want her buried at his place.

I want her here with me.

I grabbed my phone: *You don't get to decide where to bury her. Give me back my cat!*

I was so flipping mad at him right now.

I was back in the bathroom re-reading. Wash the mirrors. "You friggen wash the mirrors, pal. You wrote all over them!"

I was fit to be tied. How dare he come in here and order me around and then move me out. "Go to work"... Grrrr, I was so mad!

"What I have been waiting for is coming."

I'm not waiting for him anymore. He does not get to decide that he can come and go whenever he wants.

I yelled out, "I'm not waiting for you anymore, ANDY."

I shook my fist upward. That son of a bitch TOOK MY CAT!

I needed coffee. I dumped his ready to go mix out and made my own.

Hannah was calling. "I have the number to that pet crematory."

"Andy took my cat."

"What do you mean he took your cat?"

"He's going to bury her on his range."

"What? On his what? Range?"

"He's got a shooting range at his house."

"So, that's nice of him?"

"Maybe? But he did it without asking me or talking to me about it. He did it while I was sleeping. I haven't seen him, and he just comes in here, does whatever he wants, and leaves with no word or explanation..."

I looked at the keys and remembered the bathroom notes. "Well, sometimes he half explains. Still, it's not good enough. Then he tells me what I have been waiting for is coming. What is that Hannah? I don't understand guy code."

"Did you two talk about moving in?"

"No." I picked up my duffel and started to empty it to see what I was going to pack. My hospital scanner was in my hand as I was placing it on my table.

"I couldn't begin to tell you about George's code, so don't feel like you are the only one."

"I'm staying with my parents for a few days."

Hannah chuckled. "I think that's a good idea. Do you have your key code?"

I looked at the scanner, "Code."

"What sweetie?"

"Damn it!" I ran to my bathroom, mumbling the words, "Go to work. What you have been waiting for is coming. SHIT! I got to go. Call you later."

I hung up, reading the note one more time. I washed the mirror clean, grumbling, "I can't believe he took my cat."

I wrote the plate numbers on my wrist. It looked like a tattoo. One of my college friends taught us this over a whole semester. I called my mother to tell her I was staying for a few days. She was thrilled.

I packed a few days of clothes, all my weapons, necessities and I wore my uniform out with my new flak jacket underneath. We were getting hit.

How did he know what shift? I was assuming it was mine. Did he arrange for this hit to go down so I could grab Audrey's liver? Damn it, I didn't have Michael, and I had Taylor to babysit.

I think this was the final phase of the flu blowing through our company. There were only six of us that were unaffected by it. Everyone else had it or was over it. No overtime shifts came available. They gave me Calvin to fill in for Michael. Michael jumped in with Kyle because Jason was out sick with the flu.

I would love to be a fly on the wall in that ambulance. I know Michael still had my back even thought he was acting childishly at the moment.

I am so glad Taylor was now an expert in everything. If anyone shot at me, I was going to use her as a shield. I was quiet and Calvin was quiet, but Taylor, just could not stop talking. I sent her in with him on every delivery. One time, one of the nurses came running out ahead of them, throwing me into liver alert. It was Maggie with the information I have been asking for concerning Doctor Paris. She was worried, telling me he was engaged to the city girl. Oh, my God!!! I walked in a circle, calming myself down. "Don't do that!" I held my chest.

She touched me. "Are you okay? I thought you would like to know."

"Yes, I wanted to know. Thank you."

Calvin argued that Taylor was not going in on the next delivery. I smiled. "She has to learn this stuff, buddy." He mumbled and grumbled under his breath.

"Hey, a few more hours and we go home."

He nodded "Fine."

The construction workers and trucks on this part of the route were jerks. No doubt about it. This looked like how they got their amusement... by harassing people. I made Calvin take down the name of the trucking company. I was going to put in a complaint. Enough with these guys. I was sick of them. I got out again and yelled at them. Calvin and Taylor were protesting like Allen had. I told them both to shut up and said that I have been dealing with these jerks for a week now.

One of them followed us really closely for nearly three miles. Taylor was scared and Calvin didn't like the fact that they were right on our bumper. I wanted to slam on my brakes so bad, but then I would have another truck out of commission. I hated these construction workers.

No chance of getting out of here on time. Taylor ratted me out. I told Donovan that I was reporting the construction company as soon as they opened. He also wrote the number down and was going to make a formal complaint on behalf of the company.

Taylor described how scary it was. I rolled my eyes. They reprimanded me about leaving the ambulance.

I talked to Donovan in private. I described them as a bunch of cowboys, and he nodded. He got where I was coming from. The second shift opened up. Michael grabbed it. That made him on a double again. The weekend was coming up, and I bet that was the target. Most people were going away because of the holiday perfect set up for a heist.

I called my mother to let her know I was going to be there in an hour. Then I gave her the plate number of the car I would drive in on. She had a lot of questions. I did not want her to worry about me and told her it was Andy's car. Wrong move. She hoped Andy had a decent car at least and why wasn't I driving the one they bought me?

I pulled up next to a silver older model Camry. This must have been from the early 1990s. At least it was clean. That's all I could say about it.

This was nothing like my Lexus. There was a smiley sticker in the middle of the steering wheel. Ha, ha, ha, hilarious.

Jack worked the lobby of my parents' building. I knew they had updated the key cards. I handed him mine, and he gave me back a new one. "New style suits you, Miss."

"Thanks Jack, how's the wife?"

"Overworked, underpaid. Now, they're cutting more of the school budget. It's not worth her stress. Number one cause of death in women. I keep telling her to quit."

"Hey, I know a few companies that are hiring. She's well qualified." I wrote my phone number down. "Have her call me."

He nodded, opening the door for another resident.

*　*　*

Greg was texting me: *Tiff I have my full crew back. Take a few days off.*

I laughed, that was code for get your ass in here. I think Danny was teaching him how to use his phone.

I replied: *I need sleep. I'll be in around four.*

K

Was this one letter thing adapted by all men? I thought it was just an Andy thing.

Mother had a full breakfast ready and waiting for me. "Mother, this is very nice of you, but I am going to bed."

"When's the last time you ate?"

Good question. "All right, you win, thank you."

"The Girls' Club, fired Mandy. They also reconsidered the idea of a new facility. What exactly was said between all of you?"

"What needed to be said. Mandy poisoned them. She is very persuasive and a good liar."

"I see."

"How were you able to hold it together with her there parading around?"

"Decades of dealing with this nonsense; this crowd knows how to test limits. Besides, your father was very attentive to me."

That, I understood.

I was hungrier than I realized, shoveling the food into my mouth. Mother watched me, not commenting.

"Your father has agreed to go to couples counseling."

"Do you forgive him?"

"The problem is not the forgiving part. We have lived apart for a good decade. I think the hard part is coming back to each other. We will try, but enough of that. Here is what is going on over at Henshaw."

* * *

I woke up back in my old bed. This wasn't as bad as I thought it was going to be. Mother was out. I had the place to myself.

Greg looked at the clock. I was ten minutes late. He grumbled, "Those three need oil changes. Go see what the kid did to your truck."

I slipped into my mechanic suit, and dropped my keys on the shelf, then I walked over, inspecting his progress. Wow, this kid had talent. I stepped up into the back of the cab looking around. There was an odd shaped metal container spread out over the cooler. Seven total, all different shapes. I picked up the oval one, checking it out.

Greg was stepping up in the back, making "oofing" noises.

"You need help, old man?"

"No, no, I got it. Kid's got talent huh?"

"I'll say. What are these?"

Greg laughed "Armor for organs. Kid was playing around with the welder."

This is just what I needed. Holy smokes. Why didn't I think of this? I bet this would fit under my vest.

"What a clever idea." I examined all of them.

"He comes up with stuff like this, and it scares the hell out of me; what else is in that head of his?"

"This is seriously cool. Can I take one of these? I would like to show some people."

"Sure, I think he would like that you like his stuff enough to show it off."

"I'll give it back in a few days."

"Hey, did I hear it right? Michael put in for a transfer?"

"Yes, you did, Sir."

"What's going on there?"

"I don't know what's going on with him."

"That's too bad. You two make a great team. You were made for each other."

I shrugged. "Work-wise at least."

I tucked the half-moon organ armor in my bag and started on the oil changes.

Two shifts opened for tonight. Jason was out again and Calvin called out. I think he didn't want to work with Taylor. I couldn't blame him for that.

We had a dilemma. No one was taking either shift. Mark summoned, Kyle, Taylor, and me into the boardroom.

"Listen, we've never had this happen before. This flu has wiped out most of the crew. They're either getting over it, have it or are coming down with it. You three are gonna run a truck solo."

Kyle jumped up. "What about Michael? He can ride with me, and get a dispatcher in."

"That would leave Tiffany unprotected. Taylor isn't ready."

She protested. "I'm ready. I've got this; it's easy."

"No, Taylor, to tell you the truth, we are not happy with your scores at the academy. You are on probation for a while."

"I can handle this. I did all the deliveries with Calvin last night. Tell him, Tiffany."

I stared at her. "Definitely not ready, Mark."

Taylor gasped. "That's not fair. She doesn't like me. Besides, she put us in danger last night."

I raised a brow at Mark. He addressed Taylor. "Tiffany is one of our top guards. You were in no danger."

"Then she and I should be fine tonight."

Kyle added, "I agree."

Mark looked down at all the paperwork. "We have cut your loads in half. All the hospitals have been working with us for the past two hours. There are only six deliveries that must be made. Two are in Kyle's district and four in Tiffany's. You guys are all over the map tonight. Next few shifts will make up for the cargo that is not being delivered."

He handed me the paperwork.

Kyle protested. "Why are you handing her the paperwork? I have seniority."

"She outranks your seniority. Tiffany is driving. She is the team leader tonight."

"Oh, come on! I'll do dispatch; let me trade with Michael."

"No, Kyle. Go pick up your lists. We are done here. Tiffany, I want to speak with you for a moment."

Kyle shot out of his chair and out the door. Taylor sat, waiting.

"Taylor, excuse us for a moment."

"Okay?" She picked up her phone and started texting.

Mark looked from me to her. I shook my head.

"Taylor, leave."

"Fine!" She stood up, insulted.

Mark turned into me. "I know this isn't the ideal situation, and if there was one doubt in my mind that you could handle this, I would have made other arrangements."

"I've got this, Sir."

"I know you do. I'm sorry you and Michael didn't work out."

"I'm fine, really. If Michael wants a transfer, then so be it. Just don't make Taylor my permanent partner."

"Will do. I'm not sure if we're keeping her. She just about failed the academy. We're either going to send her back for a second chance or cut her."

"Do I get to vote?"

"No. Be careful out there. None of this, take the bull by the horns stuff tonight. Just make it slow and steady. Give me a boring evening. I love it nice and boring."

I chuckled. "Will do, Sir."

"Call in to Michael if you see anything suspicious. He has the police as your backup."

"Got it."

"And one more thing."

Grrr! "Yes?"

"Don't kill Kyle."

I laughed. "No promises."

"Boring, Chanler! I want boring."

Mark walked away. I looked down at my papers. I was Queen!

CHAPTER TWENTY-EIGHT

I walked past Michael, hearing him shout, "Good luck, Chanler."

"No luck needed, Michael." I cleared the doors. Kyle was in the passenger seat and Taylor in the jump seat, singing with her headphones on.

I turned to her. "You do know we're working, right?"

She pulled one out. "What?"

"Put those damn headphones away and shut your music off. You are supposed to be watching and not be a distraction."

"We're still in the garage."

"I can leave you here, you know."

Kyle looked back. "Taylor, do as she says. I don't want to be stuck alone with her tonight."

Taylor laughed. "You are so cute, Kyle."

She did what I asked, and we rolled to our first run in Kyle's district. Easy cargo was easy cargo. Only two containers. Kyle was talking with the nurse and Taylor.

I pulled the scanner. I was carrying organs. Oh, geez. This must be the only thing we are delivering tonight. Neither one matched my code. Ish had programmed the liver to blink when the code came up. I went over to the shotgun and looked over my shoulder. They were finished conversing. I closed the cooler and Kyle sealed the door. Next stop. I was going to load the shotgun to full capacity.

"Let's go, Kyle commanded."

Taylor was jabbering away about nothing. "Taylor, enough talking, more observing."

"You are just so anti-social, Tiffany."

"And you are anti-working. Shut up and do your job."

Kyle did a little half wave for her not to talk back.

I sent them both in. As soon as they cleared the door, I loaded the shotgun with two more slugs and put a bullet in the chamber. I tested to see if Danny's organ armor fit under my vest. It didn't. It did fit down the back of my pants if I loosened my belt buckle, but it stuck out a few inches.

They were coming back. I grabbed the coolers as they were talking to this nurse as well. I pulled the scanner out. No matches. We had four more stops, all on my route. This was like playing Russian roulette. No wonder we weren't supposed to know what we were carrying. I was anxious. I needed to calm down. I hope I didn't look out of character.

Now, we moved over to my district. I had all that construction to deal with. And Burbank was my third stop over here. It was going to happen either now or the next stop.

I was pacing and shaking my hands out, trying to stay loose and limber. Kyle walked out with the carts, and there was a loud pop.

We all crouched down at the same time. The nurse screamed the loudest. She nervously pointed. "That transformer just blew. Holy smokes, that scared the crap out of me."

All of us stood up, having the same reaction. I took over the hand cart from Kyle and scanned three containers. No match. This was getting unnerving. Taylor was texting.

"Put your phone away and pay attention, Taylor."

"To what? The one car, that is passing us in the opposite direction?"

"I'll make sure to include that answer on my report tonight."

"Fine." She put down her phone and watched the road.

Hospital number four was quiet. We had four coolers going. My heart raced as I scanned each one.

Nothing?

I didn't get it. Maybe the scanner was broken. Maybe Ish broke it.

I was sure we were carrying Audrey's liver.

Nothing was happening. Everything was normal and quiet. Burbank was a breeze. Two coolers were going to our last stop. I scanned them, and nothing.

What the heck.

This is the perfect setup night. I relaxed until we came upon the construction part of the trip.

Slow, redirections, stops, more redirections, crew fucking with me again. Taylor was filling Kyle in on last night and the other day.

Kyle pulled the talkie over to him. "I have to call into Michael that they are rerouting us."

"Please do." I agreed.

Michael came back with a, "Hold tight."

Kyle answered, "We can't; they're pushing us."

After five minutes Michael said, "All clear"

Taylor asked, "Shouldn't we have waited back there?"

Kyle responded, "Not in this situation."

"I don't get your rules. One minute it's by the book and the next minute it is okay to break them? Which is it? Okay or not okay? This is that part that will drive me crazy. Who gets in trouble if the person driving breaks the rules and you don't agree?"

Kyle turned his head. "It's from experience when you decide to bend the rules. All drivers have seniority, so what the driver does or says goes."

"That makes no sense to me, Kyle. Then why are they drilling 'follow the rules' so much?"

Kyle turned back, looking out the window. "Just learn what they teach you. The rest will develop naturally."

She huffed out with frustration.

We arrived fifteen minutes late to our last delivery, and they held us.

We waited and waited and waited. Michael was calling over the scanner to hold our position.

I picked up the talkie, "No shit."

I turned my head to the right to see a nurse, guard, Kyle, and Taylor, all running in my direction. The guard handed me the cooler.

The nurse was shouting "Back to Burbank STAT." I turned and scanned.

My scanner lit up like Christmas. This was Audrey's liver. Shit! I didn't have time to put it in the organ armor. Taylor and Kyle were climbing in.

I secured the cooler and threw the organ armor on top. Fixating my eyes on the container, I didn't want to leave it, but we had to get out of here.

As I jumped into my seat, Kyle hit the lights. Taylor was grinning. "Finally, some excitement tonight."

I shook my head. "You are clueless."

Kyle was calling in the extra delivery with Michael swearing on the other end. The construction had us all over the map. Detours and trucks blocked us. We were not on the same route to the last hospital. This was another new route.

Kyle called it in.

Michael demanded that we hold tight again.

I heard, "Tiffany, do not proceed, so help me fucking God! Hold your position! Hold your position!"

We had to move, even Kyle agreed, "I'll take the hit; keep going."

Just as he finished his sentence, they hit us hard from the back-end. I did everything I could to hold the road.

Taylor started screaming.

Kyle said something, making her stop for a moment.

I got my ambulance straight and hit the pedal to the floor. Taylor screamed again as she saw the big truck behind us with the headlights closing in. "He's hitting us again!" We all braced, and I turned and threw my full body weight into holding the wheel steady.

A bullet pierced through my front windshield, and right past my left ear. I heard it pierce the metal behind me; as they rammed again from behind, spinning my ambulance as I tried not to flip it.

Taylor was screaming hysterically.

Kyle's shoulder blew apart, pieces of it spattering the inside of our cabin. Blood and flesh landed everywhere. Some had hit the side of my face as I tried to keep all four tires on the ground.

Taylor was screaming uncontrollably.

"I'm hit," Kyle said as he slumped, dropping the talkie.

I finally stopped the ambulance, unbuckled, and climbed over Taylor. I pushed her toward Kyle, ordering her to take care of him.

I broke the seal of the cooler and slid the organ into Danny's organ armor, stuffing it between my breasts. It hurt like hell shoving it down but it was in, then I fixed the cooler lid back on, snugly closing the box back up like we still had cargo in it. I reached over and pulled the shotgun lock, securing my weapon, ready for what came next.

I looked in all directions and heard a whistling sound as a metal objected came through the back window. I looked down at the grappling hook.

This was the eeriest feeling. I knew what was coming next.

Taylor was quiet for a second and pleaded with me, "Don't let me die. Don't let me die." She sobbed uncontrollably.

The doors flew off the back of the ambulance as Taylor screamed again for Michael to help.

I saw a figure through the smoke, and I fired. I fired again and listened. Now was not the time to waste any ammo. All the lights within a short distance went out. With the butt of my shotgun, I smashed the light out above me.

I was trapped and in the dark now. I heard the shot that pierced my left thigh, making me collapse as I grunted out in pain.

I was hit.

Someone approached. I wait until the last second, firing twice, not waiting to see if I was successful.

No one else approached; I needed to reload the shotgun, and I didn't have time. I crawled to the opening, hearing more voices further away. I hobbled down; my leg nearly useless as I dragged it along.

I heard cop cars in the distance and Taylor crying; whoever this was, they were not approaching the front cab.

I managed to make it to the ground and crawled to the front of my ambulance. I heard more men; my gun was ready.

They jumped into the back. Taylor was pleading.

I heard one gunman say, "Shut up bitch," and he must have smacked her because she cried out, then she went silent. No guns went off.

I felt the ambulance rock as they jumped out the back and ran off.

I was losing a lot of blood. All fell quiet as I snapped a compartment open and pulled my parachute cord from the back of my gun belt.

I tried to tie it. I sat on the ground. I was going to pass out. I couldn't; I had to stay alert. It seemed like forever as I waited, hearing the sirens in the distance getting closer.

Startled, I pointed my gun.

Andy crouched down in front of me.

"Shh." He raised his finger to his lips.

Tears swelled in my eyes. He looked down at my leg and started to tie a proper tourniquet.

I took his hand and brought it to my chest.

"Audrey's liver. Please, get this to her."

He stared at me, confused.

I tapped my finger on the metal. He opened my shirt up and reached in, but it hurt me too much when he tried to pull it out.

He stopped and undid my buckle and pulled my shirt free. I heard material tearing. It was the vest straps as they pulled toward him and released as he cut. Relief eased my body as the vest opened.

He held the organ armor, examining it. He shook his head like I had surprised him as he studied the case.

"Please, save Audrey. I don't want to lose her."

He stared right into my eyes, brushing his finger down my cheek.

I couldn't help it as I declared to him again, "I love you."

He lifted my chin and kissed my swollen lips, "You're mine, babe." And I passed out.

CHAPTER TWENTY-NINE

I vaguely remembered arriving at the hospital. I knew I was moving on a stretcher. The lights were so bright hurting my eyes and making me squint. Michael was holding my hand leaning over me.

"Stay strong, Tiffany; you can do this. I am not going to lose you."

I felt the release of his grip on my hand, hearing him arguing with someone that he was not leaving me. It was cold in here, and the smell of rubbing alcohol filled my nose.

I heard. "I love you, Tiffany."

And everything went blank.

* * *

My head pounded. My leg felt uncomfortably hot, itchy even. I tried opening my eyes, but the light took a moment to adjust. I felt something on my face. I reached to yank it away.

"She's coming to. Tiffany, just stay still. Betty! Betty, she's waking up. Tiffany, stop that!"

It was Hannah's voice. She grabbed ahold of my hand. "It's oxygen, for the love of God, Tiffany! Stop it!"

I stopped pulling at it as my eyes adjusted better. She let go of my hand and put her phone to her ear. "George, yes, she's waking up. I don't care; get up here."

I looked around and the window indicated that it was daytime. Oh, my gosh, my leg hurt more. I was adjusting to a different angle and focused a little more.

I grabbed my chest, panicking, swinging my legs over the bed. "AUDREY!"

Michael was at my side, holding my shoulders to make me stay in bed. "Tiff, she is in recovery. Doing great. No worries."

"What? What happened? Where am I?"

Mother came into view, "Burbank Hospital Tiffany. It's Thursday morning, ten o'clock. You were in surgery for an hour, recovery for two hours, and now you are in your hospital room. You saved Audrey's life. Her surgery was successful. She's still in recovery."

"Andy, Andy got her the liver."

"No, dear. You were holding it to your chest in the metal container."

"The liver?"

"Yes, it was just a lobe, though. It's enough. She'll be back one hundred percent."

"Good."

I sat back in bed, Michael helping me swing my legs back. I closed my eyes. I must have fallen back asleep, because when I woke up again, it was just Hannah and Michael in the room.

Oh, for the love of God, my leg was on fire.

Hannah called out. "Betty! She needs pain meds. I think she's feeling it now."

I looked at Hannah while grabbing my leg. "Audrey? What about Audrey? Is she okay?"

"Still in recovery but doing well. George said this leg will take some time. Bullet traveled a nasty route. You're not going to be running any-time soon, and it looks like I'll have to pick a maid of honor dress that you can wear with sneakers."

I smiled; only Hannah would be thinking ahead like that.

"Michael." I looked over at him.

He stood and walked to me. He sat on the edge of my bed.

"I'm so sorry, Tiff. This is all my fault. I've been so stupid lately."

"Michael, no. Stop."

"No, Tiffany, I should have been there. I bailed on you. I will never forgive myself for that."

"Michael, hey, Michael? This is not your fault. Were you with me when we arrived here?"

"I drove you here. Carried you in."

"What? How did you find me?"

"I arrived first. I found you."

"You arrived before the cops?"

"Yes, as soon as I told you to hold your position, I knew you wouldn't listen, so I grabbed my keys."

"You abandoned post?"

"Yes, I'll tell you more on that later."

I cracked a smile, making me move my leg slightly. "Ouch! Damn, that hurts!"

Nurse Betty came in and injected something that eased the pain nearly instantly. I looked over to the window. It was now dark outside. I reached my hand up touching, Michael's arm. He covered his other hand over mine.

I asked. "Kyle? Where is Kyle?"

"Lost his arm. He's still in critical."

"The bullet came right through the windshield. Blew his shoulder to bits. I think it was meant for me."

"There are two bullet holes through the windshield. One was aimed at you, but missed."

I felt queasy. "I heard it pass my right ear."

"It pierced in and out clean. You are very lucky, Tiffany."

"Taylor? Where is Taylor?"

"Up in the psych ward; she won't talk."

"What do you mean she won't talk?"

"She won't talk, nothing. They can't get her to say anything. She's having a breakdown."

I shook my head over that irony. I wondered if seeing me would help her.

"Where is Mother?"

"She's hopping between you and Audrey. Your father came in to check on both of you, too. Mildred is floating around somewhere. Probably with your mother."

"Good."

"You are going to be in here for a few days, Tiff. Do you want me to collect anything from your condo?"

"Does anyone have my phone?'

Hannah pointed, and Michael picked it up. "Right here, Tiff."

He handed it to me. No message from Andy. Figures.

* * *

I wanted to go home. Mother insisted I say at her house a few more days. I caved and let her be my mother. The food was good, but by the third day, I was getting antsy. I needed something to do.

Father brought me into the investigation. That kept me busy for a few more days, but I was getting bored with that. All three of us were talking one night, and my father recommended that I come in on the engine project.

He said it would be a lot of work. Half the team had been fired, and I would have to make a lot of business trips to the plant out west.

Mother protested that I was months away from being able to anything like that. Father disagreed, and said I would be ready in a few days if my physical therapist approved.

I liked that idea. I couldn't go back to work yet. I was on a four-month paid leave. This would give me something to do. I liked this idea.

Michael arrived, apologizing for being late. He blamed my accident and his mandatory overtime. I checked my phone as I checked it twenty times a day. Nothing from Andy. I was getting around with the crutch just fine and wanted to go back to my own home.

Michael listened to all the plans my father was making, and my mother was arguing that I wasn't ready. I wanted to get out of here. We were finished with the meal, and Michael leaned over and said, "Want to go for a drive, get out of here?"

"You need to sleep. You've been working too much."

"I'm fine. Come on."

He turned to my parents. "I'm taking Tiffany for a drive. Give her a change of scenery."

Mother stood up. "When will you be back? It's dark out. She needs to rest."

I glared at her. "I think I would like you to take me to my own place now, Michael."

Mother went to protest. She was becoming too possessive of me, and it was time for me to go.

Father held his hand out to stop her from saying anything. "It is really nice having you home while you recover, but if being back in your own condo is more comfortable for you, then will you at least let us provide a driver for you? The doctor said no driving for a while."

I nodded. "Yes, I will agree to a driver."

Michael interrupted. "I can get her around. We don't need a driver."

I laughed. "You work; I do need a driver. That's very generous Father, and I will take you up on the offer. I am interested in your work proposal temporarily. I like my job; I like what I do and the people I work with and get to see every day. Sorry Mother, I would like to go back to my own place now. Michael, can you help me pack?"

"Of course."

"And give me a ride back to my condo?"

He nodded.

Mother did not like this at all, but stood silent.

I texted Andy: *Returning home and my father is hiring a driver for me, while I temporarily work at Henshaw, until I can return to Angel Wings.*

Nothing.

Michael was quiet for the most part, on the way to my condo. When we were close, he turned to me. "We make sense, Tiffany."

"You are one of my best friends, Michael."

"If you let me, we could be more than friends."

I turned my head to the outside, looking out the passenger window. "I know, Michael."

"Why are you fighting it?"

"Because."

"Because of him?" Michael's tone grew angry and sarcastic.

I didn't answer. Just stared out at nothing.

"Has he even contacted you in the last two weeks?"

I didn't answer as a tear escaped the corner of my right eye. I slowly rubbed it into my face.

"Tiff, all I am saying is that I want to be the one here for you. I get along with your family, your friends; we get along."

"I don't want to talk about this. I'm not ready."

"Okay Tiff, will you think about it though?"

"Yes."

He let out a big sigh. "Thank you."

Michael was about to turn into Andy's spot when I ordered him to take mine. He turned in and retrieved my bag from the back. He walked alongside me, then opened the doors and held them for me.

"Are you going to be able to manage these doors all by yourself?"

I shot him a look. "I could manage them right now if you would let me."

"Come on, grumpy. Be happy; you're home now."

Everything was just as I left it.

No sign of Andy being here. "Listen, Michael, thank you for everything. I just want to be alone okay?"

"Ah, hang on, Tiff? Do you have food? Because your car isn't here; you can't drive yet. I'm sure your father will have your driver in the morning, but what about right now?"

"I'm fine. Thank you."

He bent down and kissed my forehead. "I am a phone call away."

"Go home and get some sleep."

Michael reluctantly left.

* * *

Everyone was checking up on me except the one man I wanted to. Father called and asked when I wanted to start work. The day after tomorrow sounded good to me. Tomorrow was my physical therapy and while I was at the same hospital, I planned on going to check in on Audrey.

He gave me my drivers' names and phone numbers. I scheduled my day tomorrow and rested for the rest of the night. My new plan was to push myself a little more each day and not be at the mercy of others.

My first day alone was a success. Michael wanted to come over, but I reminded him that I needed time alone.

The next day was my first day working for Henshaw. I liked it better than I thought I would.

Father appreciated me being there too. Audrey was Little Miss Bossy with her video chats, and I loved every bit of it.

Tired from a long day of moving around, I was ready to relax. I pushed my door open.

Rose petals were scattered on the floor freezing me in my tracks.

I didn't realize I was holding my breath as my gaze followed the trail to the kitchen. I moved as quickly as my crutches would take me.

What I saw, I couldn't believe, causing me to gasp.

There was a new cat carrier sitting on my counter with something very alive inside.

I opened the door to a tiny black puffball of furry kitten, squeaking in a tiny kitten voice.

It was so adorable, meowing tiny little baby mew. I held him to my chest, tears glossing over my eyes. Andy was closing the door and walking toward me.

"You can't leave the door open any more. This little girl is an escape artist. She wants an adventure."

I turned to him already giving away my emotions.

He closed in, "I'm thinking, you, me, her?"

I looked up at him, tears running down my face.

He reached up, wiping my left cheek.

"It's going to be tough at times. You're going to be wondering where I am. Why am I not answering? Why am I not here?"

He brushed his thumb over my bottom lip.

"If you can handle that and let that go and focus on the big money, then I think we can make this work."

He stepped closer as I nuzzled into his hand, holding my new kitten snug to me. She was purring and looking around.

We were now at kissing distance. He looked down. "Any ideas for her name?"

I looked at her, then back to him.

"Kitten."

He kissed me like it was our last.

My door buzzer was sounding. Kitten freaked out, digging in her claws as she tried to scramble away. She did not like that noise.

We both turned. I pulled her claws off of my shirt looking at the time, holding on to Kitten snugly.

"That would be Michael."

Andy held my shoulders, kissed me swiftly again, and gazed into my eyes. He nodded, then turned, heading to my door.

"I'll take care of this."

Acknowledgements

I thank my children for understanding that I need a quiet house while I write. They even help bouncing ideas as I worked through scenes. My kids are amazing.

To my man who has a crazy, wealth of information on the most intriguing topics, I would never study. I think you are the sexiest guy alive. I thank my stars that you chose me to love.

To my friends for their support, answering my random texts, and dealing with me missing from the group, and becoming a total introvert. I miss you and thank you for your friendship.

To my writing groups and the Romance Writers of America. The information I have access to; that you share, helps advance me in my writing career. I am so happy to have stumbled upon this amazing organization.

The Kate and Robert Chronicles
Inceptions
You and I
Beckham 101
She's Got The Jack
How to Train a Bullet

The Dating Policy
The Marriage Contract

Hooker Line Sink Her
The Bait

Made in the USA
Middletown, DE
07 November 2019

78129025R00144